TOO
MUCH
DRAMA

Also by Debra Phillips

The High Price of a Good Man

TOO MUCH DRAMA

DEBRA PHILLIPS

St. Martin's Griffin
New York

www.stmartins.com

Library of Congress Cataloging-in-Publication Data

Phillips, Debra.
    Too much drama / Debra Phillips.—1st ed.
      p. cm.
    ISBN 0-312-30526-5
    EAN 978-0312-30526-0
    1. African American businesspeople—Fiction. 2. African American families—Fiction. 3. African American women—Fiction. 4. Mothers and daughters—Fiction. 5. Cosmetics industry—Fiction. I. Title.

PS3566.H4772T66 2005
813'.54—dc22
                               2004051439

First Edition: April 2005

10 9 8 7 6 5 4 3 2 1

*This book is dedicated to my three sisters,
Sharon, Edna, and Eva.
Friends may come and friends may go,
but sisters are forever.*

Acknowledgments

With so much tragedy around us, each new day is truly a blessing. For this, I have to continue to give first thanks to the good Lord above. Without him, I wouldn't be able to write the stories that plant themselves like seeds in my head.

A special shout-out to one of my favorite authors and e-mail pal, Reon Laudat. From her has come a wealth of information. Thanks, Reon, for being there when I need someone to vent to. Your encouraging words mean more than you know.

Thanks to my agent, Dorian, for always having the answers to my impatient inquiries, and sometimes the silly ones as well. You are such a sweetie.

It's the readers who take a writer to that place called "success." Hopefully, I'm on my way. I would like to take this time to thank each and every one of you.

ACKNOWLEDGMENTS

And last, but certainly not least, I want to acknowledge and thank my editor, Monique Patterson, for being so patient, and for not "shaking" my cage when I'm late with revisions. Lady, I keep asking myself this: "How can I be so lucky?"

TOO
MUCH
DRAMA

CHAPTER ONE

Stepping out from her steamy shower, Donneeka Lebeau wiped a spot in the bathroom's mirror and took a good look at herself. Smiling, she liked what she saw. Granted, she probably wouldn't be winning any beauty contests. But on the other hand, she could see herself as a runner-up. *Looks like all those trips to the gym are paying off*, she thought, patting the flat plane of her stomach.

She had her mother's eyes. Large and expressive. Big legs. A tight body. But if it were left up to her, her rear end, the same one her male cousins had always referred to as her "junk in the trunk," could stand to be a tad smaller. On the flip side, she mused, nothing's wrong with a big behind if a woman knows what to do with it. Which was all the reason why she should have been the dancer she was meant to be.

"That's right, girl. Shake your moneymaker." Feeling wild and free, she slapped the wetness along her hip. A dance beat started in her head. To help it along, Neeka pushed the Play button on her boom box and caught the upbeat rhythm as she rocked her slender hips. Snatching a plush towel from the rack behind her, she lip-synched the words to "Who Let the Dogs Out." Then she secured the towel at her bosom so she could really get into the music.

"That's what I'm talking about. Roll it, and twirl it, and tootsie and roll it." She let her knees bend slightly, putting all her emotion into a raunchy-looking tootsie roll that would make the *Soul Train* dancers she watched on Saturday mornings look like hallelujah-happy choir-girls. If she were a real exotic dancer, the tootsie roll would be her specialty because no one she knew could work a roll like she could. That same dance had gotten her seven-year-old cousin three weeks of hard punishment when her mother had glimpsed her showing Neeka how to do it at a family dinner. According to her mother, "Only hookers and street tramps dance like that!" *Well, too bad, because now it's my favorite exercise routine. So there, Mama. Deal with that! And check this out, Mama. Watch me roll it and twirl it and roll it.*

Neeka felt an odd shiver zip up her backside, but she was too into her dance routine to stop. The music was doing its best to keep her locked in its groove, but the minute she turned around and opened her eyes, her damp pelvis still gyrating to the loud music, she was staring into a familiar pair of disapproving eyes.

"And roll it, and twirl it, and—" The beat in her head screeched to a halt. The last two words of the lyrics were caught for a second, then released: "And mama?"

"Goodness, Neeka, what on earth are you doing?" Adeena regarded her with a stern face.

"Dancing—I mean exercising—I mean dancercising." It wasn't just the shock that her mother had caught her doing the forbidden dance of street tramps, but once again her mother had used her key to enter Neeka's house.

"Mama, what are you doing here?"

"Need you ask?" Adeena challenged. Her eyes became slits. "You would think that a woman who spent twenty-two hours in labor with you would always be welcome in your home."

"Mama, you are." A little voice in her head said to let it go, but she couldn't. "Being a welcomed guest is one thing, but you can't just barge up into my place anytime you feel like it!" Suddenly Neeka realized her mother was not alone. Standing behind her, peeking over her mother's stiff shoulders, was a man. A smiling man. There was something oddly familiar about him, but not enough to warrant an unexpected visit on her day off.

Embarrassed, Neeka clutched her large towel tighter and cleared her suddenly dry throat. "Mama, this so wrong! I thought we agreed that you would use your key only in case of an emergency." She fought back angry tears.

"Looks like I came just in time because it appears you're having an emergency right now." Sniffing, her mother's eyes widened as she scanned her daughter from head to toe. "Isn't it a little early in the morning for rump shaking and stripteasing? Lord only knows where you pick this stuff up." Turning up her nose, Adeena added, "And for heaven's sake, Neeka, turn that god-awful music off and make yourself decent. We have company."

We? A bell in Neeka's head ended round one. "Excuse me a minute." Closing the door to the bathroom, Neeka slipped into her white terry robe and returned for what she felt would be round two. "Mama, this isn't fair. It's Saturday, my day off. My whole day is planned, and I'm not in the mood for company right now."

Adeena fanned her face. "Everyone is busy, dear. I know I am. But you need to turn the music down a bit. I'm surprised your sisters next door haven't called city ordinance out. And why is it so hot and stuffy in here? Let's open a window."

As usual her mother was overdressed in one of her many velvet leisure suits. This particular one was the color of dark avocados. An expensive gold chain sparkled from her regal neck. "If I had known you would be dropping by unannounced—again—I would have been prepared." *Like been away on a weekend cruise.* "Next time, Mama, I'd appreciate a call first. I mean, if this is my home, you can't just pop up anytime you feel like it." There. She'd said it. She felt better, even if she knew it wouldn't do any good.

"One can if one pays the mortgage," Adeena gleefully responded after opening the living room blinds and a window. "But that's a subject for later, dear. I have a wonderful surprise. You won't believe who I ran into a few months back. Are you going to make yourself decent or what?"

Oh, Lord. This woman is like the Energizer Bunny. She never stops. Neeka fumbled with the robe's thick belt. "Mama, this is really not a good time. Can't you share your little surprise another time?" Not that she was some five-year-old following her mommy's command, but she couldn't hear herself think with the music so loud. The dogs would have to go back in. She darted back into the bathroom to turn down the music. Then she coughed. "And I think I'm coming down with the flu or something."

Adeena removed her sunglasses. "Probably so, dear, but I like right now better. Besides, I've had my flu shot. And I have some plans for later myself. I had to come right over because I wanted you to be the first." She fanned her face. "And I would hardly call my surprise little."

"The first?" *What the heck is she talking about now?* The man, from what Neeka could see, had made himself comfortable on her sofa. He kept straining to peer around Adeena. If he craned his neck out any farther, the thing would surely break and spill his fool head onto her tiled floor. And those eyes. Where did she know those eyes from?

"Mama, I have to leave in fifteen minutes." Out of habit Neeka glanced at her wristwatch, only to be reminded that she didn't have one on. *Dang it.* She resisted the urge to snatch back her door key from her mother's hand while it still dangled in her sight. That should teach her to stop barging in. But that would be pointless. Knowing her mother, Neeka figured the woman probably had a drawer full of copies of her key by now.

"Don't worry, sweetie. All is well." Adeena made a wry face before pushing past her through the narrow hallway. "Excuse me, dear, but I simply must use your powder room."

"You mean the restroom," Neeka corrected, but only because she knew that her mother hated when she did so. The sound of her mother's clicking heels on tile echoed away from her.

Back to that fool staring at her. Not bad-looking though. Not bad at all. The man was obviously removing her robe with his eyes. Her mother sure knew how to pick her men.

"Excuse me one minute," Neeka said, clutching the top of her robe tighter. "Would you care for some coffee or some tea?"

"You really don't remember me, do you?" Smiling ear-to-ear, the man stood and moved over to where she stood. Holding out a hand, he eased it back slowly when Neeka wouldn't take it. "Braxton. Remember? Braxton Dupree."

"Dupree? No, I'm afraid not. Is that the name of some new hip-hop coffee or tea? Because if it is, sorry, I'm afraid I'm fresh out." Small humor, but she could tell that he wasn't impressed one bit, and she certainly didn't recall asking him what his name was. *Umph.*

"Think hard now. It'll come to you."

Pompous. Just like Mama likes 'em. Must be a new member of the club. She stared, hoping to recollect. Tall. Handsome. The dark blue Dockers, dark knit shirt, and black leather jacket he wore gave a ruggedness to his looks. His moustache was thin and shaped to perfection. The strong jawline and facial features were like those of so many good-looking men she'd seen. "Nope. Not one clue." Still, there was something about those eyes. It wasn't easy to forget light brown crystals on a man. She blew out an irritated breath. "I give up. Refresh my memory."

"Remember Compton? The blue house two doors down on Halo Street? The boy that kept a frog in a box?"

Neeka's eyes lit up. "Oh, my goodness! You're the one who kept a bug hospital and handed out candy with frog juice on it for Halloween? Yuck Boy?"

Braxton looked sheepish. "It wasn't really frog juice. Green Jell-O and lime juice. And I haven't been called Yuck Boy in ages."

"I can't believe it! You always wore those dusty-looking clothes and were forever chasing girls through the neighborhood with some weird-looking bug in hand. I remember now."

"Me in the flesh." Braxton shifted the subject. "But enough about that. You certainly have blossomed into a lovely young lady. But that's no surprise."

"Thank you." No wonder the name didn't ring a bell at first. The four years she'd lived two doors down from him she'd known him by the nickname the neighborhood kids called him. And that name wasn't Braxton. By the time her teen years hit, her mother had made enough money to move them into a better neighborhood. For years Neeka made attempts to keep in touch with her old friends. Girls talked. The last she had heard, Braxton was dating two of her old friends and trying to hook up with another. She should have known he'd end up a gigolo-player. "What about that crazy brother of yours? What was his name? Dummy?"

"Quamee."

"Yes, of course." Neeka moved closer for a customary hug. It was all coming back to her. He had been touted as a good-looker even back then, and Neeka recalled that many squabbles between her friends had been over the playful attention of one Braxton Dupree. Three years younger, she couldn't have been more than twelve or thirteen the last time she saw him. The same coal black, wavy hair. The same flawless complexion. What had once been boyish good looks was now aged handsome in a ripe package. "It's really good to see you again." She was still shaking his hand and smiling ear-to-ear when the sound of Adeena's voice reminded her she wasn't supposed to be happy about their unexpected visit.

"I see you two have done some catching up. Wonderful," Adeena said as she headed straight to the kitchen, while Braxton took the liberty of taking a seat again. "Sweetie, you have anything to snack on in this place? I'm a bit famished. Anything low-carb in your refrigerator? Some coffee would be nice."

"Excuse me while I change into something more decent," Neeka said, ignoring Adeena's inquiry. She clutched her robe shut as she hurried up the stairway into her spacious bedroom and opened the closet door to search for something simple to put on.

The nerve of her mother, she thought, throwing off her robe and sliding into the black spandex pants she normally wore to the gym. *What's the point in having phones if you can't call first?* She located one of her white workout T-shirts and slipped on some black ankle socks.

"Mama, I'll be down in five minutes!" she called out. Outside her window the October morning beckoned. Neeka stood gazing for a few seconds. She could try climbing out. But the thought of breaking a limb or two was a turnoff.

Doing her best to put on a pleasant facade, Neeka trudged back down the stairs to her living room. "I'm supposed to be going to the gym with Mercy around twelve."

"That's nice, sweetie, but there will be plenty of days for body toning," her mother replied between sips of bottled water. She stopped to scrutinize Neeka's attire with obvious disapproval. "Oh, sweetie, why didn't you wear one of your nice dresses? They make you look sophisticated."

Ignoring her mother's comment, Neeka fought off a frown. "I

haven't had time to do grocery shopping, but I might have some coffee cake left over. I'll make that coffee now."

"That would be lovely, dear. I do hope it's that brand I like. You know, that Gevalia coffee. It's heavenly tasting. Anything else gives me gas."

"Anything for you, Mama." *And thanks for sharing that lovely tidbit.*

Padding into her newly retiled and sunny kitchen, she briefly entertained the thought of brewing up a pot of her gourmet Gevalia coffee—the good stuff, the stuff her mother spoke of. But no. Mother and Braxton being unwanted drop-ins, she wasn't feeling it. Gas or no gas, good old instant coffee would have to do.

Neeka felt a heaviness come over her. Her weekends were for her. That's all she asked for. Working with Adeena five days a week was enough. She loved her mother dearly, but that same love was constantly being tested.

"Braxton, I'm sure you remember that Neeka here is the oldest of my three daughters," her mother was saying, like a car salesman throwing his best pitch. "Not to toot my own horn, but she's turned out to be the smartest and the prettiest of the lot. She's a certified accountant and has her BA in business, thanks to my encouraging her to go to school. A mind is a terrible thing to waste."

So is a daughter's time, Neeka mused.

Adeena called out, "Isn't that right, Neeka?"

"Mama, please," Neeka called back. It took all her strength to keep from bolting from the room and running straight out her front door and up the street screaming, *Somebody help me please!* A bolus of resentment welled up in Neeka's throat. It was obvious her mother was up to something. "I'm sure you can come up with a better topic for Mr. Dupree." Any minute, any second, Adeena might pull a printed account out from her black Prada purse listing all her motherly accolades over the years. *Unbelievable.* Neeka shook her head as she plugged in an electric pot to heat some water.

"And not only did all three of my daughters attend the best college," Adeena was saying, like she was taping a documentary on the successful woman in need of a husband. "They were raised as proper ladies of the church. Not a Sunday went by that my girls didn't attend morning or evening service."

"Yes, ma'am." Braxton nodded. "I can see you've done a fine job." He seemed amused at most.

Peeking around a corner at the two, Neeka took it all in and tried to analyze it. Her mother at her house so early; her mother's perfectly made-up face lit by pride. Braxton's face frozen in rapt attention. *Holy Moses. The man is like a new puppy waiting for another tasty morsel.* The two were up to something. She could feel it.

Finishing her task, Neeka walked quietly back into the room and placed an oak tray containing three steaming cups of coffee on the glass coffee table. "Here we go, Mama. I added a splash of cream and two packs of Equal to yours, just the way you like it." To Braxton, she said, "I wasn't sure about you, Braxton, so yours is black." *The harsher the better for you.*

"Black is fine," assured Braxton, smiling up at her. His eyes took her in with genuine interest. "I like mine black every time."

"Well, good for you," she said. Something in his tone of voice and that silly mischievous look in his eyes made Neeka wonder if he was talking about his coffee or his women. She supposed that a gigolo couldn't be choosy. Either way, she didn't care what he liked. She took a seat in one of two chairs across from the brown suede sofa where they sat.

Adeena squinted at her cup. "Sweetheart, that coffee sure did brew fast. I'm telling you, Braxton, my Neeka turned out to be an excellent cook. She's even taken some culinary classes. Cooks like a professional chef. Makes a mean chocolate cake to die for." She sipped. "Sweetie, this coffee is a bit strong."

"I wouldn't have it any other way, Mama." Neeka felt too restless to stay rooted in her chair but did so anyway. For crying out loud, why would her mother be telling Braxton all her business? She looked around the room for something to rest her eyes on but found nothing more engrossing than her mother's face beaming with maternal pride. If the wattage climbed any higher, Adeena's face would be a Christmas tree. Neeka shifted her weight in the chair. Braxton, on the other hand, looked to be sitting at attention. Adeena had that kind of effect on people. It proved to be the same at work. She ran her cosmetic business with an iron fist. Employees perked up and hopped to attention when Adeena Lebeau was on the prowl. Gossip halted, and "idle minds" kicked back into gear. Her mother's presence in the posh office was akin to the pope coming to America.

"So, Neeka. What's been going on with you?" Braxton threw her a question.

Adeena intercepted. "She keeps herself busy. You know idle minds. The devil's workshop. Isn't that right, Neeka?"

"Mama, I believe he asked *me*." She dared not roll her eyes. "Just working hard everyday. Taking one day at a time. Mama here is like a modern-day slave driver."

"Neeka!" Adeena blushed, then soon recovered.

"Mama, you know I don't lie." True, working for her mother hadn't been her goal in life, but Neeka felt reasonably certain that it had been something she had been groomed for since childhood. It wasn't her lifelong dream, but it had its benefits. Fair to say, the salary that her mother paid her as chief controller for Diva Four Cosmetics couldn't be matched if she worked somewhere else. The perks were good as well. She lived in a new, gated community in Ladera Heights.

TOO MUCH DRAMA   11

A modest three-bedroom condo, expense-free. She drove the latest Lexus SUV, a pearl-white RX 330. That too was expense-paid. How many twenty-four-year-olds had a hookup that could measure up to that? Unfortunately, her mother's constant intrusion into her life was part of the package deal.

"Braxton here was telling me that he's single and looking to find a nice young lady to settle down with." Adeena paused and looked at each face. "And of course, I thought about you," she said, lifting her cup daintily to her lips, then frowned. "Oh, my. Are you sure this is the good stuff, Neeka? This coffee is rather harsh and bitter on the tongue."

"Give it a chance on the palate, Mama. It's the good stuff."

"Lord." Adeena made a face. "If you insist. Tastes more like hot mop water."

"Mama, please. It's the good stuff." *Never tried hot mop water myself, so I really wouldn't know.* Smiling inward, Neeka settled back in her seat and watched her guests' faces.

"So, Neeka," Braxton chimed in, obviously making some lame attempt at conversation. "What sort of things do you like to do for recreation?"

Neeka took up her cup and paused. "Oh, I don't know. The usual. Shopping, working. I do a lot of dodge-all playing. I should be an expert at it by now."

"Dodge-all?" Braxton frowned lightly. He couldn't take his eyes off her. "Is that something like dodgeball?" He looked as if he vaguely recalled playing a game with a similar name when he was in grade school.

"You could say that," Neeka half smirked, trying to be witty. "I spend a lot of my time dodging family. You know . . . begging cousins, pesky sisters, and such." She dare not put her mother in the mix, even if she was the main culprit to be dodged. "And then there's my scuba diving, snow skiing, and bungee jumping. The usual stuff."

"Now, Neeka," her mother chided softly, shaking her head, "let's be serious here. You have never scuba dived in your life. Nor have you bungee jumped, and you know it. Braxton, see what I mean? She's such a kidder now."

"I see." Braxton sipped his coffee. His eyes stayed glued to Neeka's face.

Adeena took the ball and ran with it. "As you can very well see, not only is my Neeka imaginative, but she's quite the socialite. Oh, and did I mention that she's a good cook? I tell you, the girl can bake a cake from scratch, and not many young women can do that."

It was the third mention of cooking. "Okay, Mama, I give up." Neeka placed her cup down. "What's going on?" The way her mother kept throwing out tidbits of information about her, she half expected her mother to leap into her tired rendition of how she and she alone had saved Neeka's virginity when Neeka was at the tender age of sweet sixteen. *Holy Moses. What a thing to think of now.* Understandably, it was the kind of childhood memory that Neeka wished would become lost somewhere in the catacombs of her mother's mind. But no such luck. And how could Neeka herself forget such a painfully humiliating experience when she had to discuss it in therapy once a month? So clear in her mind that it could have happened yesterday instead of eight years ago. Eight years, nine months, two weeks, and four days to be exact.

It had all started with sneaking her boyfriend Petey into her bedroom late one night. She admitted that it had been a bold move on her part, but the situation started out so perfect, and they had waited long enough. She still remembered the tingly skin of excitement and the hormone-rich heat that her young body had felt when they had taken their clothes off and had lain together beneath the cool cotton sheets of her bed. It was Petey's first time as well, and so the night was supposed to be a tender and magical time that she would cherish forever.

Soft music in the background had lulled them as they held each other, trying to work their way through first-time jitters and awkwardness. Petey, sweaty-palmed and nervous, had kissed her lightly on her waiting lips, a kiss so soft, so delicate, that it had been more like a feather across her skin. His hands had fumbled and found the hardened nipples of her breasts, had caressed them, massaged them until her body slipped into complete relaxation. She couldn't wait to experience her first time.

And then the unthinkable happened. The next thing they knew, there was a floodlight in the room brighter than the sun itself. Adeena! Her mother had burst into her bedroom with a humongous flashlight and shone the dang thing straight into Neeka's guilty face, then into Petey's frightened face, while screaming, "Good girls do not fornicate!" Those five loud words, over and over again. Neeka felt certain that those same five words were etched permanently into her mind.

The madness didn't end, however. Adeena went to the bedroom wall and clicked on the light switch. She spotted Neeka's Instamatic camera, kept faithfully on her vanity, and picked it up. Neeka still experienced that swell of horror she'd felt as she watched her mother walk back over to the bed, snatch the covers away, and snap a picture.

"For your mother, Petey. Just in case she don't believe me when I tell her about this, and I will be informing her. Pictures don't lie!" Adeena had craned her head for a closer look. "At least you had sense enough to use a condom. Lord knows there are enough unwanted people on this planet. Now, you get yourself up and out of my house, and don't you dare come back!"

Good girls do not fornicate! The flashback made Neeka close her eyes tight and tense all her muscles for a few seconds. She knew now that even if she lived another twenty-four years, she could never feel more humiliated than she had that night, by her own mother, who had the nerve to make her get up and shower for an hour, get dressed, read the Bible, and say ten Hail Marys. And they weren't even Catholic! All for the saving of her virginity.

"And what do you think, sweetie?" Adeena inquired. "Neeka? Are you alright, dear? You look like you're in some kind of pain."

"What? I mean, excuse me?" Embarrassed, Neeka smiled half-heartedly. As much as she didn't feel like doing so, she made herself focus on the present. "I'm sorry, Mama. I didn't hear you. What were you saying?"

"I said, my dear, that Braxton here will be spending a lot of time with us, seeing how he will be joining the family. What do you think about that?"

"Wonderful." Neeka managed a smile, but didn't feel it. *Heck. Hand the whole darn company over to him for all I care.* "Mama, I think it's great. Nothing like new family members . . . I mean—" She stopped to look from one face to the other. "Wait a minute. Joining *whose* family?" Her expression turned serious. "*Our* family?"

"Exactly. And he'll make a fine addition." Adeena patted Braxton's knee, with the man smiling like her announcement was all a head game.

"Mama, you can't be serious. Taking a husband is nothing to take lightly. I mean, that silly dream is no excuse for rash decisions. And you hardly know this man." Not to mention the difference in their age. Braxton was young enough to be her son.

Adeena dismissed her remark with a wave of her hand. "My dear daughter, you are simply a riot at times. And what would make you think that I'm the one who needs a husband?" She chuckled, then grinned. She shook her head. "Don't be silly."

Neeka looked confused. "I don't get it; you just said that he was joining our family. Mama, I heard you."

"It just makes perfect sense," Adeena continued, ignoring her daughter's pleading eyes as she bored her own into Braxton's. "Good and wholesome women are hard to find these days, and Braxton here is looking to find a nice young woman to settle down with, and praise the Lord, I just happen to have three wonderful daughters. You do the math, Neeka." She paused to sip her coffee before adding, with an air of snobbery, "And my dreams are never silly."

Okay. Enough is enough! "Braxton, would you excuse us? Mama, can I see you a minute in the kitchen?"

"Sweetheart, can't it wait? We have company. As I was saying . . ."

"Now, Mama!" Neeka yelled, shocking herself by doing so. Not only was it serious business to raise her voice to her mother, but a tad risky. At the same time it was a risk worth taking because she couldn't stand another minute of her mother manipulating her love life. Not that she had one, but she still didn't need her mother intruding into it.

In the kitchen the two kept their voices as low as possible. "Mama, I thought we went through this before. Remember Alton? The man you matched me up with who gave me a rash on my neck that took three weeks to get rid of? Remember?"

Adeena looked amused. "What? And now you blame me for him picking up some bug from his international travels? I think not."

"Mama, that's not the point! The point is I don't need my mommy to find a man for me. I'm perfectly capable of finding my own."

"Young lady, you keep your voice down! Everyone needs a little help sometimes. First the boyfriend, then the marriage, then the babies. Your mother is not as young as she used to be, my dear. I can't wait for grandbabies forever."

"Mama, for the umpteenth time, I'm perfectly capable of finding my own man."

"Do you happen to see a line of eligible bachelors outside your front door?"

"Well . . . uh . . . no," Neeka stammered under her gaze. "No, but still—"

Hearing part of their harsh whispering, Braxton called out, "Is everything okay in there?"

The two peeked around the corner of the kitchen and replied simultaneously, "Everything is great. Be out in minute."

Neeka wasn't finished. "And that John Paul fella you tried to match me up with, the one you called, 'Mr. Wonderful.' Uh-huh, him. He stole five hundred dollars from my purse."

"That's horrible, dear, but I'm afraid I don't see the point you're making."

Neeka shot her hands to her head and rolled her eyes. She wanted to scream. She felt like she was talking to a tree. It was obvious that her mother would be up to her matchmaking tricks until she was married with two kids and pregnant with the third. "Mama, the point is I want to be left alone. I will find my own baby-making husband myself!"

"I'm sure that one day you will. But in the meantime, there's a perfectly charming man in your living room." Adeena stood her ground. "And there's nothing wrong with that."

"Mama! We are not finished talking about this!"

"You know the old saying: One man in the hand is better than two on the burner." Adeena turned to leave, then halted. "Oh, and before I forget, the two of you have a date for next Saturday."

CHAPTER TWO

O h, God, my head." Neeka made an attempt to sit up, but that smell, so pungent in her nose, was pushing her back down. Every breath she pulled into her lungs was an effort. It was right in her face, horrific and stinging at her eyes. "Will you please get those smelling salts away from me?" She flailed her arms trying to knock the offender away. "Air. I need some fresh air."

"My poor baby," Adeena crooned. Concern crinkled her perfectly made up face. "Are you alright?"

"I'm . . . I'm alright," Neeka mumbled. "I just need some fresh—" Before she could finish her sentence, she heard the click of a camera. Split-second flash blinded her. *Oh God, pictures. She's taking more pictures.* Her eyes had to be red, her hair a mess. There should be a law. "Mama, please, not now. Not like this. I need fresh air."

"Of course you do, dear." Stashing her camera in her tote, Adeena went back to doting. "You know me. I have to keep up my family scrapbooks. Here. Let me open another window or two."

"I don't know what happened." Neeka ran fingers through her hair. "I was okay one minute, and the next thing I knew—" Either the room was spinning, or there was a whirlwind turning inside her head.

Someone had been kind enough to drag her to one of the downstairs bedrooms. *Lord, please let this be a bad dream. Please let them be gone, please, please.* She blinked her eyes trying to clear away the fuzziness and that feeling like someone had placed a thin layer of gauze over her face, but the clearer her sight became, the clearer she could see Adeena and Braxton standing over her bed and sucking up the vital fresh air she needed. Her mother's face was contorted with concern, which was understandable. But Braxton, like a doctor on a house call, had taken a seat on her bed, so close she could even inhale the fragrance he wore, which, she had to admit, was delightful. She recognized it right away: *Mambo. Mambo for men.* Her mother looked worried; Braxton felt her forehead for fever. The whole scenario was unnerving. "Water. Some water, please." Neeka's voice was barely a whisper.

"Mother is right here, sweetie. You just became light-headed again, that's all."

"Mama?" She was dying from thirst, and she could hear her front door open, but neither Braxton nor her mother seemed to hear her whisper for water. "Water, please."

"Mother? What's going on?" her sister Mercy asked, looking fresh as a spring flower in her two-piece denim outfit. "What's wrong with Neeka?"

Oh, this is great. Neeka sighed. Now there were three faces staring down at her: her mother's, her sister's and Braxton's.

"She'll be okay," Braxton offered, fanning his hand over her face, stirring up more dust particles than fresh air. "A little air should do it."

"What happened this time? Did somebody say 'boo' too loud?" To get a better look, Mercy leaned over her mother. "She should see a doctor about those fainting spells of hers. Could be something serious."

"Not as serious as you putting my back in traction, Mercy." Adeena twisted around for a reprimanding frown. "Will you please remove your weight from my back? Girl, what's wrong with you?" Adeena straightened and pulled at the jacket of her ensemble. "Honestly, sometimes you have the common sense of a carrot."

"Oh, sorry about that, Mother." Her feelings temporarily wounded, Mercy moved to the side of Adeena, seemingly oblivious to Braxton. "She doesn't look too good. Maybe we should call for an ambulance."

"For your information, young lady, your sister has seen a doctor. In fact, many times," Adeena hastily threw in. "Donneeka is perfectly healthy. She just has spikes in her blood-sugar levels that cause light-headedness at times. That's all. She's healthy as an ox."

Mercy rolled her eyes to heaven. "Mother, even an ox can get sick."

"Mercedes, I didn't say she was an ox; I said she's healthy as one! Your sister is fine. End of discussion." Adeena flipped the switch on her expression and smiled down at Braxton, making sure that he understood. "Probably didn't eat her breakfast yet. That's all. Am I right, Neeka?"

Neeka cleared her throat. "Right." Deep breath. Exhale. "But I'm okay now, so everyone can go back to what they were doing." Clearly the latter remark was meant for her nosy and prying sister to go back to her own condo. For her mother to go back to what she was doing would mean going back to interfering and trying to control Neeka's life. "Really, I feel better." Neeka sat up in time to see her baby sister, Princess, looking cheerful as she strolled through her bedroom door. Good grief, the girl had on a form-fitting yellow knit jumpsuit that made her look like Big Bird's anorexic sister. Neeka could see the protrusion of hipbones. *Great. Just what I need—another body surrounding me.* Maybe someone should place an Open House sign in front of her condo.

"What's going on?" Princess's eyes grew wide. "Is Nee okay?"

"She's fine," Adeena snapped, more to herself than to her baby girl. "She just needs to rest a minute." Huffily, she pulled at the lapel of her velour jacket. "Your sister has never had a true sick day in her life."

Neeka closed her eyes, wishing she could block out their presence. What in the world had she been thinking when she let her mother convince her that living next door to her sisters would be a good thing? True, there were days when she enjoyed peeking over her fence to see if one of her sisters was out basking in the California sunlight that blessed their adjacent patios. Sometimes she even opened the wrought-iron gate that separated their dwellings and joined them.

During the summer months they could sit out on one of three patios and sip lemonade and talk until the moonlight and hungry mosquitoes told them it was time to call it a night. It was a clean and quiet neighborhood that fit her lifestyle to a tee. A potpourri of culture. She especially liked the fact that Ladera Heights wasn't as stuffy and pretentious as Brentwood, where her mother lived. Even Neeka had to admit that there were times she found herself enjoying the idea of always having someone close by to talk to. She respected her sisters' privacy and had hoped to have the same reciprocated. Respect was the name of the game. The way it should be when families tried "compound" living. But where was that respect now?

"Hey, Mommie," Princess said, her tone a clear indication of joy. "I saw your Bentley outside and had to come see what was going on." Ignoring Neeka reclined along the bed, she went straight over and kissed Adeena's cheek. "Love you. You feeling okay?"

Adeena's face lit up. "Of course, sweetie. Mother loves you too. How are you this morning? Did you sleep well?"

"You know I did. I was planning to bring you a surprise later. I found a wonderful bakery that specializes in those low-carb sweets you love so much."

"Oh, how thoughtful. Always thinking about your dear mother."

Neeka felt her stomach churn. A twenty-one-year-old woman still calling her mother "Mommie" was enough to make her puke. Mommie this, Mommie that. It was all so sickening the way her mother fussed over her youngest child, brushing strands of hair from her face, gazing fondly into her eyes like the two of them hadn't seen one another for months. Sometimes she treated Princess like she was a five-year-old instead of a twenty-one-year-old.

"I have the goodies at my house. I can go get them now if you like. I missed you."

"Maybe later, Princess. And I missed you, too." She patted her youngest daughter's face gently. "But one issue at a time."

Mercy sucked her teeth and rolled her eyes. "Give us a break. How can you two be doing all this missing when you just saw each other yesterday at work?"

"I can miss my mother if I want," Princess snapped. Then she softened her voice. "Don't be hating because I'm close with my mother and you're not. Jealousy is an ugly color, even on you, Mercy."

"Girl, I am not hating," Mercy retorted, tossing back her thick hair. "Why be jealous of a baby trapped in a woman's body?" She folded her arms at her chest.

"Okay now. You both stop this nonsense!" Adeena snapped. "Can't this family get together just once without you and Prin having words?"

"You need to tell Prin to watch her mouth, saying we're not close. Mother and I are very close. Aren't we, Mother?"

Ignoring her middle daughter, Adeena focused on her youngest. "Sweetie, are you taking the supplements I bought for you? I mean, it's been over three months, and you still look a tad too thin. You have to take the vitamins every single day for them to work."

"Mommie, I do take them." The sound of Princess's voice was already grinding on Neeka's nerves. "Maybe it will just take time for the vitamins to help me gain weight, but I do take them every day."

Neeka put a pillow over her head to try to drown out their voices. No such luck.

"Maybe they don't work well when they're thrown back up in the toilet everyday." Mercy's lips slipped easily into a mischievous smile.

"Mercedes Lebeau, you need to hush your mouth!" Adeena snapped. "Must you always be the bearer of lies and bad news?"

"Hmph. Call 'em lies if you want, Mother. I only speak the truth."

"Well, I wish you'd speak it someplace else." Adeena followed her words with a stern look. "There's a time to talk and a time to hush your potato trap. Lord forgive me. 'Bout to make me forget my religion up in here." She tugged hard at the lapel of her jacket.

Sick of the whole scene, Neeka removed the pillow and shouted, "Excuse me! But will someone please get me some water!"

Stunned, four pairs of eyes shot to her face.

"Neeka, dear," Adeena chided, annoyed. "Honey, don't shout, and please don't frown like that. It makes more wrinkles set in."

"Here," announced Braxton, getting up from his place along the bed, "I'll get you something to drink." He stood up and gave Neeka his warmest smile before strolling from the room.

"Good Lord," whispered Mercy the moment she felt the man was out of earshot. "Neeka, who is that? He looks a little familiar."

And then Princess said, "Whoever he is, he's certainly a looker." She couldn't resist one of her giggles. "He looks like an old boyfriend of hers. Right?"

"Why you asking me?" Neeka snapped, then felt bad for doing so. After all, it wasn't her sister's fault her Saturday was practically ruined. "Ask our dear mother. On second thought, take a good look at his face and think back to when we lived in Compton. Mama dug him up."

"Neeka, stop it," Adeena reprimanded. "That's not nice. I didn't dig up anything."

Mercy looked puzzled. "He's someone from the ghetto?"

"Mercy," sighed Adeena. She shook her head. "All of Compton is not the ghetto. I don't ever want to hear you saying things like that."

"Okay then, Mother. Who is he?"

Proud of finding what she felt was the perfect specimen, Adeena allowed a full smile to shape her magenta lips. "Well, if you two must know, he's an old neighbor, and yes, he's from Compton. Remember Braxton? Lived on the same block we lived on—Halo Street. Always dusty-looking then. But look at him now. He's single, a business owner, available, and he could very well be the man I saw in my dream. My future son-in-law."

Mercy looked perplexed. "Braxton? Your future what?"

"She said, 'son-in-law,' Mercy. You heard Mommie."

"No shit!" Mercy squealed, a slip of the tongue she immediately corrected. "Oops, I mean, you don't say. Oh, my goodness. Looks like Mother's dream might be coming true. This is so phat. I'm taking a big guess that the lucky bride is Neeka. Am I right?"

"Oh, God. I feel nauseous." Neeka felt like she could faint all over again. This was one of the reasons she never watched any of the "reality" television shows. There was no need to when she was one of the main characters in her own show: *My Crazy and Obnoxious Family*. Ever since her mother had a dream of a magnificent wedding four months back, she hadn't let up with her ploy to see at least one of her daughters walk down the aisle in December. Neeka didn't see what the big deal was about getting married.

Neeka shot daggers with her eyes. "Please. No more talk about that silly dream."

"I love weddings." Mercy leaned into the bed to give her big sister a hug and a peck on the cheek. "Girl, you have always been good with keeping secrets, but it looks like the cat is out the bag. He seems so nice—and good-looking too. Before or after Christmas? Will the wedding be large? You know me, the bigger the better. Oh, and what about the honeymoon? The Bahamas, my sister. That's the place to go."

Adeena huffed, "Who says it has to be Neeka?" Smiling, she looked from one face to another. "The Bible says it's better to marry than to burn."

Neeka's face had to be looking like stone, but she couldn't help it. All the good feelings she had felt earlier had gelled and hardened into a mass inside her. "Yeah," she nodded, "the Bahamas sounds like heaven on earth. Maybe you can tag along when we go, Mercy." Blowing out a long and hard breath, she folded her arms at her chest. And what was with her mother taking pictures of her while she was half-conscious? Like she didn't have enough photos to wallpaper the White House. Why couldn't they all just leave her place and go back to their own?

"This is so exciting," exclaimed Princess. "December weddings can be so magical."

Neeka glared at her. The youngest of the three, her sister Princess was the one most likely never to grow up and away from her mother. Sometimes, looking at her two sisters, it was hard to believe they had come from the same womb.

Neeka couldn't count the times she'd been told how much her sisters looked like her. All three shared the same large doe eyes; the same smooth complexions akin to creamy peanut butter; thin oval faces punctuated by perfectly shaped and proportioned lips. Each sister had reddish brown hair, but each styled it a different way. While Mercy wore hers in a straight hang with precision-cut bangs, Princess favored ponytails and twisted buns. Neeka preferred a simple hang to her shoulders without bangs. Of the three, Princess was the smallest in weight and height, giving her the perpetual illusion of being delicate and fragile.

"I can't wait for the babies to come." Princess giggled with excitement. She did a little clap for emphasis. "I love babies, the smell of them, their unspoiled innocence. Babies are so special."

"Takes one to know," Neeka mumbled as she looked up to see Braxton entering the room with a tall glass of orange juice and a plate of saltines, some with their tops smeared with strawberry jam. *It's about time. It took you long enough.*

"Sorry it took so long," Braxton said, "but I thought a sweet snack and some juice might help you feel better. I hope you don't mind me making myself at home in your kitchen."

"How thoughtful," squealed Adeena, smiling from ear-to-ear. "Of course she doesn't, my dear. You're practically family already."

"My goodness," teased Mercy, "and the man is attentive to a woman's needs. Good sign. My type of man." She stared at Braxton's head as if an answer to her question would appear in print on the side of it. "Halo Street. Oh, my goodness. I remember you now. The bug boy."

Adeena looked away, annoyed. "Mercy, the man's name is Braxton."

"Mother, I know, and he's the boy who used to make the girls run home crying. What was that name they used to call you? Suck Boy?"

Adeena gasped. "Mercy! Please!"

"Mother, that's what they called him. It's not like I'm making this up." She took a seat in a chair next to the bed.

Princess surprised them all by throwing in, "They called him Yuck Boy." Immediately she looked slightly embarrassed.

"Goodness," said Mercy, batting her eyes in bold flirtation, "time sure has been good to you. Somebody's been drinking plenty of milk 'cause I certainly don't see a darn thing yucky about you now."

Braxton defended himself. "Thanks, but that was a long time ago." He placed the tray on Neeka's lap. "You know how rambunctious young boys can be?"

"Not really, but I wouldn't mind finding out." Mercy did a sly scan from head to toe. Her scandalous eyes lingered a few seconds at the man's backside.

Look at her, Neeka mused. Always checking for a man, but can't boil water without scorching it. If it wasn't for their mother being in the room, Mercy's true color would turn blinding.

Neeka gulped the glass of juice. "Now that everyone is reacquainted we can call it a day. I feel so much better. It's been great." She chanced a smile, but it wasn't enough to make her nervous stomach settle down. Too many people crowded around her had a tendency to make her stomach feel fluttery, like dozens of restless butterflies had been set free. *Everyone, please go home now.* She picked up a plain cracker. Tasted like thin cardboard. "I'm sure everyone has some errands to run today. I know I do. And what about you, Mercy? You still up for that swim at the gym?"

Mercy couldn't answer because she was so busy checking out Braxton.

Princess asked softly, "Will Mr. Dupree be staying for dinner?"

You must be crazy! "Dinner? Prin, I'm sure Mr. Dupree has a busy schedule." What was wrong with her sister? They were all behaving like Braxton was some VIP. If she remembered well, she didn't care much for Mr. Braxton Dupree when they were kids. As far as she was concerned, not much had changed.

"Dinner at whose house?" Mercy asked.

Neeka coughed, almost choking on her cracker.

"Sounds nice," Braxton spoke up, the plate of crackers in his hands. "But not today with my schedule."

Mercy's inquiry was Adeena's cue. "Don't worry yourself about it, my dear. I've made plans for us to get together at my house on Sunday after church service. I want you all there. That means you too, Neeka."

"Mama, I have plans already." She didn't, but it was worth a try. She glanced at Braxton to find him ogling her. And what was that cocky look on his face? He held a cracker in his hand like he would feed it to her.

Adeena smiled, but the sternness in her face was mixed in with the smile. "You certainly do have plans—plans to be at the family dinner. A family that dines together stays together."

Mercy mocked a deep sigh. "And you, our mother goddess, should know." She sat up and moved to the window to gaze out.

Oh, no, Neeka cringed. *Not that mother-goddess mess again. Not now.* "Okay, enough is enough," Neeka said, jumping up from bed with one fluid movement. She couldn't think of where her sudden burst of energy was coming from, but she almost knocked the plate from Braxton's hands. "I'm a little tired, and I think I need some rest. It's okay for you all to leave now. Really."

"Rest?" queried Princess, her thin fingers smoothing Adeena's perfect hair. "Sis, you've barely started your day. How tired can you be?"

Neeka resisted rolling her eyes. "More than you'll ever know." She wasn't physically tired, but mentally she was exhausted.

Braxton stood. "Look, it's been really nice seeing all of you again, but I have to be getting back to my office."

Neeka was tempted to ask just what kind of business that would be. Gigolo Incorporated? But why would she care? "For our mother here, I'm sure that it's been a pleasure."

"Neeka, I can speak for myself. Thank you."

"Whatever, Mama." She clasped her hands before her and tapped her foot in tune to her impatience. If it weren't for her mother playing matchmaker, Braxton's reappearance might have been nice. "I'm just saying that it's been interesting."

"Still spicy, I see." Braxton turned to Adeena. "Until I see you again, Mother Lebeau, take care." He kissed her offered cheek. Then he kissed the hand of each of Neeka's sisters to their silly smiling delight. "You both have turned out as lovely as your mother described you."

"Thank you," they both said simultaneously. They both wore big Kool-Aid smiles.

"Take care of yourself, Braxton," Adeena said graciously. "I'll be in touch with you regarding that business we discussed earlier." She gave him her fondest look.

Braxton tried reaching for Neeka's hand and looked slighted when she pulled it back. "And later for you."

Neeka tried smiling. *I can think of a couple of places you could kiss with those lips.* The feeling was so odd as she watched him leave, his surefooted stroll a sign of his cocky confidence. "Later? Yeah, right," she mumbled. "We'll have to see about that."

Adeena put on her no-nonsense face. "Mercy and Princess, come now. We have a supper party to plan. Not to mention a few other topics I need to discuss." She spoke; they hopped. The two followed her out of the room like waddling ducklings following the mother duck, but not before Adeena called back over her shoulders, "Do eat some breakfast right away, Neeka. We'll be at my house in case you wish to join us—and I'm sure you will." She sniffed and braced her regal frame. "Come, ladies."

Mercy stood, turned, and whispered, "Girl, that man turned out to be fine. If you don't want the hookup, I'll take him."

Glad to be alone, Neeka waved her off. "Be my guest."

CHAPTER THREE

It was well after noon when Braxton pulled his battered Chevy El Camino into the parking lot of Dupree Trucking. Turning off the engine, he sat for a minute to reflect. He had to admit, life had been good to him. Who would have thought that the trucking business would have turned out to be so profitable? Most days he felt like his life was going in the right direction, and then there were other days he felt just the opposite. True, he had all the trappings of what most people thought made a happy life: his own successful business, a nice house, luxury cars, and enough money to live comfortably for the rest of his life. But if that was all it took, why then did he always feel like something was missing?

Braxton climbed out and set the El Camino's alarm. It probably seemed silly to some, considering that the 1984 vehicle had seen better days and could stand a new paint job, new tires, and a new interior. It had been his first car, the offspring of hard work and determination, and the beat-up Chevy was still his favorite. He chose to drive it over his luxury cars because it kept him grounded, reminded him of humble beginnings. Besides, looking like another financially challenged man was the perfect deterrent to female gold diggers.

"Good afternoon, Mr. Dupree. What a beautiful day," his secretary greeted him from her neat desk dotted with family pictures and a small covered basket filled with the sweets that had become a weekly ritual around the place.

"Mertle, good afternoon." Braxton sniffed the air. "Something smells good in here." He took his jacket off and slung it over his shoulders. Changes were going on around him all the time, but one thing that had been constant was Mertle's homemade cookies and cinnamon rolls. "Any messages?" He took the small stash of phone messages she held out, keeping his eyes averted. She would be leaving soon. Already he found himself missing the short thick woman with the perpetual smile.

Mertle handed him the basket. "And here you go. I baked these for you."

"What's this for?" Braxton didn't have to ask. Every Saturday for over four years there was a basket of something warm and sweet scenting the air, compliments of Mertle. With all the office work and busy home life, Braxton couldn't figure out how the woman found the time or energy.

"Just for being such a good boss." Warm dark brown eyes smiled up at him.

"Woman, you have been spoiling me for too many years now. I might have to close the business and move in with you and Melvin."

Knowingly, he took the basket. Any other time her cinnamon rolls would have been the perfect treat with coffee to jump-start his day. But not this time. It had been a week since Mertle had dropped the bomb, giving him three weeks' notice that she was quitting to care for her ill husband and two grandchildren. Now every time he looked in her face, it brought him down to think that he would be losing the most efficient secretary he'd ever had. *Heck*, he mused, *if she was thirty*

years younger and single, I'd ask for her hand in marriage just to keep
her around.

Mertle grinned along with him. "We have plenty of room. You
know you're always welcome at our place."

"Thanks, Mertle. I don't know what I'll miss the most when you're
gone: your smiling face, your professionalism, or your homemade
sweets." Always on time, always willing to go that extra mile to help
him out of a bind, she had been simply the best. Even with ten more
employees in the main office, not one could hold a candle to Mertle.
As much as Braxton tried, he couldn't bear the thought of her leaving
the company. Twice he tried talking her out of it, even offering more
vacation days and a salary increase. But she was raising two of her
grandchildren to keep them from going into the foster care system, so
she didn't have much of a choice. A woman did what she had to do.
There was a soft spot in his heart for women like that: women who
stepped up to the plate. He'd take a mother like Mertle any day over
the one that life had dealt him.

Mertle dabbed at her cap of salt-and-pepper curls. "Probably the
sweets."

To show appreciation, he took out a roll and bit into it. "Umm,
heavenly . . . So whatcha got for me?"

Mertle summoned her professional voice. "You have a transport
down on Interstate 5. I dispatched a tow mechanic an hour ago. Your
presence is needed in department two. Your brother called. Said he'll
try you later. I left this week's payroll and the invoices to be signed on
your desk." She paused then added, "Oh, yeah, that young lady, Miss
Marshall, she called again. She seems to think I'm not giving you her
messages. The woman threatened to drive down from San Diego to
see you in person. So please return her call. I tell you, that woman is
something else."

Braxton snorted. "Yes. She's certainly one persistent woman, but I wouldn't worry about it." He supposed that men made bad decisions all the time. Miss Marshall—Layla—had been just that. A few months back, on a whim, he tried a dating service for the first time. Despite his reserve about it, some of the women he'd met had been okay. Nothing to write home about. But Layla had struck him as special. Special until her needy side emerged. Being a man of means, he didn't mind paying for dinners or a few gifts, but when she started talking about him paying for a lavish vacation, her car loan, and her rent the first month of their acquaintance, it was time to look elsewhere. He stopped calling Layla, but Layla Marshall hadn't stopped calling him.

"I'll call her when I get a chance." A small lie. "That gold digger," he mumbled. He strolled to the sanctum of his office. His private office was his home away from home, and it was filled with the things he enjoyed. The second he stepped inside, rich mahogany paneling cocooned him; a large and sweeping window was generous with sunlight. Exotic-looking palm trees and an expensive sculpture he'd found on a trip to Hawaii occupied one corner. It was all good, but somehow it didn't seem to be enough to sustain him.

Braxton had counted on the trucking business being profitable, but what he hadn't counted on was it being overly competitive. Wearing him down. That's what it was doing. More and more, he was plagued with the feeling that it was time to try his entrepreneurial skills at something else, but for the life of him, he couldn't come up with what new venture to try. It seemed that every time he looked around, one of his drivers was leaving to go haul for a new company or starting his own trucking business.

One thing Braxton was sure of was that he needed something new and exciting in his life, which made his mind wander to Donneeka Lebeau. Now *she* was something to think about. Braxton took a seat and leaned back in the soft leather. His mind floated on sweet memo-

ries. He'd never told a soul, but back in the day when they were young-
sters living a few doors down from one another, he had such a crush
on the sweet-faced Donneeka. Tomboyish then. Flat-chested. Thin
and shapeless back then, he had no idea she would turn into such a
beauty. Of all the girls in the neighborhood, she was the one he most
wanted to squirt his fake bug juice on. Unfortunately, she wouldn't
give him the time of day. From what he could tell from his visit, not
much had changed in that department. The girl still wouldn't give
him the time of day, but boy had she blossomed. Big pretty eyes, large
and shapely legs, a nice big be . . . Dang. *Enough room in her trunk for
two small duffle bags and an emergency kit in case somebody get hurt.*
The woman had a body that could stop a Mack truck with bad brakes
on an icy road. She sure knew how to move that body of hers too. Just
thinking about Neeka's dancing earlier that day stirred his loins.

To channel his thoughts in a different direction, Braxton got up
from his seat, stood at the magnificent sweep of window, and gazed
out. Dupree Trucking, located in the city of Santa Monica, was sand-
wiched between a small toy factory and a modest-sized printing company that catered heavily to nearby businesses and schools. Trucks
from both companies came and went in daily confirmation that each
business was doing fairly well even in an uncertain economy. From
his vantage point, he could see part of his fleet of diesels. This had
once been a prime location: cheap land and close to the interstate. But
now . . . He shook his head just thinking about it. Too many changes
going on around him. Across the way construction workers were busy
raising the new Super Wal-Mart. Soon there would be more traffic to
deal with and higher insurance rates. An offer to buy him out was still
on the table, and something inside him wanted to take the money and
run. A good offer. But losing Mertle and giving up his business produced something close to a stab to his heart.

Trucking had been in his blood for so long it was hard to let go.

Something about large trucks had fascinated him since the age of eight. He had his first ride in one when his foster father had taken him along on a two-day run to Texas. Braxton still recalled the magic of it all, the exhilaration of restless wind dancing softly over his face as his dad's powerful truck rumbled along the stretch of highway. He wasn't concerned with what the truck's haul was, or when delivery was due, but rather with the sense of ultimate power of being in something so huge and fast-moving and yet so graceful.

And then at night when he knew he should have been sleeping, he remembered staying awake in the truck's cabin to glimpse the procession of huge and magnificent twelve-wheelers lumbering by, or slowly pulling out from some rest stop. It had all been fascinating enough to steer him to save every dollar he ever made for the day he could buy his own truck. First one at the age of twenty-three and then another a year later. And for a while business had been good. Satisfying. But he was tired now and much in need of a change.

Mertle buzzed him on the intercom. "Your brother Quamee is here to see you."

Moving back to his desk, Braxton answered her page. "Thanks, Mertle. Tell 'im to come right on in." He took a seat and made himself look busy by straightening a stack of invoices. Quamee Liston wasn't his brother by blood, but the two had been raised for over ten years in the same foster home. Three years his senior, Quamee had been the one who taught him the ropes of his new foster-care placement— what to do and what not to do. Braxton was around nine then, and Quamee had to be twelve. When another foster brother, a bully, had jumped in his face threatening to knock his lights out, it had been Quamee who went to his rescue. A few wrestling matches and fist-fights later, the two had became the best of friends, inseparable. They even referred to one another as brothers. Braxton was always happy to see him, and he often thought that if he could have a true blood brother, Quamee would definitely be his choice.

Braxton's office door cracked open, and Quamee's red-haired head appeared through it. "Hey, bro-man, you busy?"

"Never too busy for you, Quam. Step on in." Braxton leaned in his chair, grinning up at his brother. Quamee didn't have a lick of fashion sense. The man had on an old dark brown leisure suit that looked too outdated to still be in somebody's closet, some run-down brown shoes, and a black Kangaroo hat that made his head appear larger than it was. There was something about the look on his brother's face that suggested he was going to ask for something—more money perhaps. Braxton hoped not. He hated having to turn people down in their time of need, but some people mistook him for the Bank of America. "What's popping, Quamee?"

"You the man. Just in the neighborhood and thought I'd come check my favorite brother out."

"Your favorite—or your only?"

"Same thing." The two double-bumped knuckles.

"What's going on, Quamee? What you know good?" God, he hoped this visit wasn't about money. He loved Quamee like a brother, but what he didn't care much for was Quamee's gambling problem. Gambling was okay when a person sometimes won, but winning wasn't Quamee's forte—losing was. Too many times in the past he had come to his brother's rescue, lending out thousands of dollars so Quamee could continue to pay his rent, pay his car loan, buy food, and maybe update his wardrobe. But obviously the man didn't care much for shopping for clothes. Still, it was all money that Braxton hadn't seen in the form of repayment. Quamee had that "can-you-help-me-out?" look now. "How much is it this time, Quam?"

Quamee clutched his chest, faking wounded feelings. "What? Ah, man see . . . I can't believe you would say such a thing."

"Cut the crap, Quam, and get to the point." Braxton picked up a pen and tapped it along the edge of his desk. He refused to feel guilt for being successful. Several times in the past he'd offered his brother a better-paying job to help support his vice. Even offered to pay for career training. Both to no avail.

"Ahh, little bro, don't be that way. You know I'm keeping tabs. Every dollar, every nickel, and every cent you loan me. You will get it all back, and with interest. I mean that from the bottom of my heart," he added smartly, patting at his chest.

Braxton shook his head. "Look, man, I'm not your daddy, and I'm not trying to tell you what to do with your life or nothing, but maybe you need to try going back to school to train for a better job and leave those horses alone."

"Maybe one day, but not now, little bro. Not when I'm so close I can feel it. I'm telling you, my ship is about to come in. I know it."

"Look," Braxton said, trying to talk some sense into him. "You might think it's okay to take chances with your rent and food money, but face it, when you lose, can your broke behind go home with those horses?"

"Man, I'm not trying to go home with no horse! And this time is different. This is the winner race. I can feel it."

"The winner, huh?" Braxton knew it was pointless trying to convince his brother any other way. "Man, sit down and rest yourself for a minute."

Quamee took a seat across from him. "Look, I promise, this is the last time I'll come to you. This is a sure thing this time. I promise I'll never ask you for another dime. But I'm drowning right now, and you're the only lifeboat in the water. You know me, Brax. I wouldn't ask if I didn't need it."

"The only one you feel comfortable asking?" Was that a good thing or a bad thing? Braxton wasn't so sure. He didn't want to know the details of his brother's sure thing. If he gave Quamee the money, he felt bad, and if he didn't give his brother the money, he would feel worse.

"Man, like I said, I wouldn't ask if I didn't really need it."

He should have known. "How much, Quamee?"

"Before I ask you for another dime, I'd just as well take my own head off. I'm talking actually removing my head from my body."

"Promises, promises. But if you do, don't be coming around here without your head because it'll freak too many people out. So skip the drama and tell me how much." Braxton tapped harder along his paper-blotted desk. Waiting, he looked up at his brother and tried keeping his expression neutral.

"Six thousand."

"What! Are you on crack? Because if you are, Quamee, I'm not down with supporting a drug habit. I'm sorry."

"Brax, it's not like you hurting for money. You have to trust me on this, man. I'll pay you back every penny and then some. You'll see."

Braxton took a deep agitated breath and pushed it out slowly. Who was he fooling? Of course, he would loan him the money. They were brothers, at least in spirit. If his brother was in need and Braxton had the means to help, he had to.

"Brax, I'm telling you, man, you won't be sorry for this one."

"I hope you know what you're doing, Quamee." Pulling his checkbook from the desk, Braxton wrote out a check on his company's account. The idea of selling his business and moving away from California was looking more and more inviting each day.

Quamee's eyes lit up as he accepted the check and put it away in his leisure suit pocket. "Trust me when I say I will pay you back. You won't be disappointed."

Braxton doubted it, but said nothing as he put his checkbook away.

Quamee's face slipped from serious to playful. "So, little brother, what else is kicking with you?" A devilish smile tugged at the corners of his lips. "Oh, yeah, did you get to have your little trip down memory lane? How did she look?" Easing back in his seat, he crossed his legs.

"Who?" Braxton looked puzzled. It occurred to him then that he and Quamee had spoken on the phone the week before, but somehow he had forgotten that he had mentioned running into Donneeka's mother.

"Man, don't play dumb on me. Did you get to see her again or what?"

"Might you be referring to entrepreneur Adeena Lebeau or one of her daughters?"

"Yeah, right. I wanna know about the mama. I'm talking about Mercedes. How did she look? Is she still pretty? That girl was a sight for sore eyes back in Compton. You thought I forgot, huh? Quamee never forgets."

"For sure." *Except when it comes to paying my money back.* "I don't know about Mercedes, but remember the oldest one, Donneeka? She's something else now. Working for her mother, has her own place. Beautiful and independent. I like that in a woman."

"What about her sister? She still have those big pretty eyes?"

What a silly question. "Nah. She had some new slanted ones put in." He waited for a response that didn't come. "Of course she does. All three girls do."

"All single, huh?"

"Yeah. It looks that way." Braxton opened a side drawer and took out one of several loose cigarettes. He had no intention of lighting the thing, not after quitting the nasty habit over three years ago. Going cold turkey hadn't been easy, but determination could be his middle name. After witnessing the slow and painful death of his foster father from lung cancer, he had made up his mind that he wouldn't put another lit cigarette in his mouth. Never. However, every now and then he pulled one of his cancer sticks out and sniffed its aroma. It was crazy, but he could almost swear that sniffing a cigarette gave him strength, kept him from falling back into the undesirable habit. "I know one thing. They were an interesting bunch even back in the day, especially the mother, always walking around with a camera in one hand, taking pictures. Thought she was crazy. Kind of like the Godfather with a camera instead of a gun."

"Yeah? And no fiancé yet?"

"The mother?"

"Man, forget the mother. I'm talking 'bout that second daughter, Mercedes. Is she betrothed or not?"

"Man, how should I know? I didn't stay that long. And I was there to rekindle my interest in Donneeka. God, she was such a cutie in her teens. She used to send pictures of herself to her friends. Sometimes they would share."

Quamee's reddish brown face, complete with a splash of freckles, lit up. "You were the one went to her house. You should have asked questions. Always get the facts. Keeps you from wasting time."

Braxton leaned back in his chair as far as the mechanism would allow. "I know one thing. I know a lot of women, but this feels different to me."

"Where did I hear that before?"

Braxton let the remark slide. "Come on," he said, getting up from his seat. "Let's go find something to eat. My treat."

"Sounds like a plan to me. Maybe you can invite the ladies to your house for dinner so I can hook up with Mercedes. If she still looks like she did when we were neighbors, you need to hook a brother up."

A loose-at-the-lips and snobby-acting woman like Mercy hooking up with a hopeless gambler like Quamee? *That should be an interest-*

ing match. Braxton wanted to burst out laughing. To keep from bruising Quamee's feelings, he fought the urge. "Hold your horses on that one," he replied jovially, picking up his jacket and feeling for his wallet to make sure he had some spending money. "One sister at a time for now."

CHAPTER FOUR

Excuse me, young man, but I do believe I spotted that parking space first!" Adeena Lebeau didn't dare take her eyes off the black Honda that was halfway into her favorite parking spot at the Baldwin Hills Crenshaw Plaza. One of the main reasons she'd risen early for a Sunday morning and driven her silver Mercedes instead of her pearl-white Bentley was to acquire the first parking spot outside of Sears. Not the second one or the third one; it had to be the first one. It was the same spot she'd parked in ever since her first time visiting the center where her beautician, Undra Parks, insisted on running her salon. It wasn't like Adeena had a deed as proof of ownership, or paid out any cash for the title of ownership, but as far as she was concerned, the parking spot belonged exclusively to her.

"You there. Young man," she shouted over to the intruder, "would you kindly remove yourself?" Then almost as an afterthought she picked up the camera from the seat, aimed it in the driver's direction, and clicked.

"No. No, I won't. And you can take all the pictures you want!" The driver of the black Honda, young and defiant-looking, fixed his face as if to say, *Lady, get real. I'm not budging.*

Adeena put the camera down on the seat. She could feel her annoyance slowly rising like drifting steam. She gritted her teeth while mentally calculating that the driver couldn't be more than nineteen or twenty. Still testing the waters. The young were like that. *Such a disappointment.*

She pressed down lightly on her horn, but the driver acted like he couldn't hear. Unfortunately, if her car moved in any closer, she would surely hit his vehicle and no doubt do damage to hers. The two cars were stuck at a point on entry that neither could achieve without the other backing down.

"Dreadful young man," Adeena mumbled under her breath. This was one of the reasons why she hated coming to this very mall—too many dreadful young people. This is what she got for trying to be supportive of her people. There certainly were plenty of high-tech and opulent hair salons in Brentwood that she could very well give her business to, and hiring a stylist to come to her home was another option. But needing to get out from time to time, needing to spend money and see where her money was going, steered her efforts in keeping the revenue flowing in the black communities. It was her staunch opinion that more blacks should support African-American businesses in order to help their own communities, but she thought that for some odd reason those same communities always let in the "undesirables." It was no secret that the Baldwin Hills Crenshaw Plaza was once hurting for more business, and it was a wonder how the small shops had managed to stay afloat in the dull shine of only two major stores: Robinsons-May and Sears.

Adeena avidly believed in patronizing the smaller, independently owned black businesses, but it was becoming increasingly harder to do when she had to constantly deal with young hoodlums, loud and obnoxious thug wannabes, and rude airheaded hoochie mamas who frequented the small mall, especially on the weekends. Not only that, but now that the mall boasted a brand-new Wal-Mart and McDonald's, she could see that more foot traffic was likely.

This is ridiculous. From her open window Adeena leaned forward and shouted, "Young man, would you please move your vehicle!" It was a good thing she was a strong Christian woman or she would have been out of her car and in his face with some words that would shame a sailor. *The nerve of him!* She didn't know what his problem was, seeing as how there were numerous empty parking spots available. His trying to park in her favorite spot was downright ludicrous.

Adeena took a deep breath to settle her nerves. She looked up at the somber October sky where a light overcast held the sun hostage. *What a dreadful young man.* Obviously the driver of the black Honda had not had a solid upbringing by a good mother. Perhaps no strong father figure in the home either. If he had, he would know about respecting his elders. Adeena blew her horn. The Honda driver blew his horn back at her.

Neither car budged.

"Young man, I really don't have all day for this!" Another glance over into his dark face and she could almost see a smirk sliding in. *Oh, I see. You're trying to be difficult.* But she wasn't having it. Oh, who was she fooling? The only thing his kind probably understood was violence and money, which prompted her to reach into her open purse for her wallet. Her French-tipped nailed hand pulled out a crisp bill and folded it in her hand. She put the car's gear in park. *This should do the trick,* she thought as she opened her door and climbed out, leaving her door open to chime in protest.

"Only a fool turns down money," she mumbled as she made her way to the black Honda. Right away she noticed that the driver's face was slowly changing. What had first been some kind of smirk of defiance for the standoff was now metamorphosing into suspicion at her approach. She walked straight up to the driver's side. "Excuse me, young man," she said as she tapped lightly on the glass. It inched down a bit more, but not enough. She could clearly see his apple-red eyes bulging as they sized her up. They seemed to cry out, *Lady, what the hell are you doing?*

"Look, lady, I saw this spot first, and . . ."

Adeena held the crisp hundred-dollar bill up for the young man's eyes to feast on. Oh, yeah, she knew that would do it. She could see the spark of hunger flickering at the back of his beady eyes. Money was a language that everyone spoke. "The Lord certainly is good. Isn't he?" Adeena said.

The Honda driver looked skeptical, like her generous offer might somehow be a trick; then greed kicked in, just like Adeena knew it would.

"For real?" The driver's dark eyes lit up. "You wouldn't be playing now, would you?"

"I don't play," Adeena replied, allowing the driver to slide the money from her hand through the window's slit. "Now can you be a dear and move your car?"

"Hey, no problem, lady. It's all good. Hell, I wish my mama was this generous when she wants her way. You alright, lady."

"I'm sure." Smiling, Adeena braced her thin and regal body and walked slowly and gracefully back to her car while the black Honda retreated.

"Hey, thanks a lot, lady."

"You're welcome," Adeena called back without turning around. "And God loves you too." She slid back into her supple leather seat. "Now move that piece of junk," she mumbled. It never fails, she mused, guiding her Mercedes into her favorite spot. It all boiled down to one fact that she'd personally proven over and over again during her fifty-eight years on God's good earth: Everyone has a price. Everyone. No matter what the situation was, money could change it. It's all a matter of coming up with the right amount.

Adeena got out and made her way to the mall's entrance. Despite it being overcast, there was a hint of warmth in the air, a promise of the heat and humidity to come later. She smoothed the dark pink silk of her flowing two-piece ensemble and picked up her pace. Undra never complained about Adeena's tardiness, but still Adeena didn't want the young woman to get the impression that she thought her time wasn't valuable.

She was twenty minutes late for her hair appointment thanks to the parking ordeal, but Adeena felt confident that it would be okay because she was the only patron who paid her beautician a nice stipend to open shop before business hours. Being a private person, she never felt like she was one of the regular clients; therefore, there was no reason for her to have to sit among them as they waited to get some ridiculous color put in their hair. She'd seen the tones with her own eyes, right in Undra's shop: the shocking pinks, the flaming reds, the blues, the greens. Colors that had no place on human hair. She had no tolerance for being around such nonsense, and because she was a woman so used to preferential treatment, it was nothing for her to toss out a few hundred bucks in tips if it helped to facilitate being treated special. A few times in the past, she'd paid Undra four times the price for doing her weave on a Monday, which was the only day of the week the poor woman had to rest. Her girls would pass out if they only knew, but what the heck. It was her money and her business.

"Where have you been?" Undra Parks mouthed through her glass shop door.

Adeena tinkered with placing her keys in the right compartment of her expensive bag while she waited for Undra to undo the lock, but the minute she stepped inside she noticed right away that one of

Undra's eyes looked red and slightly swollen. *The poor child.* For as long as Adeena had been coming to the Classy Look Salon, Undra had been having marital problems that included episodes of infidelity, outside baby-mama drama, and domestic violence. Why the woman didn't get it over with and leave the man was a mystery. She herself would rather be penniless and left alone than share her bed with a man who constantly abused her and made her feel ugly and unloved.

"Sorry to keep you waiting." Adeena knew she was in for an earful once Undra got started on her hair, but sometimes she didn't mind. She had plenty of advice to offer, but her foolish hairdresser never applied any of it.

"No problem. So how you doing this beautiful Sunday morning, Miss. A.?" Weary, but still smiling, Undra led the way to her shampoo area and stood waiting for Adeena to get settled.

"I can't complain," Adeena responded, looking around for a spot to place her Gucci bag. She dare not place her bag along the floor like some women would do. She wouldn't have half the wealth she had today if she were so careless as to allow her purse to touch a floor, especially a horrible black-and-white checkered one. Superstitious or not, she moved to the next shampoo chair and placed her bag on it. "You doing okay yourself?"

"I'm fine, thank you. Maybe a little tired."

"Hopefully I won't take up too much of your time." Adeena patted at the top of her hair, feeling for tracks. One of the reasons she'd been coming to Undra for so long was that the woman was the best at what she did. Undra had a way of hooking up a weave that even the devil himself would be hard-pressed in locating her scalp-grown hair from the added extensions. Not only that, but over the years the two had developed a mutual closeness, and it often felt to Adeena that they could confide in one another, no matter how delicate the topic.

True, she wished that the salon was in a better location and had a more opulent environment, but there didn't seem to be much she could do about it. More than once, she'd even tried offering Undra the down payment on a brand-new salon in Brentwood, five blocks from her own house. But Undra always said, "Oh, no, Miss Adeena. I couldn't let you do that, but thanks so much for offering!" Undra's staunch refusal had been a soft slap in the face each time, but Adeena quickly got over it. Actually, she could see how Undra's southern upbringing might stick out in an upscale city like Brentwood.

"Don't forget my deep conditioner." Adeena sat back in her chair, while Undra fixed a black apron around her own thick waist and went about the business of securing a plastic shampoo cape around Adeena's neck. Undra always wore black. Black pants, black blouse, black shoes, and black apron. Adeena saw it as an attempt to make her size twenty-four frame look more slender, but it wasn't working. Only exercising, detoxing the liver, and cutting down on carb intake, fat, and dairy products could do that.

Undra fluffed her dark wine curls. "Now, Miss Adeena, I do the same service on you every week, and you remind me of the same thing every time you come. You know I have the memory of an elephant. I never forget your deep conditioner, and ooh, I really like that outfit you have on. It sure is nice."

"Thank you." No sense in telling the woman that she had three more at home just like it, only in different colors. While Undra fussed with her hair and talked about her latest marital crisis, Adeena listened in silence. She felt confident that the woman would have her fixed up and out of her shop by ten A.M. Perfect. Church service was at noon, and she hated being late.

Undra's hands felt like pure magic on her scalp as she manipulated her fingers through the shampoo suds. Adeena detected the delicate scent of coconut swirling and mingling with the air. "That smells good," she said.

"I knew you would like it. It's something new I'm trying." Undra went quiet a moment before asking, "How's your family?"

"Everyone is fine," Adeena sighed gently. "Thank you for asking." This was the part that Adeena wasn't so sure she liked. It was one thing for Undra to slip into details about her own private life, but it was an entirely different matter when the woman tried to ease her way into Adeena's like they were in the same league, as if they had more in common than the beautifying of her hair.

"Any grandchildren on the way?" Undra inquired, her fingers making curly circles along Adeena's scalp.

Adeena had her eyes closed. She felt like she could drift off to sleep, but the mention of grandchildren jolted her alert. It reminded her that she had planned to call Braxton to confirm that he could join her family for morning worship. "There's no bun in the oven yet, but all that could be changing soon enough because the cooks are beginning to gather in the kitchen."

"Sounds like your little plan is in action," Undra said, speeding up her shampoo massage. "So, which one of your daughters will be getting married first?"

Goodness, thought Adeena, mocking disbelief that the woman still recalled a conversation they'd had long ago. Three months earlier, when Adeena had first started doing business with Braxton Dupree, she'd made the mistake of mentioning the man to Undra while the woman was manipulating her scalp.

She must have slipped beyond relaxation because she had meant to keep the whole ordeal to herself until she could see if her plan would work or not. Vaguely, she recalled telling her hairdresser she had discovered the perfect man for one of her daughters—hopefully for Neeka. Sweet mercy, that Undra had a way of working with her scalp; working her into a state of mind that could make her tell secrets from her own past.

"Let's just say that my Mercy is quite interested, and Princess, my youngest, is nowhere near ready for a husband. However, the man is perfect for my oldest. Just perfect. Unfortunately, I can tell that she doesn't care much for him." Adeena could feel her guard slide down, and she felt extremely relaxed. Maybe this was why some hairdressers were made privy to their clients' deepest and most intimate secrets. It started with the heavenly manipulation of the scalp, much like stroking the soft bottom of a fussy baby to soothe it. What the heck. It couldn't hurt to discuss the matter with Undra. After all, it wasn't like they ran with the same crowd or associated with the same family members. And if she did divulge intimate tidbits of her personal life, who could Undra possibly repeat such information to anyway? The supply deliveryman perhaps?

Adeena felt confidence and pride swell her chest. The kind of maternal pride that loosened lips. "Neeka can't stand the man right now, but I know my Neeka like a book. She tries so hard to appear strong and complicated, but the truth is, she simply can't resist a good thing. And it's like they say, a mother knows best. Braxton is as good as it gets." Thoughts of the sweet babies they would make—after marriage, of course—brought a glow to her face. An out-of-wedlock child was something she couldn't tolerate. Not after all the work she'd invested in her girls. "I'm planning a wedding on the water at sunset. Perris Lake perhaps. I have a few rental homes out that way."

"Sounds so romantic. It reminds me of the historical days when arranged marriages were the norm. Shoots, in some third world countries they still honor arranged marriages today. Who knows? If I had let my own mother pick out a husband for me, I probably wouldn't be married to the fool I'm with today."

Adeena sniffed. "Oh, what a shame. But that is something to consider, my dear. And what was your husband's name again? Harry?" Undra had no doubt told her that man's name over a dozen times, but because she really held no interest in Undra's husband or his barbaric tendencies, she could never remember the man's name.

"Harold the fool."

"Yes, of course," Adeena snorted. "Neeka might not see it now, but eventually she will. Braxton is the one. Handsome, smart, and he has the patience of Job. Not the highest education, but enough to run his own business. No ex-wife or baby-mama drama, and you know how important that can be."

"Works for me. Shoots, as long as he's good to her and treats her with respect, it could work," Undra said, looking off in reflection. "Maybe you can give me some tips on finding a good man. Lord knows I need to find one."

Adeena huffed. "What's stopping you?"

"I keep asking myself that same thing, Miss. A. I mean, I'm a good woman. I may not be perfect, but I'm a good person. I keep my house clean. I keep myself looking decent. I take care of my kids. Shoots. It's my time to have a worthy man in my life. Am I wrong to want Mr. Right to come into my life?"

Amused, Adeena allowed herself a light chuckle. *Poor dear probably wouldn't know a worthy man from a hole in the wall.* She couldn't blame the woman for wanting better though. What woman in her right frame of mind wouldn't? "Quite the contrary, sweetie. You see, I prayed about finding the right son-in-law. I prayed and prayed and waited for him to come along. I saw my Neeka getting married in a dream. It was so extraordinarily real and so beautiful. It was right before Christmas and very festive. I can recall every detail. She with this bright halo of light that followed her down the aisle. She wore light silver instead of white. Nighttime overlooking the water. Stars blinking above. Moonlight bathing her face."

"And did she look happy in this dream of yours?"

Silly woman. No, she kept her arms folded stubbornly and was frowning through the whole ceremony. "My dear," chuckled Adeena, "of course she looked happy. She was stunning, proud and so happy. Those two emotions should always go together."

"And what else?" Undra appeared to be all ears.

"I needed cosmetics delivered. He owns a trucking company that delivers. I believe it's destiny." Adeena stopped to cough a few times, making sounds of clearing her throat. She patted at her chest. "Ooh, my. Water. May I please have some water?" It was a ruse to steer Undra's focus away from her family business. Maybe she could change the subject and talk about something else, like weight-loss tips or, perhaps, how Undra had acquired her swollen eye.

"Hold on, Miss Adeena, I'll get you some water." Undra dried her hands, hurried over to the watercooler, and was back pronto to hand her client a small paper cup of cold liquid. "Here you go. Take your time now. You need more, just let me know." Picking up her tube of conditioner, she squeezed some of the light pink crème onto Adeena's head.

"Thank you," said Adeena, hoping she could now rest her lips. Too much talking had a tendency to dry out her throat.

Undra removed the paper cup from her hand. "So, this guy . . . this Braxton guy delivered your cosmetics, and then what happened?"

Mercy, Jesus. This woman never stops running her potato trap. "Oh, yes . . . I plum forgot what I was talking about. Must be old age. Let me see now. Oh, that's how I ran into him. I went to his place of business myself. I make it a habit to meet with anyone handling my merchandise. We got to talking about our hometown. Of course, he wanted to see the girls again."

"Of course," agreed Undra.

"I could see the sincerity in his eyes. The eyes lead straight to the soul, and they rarely lie."

"That's true, Miss Adeena." Undra stopped and stood back on

thick legs. "Now take my husband, Harold; he has devil eyes. His mama said he was born with 'em."

"Devil eyes?" Adeena raised a perfect-shaped brow and fanned her face. "My dear, what on earth—"

"It's true," confirmed Undra, massaging conditioner through Adeena's hair. "Harold's mama said he was born with apple-red eyes, like he might have been smoking funny weed or something while he was inside her womb. His eyes stayed that way, red on red. But what freaked me out in the beginning was that when he slept, his eyes stayed half-open. They never close completely."

Yeah, that certainly sounds like some devil eyes. "Well, isn't that amusing. But Undra, sweetie, I have to ask you this now. Didn't you know all this before you married him and had four children by the man?"

"Give me a 'g,' and call me guilty. Yes, I did. But what can I say? He was good in bed. Guess he had the devil in him when it came to that too." They laughed again.

"Sometimes it takes more than a good romp between the sheets."

"I thought he was special."

"Well, good for you, Undra. Some women never find that one special man. Devil eyes and all."

"I wish I could agree with you, Miss. A, but ain't a damn thang special 'bout that man anymore! Excuse my profanity—I mean, I know you a strong Christian woman and all—but I have to tell the truth about this. If he were a car, he used to be a Lexus, but now he's a Yugo that just won't go."

"Oh, dear. I'm so sorry to hear that. But anyway, to shorten my story, Braxton has never been married. I even had a private detective check him out further—you know, leisure time—and see if there was any baby-mama drama on the horizon. He checked out. He and I have been talking since. I don't know if I mentioned this to you before, but

I'm a mother goddess, and we goddesses of motherhood take a dedicated interest in our children that goes beyond rearing them to adulthood. Just because your children become of legal and consenting age does not eliminate the need for guidance in their lives. She may not know it, but my Donneeka needs my help."

"Wow." Undra grinned. "Maybe that's why I turned out the way I did. I needed a mother goddess, not just a plain old mean mama in my life." She made sure that Adeena's head was completely covered in conditioner. "Donneeka. I like that name. What about your other two daughters? What are their names again?"

"Mercedes and Princess Ferrari, but we call her Princess."

"Oh, that's right. You have that car-theme thingy going on with their names. That's . . . well, it's different," Undra said. She placed a clear plastic cap on Adeena's head and made sure that all her hair was neatly tucked in. While Adeena's hair soaked up the silky conditioner, Undra turned her attention to some light cleaning-up. "Sounds like some lucky girls if it's true what they say about a mother knowing what's best."

"It's true," Adeena confirmed, a warm glow illuminating her honey-brown face. She checked her Rolex and noted that it was eight A.M. "Oh, my, look at the time. Undra, be a dear and pass me my bag. I need to make a call."

"Sure thing." Undra fetched Adeena's bag from the next chair and held it up for inspection. "I love this bag. This is really nice. Shoots, I think I like this one better than the Prada you had last week. Here you go."

Sounded like another pre-Christmas hint. "Thank you, dear," Adeena said. Then, removing her phone, she pressed for the stored number that would ring Braxton's place. She hoped he hadn't forgotten about the noon service. The devil stayed busy in the lives of young single men, and any potential son-in-law of hers was one who believed in the goodness of God and regular church attendance. She wouldn't have it any other way.

After four rings she heard his deep, sexy, sleepy-sounding voice on the line. "Braxton? Hello, dear," she said. "Shall I expect you at church at twelve today? Good. Of course, Neeka will be there. And Mercy as well. And do be prompt now. Rev. Clayton is a stickler for promptness. Okay then. We'll see you there."

CHAPTER FIVE

I will not be told who to date. I'm a grown-assed woman!" No. Better to leave out the a-word. "Mama, I'm a grown-behind woman, and I resent you constantly trying to fix me up with some man!"

She was standing in the full-length mirror of her downstairs guestroom. It was Sunday morning, and Neeka had been rehearsing her lines for a good five minutes. When dealing with her mother, not only did her words have to be just right, but the tone of her voice needed to be serious, but in a careful kind of way. True enough, her mother had always presented herself as nothing less than a devout Christian woman of high morals and equally high standards, but she could also be a chameleon. Adeena could be soft like a yellow baby chick one minute, and in the blink of an eye, she could turn flashing red like a stoplight.

"Instead of worrying about who I marry, you need to find a husband for yourself! That's what you need to do." Not only was her mother a person who didn't take criticism too well, she possessed a crouching temper that was constantly obscured by her soft-spoken kindness. For too many years Neeka and Mercy had joked that Adeena would climb in the ring with Mike Tyson for a few rounds if the man spoke to her in the wrong tone.

Neeka stood straight and cleared her throat. If she faltered, tears could rush up and claim her. She threw her head back with pride. "Mama, I'm an adult now, and I don't think I have to do what you say anymore." Turning for a side view, she took another deep inhale. "Mother, begone with your talk of marriage and babies, and leave me be. In case you haven't noticed lately, I'm a grown-butt woman! My butt is grown. Heck, my butt is all wrong." *Oh, heck, who am I fooling?*

She stared at her reflection. She felt sixteen years old again, begging her mother to let her wear her hair in a sexy-looking French roll with a side-hang. The more she asked, the more her mother's answer had been no. Taking matters into her own hands, Neeka had put her hair up in that French roll early one morning and come downstairs dressed and ready to go to school. It didn't take long for her mother to snatch her roll, get her camera, and take a picture. Half an hour later she was dropped off in front of her school with her hair looking like a tousled bird's nest. Her mother was a hopeless control freak. It always had to be Adeena's way or no way. Tears threatened to pool in Neeka's eyes. She had had no control back then, and not much had changed.

Smoothing the sides of the skirt of her navy blue two-piece suit, she tried her speech with a hand on her hip, sassy. No. Mama don't play that. She tried a hand off her hip, one hand behind her back. "Mama, I refuse to be part of your matchmaking plans. No, I will not be part of your asinine plot to hurry up and marry me off! I don't care how nice or good-looking you think a guy is. I am not feeding into your madness, and furthermore, Mama, if you think Braxton is so wonderful, perhaps you"—she jabbed her finger, pointing for emphasis at her reflection—"yes, you, Mama! You should marry the man and have his baby!"

Heck, no. Maybe not that last part; after all, her mother was a fifty-eight-year-old woman. A pregnancy at her age, if such a thing was even possible, would probably kill her for sure. "Then, mother dearest, you should marry the man and adopt a baby, because I refuse to be part of a marriage just to satisfy you. There! I said it! And I'm not marrying anyone until I get good and ready." *Actually, until I get ready, because I'm already good.* She winked at her reflection.

Standing before the mirror, she felt victorious, but her triumph was cut short by the sound of clapping. Spinning around, Neeka held her breath, but quickly released it at the sight of Mercy dressed in a baby-blue chiffon dress, ready for Sunday services. "Dang, Mercy! Don't be sneaking up on me like that. You scared me half to death!"

"And good morning to you too, big sister." Mercy leaned against the door entrance, her hands folded at her chest, observing. It was obvious from her expression that she was fighting back laughter. "Poor Neeka. If that's the best you can say to your sweet and dear mama, I better get started on some wedding invitations now."

Forget that. "Wait a minute here. Please follow me."

"What?" Mercy feigned ignorance and moved aside to allow Neeka to pass. Rolling her eyes, she followed Neeka back into the living room. "What is it?"

"Be patient. I want to show you something important." Neeka opened her front door, stepped outside, and closed the door lightly behind her. She pressed the lit doorbell and listened for its distinct chime, then entered back into her condo. "Do you know what that is?"

"Umm. A doorbell?"

"You're absolutely right, Mercy. A doorbell. And do you know why they place doorbells on the outside next to doors?"

"Umm. Could it be to annoy people when they are trying to rest or sleep?"

"Very funny, Mercy. Here's another question for you: Have you noticed that I always ring your doorbell when I come over to your place?" She waited for a response.

"Come to think of it, sis, yes, you do. How thoughtful of you."

"I always ring because I respect your privacy." She walked over and took Mercy by the hand and led her to the front door. "Now, let's see you try ringing my doorbell for yourself. It's really not hard to do."

"Okay, okay, I get it," Mercy protested, snatching her hand back. "It's not like you have a real life or something I haven't seen before."

"No, I want you to try it. You know the saying that practice makes perfect? It's so true. Now try it." Unfortunately, before she could show Mercy out, her front door opened and in bounced Princess, looking flustered.

Unbelievable. "Can someone please tell me what's the point in having a door if no one knocks?"

"Oh, uh, sorry. Can I get a ride to church with you two?" Princess looked from one sister's face to the other. "I feel a little dizzy this morning."

Neeka resisted the urge to repeat her learn-to-knock lesson. "You poor thing."

"So, what else is new?" Mercy crossed her arms at her bosom and headed for the kitchen.

"I must live in a barn. That's what it is. This is not my condo; this is a barn open to the public." Neeka channeled negative energy into tidying up her living room. She fluffed a pillow on her sofa, then removed an empty glass from the coffee table. The place could stand a thorough dusting, but she didn't have the time.

"Stop being so dramatic." Mercy came out from the kitchen with a piece of bologna folded between one slice of wheat bread. "This will never be your condo until Mother hands over the deed in your name. And to be honest, I don't see that happening anytime soon. But if our coming to visit bothers you so much, maybe you should practice locking your front door more often. This may be a nice area of Ladera Heights, but crime is like a fungus, my dear sister. It's growing everywhere."

"In more ways than you know," Neeka snorted, heading for her kitchen to run water in the sink.

"Neeka, can I get a ride to church with you?" Princess asked again. She held a hand to her head like it might tip over. "My head feels awful, and I really don't think I can drive this morning."

"Let's see now," Mercy said, pausing for a moment. Then, eyes squinting, she pinched up her pink lips. "With three moving violations in two months, and one fender bender, I would have to say that your driving can't get any worst."

"Mercy, stop picking on her," Neeka chided softly. "If you can't say anything nice, why say anything at all?" Sometimes it seemed to her that from the day their mother brought Princess home from the hospital, Mercy had appointed herself as the picker. At the end of every statement Princess uttered, Mercy made some kind of taunting remark. Maybe because she was so darn good at it. At any rate, Neeka often found her belittling remarks annoying, but then again, Mercy picked at everyone she came in contact with, not just their youngest sister. Neeka continued, "And I'm not done with the matter of you just walking into my place all the time. If you feel like discussing something, let's discuss that." Then Neeka turned her attention to Princess. "What's wrong with you?"

Mercy looked in their direction and snorted, "Oh please. There's nothing wrong with her except she had too much to drink last night at the club."

Oh, my God, did her sister just say "the club"? From the time Neeka was in Pampers, her mother had preached and preached about the evils of socializing in bars and clubs: "Only serial killers hang out in clubs," and "To play in the devil's playground, one only needs to go to a bar or a club." Neeka still remembered those one-liners as if they were scrolling neon signs in her head. Once, maybe twice, she had been inside a club, and that was only to use a pay phone or the restroom. "I know you are not standing over there saying you and Princess went to a club. A nightclub?"

"No, Neeka, we went to a Girl Scout club meeting," Mercy said flippantly. "Of course it was a nightclub!" Mercy tossed her loose hair and did a little wiggle-hip dance to bring her point home. "Girl, baby sister and I danced, and we drank, and we partied like it was nineteen ninety-nine, whatever that means."

Princess looked queasy. "Mercy, I wish you would stop talking about it. I just want to forget we went there."

"And Mama will have a cow when she finds out." Neeka took up a towel and dried her hands. "Thought you two were at Mama's place discussing my pending courtship with Braxton."

"We were," Mercy grumbled, making a face at the mention of their mother. "Wasn't like it was a sleepover. We started off discussing you hooking up with that fine Braxton. And finished with the possibility of Braxton and me hooking up. All that talk had me all heated up." She fanned her face. "A night out was the perfect antidote. Danced my behind off. See?" She turned around for a view of her derriere. "Besides, what Mama don't know won't hurt us. Knowing her, if she had known, she probably would have arrived at the club with her Bible in one hand and her trusty camera so she could take our picture to add to her collection of do-wrongs over the years."

Neeka grinned at her words; she knew them to be so true. "It's nothing to laugh about. I'm still looking for that infamous picture of me and Petey every time I go to her house. I can't seem to find it. But when I do, I plan to burn that darn thing on her front lawn. Maybe even find that photo of you in that police car after that shoplifting incident. Burn it all!" She lined up sugar and creamer before turning on her coffeemaker.

"Good grief. I was just a kid acting out. I mean, it wasn't like I didn't have the money to pay for that stupid blouse. Mother didn't have to come out to that squad car with that darn camera. I don't care what nobody says, she was wrong for that."

"And you looked so frightened. I get a kick out of it every time I see that picture of you. But don't worry. Like I said, when I find where Mama keeps her stash of pictures, I will burn that one right along with the one of me and Petey. Right on her front lawn. Watch me."

"Yeah," Mercy said, joining in. "Burning pictures out on the front lawn in Brentwood should be quite interesting, especially when the police arrive and haul your crazy behind away. Let me know in advance so I can bring a chair and some popcorn."

"I think I need some aspirin." Princess took a seat at the small kitchen table, demurely folding her hands in her lap. "Where were you, Nee-nee? We waited for you to come to Mommie's and help with wedding plans. Mommie seems to think that one of us will be having a grand wedding out on the lake. She wants white doves released over the water, but I think butterflies are better. She's such a romantic at heart."

"Right," Neeka said, opening a cabinet, reaching up, and pulling out her favorite yellow mug. "Obviously Mama has forgotten that this is America, and we have the freedom of choice." She banged her ceramic mug down hard along the tile. "Crazy woman!" Every muscle in Neeka's body tensed up. "I don't know about you two, but Mama is insane if she thinks she'll get to pick out a husband for me."

"Amen," Mercy agreed with sly smile. "But you have to admit, Braxton is worth checking out. I'm up for it."

"Well, good luck with it. Anyway, that woman is not stealing my joy today." Neeka turned and noticed the periwinkle Evan Picone suit Princess had on. It was such a pleasing color on her, and the matching shoes and gloves gave the outfit a nice finishing touch. Her sister might have a hard time spelling "sophisticated," but she knew how to hook up a classy look. "You look nice, Prin."

Neeka poured herself half a cup from her coffeemaker. Last thing she needed was too much caffeine before going to church services. "So, what club was it?"

Mercy was back in the refrigerator. "That place over on Slauson and Overhill Drive. You know the one—La Louisanne or La-la land. Something like that. And it was hopping too. At first, I didn't think it would be fun, but I kept hearing about it and decided to give it a try. Cute guys all over the place, and they were buzzing around us like crazy."

"Mommie says when the first one gets married, she'll pay for the entire event." Princess removed one glove, then the other. "That could mean a large turnout, don't you think so, Nee-nee?"

"Prin, are you deaf? I don't want to hear that madness right now. Mama is crazy, I tell you!" She hadn't meant to yell, but her emotions got away from her. Her youngest sister hung her head, making her feel regretful for shouting. "Prin, I'm sorry. I just don't want to talk about that right now."

"I'm sorry. It's just that . . . well, Mommie is so happy about the possibility of having some grandchildren soon. You know how she gets." Like a child after being reprimanded, Princess lowered her eyes. "She just wants the best for all of us."

Mercy walked over and took a cup down from the cabinet. "Forget about Mother dearest for a minute. All I know is I haven't had a good time like I did last night in a long time, and I don't regret a thing. Might do it again in fact. Your mother may be two cards short of a full deck by trying to get you hooked up, but she will not be standing in the way of me getting my party on anymore. Mark my words."

Neeka looked incredulous. "My mother? You came from crazy genes too."

"If you two are going to talk bad about Mommie, I can go wait in the car." Princess stood to leave. "She gets a little carried away at times, but she means well." She plopped back down in her chair. "She deserves respect at all times."

"Yeah, and if you believe that," Mercy retaliated, "maybe you should take a space shuttle and go wait for us on another planet. She may have you fooled, Prin, but I can see through that selfish woman like glass. Trust me, that crazy dream she claims she had about one of us getting married in December is about her. Adeena."

"Mercy, stop it. Prin has a right to her own opinion." *Even if her opinion is whacked*, Neeka thought.

"Face it, Miss Princess," Mercy pressed on, "she may be our mother, but it's becoming increasingly clear that she's not going to stop with her matchmaking until she gets her way."

Princess popped up again. "Do you have aspirin in your medicine cabinet or not? I don't like hearing negative talk like this about Mommie. It's not right."

"Shall I go get the aspirin for you?" Neeka asked, placing her coffee down. *Big baby.* She half-expected Princess to start crying and say, "Yes."

"No, I know the way," Princess answered, walking from the room.

"Back to what I was saying about last night," Mercy said. "You know me; I rarely go to clubs, but I made up for it last night. And even Miss Princess had a good time. That girl even gave her digits to a couple of nice-looking gents at the club."

"Better not let Mama find out about that," Neeka warned. "She might have you both tested and put away in somebody's mental asylum. It's best to leave the man-picking to her."

"Yeah, right. You should have seen our Princess with her male friend last night. That brother was all over her practically, and she was enjoying every minute of it. If I didn't know any better, it almost looked like she knew the guy before the club scene from the way they were carrying on."

"Girl, stop. Our shy and innocent sister, Prin?" That was something to reflect on. "Must have been that drink she had."

"That's what's wrong with her head now. She had a little too much to drink, and maybe a little too much of that man."

"Mercy, please," Princess giggled, coming back into the room. "Stop announcing it. Next you'll be telling Mommie about it, and you know how she is about worldly things the day before church day—or any day for that matter. Besides, it wasn't all that great having one watered-down drink. My stomach feels funny, and my head feels even worse."

"You telling the truth about Mama," Neeka agreed, stirring more sugar into her morning brew. She could see her mother dragging a "dirty" Princess off to a steamy shower and scrubbing all the particles of club filth from her sister's fragile-looking body. Neeka still remembered the many nights that she and Mercy, as teenagers, had to resort to sneaking out of the house to go to a dance or to some innocent house party. A sleeping Princess was always left behind on such occasions for fear of betrayal later. All it would take was for their mother to ask the question and look at her daughter the right way, and Princess would crack like cheap china. She didn't think Princess knew what a nightclub was, let alone how to meet a man at one. Legal age or not, Adeena didn't approve of such behavior and would throw a righteous fit if she found out.

"I think you had too much Sex on the Beach," Mercy tossed over, obviously feeling comfortable enough to head to Neeka's refrigerator. "That's what I think."

"Oh, my God!" Neeka snapped. "She did what on the beach? You mean with a total stranger?" It was worse than she thought. "Mercy, how could you let her get tipsy and go off and have sex on a beach? What kind of sister would do—"

"Neeka!" Mercy stopped her, "Get a real life. It's the name of a mixed drink, Sex on the Beach. Goodness. You could stand to live a little and get out more often yourself."

"Oh. I knew that." Neeka felt so silly. It was just what she deserved for living such a boring life that included work, dancing around in her condo, shopping, and more work. She couldn't think of the last time she'd been out on a date.

Princess kept her head down in shame. "And I think that if we're going to service, we better get going. So, can I ride with you two?"

"No, Prin. We'll hitch up a tow and pull your car behind us."

"Mercy, stop it."

"Oh, I'm just teasing with her."

"Of course you can, Prin," Neeka sighed. "However, if we plan to get there by noon, we'd better hit the road. And Mercy, will you please close my refrigerator door? You've been standing there looking for a good three minutes now. There's no television in there."

"But I'm hungry. I haven't had time to buy groceries."

"And this is not Jack in the Box or Denny's. Close my refrigerator, and let's get going or we'll be late for service!"

"Girl, stop yelling at me! You not the mama."

"Whatever, Mercy. Let's get this train moving." Neeka put her mug down and went for her purse, Bible, and car keys. She couldn't wait to get to the end of the day. It wasn't so much the service she was thinking of, but after the service. After the service her mother always headed to her private quarters. Neeka figured it would be a good place for her to stand firm on this so-called date with Braxton on Saturday. *We'll just have to see about that too!* The sooner she made it clear to her mother that she had no intention of dating Braxton or any other suitor she picked out, the better she would feel.

CHAPTER SIX

Good Lord, it looks like a sinner's convention in here," Mercy said, scanning row after row in search of a place to sit, preferably up front. She led the way.

"This place is always packed. You would think they were giving away free stuff the way they come," Neeka whispered, but her whisper was loud enough to turn the holy heads of several faithful churchgoers. Their frowning and forbidding faces glared at her, making her feel odd and out of place for speaking her piece, but it was true. Angelic Grace Baptist was a large, newly restructured building on Crenshaw Boulevard.

Their mother had been attending the church for as long as she could remember. In fact, her mother had been a major contributor to the building fund. Still, it was too much church and not enough parking.

"I knew we should have gotten here earlier," Neeka said, as she maneuvered her way through a half-filled row of seated members.

"We could always go back home," Mercy suggested.

"Pardon us. . . . Excuse me. . . . I'm so sorry. . . . Please excuse me. . . . Oops, sorry." Finally there was a clearance along the polished wood bench for Neeka's narrow hips. Mercy sat to the right of her, Princess on the end. Neeka sat down with a sigh of relief and tried to focus on Rev. Clayton, who was already deep into his sermon on the wages of sin. From past experience she knew that before the end of his sermon the topic would slide easily into the subject of "tithes." She believed in faith, she believed in God, and she believed in the power of prayer, but the sad reality still remained that modern-day churches were more than houses of worship. They were big businesses that seemed to be more about the money. No matter how much money she put in the offering plate, it never seem to be enough. There had been times when Rev. Clayton had pushed the topic of sin and repenting to the bottom of his list and had actually preached exclusively about how members should reach deeper into their wallets and purses for the church. Never mind that Rev. Clayton lived in an eight-bedroom mansion in Anaheim Hills and drove a late-model Rolls-Royce, or that his lovely wife, Seritha, drove a late-model Range Rover. Neither one, to her knowledge, held jobs outside the church. Nothing hard to figure out about that one. Tithes and more tithes.

"Thought our dear mother was suppose to be singing her favorite solo today." Mercy whispered in Neeka's direction while looking around like she was trying to spot one of her many admirers.

"Maybe her voice needed a break from barking orders all week. Who knows." Neeka could feel a calming effect coming over her. Sitting in the Lord's house always did this for her. She had spent every Sunday in this very church ever since she could remember, and it was always the same. The preacher screaming about sin, the choir singing about sin, the deacons and the congregation praying about old sins and new sins to come. It didn't take a rocket scientist to know that most of the people sitting around her lived lives full of sin all during the week, only to push that same sin aside for one day of the week, Sunday. "Sunday Christians," she called them.

In her heart she believed in God and heaven, but for some reason still unclear to her, she had a hard time believing that a loving God could let sinners burn in a lake of fire forever. *I mean, c'mon now. Maybe they could burn for a day or two, but forever? Be for real now.* One thing she knew for sure, she didn't live a perfect Christian life, but she did the best she could.

Neeka opened the Bible that rested on her lap and tried to concentrate on Rev. Clayton's sermon, but already her mind was wandering off. Braxton. Thoughts of the date with Braxton on Saturday tried to weigh her down. Her breathing didn't feel quite right, and there was a heavy feeling in the center of her chest. Adeena had a lot of nerve arranging a date without asking her first. She wouldn't take the matter so seriously if it weren't for the fact that her mother usually got her way. Adeena was generous and she appreciated all her mother did, but in reality the money only helped to mask the truth that she didn't have a life of her own. It all belonged to Adeena. All of it. *And now the woman wants to pick out my husband too. What next? Picking out the sex of my children?*

"Darn that woman," she muttered. She massaged her temples for a few seconds. So many thoughts were giving her a mild headache. From there, her thoughts rolled over to all the work waiting for her on her desk. *Girl, pay attention!*

The fresh flowers at the front of the church caught her eye. It was an elegant collection of Asian lilies, white carnations, and bird of paradise. Some of her favorites blooms. The stained glass at the high windows was so beautiful that seeing it for the first time could literally take your breath away.

Neeka closed her eyes, and once again she was that young girl sitting beside her father in church. He always held her hand. She was his firstborn girl, special and outright spoiled, and Daddy Elton made sure that she always knew it. He had been her hero. And when her hands had become restless in his, he always had a peppermint in his pocket to give her. But he was gone now. A heart attack eighteen years ago. Every time she came to this very church, she could still smell his heady cologne like he was sitting next to her. The fragrance smelled so close to her, so real now, that she could almost reach out and feel the smooth fabric of his pants beneath her touch.

"Careful now. You wouldn't want to start a small fire you can't put out."

There was no mistaking his voice. She'd know that deep baritone anywhere. Neeka opened her eyes and chanced a peek to her left where Princess had been sitting. Braxton. *Oh no, not him!* The man had the audacity to be sitting next to her along the bench, smiling at her hand resting on his right leg. He was dressed in an expensive-looking suit, and his cologne was heavenly, a scent so light and woodsy that she felt like she could float away on it. She looked around for her sister. That traitor had given up her seat to Braxton.

"Lord, why me? Why?" Neeka mumbled. She tried to be quick with snatching her hand away, but it became trapped in place beneath his. "I beg your pardon. And for your information, Mr. Dupree, any fire I start I'm quite capable of putting out," she whispered harshly, still trying to pull her hand out from under his.

"Is that right? I'll have to remember that." Braxton leaned in and whispered in her ear. "Your hand is okay. I don't mind being touched."

"I'm sure you don't." Neeka reached for a paper fan at the back of the seat and fanned herself. Mercy, seated to her right, kept stealing peeks over at Braxton. She was obviously trying to snag his attention, but it wasn't working.

"Will you stop it?" Neeka mumbled in her direction. Then to Braxton she whispered harshly, "Release my hand, please!"

"Sure thing. And how is my lovely friend this morning?"

"I wouldn't know; I haven't seen your friend. But as for myself, I was fine until the likes of you showed up." Neeka scooted over, causing a wave effect with everyone along the bench seat. Braxton scooted closer. Neeka scooted again, huffing at his audacity. Maybe she should get up and move to another row, or another church. Determined to ignore him, she fanned harder and concentrated on Rev. Clayton.

"Did you miss me?" Braxton asked, his grin wide.

"If you mean since yesterday, I'm afraid not." His body was way too close to hers. She could almost feel a mild current running between them. She scooted over some more.

"You were on my mind all night. Felt like calling you, but I had a strong feeling you would have hung up on me."

"Then you must be psychic, Mr. Dupree." She could only guess that he'd obtained her phone number from her mother. When would her mother stop trying to play matchmaker and stay out of her personal life? "Look, Mr. Dupree, I—"

"Braxton. I prefer to be called Braxton."

"And I prefer to call you Brat. It suits you."

"Oh, a comedienne. I like that too. Nothing like a humorous woman."

She rolled her eyes. "Can you please scoot over and give me some room?"

Braxton looked to be enjoying every minute of her discomfort. "Why, of course I can." Instead, he scooted so close that his thigh was against hers, and she could feel the tautness of his muscle and warmth. It would have been alright if she liked him, but since she had made up her mind not to like him, it wasn't. *The nerve of this man! Does he really think he can pester his way into my life? Is he really that out of touch with reality?*

"I bet a beautiful lady like yourself has a lot of boyfriends. Am I right?" He kept his whisper as low as possible.

For crying out loud, Neeka thought, looking around to see who was listening. *Are we in church or at some social club?* Then she responded, "That would be for me to know and for you not to find out." Boyfriend. That was a place she didn't want to go. Her boyfriend. The last man who held that position had sweet-talked her out of thousands of dollars in the form of a loan. She had been saving herself for what she thought would be a happily-every-after union when John Paul had come along with his good-looking, sweet-talking self. *Must have lost my damn mind.* Four months of wining and dining—well, mostly dining and pining because wine gave her a headache—and the whole time she had pined for John Paul to pop that four-word question, Will you marry me? But obviously it wasn't meant to be. He didn't get around to asking for her hand, but he did manage to ask for a handout. Good thing she didn't sleep with him. John Paul may have temporarily gotten away with the bounty, but he didn't succeed with the booty.

Neeka clenched her jaw thinking about it. After four months it still pained her to think how stupid and gullible she'd been to hand over that much cash. Something about helping his sick mother with some hospital bill. Stupid, stupid, stupid! It was three weeks later, after not hearing another peep from John Paul, that she'd driven over to his place in North Hollywood only to find his apartment bare. No John Paul. Not one trace. To this day, she hadn't told one soul about her jilt. But that was his loss. She tossed her head up, refusing to wallow in shame behind the incident.

"It would be nice if I could take you to Sunday dinner later." Braxton looked hopeful, if anything. "Perhaps we could do some more catching up before our date on Saturday."

"And it would be even nicer if you would sit somewhere else," Neeka said. She had no time for boyfriends, casual lovers, or husbands. None of them, as far as she was concerned, could be trusted.

Determined not to be touching any parts of Braxton's body, she scooted farther to her right, forcing Mercy over.

Braxton leaned closer to Neeka's ear. "Is that a yes?"

"I'm afraid not," she sniffed, keeping her attention on Rev. Clayton. "It's a no for today—and a never for Saturday." That seemed to change the direction of the train.

Braxton sat quiet for a spell, looking around. "Is your mother here?"

"Are you kidding? She's usually up in the choir singing her heart out, but I don't see her up there." Neeka scanned the huge congregation. Her mother had to be somewhere at the front in the sea of flamboyant hats and fancy go-to-church outfits.

"Now before we leave here today," Rev. Clayton was saying, his voice booming through the Bose speaker system, "I want to take the time to remind everyone of the dedication services for Sister Adeena Lebeau. For those of you who don't know, Sister Lebeau has been God's instrument in renovations to this church being completed, and in being completed on time. Sister Adeena Lebeau is what we can refer to as an angel on loan. An angel on earth." He paused for time to wipe a handkerchief across his sweating forehead. "The ceremony will be held the last Sunday in November. I know it's only October and it's still early, but the dedication is going to be one of our biggest events. All in Sister Lebeau's honor. It's just our way of showing love, appreciation, and honor to a fine Christian woman who the Lord has chosen, and a person who has done so much for her church and community."

"Great," low-hissed Mercy to the right of Neeka. "Another all-about-Adeena day. Just what we need."

Princess nudged her from her seat behind. "Don't you dare speak like that. Mommie deserves way more than that!"

"Ouch. And if you poke me again with your bony finger, I'ma make sure you get more. More of my fist to your head."

"Mercy! Princess! Will you two please stop it!" Neeka admonished in a controlled whisper. "You act like children!"

"That's Mercy, not me."

Mercy sassily retorted, "Neeka, you stay out of it."

Finally a gloved usher threw a dagger of a look in their direction and followed up with a gesture of "Silence, please," followed up by "Shhh. Quiet, please."

After service, Neeka, Princess, and Mercy got up and began their migration to the church's rear, where a long hallway led to various rooms used as offices, a large lounge, a child-care facility, and a few other extravagances that had no place in a church: a juice bar, a recreation room complete with weights, and an extensive library of books and videotapes of the Bible and every biblical story told. She'd even heard once that Rev. Clayton's private quarters had marble flooring and a small chandelier. Three doors down from Rev. Clayton's posh digs was Adeena's private room.

"I'm going to see what's on the refreshment menu," Mercy announced, heading in the opposite direction.

"I'll be in Mama's room when you're ready to leave," Neeka said. *Don't that beat all,* she mused, as she hugged and cheek-kissed her way through a throng of church folks, some familiar and some not. She could hear Braxton not far behind her, greeting anyone and everyone who was curious about a new face at service—mostly females. Her mother would have to have her own private room at somebody's church. In one way she saw it as funny, but in another she saw it as a waste.

"Praise the Lord, you look beautiful today, Sister Perkins. Thank you. Excuse me, Brother Richards, can I slide by? Thank you. Excuse me." Neeka was doing her best to get to Adeena's room before Princess did. That way, she could have a few private words with her mother before her sister joined in, but people were standing around everywhere, and someone was calling her name. She didn't have to turn to know it was him. *Darn, that man is persistent.* She couldn't see four feet ahead of her, making it impossible to escape Braxton's approach.

"Hey, you," Braxton called behind her, "wait up."

Neeka halted and drew a deep, steady breath. He caught up with her and grabbed her hand lightly. "What now?" Her look was one of acute annoyance.

"Not so fast. Maybe you can tell me why you won't have dinner with me. As an old friend, don't I deserve that much?"

"Actually, Braxton, no, you don't. We may have been neighbors at one time, but I don't recall us being friends, and I don't owe you, or any other man for that matter, a darn thing."

"I don't see no reason for you to be so mean about it."

"You're a man. Of course you don't."

Braxton looked taken aback by her words. "Sounds like some deep-rooted issues. Maybe cocktails would be better?"

"No, thank you. I don't care much for drinking."

"Hot cocoa."

"Chocolate breaks my skin out."

"We could go somewhere and share a soda pop."

"Soda gives me heartburn."

"Coffee?"

"Coffee makes me hyper."

"A glass of milk perhaps?"

"Milk gives me gas."

"A cup of water then."

"Water makes me . . ." Neeka halted. She couldn't think of a darn thing. Truly, there was no solid reason for her to be so testy with the man, except that he was part of her mother's twisted scheme to marry her off. "Bottom line is, Braxton, I don't want to have dinner with you, lunch with you, or even brunch with you. I don't want to share a peanut butter sandwich with you. So, if you don't mind . . ."

His smile was cool, his demeanor a bit cocky. "Oh, a woman who plays hard to get. Good thing I'm a man who loves a good challenge." He flashed a sexy smile.

"And so do I, so it looks like we do have something in common. Have a nice day, Mr. Dupree." She threw her head back and walked away, hoping to leave him standing there looking forlorn and rejected. But instead, he walked proudly behind her, a man on a mission.

"So why can't you go out with me? Is it because of your mother?"

No reply.

"I mean, just because Mother Lebeau and I worked on a few projects together, it's not like I was dating her. It was all business."

Neeka kept walking.

"Is it because you think I'm so handsome and I might have too many women?"

No reply.

"Because I'm not a player. At least not anymore. So don't believe everything you hear."

Once a player, always a player, Neeka wanted to say, but resisted adding her comment. Give the man enough rope to hang himself.

"Or could it be you're afraid?"

Oh, my goodness, are you for real or what? She stopped and swung back around. "Afraid of what, Brat . . . I mean, Braxton?" Neeka tried a hand on a hip to give the appearance of having more confidence. When Braxton stepped closer, she could feel her knees falter. God, he was one handsome man. A moment of light-headedness tried to claim her, but soon passed. "Tell me what there is to be afraid of?"

"Oh, I don't know," he said, licking his lips, drinking her in with playful eyes. "Afraid you might have a good time perhaps. Afraid you might find me . . . how can I put it? Irresistible? You might not know it yet, but I can be very charming, witty, and so, so irresistible."

Damn, he sure could. But no, she wasn't falling for that. "Maybe to your own mother, but seeing how I'm not your mother and you're making a list, don't leave out that you can also be a pest, and so, so full of yourself." Did he have to stand so close?

He licked his lips again. "I believe it's called the three Cs: charm, charisma, and confidence."

"Or they could stand for crazy, cocky, and confused." She turned and continued to Adeena's room. "Now leave me alone. I'm sure that you can find plenty of women who would love to have dinner with you."

"That may be so, but I'd rather it be with you." Braxton walked behind her, allowing his eyes to draw in her essence, the way her slender hips swayed, the way her full and shapely legs looked in pumps.

They reached her mother's closed door. Before Neeka could knock, Adeena, seemingly clairvoyant, opened her door and stood there looking grim-faced for a few seconds, but seeing Braxton remolded her face. "Hello, Braxton, dear. A pleasure to see you."

"The pleasure is mine, Mother Lebeau." He reached for her hand and kissed it. "You're looking lovely as always."

"And you, always the handsome gent. Love your suit."

"Thank you." Braxton stepped back, looking smitten with her compliment.

Neeka made a disapproving face. "I think I'm feeling sick to my stomach."

"How exciting," Adeena said with a mock thrill. "Young budding love can make you feel queasy in the stomach from time to time."

"What love would that be, Mama?" *You mean young loathing.* "Never mind. I need to talk to you."

"Don't worry, sweetie, everything has a way of working itself out. In fact, my dear, I'm glad that you're here. I was about to have someone page you and your sisters. They are here, right?"

"Mama, of course. But I need to speak to you alone before they get here. About Saturday, Mr. Dupree here seems to be under the impression that we have a planned—"

"Neeka, not now." Adeena patted a few times at her chest before coughing.

"Mama? What is it?" Her mother had a peculiar look in her eyes, a mixture really. Worry, distress, anxiety, maybe even sadness. This was so unlike the woman who didn't back down or bite her tongue, especially under the roof of one of her favorite places. "Is everything okay?"

Adeena patted at her chest again. "I'll . . . I'll be okay, sweetie. But I want you and your sisters to meet me at the house. I have something I need to discuss with the three of you. It's very important."

"Can't you say what it is?" If Braxton knew the purpose of the impromptu meeting, his expression wasn't giving it away.

"Neeka, I can't talk about it now. I just can't, sweetie. Later at the Brentwood house will suffice."

"But Mama, I have plans—"

"Sweetie, we'll talk later. I promise." Before Neeka could get a full sentence out, her mother had turned a deaf ear and slowly closed the door, clearly dismissing her.

"Darn it. What now?" It wasn't like her mother to be so blatantly rude without due cause. Whatever it was, it had to be something major. "This better be about something serious, I know that."

Braxton regarded her with a serious look. "Is there anything I can do to help?"

Despite his sincerity, she didn't see what Braxton could possibly do except leave her alone. "No, not really. I just need to be alone."

"I think I can manage that. It was nice sharing the bench with you. If you have a change of mind about my dinner offer, let me know. I'll see you on Saturday."

"I'll keep that in mind." Neeka watched him walk away. In the past, every time some issue came up about work, her mother had been quick to call a family member, which made sense because Diva Four Cosmetics was a family-run business. Five days a week she dealt with work-related issues: accounts dropping, accounts signing on, new products not living up to their potential. Meetings to problem-solve were usually held on a Friday or Saturday evening. The last thing Neeka wanted to do was discuss work matters on what was supposed to be the Lord's day and the day of rest, but at the same time she felt helpless to change it. Looked like her talk with her mother would have to wait.

CHAPTER SEVEN

I sn't it wonderful about the dedication for Mommie?" Princess squealed before lifting another stick of carrot from her plate and taking a tiny bite. "First, Neeka and Braxton reuniting after so many years, then the possibility of a December wedding, and now Mommie's dedication from the church. It's all so exciting. I can hardly wait. I do love functions. Don't you, Neeka?"

"Sure. Love 'em." Neeka resisted the urge to throw a celery stick at her. It didn't take much to stir up Princess, who was known to get excited about fire ants invading the city. It was bad enough that Neeka hadn't been able to sit down and have a serious talk with her mother about constantly interfering with her love life—well, actually, her lack of one—but the fact that her sister seemed so cozy with Adeena's matchmaking charades was annoying to say the least.

"I can see myself married to a man like Braxton," Mercy swooned. Her eyes glazed over. "And our kids would have those pretty light brown eyes of his."

"Mommie thinks he's perfect for Nee."

"Honestly, if one more person mention the name 'Braxton' and the word 'marriage' in the same sentence, I'll scream to the top of my voice." It probably wouldn't do much good, but Neeka wasn't trying to hear such talk. "Mercy, you probably could see yourself married to Jeffrey Dahmer if he were still alive."

Mercy grinned over at her. "Girl, stop living in denial. You know you were checking that man just like he was checking you. I was checking too. Lips lie, but the eyes don't deny."

"Mercy, in your dreams. And if you know so much, you go out with him on Saturday."

"I just might do that." Mercy returned a bold, don't-dare-me look. "Just tell me the time and the place, and I'll be there."

"Good. It's all planned then." Neeka checked her watch. "For it to be so important what Mama wants to talk about, she sure is taking her sweet time about getting down here. I mean, it's not like we don't have lives of our own, and I do have other things to do today."

"Neeka," Mercy said, making a face, "you know you don't have nothing to do on a Sunday except go home and watch the grass grow in your backyard. Get real."

"Now see," Neeka chuckled lightly. She picked up a small accent pillow and tossed it over, aiming at Mercy's head but missing. "You wouldn't know that if you weren't always looking over that darn fence into my yard. Try minding your own business for a change."

"Be advised now, your business is my business. Just like Prin's and Mother's. Heck, if it wasn't for me, this family would be in the dark about a lot of things. Talk radio, the daily news, and the Internet all rolled into one. That's me, thank you very much."

"You know what?" Princess perked up with a sudden epiphany. "I think I'll write a poem or an essay for Mommie's dedication. Something nice." She took a seat on one of several large ottomans about the room.

Mercy rolled her eyes. "Ooh, wow, Prin. That should make everyone extremely happy."

"Mercy, don't start. Dang. What could Mama be doing up there?" Neeka blew out agitated air from her lungs. Waiting had never been one of her strong points. They were lounging in the family room, which was one of her favorite places in her mother's spacious house. Even when she and her sisters were growing up, Neeka had loved the idea of having her own bedroom and living in a mini mansion. With six bedrooms, each with its own private bath, the five-thousand-square-foot, two-story house, was simply too large for warmth and comfort. This was the place her mother playfully referred to as the Big House. Each time she visited Adeena's residence, Neeka sat amidst the plush carpeting, expensive handmade rugs, marble flooring, and excessive elegance and pined for the simplicity of her own place.

At her own place, she didn't have to worry about putting her foot up on the hand-chiseled, solid marble table that cost more than her car. She didn't have to feel like she was constantly surrounded by expensive things that were meant to be seen and not touched. However, in the family room filled with gold-plated frames of family memories, her mother did try to keep the ambience cozy with a large, buttery-soft, calf-leather sectional. There were potted plants, large and small, and abstract pictures adorned suede walls. No denying it, her mother's last interior decorator had outdone herself, but all the same, Neeka couldn't stop wishing for her own place as she waited for Adeena's arrival. If only Princess would hush up so she could think.

"I'm just saying that I think it's a nice thing for the church to do for Mommie," Princess said, then paused to look from one sister to the other. "The dedication that is. Mommie so deserves it. She does so much for others."

"More than she should," Mercy offered.

More like 'to' others. Neeka kept quiet.

"And having the event at the church is such a nice gesture," Princess said softly.

"Prin, get real," snapped Mercy. She dipped a slice of raw cauli-
flower into a dollop of French onion dip on her plate. "Mother owns
that whole church. She just won't say so. A dedication is the least they
could do for her."

"You don't know that," Princess snapped.

"I'll always know more than you," Mercy snorted at her. "I know
that much."

Neeka wished they both would hush up. "I think I'm going to run
upstairs and see what's taking Mama so long to come down," she
offered, but she didn't move from her spot along the sofa, where her
feet rested on a matching ottoman. At least she had been able to
change from her go-to-church suit to casual jogging attire. In the past,
there had been times deemed as "family night" when the four of them
would sit around Adeena's house and talk until the wee hours of the
morning, eating gourmet popcorn or some newly discovered snack.
For this reason, each of her sisters always kept a change of clothes at
Adeena's place, just in case.

"Please do," Mercy snorted. "I have a new credit card in my purse,
and I need to get to the mall to break that bad boy in."

"I hate to wait, and Mama should know this about me by now."
Neeka got up, moved to the buffet table, helped herself to some more
fresh fruit, sliced carrots, and celery. She thought about a tall glass of
orange juice but decided against too many carbs. Back at the sofa her
body plopped down again with discontent.

"Mother is so sorry to keep her girls waiting."

Thank God for small miracles. Neeka sat up straight as Adeena
casually strolled in followed by her "house assistant," Sarah. The
plump middle-aged woman, always dressed in a dark brown uniform, had worked for Adeena for more than nine years. To Neeka,
Sarah was more than a mere maid or housekeeper. The coffee-colored
woman was a mix of valet, accountant, butler, and full-fledged spiri-

tual advisor. Sarah did everything when it came to matters of Adeena's house: she cooked in it, cleaned it, painted it, ran it, scheduled who could visit it, dished out advice and scolded deliverymen and other hired help. The Big House would probably crumble without Sarah, who gave a nod to all three women.

"Do forgive me for taking so long, but Sarah had a difficult time locating where she had put my castor oil pack paraphernalia. I thought I would do a castor oil pack as we talked."

"It's about time, Mama." Neeka got up and headed for the buffet table to look over some cut-up fruit. Some meat would be nice, but Adeena was a vegetarian and rarely served any meat or meat products in her house. "We thought you had forgotten about us."

"Goodness, Mother, you still do castor oil packs?" Mercy asked, making a face like she was talking about eating dried bugs dipped in chocolate.

Adeena was quick with, "I know, Mercy. However, castor oil packs have been around for ages, and they are quite beneficial to my health. In fact, dear, you wouldn't have that little pouch trying to come in your stomach or the back pains you always complain of if you would do them maybe twice a month."

"No, thank you, Mother. I'd rather have a root canal."

"Suit yourself, Mercy."

Neeka moved back to the sofa. It felt like all her energy whooshed out the moment she plopped down. "Wow, Mama, I haven't seen one of those in years," she said, referring to the girdle-like contraption her mother's house assistant was holding in one hand. "Boy, does that bring back memories." She couldn't recall the first time her mother had come home with gallons of castor oil, castor oil holders, organic coffee, and two professional juicers, but if she had to guess, she would say she had been around eleven or twelve years of age.

The only thing that had been on Neeka's mind then was keeping

up with the latest fashions for teens, how to keep pimples from finding her face, and how to ask her mother if she could spend the night at
her friend's house. Then, out of the clear blue, her mother had come
home one Saturday and announced she would be introducing healthy
habits that would consist of fresh juice the first thing in the morning,
coffee enemas once a month, and castor oil packs twice a month.
Neeka still cringed at the taste of carrot, celery, and beet juice. But
once the juice of apples was added to the concoction, it wasn't so bad.
Unfortunately, she never could get into the coffee enema part, and
even now, the thought of putting coffee anyplace besides her mouth
was a turnoff, but Adeena swore by it. According to Adeena, there was
no better form of detoxing the body than organic coffee enemas. Her
skin stayed clear, her weight stayed down, and for a woman of fifty-
eight years, she always seemed full of overbearing energy. That much
she had to admit. Still, the castor oil pack was a practice older than all
of them put together, and somewhat of a messy ritual.

"Coffee enemas are good for you," Princess announced with pride.
"That's how I keep my weight down."

All eyes shot in her direction. Mercy looked tortured, resisting the
urge to add more information, but kept her lips sealed.

"Well, sweetie," said Adeena as motherly as possible, "you need to
stop. You're trying to pick up some weight, not lose some more.
Remember?"

"You're right, Mommie." Embarrassed, Princess looked away.

"Stop picking at her. As long as she's healthy, I don't see what the
problem is." Neeka ate pieces of diced fruit and tried not to gag. *Lord,
have mercy.* She stole a quick peek at Princess. Why in the world
would her sister want to lose any more weight? She was already thin
enough to hide behind a lamppost. If a strong wind were to find its
way into the house, they would have a hard time keeping that girl
from becoming airborne. She slid her attention over to watch Sarah

hook her mother up. Adeena was wearing pink spandex pants and pink socks on her small feet. Her trim and flat midriff was exposed by a pink tube top, and the garb seemed so out of character for her mother, so exposed. Neeka supposed it was the correct attire for detoxing a liver.

"You got it ready, Sarah?"

"Yes, ma'am."

"Very well. Now put the oil in place, please." Adeena waited patiently for her assistant to place the warm wool cloth saturated with castor oil along her upper right side. She offered her assistance by holding the slightly messy cloth in place while Sarah wrapped clear plastic wrap around her waist, then applied the girdle-like holder that zipped at the back. A heating pad fit snug on the inside of the holder. "Are we ready now?" After her assistant plugged the heating element up, she placed a large glass of ice water and two large towels down along the leather sofa before leaving the room. When she returned, she handed three black folders over before retreating. "There, we can get down to matters at hand while I detox."

"Good gracious, Mother. You have been doing this so long, you should have the healthiest liver in Brentwood by now." Mercy crunched down noisily on a carrot stick.

"Something like that, Mercy. Our bodies are so complex that any-thing is possible when it comes to our health." Adeena checked the contraption around her waist one last time before turning her atten-tion to her three daughters. "Now, enough about health. What I've asked you here for is important. First, I need to know where every-one's head is in reference to your jobs and how you feel about what you do for Diva Four Cosmetics."

Mercy went first. "I'm glad you brought that up, Mother. I've been wanting to talk to you about it for some time now." She stopped long enough to pick up a piece of melon between long, pink nails and drag it through some creamy dip. She batted her enhanced eyelids and smacked her pink lips before she spoke again. "I feel I should be making more money. I know you said we should never discuss our salaries with one another because it causes problems, but I know for a fact that Neeka is making more money than I do, and it's not fair."

"And your point would be?" Adeena held the folders to her bosom as she waited. A thin, dark brow raised, she didn't blink once.

"My point is, Mother, I need to be making the same salary as Neeka. Why must she always be the special one? A mother shouldn't play favorites. It's wrong. I have bills to pay and things I want. I need to make more money."

Obviously amused, Adeena's rebuttal remained calm. "You mean more money to take on more responsibility, Mercy, or more money just because?"

"I do enough on my job as it is. Overseeing personnel matters is not as easy as it looks, Mother."

"Quite the contrary, Mercy. I would hardly call a day of taking three-hour lunch breaks hard work. And please, don't sit here and act like I don't know what goes on at my own place of business. I know. Even on the days I'm not there to see for myself, I still know."

Princess gasped like it was a revelation she was hearing for the first time. "Three hours! How can she get three hours when I get only two? That's not fair!" As soon as the words escaped, she looked sorry and sunk back into her seat. "Never mind."

Neeka shook her head. *Lord have mercy.* All that education down the drain. Neither one of her sisters had a real clue. Instead of chief executive of finance, Neeka had always felt that she should oversee personnel matters. The three sisters went to work faithfully each day, but the way Neeka saw it, what Mercy and Princess did in their eight-hour day usually had little to do with actual work. Obviously the two weren't true team players.

Mercy pleaded her case saying, "True, I admit I might take longer for lunch some days, but it's not every day, Mother. Regardless, it still don't dismiss the fact that I need more money. I can't help if it takes time to get my hair and nails done." Mercy studied her perfect nails in hot pink. "It's not like I own the salon and the beautician works for me. Sometimes I have to wait just like everyone else. I need more money."

Adeena huffed. "Let's make sure we don't mix caviar with beef jerky, my dear. There's a big difference. I love each one of you equally. At the same time, family is family and business is business. True, your sister makes a little more than you, but she certainly has more duties and responsibilities. I depend on her more."

"And so now I'm beef jerky to you. Is that what I am, Mother?"

"For crying out loud, Mercy, put a sock in it. It's a metaphor. We all know you're not beef jerky." Neeka turned her head away to snicker. "More like ground turkey."

"Oh, I see where this is going. This meeting is really about me. Gang-up-on-Mercy day."

Adeena's mouth pulled into a scowl. "As much as you would like, Mercy, this meeting was not called to be a gripe session for you. You and I can discuss your salary privately at a later date, but I doubt if it will do you any good until I see more productivity. Like I said before, business is business."

"Mother, I'm not griping. I just don't like being called beef jerky—"

Princess cut her off. "Mercy, hush up and let Mommie talk." Her words were met with a disapproving glare and a roll of the eyes.

"Thank God. Now, I know you ladies think your poor mother will live forever, and that I'll always be around to help you out of one bad decision after another." Adeena paused and gazed a few seconds at each one of them, her gaze lingering more on Mercy, seeing how she was the daughter with the most issues.

"What?" Mercy looked around to see if her sisters were staring. "Why is everyone looking at me?"

Adeena grinned, shaking her head. "Guilt is a funny thing, isn't it?" She checked for warmth from the heated pack around her waist and smiled, seemingly pleased with the results. "I'll just get straight to the point. The truth is your poor mother here won't be around much longer."

Princess was the first to gasp. She got up and moved to Adeena's side, stooping; then she fair out settled on the floor in an attempt to be closer. Lovingly, she took up her mother's hand and held it gently. "Mommie, what's wrong? Is it your kidneys again?" Her eyes began to mist. "Tell us, Mommie. Is it diabetes?"

"Are you okay?" Neeka put hold on her emotions. She wanted the facts before she leaped at conclusions about her mother's condition. In the past, her mother had been on one health kick after another for as long as she could remember, and if she remembered correctly, there wasn't an organ in her mother's body that she didn't have a problem with at one time: a slow heart, a fatty liver, a bruised kidney, an infected appendix. Neeka didn't dare voice it, but her mother could very well be a recovering hypochondriac. "Mama, we can't help if we don't know what the problem is."

Mercy took up a piece of celery and bit it. "One thing for sure, if it's one of her organs, mother has enough in the bank to have a new one put in."

Neeka and Princess rolled their eyes in her direction.

"Thank you for your concern, Mercy," Adeena said mildly. "You always were the softhearted and sympathetic one."

"Dang, Mercy," chided Neeka, coming to Adeena's defense, "you sound like we're discussing the installation of new spark plugs." While her mother drove her crazy on most days, it rarely interfered with the way she felt about her. No matter how bossy, controlling, and meddlesome Adeena could be, Neeka still held the strongest love and the deepest admiration for her. If anything were to happen to her mother, she would be like a fish out of water. "Will it kill you to show a little sympathy?"

"What? What did I say that was so wrong? Mother, I didn't mean it to sound like it came out." Mercy tried sugarcoating it. "I just meant that a woman of financial means, such as yourself, rarely goes wanting for much." She took a ferocious bite of her celery. "People get organ transplants all the time. No big deal."

"Tsk-tsk." Adeena shook her head. "Money is nice to have, but it can't guarantee love, happiness, or perfect health, my child. I still have things I desire before it's my time to leave this place, which might be sooner than the three of you think."

"Mommie, please! Do you have to talk like that? I don't wanna hear talk like that." Princess scrambled up from the floor, her eyes threatening tears. "Stop talking like that!" She half ran from the room, leaving a hushed silence that was thick in the air.

"Always my sensitive one." Shaking her head, Adeena smiled weakly. "Let her be for now. She rarely stays in one of her moods for very long."

"Mama," Neeka pleaded, "stop dragging this out and tell us what's wrong. What is it?"

"That may not be the best thing, because there would be nothing that you could do anyway. When I'm gone, just know from my heart that I have wanted only the best for my girls. Only the best, and for this I have struggled to get to where I am in life." She stopped and sniffed. Seemed like a stream of tears should have come next, but dry-eyed, she continued: "All of you are so special and dear to my heart. If I could give you the world, I would."

"Mother, this is sounding too damn serious." Mercy covered her mouth. "Oops, I mean too darn serious. Sorry."

"Mercy, hush and let Mama talk," Neeka said.

"Mercy, you let this be the last time you use such language in my house! You hear me? I will not tolerate profanity in my house, and I don't care how old you think you are. Now . . ." Adeena paused to compose herself. Her voice softened. "I need to talk about the business." Adeena blurted out the last words before Mercy and Neeka got in a row. She handed each one a folder, then laid the third on the coffee table. "You, Neeka, more so than your sisters, have probably noticed that company revenues have been down for the last three months. In business, this is not a good thing."

"I know, Mama, but what does that have to do with your health?" Adeena shot a look that expressed it was the wrong question. "I mean, it's just a phase." Neeka flipped it open and took a glance at the folder's content. *Oh, no. Expenditure reports.* Sheets and sheets of them. Being head of the revenues department, her duties included the constant monitoring of accounts old and new. More times than she cared to remember, she'd had to wear more than one hat by being a field representative, a makeup consultant, and an in-your-face account collector. Having to chase down money was okay occasionally, but she was more inclined to be in her office behind her desk. True, a few accounts had been lagging in their normal acquisitions, and it didn't help matters that two large accounts had ended with no renewals. Neeka saw it as the way of business, and she wasn't in the mood for a blame party. Revenues were down but not enough to go into the heart failure over. "Mama, all companies go through a dry spell every now and then, we just—"

Sharp words cut her off. "We are not all companies! We are Diva Four Cosmetics and number three in southern California! We will be number one, end of story. I don't have to remind you ladies that I have worked too long and too hard to build this business to sit back and watch it slip away like sand through open fingers."

Mercy shifted uncomfortably in her seat. "Mother, aren't you overexaggerating?"

"I am not! And if you think I am, Mercy, you have a fool's head for business, and your college education has been a total waste of precious time and money!"

"Good grief, Mother, why I have to be a fool now? All you do is call me names!"

"Mercy!" yelled Neeka, hoping to head off a barrage of back-and-forth bickering. "Will you please hush up and just listen to Mama!" Good grief, she needed two Tylenol and a Valium just to be around the three of them. She closed her folder and placed it down along the table. She'd seen enough. "So what do you think we should do about it?"

Adeena coughed twice and scrunched up her face like she was in pain. She took a swallow of water before she spoke. "Thank you, my sweet Neeka. Always the understanding one."

"Mama, just tell us what you need done. Maybe we can plan more advertising, or do another infomercial. Remember how our infomercials helped to raise revenues last time? I'll do whatever you need me to do if it will make you feel better."

"Me, too," Mercy tossed in. Her folder was flung aside like a bad memory, and her fingers were gliding a plump strawberry to her lips.

"So sweet of you, Neeka. Just so sweet because I do need something to be done, and it has to be done right away."

"Something like what, Mama? A new ad package? Just tell me?" She couldn't imagine anything happening to her mother. Even though the woman had been like a tiny thorn in her side from the first day

Neeka knew what pain felt like, she was still a loving mother, caring and sweet, but only in a prickly kind of way. Just thinking about losing her mother made tears threaten to pool in her eyes. The thought of hope pulled at her heart. "Anything you need, Mama."

Adeena took a deep breath, allowing her words to rush out. "Good. I need you to travel to Texas to do a presentation for a major account, a group called Hope in Healing." Sniffing, she took up a tissue and dabbed at her eyes. "Major contributors will be there seeking tax write-offs, and you'll be presenting to a host of possible new clients."

"Excuse me?" Neeka frowned, eyelids fluttering fast like hummingbird wings. She couldn't regard her with a more incredulous look. "I'm not sure I heard you correctly. You need me to fly to where and do what?"

"Neeka, don't be silly. I know you have that silly little thing about flying. You can't fly, but you can certainly be driven."

Mercy snorted. "I wouldn't call fainting every time she goes near an airport silly."

A silly little thing? "Thank you, Mercy." Neeka wasn't sure what it was, but even before the September eleventh attacks, the thought of getting on a plane ignited panic attacks with shortness of breath. The thought of flying over water made her break out in hives. She had hoped during her therapy sessions that Dr. Singleton would address her phobia and cure it, but no such luck. "Driven?" Despite the room's comfortable temperature, Neeka could feel a trickle of sweat run down her backside. The cotton shirt she wore felt like it was sticking to her skin. Her mother's request wasn't sounding right. "But Mama, can't you mail the products ahead?"

"Don't be ridiculous. That's like mailing precious jewels ahead of your own arrival. It's too risky. Besides that, mailing is the same as flying them to another state. The products must be driven. There's no other way, Neeka. Now don't resolve to giving me a hard time. I've gone over this many times, and you're the only one with exquisite ora-torical and makeup skills—not to mention your outstanding market-ing skills—who can handle such a presentation. And you do remember what happened last time we had our exfoliating creams flown out to New York?"

She did. The ingredients in a newer version of their exfoliating masks had exploded in their boxes and caused enough concern with airplane security that her mother had been slapped with a small fine by the airlines. Not to mention the revenues lost from product dam-age. "Okay, you want me to go to Texas." She took a few seconds to mull it over. "A limo and chauffeur, I hope." All in the name of busi-ness. "Yeah, I can do that." *Nothing like traveling in style,* she mused, with a smile easing into place. Maybe it wouldn't be so bad. A few days away from her office, champagne to sip, caviar to sample, a pri-vate phone to her ear while rolling along the highway. How bad could it be? "Well, now that you've mentioned it, I can see myself in a limo."

"Well, no. Not quite a limo, dear. But you won't be disappointed with the traveling arrangements, I assure you. I thought of the best in the way of comfort. You'll be traveling by RV."

"But, Mama . . ." Neeka stood up to help herself think. The request was sounding more ridiculous by the minute. "Those things are nice, but they are huge. Not that I'm trying to get out of going, but what if I need to relieve the chauffeur and drive? I don't know if I can navi-gate something like that. And don't you need a special-class license to drive one?"

"Like I said, you will not be driving. You won't have to." Blinking long dark lashes, Adeena threw her head up waiting for the next excuse. "I've hired Mr. Dupree to chauffeur you. Driving large vehi-cles is what his business is about. He comes with good recommenda-tions, and it's not like he's a complete stranger. I feel quite confident he is the best man for the job."

Neeka felt like she'd been kicked in the gut. "You did *what*?"

"Now, Neeka, let's not add more drama to this. You'll have to keep in mind that this is not about you right now. This is serious. This is about saving our family-owned company. If the company is lost, there will be nothing for me to pass down to you and your sisters when I'm gone. And that may be sooner than you think. What will I have to leave my daughters?"

"Cash is always nice," Mercy added with a devilish smile.

"Mercy, shut up!" Neeka yelled. She could never understand how her sister could always make jokes when she herself felt like screaming. The girl was about as sympathetic as a fly buzzing around a slaughtered pig. This wasn't something to poke fun at; this was something to make her pull her hair out from the roots, run screaming from the house, hop in her car, and burn rubber away from. "Mama, I don't mind going out of town to handle family business. That's not a problem for me. The problem is, I don't want to go out of town with . . . with that man."

"I have faith in you, Neeka. You can do it. Not only that, but Mr. Dupree has expressed that he's interested in buying a luxury RV similar to the one you'll be traveling in. This way, he gets a chance to have a trial run with one. It's perfect."

"Mama, I can't!" If tears could have helped, she would have fair out started crying.

"Neeka, yes, you can, and yes, you will! Once again, let's not make this into an issue about you. Think about it, a fund-raiser and presentation gala. This is big and strictly business, so push all that selfishness aside, and think of business. It's dreadful enough to think that things have come to this, but they have. We need that account and any others that may jump on board. That's all there is to it. End of story."

Her mother had to be crazy or, even worse, insane.

Neeka could almost feel the fine hairs bristling along her back. The same helplessness she'd felt at the hands of her mother since child-hood was still strong inside her. If she could just say no and stand strong with her refusal, she would. But of course that wasn't an option. "And what about Prin and Mercy?" she asked. "Why can't they go?"

Mercy perked up at the mention of her name. "Nee, you must be crazy. I would love to go on a business trip with Braxton. Heck, I'd be more than happy to take your place." She licked creamy dip from a piece of celery. "Just say the word, Mother, and I'll go home and start packing today."

Adeena snorted up at her. "I'm sure you would." Her full attention turned back to Neeka. "Sweetie, I have never asked you for anything of this magnitude before. I would go myself, but . . . well, my doctor says I should take it easy for a few weeks just to be safe."

Safe from what? she wondered. *Safe from torturing your own daughter?* Neeka took a deep breath and held it. When her lungs felt like they would burst, she let air out slowly. "Shoots, I'd rather go to Mars with Bigfoot." It wasn't the trip per se; it was going on the road with Braxton. There was something about his intentions that rubbed her the wrong way.

Then Mercy spoke. "Funny you feel that way. I took the liberty of checking out Braxton's feet, and they were definitely big. Which could be a good thing, if you know what I mean." She winked at her sister.

"Mercy!" Adeena snapped. "Will you please refrain from such lewd suggestions!"

"Okay, okay, Mother dear. Don't bite my head off."

"Thank you." Adeena smiled a soft, pleading smile. "Baby, just this one thing for your poor old mother. And just because you're so good at what you do, there's a nice bonus in it for you. Trust me, you won't be sorry, and Braxton is the perfect gentleman. He's strictly business. Just think about your bonus the whole time."

Neeka focused on her mother's pleading face. *To Texas. Great.* She knew she would be going despite her reserve. That's how it was. "That bonus better be big," she said.

"Ooh, bunnies. What about big bunnies?" Munching on a peanut butter and jam sandwich, Princess walked slowly back into the room demonstrating more composure. "Whose getting a bunny?"

"Don't worry, baby sister," Mercy teased. "We'll make sure you get a nice fuzzy one with your new Easter basket come April."

Adeena called for Sarah to come assist her. "Dear Lord, I'm about to cook in this contraption."

The room's air held an odd sensation. Like any minute, any second, something large and heavy would drop on Neeka's head. Full of angst, she sat back down blowing out hard air. "Mama, we have to talk about this some more. I have plenty of work waiting on my desk. I just don't understand why my work should have to pile up when you could hire someone else to do this. It makes no sense."

"Not now, Neeka, I feel a little light-headed." Adeena hung her head, then tossed it back and called out again for her assistant. "Where is that woman? I wish she'd come free me from this monstrous heat. I swear that woman is getting too old for this job. Sarah!"

Princess was quick to her side. She sat her half-eaten sandwich down along the coffee table. "Here, Mommie, let me help you out of this thing."

"Don't worry, Mother," Mercy announced with a halfhearted smile, working hard for sincerity. "If you need me to chaperone the trip, consider it done. Anything to help out the family business. Right, Neeka?"

Yeah, right. And bite me while you're at it. Her lips pouted, Neeka looked from her mother to Mercy with a heaviness in her chest. "Of course. It shouldn't be no other way."

CHAPTER EIGHT

This is not a date. At least not for me. No matter how many times Neeka said those same five words to herself, they still felt unbelievable. Her first thought when she awoke on Saturday morning was not to show up for the scheduled meeting with Braxton at noon. But listening to Adeena insist that plans for their pending business trip needed to be discussed and the itinerary perused, not to mention Mercy begging to come along, how could she miss it? Business was business. Not only would the meeting provide Neeka with departure time, trip duration, and information on shopping places she could check out, but she could also hook up Mercy with Braxton at the same time.

"Nee, this is so nice of you to let me tag along. Mother would have a fit if she knew, but too bad. Did I ever tell you that you're the best sister a girl could have?"

"Only half a dozen times since we left the house," Neeka sighed. *Good grief. All this excitement over having lunch with Braxton? What's the big deal?* Obviously her sister had a deep interest in the man, which was nothing new. Mercy had a deep interest in all good-looking men who showed up in close proximity. If Neeka played her cards right, she'd have Mercy and Braxton dating, engaged, and married in no time. That should get her mother off her back, at least for a while.

Mercy's heels clicked along the cobblestone pavement. "I still say I should have followed you in my own car—just in case things don't work out."

"And I still say that I shouldn't be here at all." Neeka had driven her car so that she'd have more control over the situation. If the situation became too awkward, she could always get up and leave. Simple and perfect. "But I'm sure Braxton will be just as surprised to see us both," she smiled as she followed Mercy through the door of Pete's Grill in Long Beach.

The place was small, but with its antique neon signs, round bistro tables, and potted plants scattered about, it gave off the right vibes for a cozy sidewalk excursion. Neeka detected a hint of star jasmine mixed with the ocean-scented air.

Mercy asked, "How's my makeup? You think I look okay in this skirt?"

When it came to fashion, she was no prude, but who in their right mind would wear pink Blahnik stilettos and a black knit dress on a warm summer day? The short dress was meant to show off nice legs, but Neeka wouldn't be caught dead in it, which was why she had opted for a terry-cloth walking suit and sensible white Keds. "Yeah, you looking pretty sexy." No sense in hurting the girl's feelings. "Just remember not to bend over to pick up anything."

"Why not? I wore new underwear."

"Mercy, so did I, but we're not here for a peep show."

At the grill's counter they both ordered tall glasses of ice tea before making their way outside to one of numerous tables along the sidewalk. The weather was just right. Not too hot, but just enough sun. They had an ample view of cars coming and going along the busy street. Neeka was mildly surprised that there were parking slots available at the meters during the lunch hour.

"Don't hate." Mercy grinned. "You're just jealous because I can hook up a sexy look and you can't."

"You mean my secret is out. Who told?" *What a trip,* Neeka mused. Mercy was forever claiming to have the best everything, from hair down to toenail clippings. Poor thing made everything seem like a contest.

"Say what you want, but all week I dress in those church-looking suits and dresses. Don't get me wrong, I love going to church, but that don't mean I can't dress sexy every now and then." Mercy paused to fling back her loose hair. "Besides, I can tell Braxton's type. He loves the sexy look on women."

"If you say so," Neeka responded lamely. She placed her keys on the table beside her purse. Her mind was on everything but Braxton. Shopping, her favorite pastime, was calling her. Her plan was to make a beeline to her car right after eating. "I know one thing. He better not be late getting here, or you'll be sitting in wait by yourself." Unzipping her top, she removed the baby-blue terry-cloth jacket. "Five more minutes," she said. No sooner had she uttered those very words than a loud and battered-looking El Camino pulled up to one of the meters directly across the busy street. "Speak of the devil. That looks like him now."

The two watched in silence as Braxton parallel parked, got out, and fished out change to feed the meter before heading to the crossing light. Her cup suspended at red lips, eyes unblinking, Mercy said, "Isn't he supposed to be a successful businessman?"

"Something like that. Mama says he owns his own business." Neeka could feel a slight nervousness coming over her, but for what reason she wasn't sure. No denying, Braxton looked good dressed in maroon slacks and a knit shirt of the same hue. Funny she hadn't really noticed it before, but his arms looked huge and muscular. He still wore the same devilish smile he had when they were kids back in Compton. As he headed in their direction, she wondered if his confident and macho stride was an effort. *Look at 'im. A player if I ever saw one.* "Mercy, remember what we discussed. I'm not staying long. You make a suggestion that Braxton can give you a ride back to your place. I'm sure you know what to do from there."

Mercy was shaking her head. "Uh . . . there's a slight problem."

Neeka took a quick sip of her tea, which reminded her that she'd forgotten to add sugar. "What now? Isn't that what you want—to be alone with Braxton?"

"Affirmative, but there's a slight change in plans. I mean, look at that pile of junk he's driving." Mercy gestured toward his vehicle. "I like the man, but I'm not quite that desperate." She gazed at her perfect nails before looking up at Braxton's approach. "I can't be seen in that bucket."

"His car? You have a problem with his car?" Neeka hissed, keeping her voice low. She knew her sister could be superficial and shallow at times, but being a car snob was a new one. She could understand such behavior in a teenage girl, but honestly, Mercy was too old for such nonsense. Anyway, Neeka couldn't elaborate any further, because Braxton was standing before their table and smiling a smile as wide as Texas.

"Good evening, ladies. Mercy, what a pleasant surprise. Had I known you would be joining us, I would have brought Quamee. He asked about you."

"Umph. If you're referring to your red-haired, freckled-faced brother, tell him I'm married with five bad kids."

"Will do." Braxton pulled out a chair and eased into it. For a moment his gaze lingered on Neeka before he offered her a single red rose. "Glad you could make it. You both are looking pretty fly today."

"Braxton. And thank you for thinking of an insect." Neeka noticed that Mercy barely responded. In fact, her interest was like a light someone had clicked off. For a second Neeka thought she had seen a flicker of disappointment in Braxton's face when he spoke to Mercy. Maybe not. "We'll eat, get down to business, and be on our way," she said, picking up the small menu. "I'm sure this won't take long."

"I'm sure it won't," Braxton responded, looking around for someone to take their order. "They make the best grilled seafood salads here. I highly recommend the lime-grilled salmon."

Braxton pulled a folded piece of paper from his back pocket. "Neeka, this is for you." He slid it over to her. "I took the liberty of having our itinerary for Friday's trip typed up. You know, our travel route, estimated arrival time, and where the RV will dock for the night. Emergency phone numbers. Reservations have already been taken care of."

Mercy stood up with keys and purse in hand. "Nee, order me the same as yours. I'm off to the ladies room. Be right back."

"Yeah, yeah." Neeka waved her on. She unfolded and reviewed the typed sheet Braxton had given her. "What's this? Something your girlfriend typed for you?"

"Not when I have a perfectly capable secretary. And just for the record, there is no girlfriend at the moment."

"Is this it? This is the big plan we had to meet to go over?" She felt like laughing at it. Instead she pushed the typed itinerary back in his direction. "Unbelievable."

"That's all she wrote." A too-thin waitress came over and took their orders for salads. Braxton made an attempt to explain. "I know. I could have called you up and discussed the plan, but over the phone

I wouldn't get to gaze into those hypnotic eyes of yours or see your smile." He sat back in his chair watching her. "Face-to-face is always better for old friends with a lot of catching up to do."

"Ketchup is for burgers and fries. If I think back to when we were kids, you weren't exactly my favorite person." Neeka went quiet to make her food selection.

That brought a wide grin to Braxton's face. "Don't tell me you're still mad about me putting that frog down the back of your dress? We were just kids."

"It may have been fun for you, but I had nightmares for a week." Nightmares for a week was putting it lightly; the incident had kept her in the house for a whole month.

"Well," he said, his expression serious, "I know it sounds crazy, but maybe it was my way of telling you I was digging you. And if I didn't tell you I was sorry back then, I want to say it now. I was wrong. Now let's order."

Braxton chose a grilled salmon salad, while she chose Cajun swordfish. Neeka took the liberty of ordering the same for Mercy, who still wasn't back. Their meals arrived in no time. "I don't know about you, but I have to tell the truth about this. I think the idea of both of us traveling by RV is ridiculous. I mean, who does that? I tell you, my mother can be extreme at times. Once she gets an idea in that head of hers, she's like a hurricane that can't be stopped."

"Really? I seem to recall I asked her about flying, and she mentioned something about somebody having a flying phobia."

"That's not the point," Neeka huffed. Her fear of flying was her business and nothing that concerned him. "She might think her little plot is working, but I want to make it more than clear: It's not."

Braxton sprinkled pepper on his salad, ready to dig in. "Oh, I don't know. A long drive might be fun if not interesting. I've been thinking about buying an RV for years. In the beginning I didn't have the money; then I didn't have the time. This trip will give me the opportunity to finally test-drive one. I'd be lying if I said I wasn't excited about it. I can't wait to put that sweet puppy on the road."

"Well, good for you. Still, my mother isn't as cunning as she wants to be." She could see it now, Adeena somewhere reveling in the thought that she had succeeded in bringing Neeka and Braxton together for a date. Her pole might be in the water, but the fish wasn't biting. *We'll just see who gets the last laugh this time.* Neeka had her fork up to her mouth when she looked up and noticed her car passing by, Mercy behind the wheel, waving. "Hey, that's my car! Oh, no, she didn't!" She looked next to her purse. Her keys were gone. "That sneaky heifer! Ooh, wait until I get my hands on her. I'm gonna strangle her!"

"What's wrong?" Braxton was reading her alarmed expression.

"That no-good sister of mine just drove off and left me! That's what's wrong." No wonder that girl hadn't come back. She probably couldn't wait to sneak out the café's side door. "It's the last time I trust her."

"Is that all?" Braxton looked mildly amused. He blew out a breath of relief. "Good grief, no need to make a face like that. For a minute I thought you were having some kind of epileptic attack."

"I beg your pardon."

"Don't worry about it. You're in good hands. I can take you wherever you need to go."

An hour later Braxton's old and trusty El Camino rattled and coughed as it pulled up to Neeka's condo. She supposed he kept the motor running because if he turned it off it might not start again. "Braxton, thanks for driving me home."

"My pleasure."

"I'm sure." Neeka fanned exhaust fumes away from her face. Her Lexus SUV was parked out front, which meant Mercy was at her own condo, no doubt waiting for the play-by-play. Not to worry. She planned to deal with her later for pulling such a stunt. "Ouch," Neeka squirmed. Something in the raggedy seat was pinching her bottom, and if any more smoke filtered in through the car window she felt sure that she would pass out. Coughing and fanning, Neeka tried to open the passenger door to get out. "What's wrong with this door?"

"Here, let me help you. Sometimes it sticks." Braxton put the car in park, then reached across Neeka to wrestle with the handle, his thick arm brushing against her thigh. "Excuse me."

To her surprise, his touch sent small shivers through her, and there was a warmness at her center that caused a blush at her cheeks. Neeka turned her head to keep from inhaling his fresh and clean scent, while the craziest thought jumped into her mind. She felt like kissing the top of head. *Oh, my God, what's wrong with me?* A loud sound like a gun going off assaulted her ears. Her heart thumped in her chest as she ducked in the seat. "Oh, my goodness, someone is shooting at us!"

"Calm down. No one is shooting at us. It's the car backfiring."

Neeka sat up, patting her chest to calm her breathing. "Of course, backfire. You might wanna get that fixed before someone has a heart attack." If this was what a successful businessman drove, she'd hate to see the opposite.

"No way. She's an oldie but a goodie," Braxton explained with pride. "She coughs and smokes every now and then, but put this baby on the highway and she can scoot."

"Whatever." She cleared her throat and climbed out. "Oh, and before I go," she said with her face at the window, "I want to clear up a couple of things."

Braxton raised a brow. "I'm all ears."

"This was not a date."

"Of course not. Never." That silly grin of his again.

"And this trip on Friday is strictly business. So, if you have anything else in mind, I suggest you get over it before we head out."

"If you're still worried about falling in love with me, don't worry. I'll keep you on track." He revved his engine, producing a cloud of gray smoke at the rear. Just before pulling off, he said, "Oh, you might 'wanna close your mouth. Wouldn't want a fly to buzz in. See you on Friday."

CHAPTER NINE

Is this the bus leaving for Texas?"

"Man," said Braxton, grinning widely, "if this is what you think a bus looks like, you need to have your eyes examined." He turned his cell phone off and tossed it into one of several compartments along the cockpit dash. "And your bus left an hour ago."

The two men laughed.

"Had a feeling I'd see you before we left." Dressed casually in navy blue Dockers and a dark blue, knit pullover shirt, Braxton opened the hydraulic door, and got up from the leather captain's chair to greet his brother. Like a big kid in a toy store, he'd been tinkering around in the luxurious RV for a couple of hours, waiting for Neeka to show up so they could get on the road. Tired, excited, bored, and antsy, he was still happy Quamee had arrived early to deliver part of the money that he owed him. Not that he needed it, but the money would come in handy for the trip. "What's up, man? You come with good news or what?"

"You the man, little bro'. Check you out. Looks like you're ready to roll. This is way too early in the morning for me, but I wanted to holler atcha before you headed out." Quamee stepped to the top level of the vehicle.

"Nothing wrong with that. If that woman was here, I'd be long gone by now." Like most times, they did the fancy handshake: two palm slaps, then a double fist bump followed by another palm slap. Braxton knew it held little meaning, but childhood habits were sometimes hard to break. "What you waiting on, Quamee? Step in and check it out. No, hold up one minute. Let me snap your picture so you'll have proof to show your friends of you stepping into heaven on wheels."

While Braxton slipped his digital camera from his pocket and clicked, Quamee provided him with a pose to his good side, and then another of him doing his mock muscleman pose. "One more—and this time, smile. There. Now step on in. Let's get one of you in the captain's seat."

"Don't mind if I do," Quamee replied before making a mockery of wiping his feet a good ten seconds, then stepping up from the stairwell. "Whoa, will you look at this!" His eyes widened as he took it all in: a large plasma TV just beyond the cockpit; plush carpeting leading to a pathway of marble flooring with tiny running lights along the side; rich oaken cabinetry dressed with brass; a light leather sofa on one side; and above that, a minichandelier. "Whoa, will you look at that! Man, this is too much. It's bigger than my studio apartment in Culver City. This is all the comforts of home and pure opulence on wheels. I know one thing, I could really get with something like this," he looked around admiringly, shaking his head.

"It's what I've always wanted," Braxton said. "The only thing missing is the wife and kids."

Quamee was shaking his head. "Look what having money can do. Unbelievable. I wouldn't mind taking a spin in this myself."

"Maybe I'll let you borrow mine."

"What?" Quamee looked animated. "Are you saying you own this?"

"Not this one, but you could say that this bad boy is my major test drive before I select my own. I want one just like it. Top-of-the-line luxury." He looked around with pride. "Here, let me give you the deluxe tour." Braxton lead him toward the rear of the vehicle. There he could show off his favorite amenities. "This is the master suite, complete with a full-sized bed. Equipped with everything you would find in a normal bedroom, only scaled down in size." The bed was covered with an exquisite gold and white brocade, dotted with matching pillows. French-vanilla silk adorned the walls, and all the surrounding woodwork was real oak. All for me, Braxton mused. It was all rented and temporary, but he felt like he had died and gone to heaven, and he couldn't help beaming with pride as if Adeena Lebeau had actually given him the luxurious Fleetwood RV as a personal gift instead of merely hiring him to drive her eldest daughter to a business meeting. "And as you can see, the restroom to your right is located in the back with the master suite." He pushed open the door to reveal a beautiful etched-glass enclosed shower and marble sink fitted with gold-toned faucets. "It even has a regular-sized toilet, which is something you don't usually find in an RV."

"Man, oh, man," said Quamee, appreciation lighting up his face. "This is the lick. I mean, if I owned a vehicle like this, I could live like a king and be all over the place. I would go from one state to another until I'd seen all of America. It's a tight space in this sleeping area, but it sure is nice."

"Need more space? No problem. Check this out." Braxton reached up and pressed a button along the wall, and the low whirling sound of a motor could be heard as the sides of the RV advanced out five feet on each side.

"I'll be damned." Amazed, Quamee stood scratching his head. "Man, this is too much. I mean, I've seen fancy-looking RVs on the road every now and then, but I've never taken the time to check one out up close. I had no idea they could be so lavish on the inside. You have everything here—a television, stereo, a place to sleep, a stove and kitchen area, a place to sit and eat, and the shower too. I'm really impressed."

"I know," said Braxton. Actually, he was still in awe of it himself. Three weeks ago, when Adeena approached him with the idea of paying him to drive her daughter and some cosmetic products down to Texas, he had been skeptical. Although he owned his own fleet of trucks, it had been months since he had driven anything larger than his El Camino. But soon he saw the offer as an opportunity. He could do a test run before buying his own RV, spend some time with Neeka, and have a short vacation to boot. He refused the money part, but Adeena wouldn't have it any other way. How lucky could he get? "There's another large TV on the outside, in case you want to sit under the rollout canopy and watch the tube under the moonlight."

"Something like this has to be expensive, right?"

Braxton did a mental calculation of his surroundings. "If I had to guess, I would say this would run about four hundred thousand."

"Damn. More than a new house."

Braxton took a look at his watch. It was six A.M. "Just like a woman to take her sweet time. We could have been a fourth of the way there by now." Already, the impressive vehicle had been parked on the lot of Diva Four Cosmetics since four A.M. Now it was more than two hours later, and the parking lot was beginning to fill. "She know she wrong. We discussed all of this earlier in the week. I even had the schedule printed up and called to remind her last night." He should have known that she'd be difficult by the tone of her voice at dinner last Saturday. "I know one thing: I'm ready to show this proud bird off on the road." Honestly, there were only so many times he could check the cargo, check the controls, check the tires, and recheck the fuel level. Maybe the woman didn't fully understand how long a drive Austin, Texas, was from California. They should have been on the road by now. "She just trying to ruffle my feathers, that's all."

"If y'all had flown to Texas, you'd be there by now."

"True," Braxton shook his head. "But . . . she can't fly. Something about a fear of planes. I just called her house, but there was no answer. But you know me, always Mr. Patient."

"I heard that," Quamee agreed. "I don't care much for flying myself."

Braxton couldn't fathom where or why his brother would need to fly anywhere. A new racetrack perhaps? "Hey, how about some coffee while we wait? I have a pot ready." He pressed the button again to bring the massive vehicle's hydraulic slide-out walls back into place.

"Sounds like a plan to me. Make mine black with two or three lumps to sweeten." Quamee walked back and took a seat at a small table alongside a small window. "Man, this is really something special. So, where's that fine Miss Donneeka?" He eased up from his seat to reach for his wallet and placed it on the table.

Braxton went over with two Styrofoam cups of steaming black. After handing one cup to Quamee, he slid down along the bench seat facing him. "Man, how should I know where she is? But I wish she would come on. I've taken the drive to Texas over a dozen times, and I know what it's like to get a late start on the highway. She don't know it yet, but I plan to show her some of the scenic route. Some beautiful farmland in Texas."

Quamee gave him one of his sly-dog looks. "I know one thing. I only glimpsed one bed in the back. One big bed, two adults. How's that going to work out?"

"What?" What a question to be asking. Quamee didn't miss a beat.

If a bug was nesting in the crack of a wall, he would notice and have a comment. "Truth be told, I don't have a problem with sharing the bed," said Braxton. "Like you said, we're two adults. I got it all worked out in my head, and by the end of this trip, man, the lovely Neeka Lebeau will be wrapped in my arms and begging for more. You know how I do it."

Quamee raised a thick brow. "And if that don't work?"

"That leather sofa there lets down and sleeps two."

They slapped hands like men do, usually as a lead-up to bragging.

"No, but on the real side," Braxton grinned, "it's like I said: You know how I do it."

"And like I said before, no," Quamee said. "No, I don't know how you do it, but I'm sure you'll be spilling the details. Hell, I can't wait for you two to get back. Sounds like a fun trip in the making." He sipped at his steaming brew. "What about Mercy? Did she ask about me?"

"Something like that. Told me to tell you she has five kids."

"Tell her so do I. All the reason for us to hook up. Our own Brady Bunch. What she look like now? She still look good?"

"Man, hell, yeah," Braxton confirmed, placing his coffee down. His eyes took on a dreamy glaze, but his voice was serious as he spoke, his words unfaltering. "But that Neeka was always a looker to me. She had a brother feeling fiendish even back then. But I was too young and too stupid to know what to do." He'd been doing a lot of thinking about her. "You should see her now. Cute little body, long pretty hair, big pretty brown eyes, and those big legs of hers would make a blindman see. We talking sexy. Shoots, don't get me started about those big legs of hers. Don't worry, she'll be stepping her fine self up in here shortly. You'll see for yourself."

"I can hardly wait. I know one thing: I'm glad you moving on with your life after that mess that Sheila pulled. For a while you had me a little worried."

Braxton's jaw tensed up at the mention of his ex-girlfriend. "Man, I'm in a good mood, so don't bring up Sheila."

"Sorry. I didn't mean no harm."

Braxton waved the subject off. "Man, bump Sheila. Life goes on." Quamee would have to go and bring up the subject of Sheila. Sheila Ramsey had been one sneaky, conniving woman, a woman he had made the mistake of trusting too far. Boy, had she pulled the wool over his eyes, with him thinking she really cared about him, really loved him, and wanted to settle down as his wife and have a couple of kids. He had bought the five-carat ring, he had put a down payment on a bad-assed six-bedroom house, and they had planned a honeymoon trip to Jamaica. He had even been foolish enough to put her name on his bank account, which had seemed to be the right thing to do at the time. After all, she was going to be his wife and the mother of his children, and when he needed her to run errands for his company or pay bills, he wouldn't have to be around to sign off on a check. He had trusted her, but she had shown her true colors when she ran off with a tremendous chunk of his money, as well as the engagement ring, and dropped off the face of the earth. Not even the help of the private detective he'd hired to track her could find a trace.

Braxton had to admit that Sheila was good. She was damn good. Not only had she broken his trust of females, she'd also broken his bank and his heart. And she'd left him with only thirteen thousand dollars out of more than four hundred thousand. If it hadn't been for his reserve accounts, his business would have been devastated. If he never saw that she-demon again in life, it would be too soon. *Control yourself. Breathe.* Braxton took a deep breath and chanted the seven words that were the glue to his peaceful existence: "I have forgiven, and I will survive." If there ever was a time he felt like a cigarette, now was that time.

"I know, little brother. I know." Quamee paused and looked away for a few seconds. "Sorry I brought it up."

"No big deal. But, hey, that coffee would go good with a donut. I have some lemon-filled and some chocolate. Fresh from Krispy Kreme."

Quamee refused. "No thanks. Guess I should stop stalling and get to the chase. Look man, about the money I owe you—"

Oh no. Braxton didn't like the tone of his voice. *About the money.* Sounded to him like another excuse not to pay up was forming. It wasn't like he was hurting for money, but it was the principle of the situation: If a man promised to pay back a loan, he should keep that promise. Why did it seem like everybody wanted to keep Braxton's money? "Before you say more, I want you to keep in mind that it's not about the money, Quamee. It's about being a man of your word. I mean, I don't have money like Oprah, but I'm doing pretty good. Keeping your word means more than paying the money back."

"True that, true that. I hear what you're saying loud and clear. And I know you have your own problems to deal with trying to decide if you should keep the trucking company, and with your best secretary up and retiring. The last thing you need is somebody in your grill talking about they don't have all your money yet. But man . . ."

Braxton felt a tug of melancholy at the mention of his former secretary. Mertle. On her last day at the job, it felt like a good friend was turning her back on him. If he did decide to give up the company and pursue something new, he would want the best secretary or assistant at his side. "Well, even with Mertle leaving, life still goes on. She'll definitely be missed."

"I know what you mean. But anyway, little brother, as I was saying about your money. I know I owe you six grand, but I was wondering if it would be okay if I pay you half now and half in about three weeks? No later than one month."

"Did you by any chance fall and bump your head on the way over here?" This was the part where he knew he should be getting upset. Six grand? Obviously Quamee had forgotten about the three grand he'd loaned him last year, and the two grand the year before that. Braxton could get a pad and pencil and write it all down for him, but there was no sense in having his day spoiled with bad thoughts about money. "Did I mention that this vehicle has a small barbeque grill on top and a sunken seating area?"

"Man, you lying. A grill?" Glad for a change of topic, Quamee removed a cashier's check from his wallet and handed it to Braxton. "Are you serious?"

"I can show you better than I can tell you. Follow me." Reluctantly, Braxton took the check and struggled to keep his opinion to himself. If his brother said he would pay him the rest of the money, he had to take him for his word. Besides, what could he do about it now? They stood and exited the vehicle, Quamee following Braxton to the RV's rear, where a side-attached ladder could be pulled down for the climb up. As they reached the top of the vehicle, the morning sun was just peeking through some clouds, and low and behold, not only was there a small grill secured in place, but also a safety railing and leather benches where a person could sit and nurse a drink or two while waiting for the cooking to be done. "You think this is something, but you should see the model with the Jacuzzi on top."

"Unbelievable," said Quamee. "It's amazing that they can put so many gadgets on a moving vehicle. Now I wanna ask you one more big question."

"As long as it's not for more money." Braxton patted his back lightly. At that moment he felt that if his brother asked him for another dime, he'd snatch him up and throw him off the RV's roof.

"I just wanna know can I go too?"

They both laughed at that one. "Yeah, you can be on top here cooking some of those homemade sausages you love so much while I'm driving."

"Hell, yeah, man. I love those sausages, especially in that sauce you be making up. Heck, I haven't been over to Harris's place in Watts for a while, but I get to thinking about those homemade chicken sausages from time to time. It's been so long, I've forgotten how to get to the place. You still go there?"

"Are you kidding?" Braxton perked. "I have a pound of chicken, and a pound of Harris pork sausages in the refrigerator as we speak. I had to get my food shopping on. I even made up a jug of my barbecue sauce. You know me. This may be a business trip for Miss Neeka, but I plan to do some barbecuing along the way. A man gotta eat to keep his strength up; that's why I come prepared."

"Now you have me craving for those links. Make me wanna go to Harris Market for some chicken links when I leave here. Where's the place at again?"

"You have to ask?" Their foster dad used to frequent the tiny family-run place so much, Braxton wondered how could Quamee possibly forget. "It's still at Juniper and Seventh Street. Ask for Mr. Harris's daughter, Cookie. She's real cool, and if you tell her I sent you, she'll hook you up for real."

"Damn. I could stand some of your barbeque about now. Heck, I wanna go to Texas too. Let's get this show on the road. Where's that cute little passenger of yours? I can't wait to feast my eyes on her."

"Man, you know rich and spoiled women. Probably somewhere primping in a mirror or trying to decide which cute shoes she should bring on the trip." Braxton sniffed and pulled his slender digital camera out from his pocket. "Hey, Quam, smile one more time." He clicked before Quamee could protest. "Now you can tell your lady friends that you were standing on top of your own luxury RV."

"Man, you know that's not right. You could have at least waited till I said cheese."

"You don't have to. Your mouth always looks like you're saying cheese." Braxton meant that as a compliment. Even when his foster brother was upset, he was a teeth flasher, always smiling. "I'll e-mail you some digital copies once I upload the picture to my laptop." Braxton slid his digital camera back into the pocket of his shirt.

"Thanks, little brother. You alright."

"I wish this woman would come on. I don't have all day to be waiting on her." Braxton glanced anxiously at his watch again. Six-fifteen. He was just about to complain at length when a late-model Lexus RX 330 pulled up close to the RV and parked. Looking down from their perch, both men stood stiff as metal rods and watched as a petite woman got out and stood at the driver's side and removed something from her car that appeared to be a bundle tied to a stick.

"What the heck . . . ," Braxton said.

"Someone you know?" Quamee craned his neck for a better view.

"I'm not sure yet. I hope not." Amused, Braxton watched as Neeka, dressed in tattered-looking denim and a dingy, paint-splattered T-shirt, closed and locked her car door. "Oh, my God," he mumbled as she stopped and looked up at them. He could see that her hair was in a ponytail at each side, and from her disheveled attire, down to the patched-up, dirty, and dusty-looking sneakers she had on her feet, if she was going for the chic hobo look, she was right on target. It just didn't make sense. He had known that she wasn't happy about having to make the trip with him as the driver, but darn, he didn't think it was serious enough for her to be making a big deal about it. She cracked a big smile as she waved feverishly up at them.

From where he was, Braxton could see that her smile was somehow different. *Good grief*, he thought. Where did those big buckteeth come from? He blinked once, blinked again. Maybe his eyes were deceiving him. "Neeka?" This couldn't possibly be the same pretty face and beautiful smile he was used to. Could it?

She was waving up at them and saying, "Howdy. How y'all doing?"

Quamee swallowed hard. "Man . . . Ahh, is that by chance the fine Neeka you spoke of?"

"Uh, yeah." Braxton stared down at her, scratching his head. "Yep, I do believe that's her." And she had the nerve to call her own mother an extremist. Obviously the apple didn't fall too far from the tree. Too bad she didn't know that he was a man who wasn't easily intimidated or embarrassed. Still, her efforts to rouse him were, to say the least, amusing. "Ain't she something?"

"Yeah," said Quamee, refusing to take his eyes away. "She's something alright. I feel for you, my brother. If you getting paid for this trip, you might wanna ask for more money."

"Man, shut up," Braxton snapped. "She could very well be my future wife. C'mon, I'll introduce you."

"Brax, don't say I didn't warn you. Ugly women make ugly babies."

"Man, don't be so hard on yourself."

Down from the roof, the two men met Neeka at the front of the RV. Now that he was closer, Braxton felt like laughing at her appearance. Up close it was even worse. The woman couldn't have found thicker black-rimmed glasses—they magnified her eyes a good six times. Large, light brown orbits behind thick lenses. The ponytails and the buckteeth gave her a black hillbilly look. If this was an attempt to deter him from being interested in her, it wasn't working. He liked the look, and just to show her how much, he didn't allow his smile to falter. "Hello, Miss Neeka. As usual you're looking swell this morning. You remember my brother, Quamee." He paused to take up her hand and kiss the top of it.

"Ah, sure you're right. You did mention that she was a looker." Quamee appeared to be having a hard time fighting back a bout of laughter. "Pleased to teeth you . . . I mean . . . to see you again."

The hillbilly getup was one thing, but the woman even had the country accent down pat, like she had been practicing for days at trying to embarrass him. Braxton couldn't believe the lengths she'd gone to, all for him. No doubt it had taken much planning on her part. This was good. It was a sure sign that she had been thinking long and hard about him. He noticed her cute pink IceTek Valentine watch. Obviously she hadn't had the presence of mind to know that her two-thousand-dollar watch would clash with her hillbilly-hobo look. *What a shame.*

"Gosh darn," Neeka gushed, following up with a geeky laugh. "I'm mighty darn happy to see you too. Shucks now, it's been too long." She threw down her stick-bundled clothes, snatched Quamee by his yellow knit shirt, and pulled him closer for a big hug. "Sorry," she gushed, pulling away. "Shucks. Hope I don't smell too much like garlic. I ate a few cloves of the stuff before I came. I hear tell it keeps them pesky mosquitoes away, and I hear tell that Texas is full of mosquitoes. Ain't that right now, Braxton?"

"Yes, I believe that's partly so, especially at night."

"That's right." Neeka sniffed, then pretended to wipe her nose with the back of her hand. "Mosquitoes and vampires. Garlic works good on vampires too, I hear. And you know how vampires can be."

"Vampires?" Quamee stared at her like she had turned crazy in real life. "It's the first I've heard about vampires being in Texas, but you never know."

The three stood for a moment longer, looking uncomfortably from one face to the other. Braxton kept checking out the torn and tattered denim pants Neeka wore. Her pants had enough small holes in them to be mesh. *That's a darn shame, and with all the money she has too. Darn pants should be in somebody's trash. And look at her. No shame whatsoever.*

Finally, Braxton broke the spell. "Well, it's going on seven, and we'd better be on our way. Brother Quamee, thanks for showing up so early to show some love before I head out." Then to Neeka, he said, "Miss Neeka, do you have any bags that need loading?" Her amply magnified eyes were glued to Quamee, obviously making the man more uncomfortable. "Neeka?"

"Huh? . . . I mean . . . yeah?"

"Your bags," Braxton prompted. "Do you have any luggage that needs to be loaded before we leave?" The woman was something else, and a darn good actress to boot. Should be somewhere on somebody's sitcom instead of working for her mother. He fought the urge to pull out his digital camera.

"That's mighty nice of you to be asking, but no, sir. I do plans to buy myself some new duds when we gits to town. Can't wait to be doing me some shopping in one of them fancy places they call the mall. Oh, yeah, I'm ready."

Braxton straightened his frame. "Let's get this show on the road then."

"Brax," said Quamee, shaking his head before hanging it. "I'll pray for you, man."

"Yeah, big brother, you do that. Take care now." Braxton stepped up inside, took his seat in the captain's chair of the cockpit, and fired up the RV's engine. The powerful purr of technology roared to life. Looking through the door at Neeka, he felt like closing the vehicle's door and driving off without her. Hell, he had the products already loaded on the vehicle. He had the destination address and the contact person's name in Austin, and more importantly, he wasn't dressed like a hillbilly hobo. He could probably do the Diva Four's cosmetic presentation without her. "Neeka, let's get moving."

"Sure thing. And Quamee, I'm sure we'll meet again." Neeka mounted the stairs slowly. The door closed behind her. She looked at Braxton long and hard through those thick glasses, her eyes blurred ovals. Hillbilly friendliness pushed to the side, her smile slipped away. Her face attempted a frown, and Braxton knew right then that she was going to say something so profound that he would remember her words for a long time. She said, "As for you, Braxton, I'm warning you now. I have a black belt, and I'm not afraid to use it."

CHAPTER TEN

Y ou planning to stare at the side of my head until we get to Texas, or what?"

"Maybe, maybe not." Shifting in her seat to find comfort, Neeka kept her gaze focused on the side of Braxton's head, where it had been for the last six hours. Her eyes felt hot and red from it. She hadn't been able to read his thoughts or figure out his main objective for agreeing to drive her out of state, but one thing she knew for sure, he definitely had a game plan. All handsome men had a game plan, and it was only a matter of time before the truth seeped out. "I'm not making you too nervous, am I?"

Braxton ignored her question.

"I read somewhere that if you stare at a person's head long enough, you can see their thoughts forming. You think it's true?"

"No, I'm afraid I don't." Braxton's hands tightened on the steering wheel.

"You never know." She couldn't read his thoughts, but what she did notice in three hundred and sixty minutes of staring was that he had the cutest sideburns of dark, baby-fine hair she'd ever seen on a grown man. Judging by the curly texture, he probably had a lot of chest hair as well. Something she liked in a man. Not only that, but she was convinced that his mother must have birthed him by way of Caesarean section because no head squeezed through the natural path could possibly be so perfect in shape. Not too round, not too square, and no dings, dents, or grooves where his hair faded at the back. The shape of his head was beautiful in its own perfection. An inside smile warmed her.

Braxton cleared his throat. "I think that the television in the sleeping quarters would be better entertainment than my head. Don't you agree?" He chanced a quick peek at her, but only to try to judge what her mood might be.

"Probably so. Nothing wrong with the view I have now. Maybe I'm looking for answers." She shifted her weight in the swerving leather chair across from him. Sitting for too long had produced a dull ache in her lower back. He was one smooth operator alright. Most people having someone stare at the side of their head for six hours would have no doubt swerved off the highway or crossed the centerline into head-on traffic. But not Braxton. Smooth, calm, collected. He appeared to be in perfect control.

"Look," he said, calm as water sitting in a glass, "I know it's been a long time, but anything you feel you need to know, you can just ask. Consider me an open book."

"Open book, huh? Okay, Braxton, if you're an open book, let's turn to the chapter on reality, page now. Why are you doing this?"

"This?" He chanced a quick peek over at her. "This, as in sitting here minding my own business? Or do you mean this, as in trying to drive you to Texas for business?"

"This, as in pretending that you want to get to know me all over again, and this, as in pretending that this whole thing isn't about money."

He produced a single cigarette from the top pocket of his shirt.

"For your information, Miss Lebeau, I'm a professional driver of large vehicles, and a darn good one at that. That's what my business is about." He considered telling her about his financial success, but then decided it was better to let her think what she wanted. He took in two long whiffs of the cigarette before placing it back in his pocket. Out came a stick of mint-flavored gum. "Care for a piece?"

"No, thank you."

"Your mother needed someone she could trust to drive, and that's where I come in. That's what I do. You make the deal. Your company prospers. So, in a way you're right. This trip *is* about money."

"Never mind the stupid trip, Braxton. I'm talking about showing up at my place with my mentally twisted mother—who means well, of course—and she implying that we could somehow hook up, get married, and have two children and a little white house with a little white picket fence around it. I want to know what's up with that?"

Grinning, he looked back over at her. "Only two kids? Darn, I was thinking more along the way of seven or eight."

"You're crazier than I thought if you think I would have seven children. With the state of the world today, no one in their right frame of mind would have that many children. Kids are okay, but to be honest, I don't even see myself being somebody's wife."

"Why not? I mean, what, you have something against the institution of marriage?"

"Funny you should use that word, 'institution.'" She was about to roll her eyes but remembered how awful her sister looked when she did it. "As far as I'm concerned, only crazy people get married; then they're ready for an institution alright. A mental institution."

He chuckled at her words, but only briefly. "I don't know about that. A man can get pretty tired of not having roots. Dating starts out fun, but after a while it becomes an empty challenge. Eventually a man wants to put down his roots. A loving wife, a few kids running around. A family provides plenty of roots. Besides"—he looked over for her full reaction—"I need to settle down with a nice young lady, and maybe, just maybe, your mother is thinking the same about you."

"There won't be any settling down with a nice young lady for me!"

A few chuckles. "Neeka, I think you know what I mean. A female for me, and a male for you. The circle of life that's meant to be."

Oh, no. He wasn't getting off that easy. "C'mon now, Braxton. Do I have the word 'stupid' stamped on my forehead?"

A quick look at her. Her huge eyes through the thick lens looking back. Laughter tried to bubble up inside him. "Well . . . I mean . . . of course not."

"You think I don't have sense enough to know what you're after? You're no different from the rest of the men who smell the sweet aroma of a family with money and think they can ease their way into it. Only you're the worst kind because you're trying to slither your way in through my mother. You're an open book alright. An open pocketbook."

"And what's that supposed to mean?" Coming from anyone else, her last remark would have fallen into the category of fighting words. For too many years he'd worked at his financial independence, and just because he didn't go around flaunting his success didn't make him some kind of gold digger. "Now, see, you could be so off target. You should never judge a book by its cover."

"Sometimes you don't have to judge when the cover is already ripped off, Mr. Dupree. You are so like glass, fragile and transparent. You're wide open."

Not certain what she was referring to, he looked down at his zipper. "No, no. I'm afraid you have it all twisted." He wanted to take her seriously. He really did, but that get-up she had on was making it impossible. It was hard to look into her magnified eyes without wanting to laugh. "I can honestly say that I have not taken any money from your mother, except for her paying for the rental of this vehicle and the operational costs. And that was her idea."

"I'm sure," Neeka huffed.

"Maybe she thinks we'll click and make a cute couple. I mean, I'm not involved, and she seems to think that you're not involved with anyone. However, I can assure you that no one is going to hog-tie you, nor pull a gun on you and make you do anything that you don't wish to do. Innocent matchmaking, that's all she's up to."

"Matchmaking?" she hooted, ready to tear him down like a condemned building. But no. She softened her tone. "Maybe to you it might be making a match, but to me it's pure making madness of my life. Don't get me wrong now. I love my dear mother, and she's a good person in her own way, but sometimes she's like the mother from the far side of hell." She studied her nails. "Trust me, I know what I'm saying. I've known the woman for twenty-four years now. She hasn't changed one bit."

Braxton shook his head, still smiling. "She seems harmless. She's like most mothers; she only wants the best for her daughters."

"You don't know her like I know her, so don't make lame excuses for her."

"You're just being overly sensitive."

Neeka bristled. "Who told you I was sensitive? Did my mama tell you that? She did, didn't she?"

"No, not really. Your mother always brags and speaks very highly of you. She's very proud of her daughters. Especially you. You don't know how lucky you are." He kept his hands tight on the steering wheel, his eyes straight ahead. Getting a late start was turning out just like he knew it would, and the noon traffic on Highway 10 was getting heavy.

"You're just saying that because she'll be paying you good

money." Neeka snorted and unbuckled her seat belt. "If it wasn't for the money, we would not be here together in this . . . this." She swirled her seat around and gestured with her hands, stopping to gaze into the cavern of the vehicle. "Good golly, Miss Molly!" she exclaimed. She had been so preoccupied with dressing like a "bummette" and with how she could make Braxton's trip as miserable as possible that until now she really hadn't paid much attention to the interior. It wasn't like she'd never been in a nice RV before.

When she and her sister were younger, her mother had rented an RV every two years for camping trips. Of course, Adeena, being the self-made diva that she was, never actually drove the massive vehicle herself. Instead she always hired some English-challenged foreigner as a driver, which ultimately took away from the essence of a true family vacation. Those RVs had been nice, and some even better than just nice, but this . . . well, this was something else. "Wow . . . this is really grand. Looks like mama dearest really outdone herself this time." Stretching her legs, she took a deep breath and stood up.

Alarmed, Braxton asked, "What are you doing?"

"What does it look like I'm doing? I'm stretching the kinks out of my legs and back." She stepped away from the leather seat and stood for a few seconds, then walked toward the center of the RV looking around at how her mother loved to waste money. Children were starving in Africa. The homeless were cold at night and hungry during the day, and this was how her mother wasted money. *Must be nice to squander money.*

"Look, uh, Neeka, I don't think it's a good idea to stand or walk around while the vehicle is moving. It's smart to stay buckled up, especially while we're on the freeway."

"And I think that bottled water should be free, but I guess I'm not as smart as you, Mr. Dupree. But don't you worry none, I'm a big girl and I can take care of myself. Thank you. You worry about Braxton, and I'll worry about Neeka." She spun her backside to him and headed toward the sleeping quarter in search of the restroom.

"Suit yourself," said Braxton, with a sly smirk. "I know one thing; your mother forgot to mention how sassy at the mouth you've become." No sooner had he uttered the words than the car before him braked hard, causing him to do the same. The massive vehicle screeched at the brakes and lurched to a forceful jerk that sent Neeka backward, then forward, and then straight against a divider wall where she took a hard bump to the head.

The bump was so hard, in fact, that Neeka could almost swear that she saw stars. "Ow, Braxton. You did that on purpose!"

"No, I did not. It was the car ahead of me!" Traffic kicked into a crawl slow enough for him to pull the RV safely over to the shoulder. He stopped, put the transmission in park, and engaged the emergency brakes. In a flash he was unbuckled and out of his seat and at Neeka's side, kneeling at the table where she sat holding her head. "You okay? See? I tried to warn you. Just because an RV is like a house doesn't mean that you should be walking around in it while it's in motion. You could really get hurt." He made an attempt to look at the small bump rising on her forehead, but stubbornly she pulled away. "Will you stop being so difficult and let me have a look at it?"

"Wait until my mother hears you tried to kill me."

"Let's not be so dramatic. It was an accident. The guy in front of me stopped short. I had to do one of two things, either stop the vehicle or plow straight into the back of him."

"Yeah, well, you thought about me getting hurt, and it happened." Rubbing her bruised forehead, she stood and moved over to the leather sofa and sat at the edge. It didn't feel like the skin was broken where her head had made contact with the solid divider wall, but she felt sure that the impact was hard enough to loosen a few teeth.

Wasn't his fault. Yeah, right. If not his, whose fault was it? "And you call yourself a good driver."

"Here, I'll go get some ice in a towel to put over it."

"Braxton, never mind," she huffed. "I can take care of myself."

"I know you can, but sit tight for a minute. It's not a problem for me. We have plenty of ice in the small freezer over there. Some ice, a Band-Aid, and some aspirin. Whatever you need. I have it." Despite her protest, he went to the freezer and withdrew a few cubes to wrap in a large red towel.

"I bet you do," Neeka snipped. She was being a stone brat about it, but too bad. No one invited this man to be in her family business— well, maybe her mother did—but she certainly didn't. If he didn't like her attitude, he could always quit.

"Here, let me put this on your head."

Cringing, she leaned away like he was offering a poison dart. "I'll do it myself. Thank you." She sniffed and held her reserve. *Look at him. Trying to be all sympathetic and helpful and smelling good enough to make me pass out.* She took the towel and held it to her head. "I'll be okay in a minute. You just go on and do what you were hired to do, drive this baby. The quicker we get to Texas and back, the better."

"Are you sure?"

"I'm positive, Braxton. Just drive!"

"Okay, but before I do, I can't pass up a Kodak moment, and this is definitely one of them."

Before her lips could sag open, before the horror of his intention could fully register in his eyes, he slid his digital camera out of his pocket, aimed, and clicked. Maybe it was something they could laugh about later, he hoped. He expected that the mood would be lightening up, but what he didn't expect was her reaction to his taking a couple of measly pictures.

"Say cheeseburger." Click.

"Braxton, no! No pictures! Who told you to take pictures?" Her look of sheer protest didn't stop him.

"Just one more. Say cheesecake." Click.

"Don't you dare!" She shot up from her seat, her face more serious than her words. "No pictures, never again! I'm not playing! I will get off this carnival ride right now and walk back to my condo if I have to!"

"What's wrong with you? It's just a couple of pictures."

"And I said no. No pictures!" Jumping up in his face, her hand grabbed the small camera. She hauled back and flung the thing with all her might against the wall, where it shattered into two pieces.

"Why the heck did you do that? That was a new camera!"

"Because I hate having my picture taken!" she screamed back.

"That doesn't make it okay to destroy my property. I just bought that camera two weeks ago."

"So. You can get another one. I'll pay. I'm sorry, but I don't do pictures."

"Woman . . . what in the world . . ." He stood a few seconds, scratching his head, then walked over and stooped to retrieve his damaged property. The shutter eye was broken, and the back panel was cracked in half. Damn her! He tried pushing the button to see what would happen. Nothing. *I cannot believe this! The nerve of her!* "Unbelievable. You act like you've been featured on *America's Most Wanted*. Only criminals hate to have their picture taken."

"Give me a break. Do I look like a wanted criminal?" She tossed her head back, then hung it to avoid his eyes. "Can we please get this vehicle back on the road? And when we get to the city, can we stop at the mall? I need to do a little shopping. I'm sorry about your camera, but I'll replace it later. Like I said, I don't do pictures, so don't ask."

"You don't do pictures?" He stood there looking at her like he wanted to say something else, wanted to ask something. Something about the look in her eyes held him back. "Alright, Miss Neeka. If you say so."

"Look, it's a long story from childhood. I don't like having my picture taken."

"You just broke my property; I think I deserve an explanation. I want one, long version or short."

"And I want to be a contemporary dancer and open up my own dance school. We all have something that we want in life, Braxton. Can we please just go?"

He looked down, noticing the tiny running lights embedded in the vehicle's floor. They would look nice once the lights were out. Maybe calming too. "Look, I don't know what's going on with you, but when you get to that place where you want to talk about it, I'm a good listener."

Neeka kept her head down, too embarrassed by her own behavior. "I'll remember that."

"I still think you need to buckle up. Just to be on the safe side. The freeway is getting a little hectic." He headed back to the captain's chair and waited.

"Restroom first." Neeka sprinted up and hurried to the restroom. Then she got back in her seat and buckled up, like a wayward kid ready to please. "How's that, Daddy? I'm all buckled up. Can we go now?"

Braxton mumbled under his breath, "Yeah, I'll be your daddy alright." *Maybe this trip wasn't such a good idea after all*, he mused. Not if all he had to look forward to were sassy comments, snippy remarks, and a bad attitude. "Look, I'm not trying to give you a hard time or act like I'm controlling your life here. I'm only trying to make sure we get to Texas and back safe, that's all."

"What?" Neeka said, feigning innocence. "All I said was I'm all buckled up."

"I mean, despite how you might feel about me, I'm sure that we can keep this trip as professional as possible."

She tensed up. "What makes you think I feel anything about you? That's being a tad presumptuous, don't you think?"

"Maybe so. But still, let's keep our ill feelings in check and strive for a more professional disposition."

"I agree one hundred percent, Mr. Dupree. Professional it is then."

"Good."

Obviously she was used to having the last word, so he let it be when she beamed, "Great."

CHAPTER ELEVEN

Please forgive me, Father. Forgive me. This is wrong, and I know it, but I can't . . . I just can't help myself."

Princess Lebeau relaxed her face as she stared into the small mirror of her bathroom. *Sinner! Big sinner!* It seemed to shout back at her. Why did there have to be such thing as sin? Lord, why? Squeezing her eyes shut, she opened them slowly and tried a happy smile, but all she could see gazing back at her was the reflection of an anxious and horny sinner. "Oh, Lord, I'ma burn in hell for this. I just know it."

It was so wrong what she was about to do. All sins were considered wrong in God's eyes. And how many times, how many years had her mother drilled that very thing into her head? Forever, it seemed. But even the fleeting thought of flames licking at her rear side from a pit of eternal damnation couldn't deter her from what waited on the opposite side of her bathroom door. "Just this last time. I promise never again, Lord. This is absolutely and positively the last time. I promise, so help me."

Her stomach felt like it was being twisted and then stretched far beyond its limit. And her sweaty palms. Lord, why did she have to have sweaty palms every time that man was near her? She tried steadying her breath with controlled breathing; after all, Tee was waiting for her, and she couldn't stay locked up and stalling for time forever.

Timidly, she unlocked the door and eased out of the room to be with her guest. Just like on other occasions, Tee would be expecting her to come out dressed in her sure-nuff birthday suit, but it always took some coaxing and sometimes even half a glass of sherry to help her.

So far, after being locked in the restroom for all of twenty minutes, she'd only managed to remove her navy blue pumps and blue jacket. Two-hour lunch breaks didn't seem like enough time to get butt naked, but Tee wouldn't have it any other way.

"Are you ready for me?" Princess was asking Tee the question, but really it should have been the other way around. It was midafternoon, and she'd done her best to darken the room before Tee came over, but traces of sneaky sunlight still found its way into her bedroom. It splashed against the cream-hued comforter that matched her drapes. "You sure you don't want something to eat first?" she asked him, stalling. She was always stalling, even though she should be so used to him by now. Six months now. That's how long they'd been doing "it." Princess still liked to refer to what they did beneath her silken sheets as "it," because referring to it as "sex" would make it seem more like pure sin and fornication. "It" was safer. "It" gave the impression of something sweet, something innocent, and something necessary, like springwater. "I could scramble us some eggs and make some toast."

Tee, one hundred and seventy pounds of taut brown muscle, was sprawled along her bed. He looked at her, smacking his lips. "Oh, I want something to eat alright, but it's not in the food group." His devil-in-me-now smile took up most of his clean-shaven face. "You can take those clothes off nice and slow. You don't need no clothes for what I have in mind. Take 'em off, and do it slow now. Just like Tee showed you. You know what I like."

He was a man who could bring out the long-hidden friskiness in her. "Make me," she said. Her hand paused at the second button of her pink silk blouse. Taking off her garments in front of him always ignited a sensation of being naughty, a schoolgirl gone bad. And Tee was a man who didn't mind showing her some incentive by throwing the cover off his chocolate body. His swollen penis stood to attention, pointing stiffly to the heavens as if to remind her of where it could take her emotions. "Now," he said, making sure she had a full-sized view, "be a good girl, and take your clothes off nice and slow."

"You mean like this?" The sweet sight of his perky member, frisky and waving, always did the trick. Reservation slid away. Inhibitions were pushed back into the catacombs of her mind as she removed her blouse, revealing her small breasts straining in her push-up glory, thanks to Victoria's Secret. Her skirt slid down to the carpet. "This is the last time, Tee." She slowly peeled off the rest of her clothing, never taking her eyes off the prize. "We can't keep giving in to lust this way. It's not right."

"I know, baby," said Tee, licking his lips.

Naked, she stood a few seconds allowing his eyes to drink her in, but only because she knew he enjoyed it so much. Then she hurried to the bed, fumbling with the covers.

"Oh, no, you don't," Tee insisted firmly. "I want to see every inch of you." Tee, not too tall and not too short, maneuvered himself to Princess's side. He perched his head in his hand. "You are so beautiful that it hurts my eyes to look at you for too long."

"Thank you," she giggled. But Princess didn't feel so beautiful. She knew that she was too thin for that. She had narrow hips and small breasts, but even in her thinness there were curves in the right places. What she felt was exposed. It was hard to look at him and see his eyes drinking her in, intoxicating him. She kept expecting him to pull out a big spotlight and shine it between her thighs the way the doctor some-times did at her gynecology exam. Exams she saw as so embarrassing.

"I think you have a spell on me. You have something." Her words were low and nonaccusing. "Whatever it is, it finds the bad in me and draws it out and into the open. I don't know if that's a good thing, Tee. I just don't know. Is it a spell?"

"A spell?" Tee regarded her with a quizzical look.

"I really do feel that way. I mean, my friend Jessie . . . I told her about us. Don't worry. Jessie is cool. She's the only one I can trust. Anyway"—she stopped to fight back a giggle.—"Jessie says that you have me—" She halted, embarrassed to use the word Jessie had used. Jessie could say anything with that mouth of hers.

"I have you what?" He reached over and touched her soft middle with a gentle stroke of his finger, dipping into the warmth of pink.

Silly her, giggling like some underage schoolgirl. Tee's touch could make her shiver on a hot day. "Well, my friend Jessie said that you have me dicknotized." There, she'd said it. She said the word, "dicknotized." He looked amused but not too shocked. Princess didn't see him as a strongly handsome man, but good-looking in his own way. He had those dark eyes that always looked as if he was being sexually suggestive when you looked into them. Maybe it was the way he cocked his head sometimes when he talked, or it could be his smile. He had such a sexy smile that she was sure other women misunderstood it to mean he was interested in them. Women were silly like that. A man smiles at them, and right away they think he wants to bed them.

"Never heard it put like that before, but your friend Jessie could be right. Maybe it does have the power to hypnotize." He lifted his penis for her view. "You do like it, right?"

One thing she liked about him was that he had no shame. "I do," she stammered, "I really do." The more Princess stared at it, the more warm and curious she felt about it. The more she stared, the more she wished she could make herself want to touch it. Heck, she wished she could screw the darn thing off Tee's body and put it away in the drawer of her nightstand for later. Later, she could have more time to study it up close without Tee being around observing.

"This is still our little secret, right?"

"Don't be silly," Princess assured him. "My sisters would die, and my mother would kill us."

"Yes, she probably would," he said, his dark face moving closer to her breast. "What we do behind closed doors is only for us to know about, our sweet little secret."

"But . . . is it really wrong what we're doing? I mean, being the Christians that we are and all."

"No . . . no, of course not. Not when a man and a woman love each other. This is what they do. God gave us this gift. Think about it, Prin. If the man above didn't want a man and a woman to do this, why would he make it feel so good? Why would he make it such a natural thing that our bodies crave?"

"Are you sure?"

"Of course I'm sure. And it's okay to touch it. It was meant to be touched. Go ahead, touch it."

She didn't see his member as a penis—oh, no, not that hardcore and unsavory word. Instead, his swollen flesh waiting for her was more like a wand. A magic wand. It was warm and thick and it had powers. Those same powers had taken complete control of her senses. "You know I have to be back at work by two? Friday is our busiest day of the week, and with Mercy out with a cold and Neeka in Texas, it's all on me and Mommie . . . I mean, my mother."

"Trust me, you'll be back by one-thirty. Relax."

"You like what you see?" She angled her head, trying to appear sexy as she shifted along her 600-thread-count sheet. "You make me feel so free."

He'd been her first and only lover, and even though the first few times hadn't been the greatest, she'd learned to relax and move with the rhythm he created. That was how his magic wand worked. It was like a pressure gauge moving up inside, further and further up her until she could think of nothing else but getting to the top of love's journey.

Tee was such a pro. He always knew what to do, what to say, where to touch. It was almost as if he knew more about her body than she did after living with it for twenty-two years. She wanted to be more aggressive, but something lurking in the back of her mind was holding her back. Thoughts. The thought of someone with loose lips finding out about their affair and telling her mother; the thought of her sisters finding out and telling her mother. Her mother thought so much of her that no man went without scrutiny. It would break Adeena's heart to find out that one of her daughters, the youngest one at that, wasn't as pure and untouched as she imagined. A failure in a mother's eyes. Princess couldn't bear the thought.

"Does this feel good?" Tee asked, kissing the delicate spots along her neck.

"I think so. I mean, of course it does." Her body would tense up with too much thinking, but Tee always knew what to do. His warm mouth slurped up her pink and engorged nipple, his expert tongue flicking around its darkened bulb. Her tendency to clamp her thighs together melted away as his hand gently stroked them. His hands were like matches as they ignited a fire inside her.

"What about protection?" Taking a chance with sin was one thing, but starting a family was another.

"Here, let me prepare myself right now."

She never saw him breaking open the foil packet, but assumed he had done so while she was in the restroom. She didn't have to check to see if he had fitted himself with the thing properly. She didn't have to because Tee knew what he was doing. Tee could handle it. Even this faded away to the back of her mind the moment he fixed himself above her. Nothing but good feeling flooded through her.

"Let me show you how much I care about you."

Princess could feel her back trying to arch; then it relaxed. What Tee said made sense. That was another thing she liked about him. He always knew what to say. Tee knew how to make it all so right. "Ooh, Tee, like that." All thoughts of right and wrong floated away from her mind when his warm lips, then his hot probing tongue, touched her thigh. Even wrong turned to right. She closed her eyes. Thank goodness. Tee always knew what to do.

CHAPTER TWELVE

Neeka stood up and looked at her heart-shaped IceTek watch for what had to be the twentieth time. "What could possibly be keeping that man?" She forced hard air from her lungs as she peered across the mall's massive parking lot hoping to spot the RV. Something that big couldn't possibly be hard to see, which only meant that it was nowhere to be found. "Ooh, I could strangle him!"

The more it registered that the RV was nowhere in sight, the more irritated she became. *Great. Nothing like being stranded in El Paso, Texas.* "Stupid man," she muttered, "I can't believe he could do this." Sitting back along the cold hard bench to wait, she shivered. She'd tried his cell phone twice with no answer. With nightfall creeping in, the tattered-looking jeans she wore were barely keeping her legs warm and the paint-stained cotton top that had meant to be a joke wasn't so funny anymore.

She felt so silly. The objective behind her hobo outfit had been to look as unattractive as possible, but the reaction from Braxton hadn't been what she had hoped. In fact, he seemed genuinely happy that she was dressed so outrageously. The fake buckteeth had to go, as well as the blurry glasses and two sideway ponytails. Now, waiting outside in the cold for Braxton to show up, the skimpy outfit was another reminder of another bad choice. *Good grief, why can't I get it right? For once I need to make the right decision. Now look at me. And wouldn't it be funny if Braxton had enough of my mess and left my behind out here to get back to California the best way I can? If he did, I wouldn't blame him.*

"Still, I'll strangle him. Just wait until I see him!" Using her hands, she rubbed friction along her arms, trying to warm over the tiny rise of goosebumps. In a sad little way, she had some nerve getting upset when she was the one who had insisted that he stop off at the mall to begin with. That stunt of showing up with a few pairs of underwear and a sleep-shirt bundled to a stick had been the silliest idea she'd ever had. It had taken her a few days to come up with the idea of not packing the things she needed for the trip. Her rationale: What man would try any romantic moves with a half-blind, bucktoothed, dirty-looking woman who looked like she might be homeless?

Obviously, it was a plan that had turned sour, and now, being stranded outside Cielo Vista Mall in El Paso, waiting with her purchases, was proof enough. His late show was probably his way of paying her back for her late arrival earlier. *Umph. He obviously don't know who he's dealing with.*

Neeka stood up again, hoping that doing so would help her to see something. Shoppers walked to and from the shopping center. Occasionally, a mother hurried her child away from her like she might be contaminated. She focused hard on searching for a small glimpse of hope, anything. Finally, a sight for sore eyes—she spotted the mini-mansion on wheels turning into the parking structure. *Thank God, here his crazy butt comes now.*

She didn't wait for the vehicle's doors to open before she verbally tore into him. "If this is your idea of playing a joke, Braxton, I am not laughing. How dare you drive off and leave me at this mall!"

"Look," he said, calm and collected, "I fell asleep after locating the RV park we're booked to stay at for the night. I was tired and I overslept. I apologize."

"Braxton, stop lying! You wanted to make me wait as some form of punishment for having you stop at the mall. I even tried to call your cell. Be a man and be honest about it."

"No." Braxton shook his head. "It wasn't like that. I fell asleep. And while I'm on vacation, I prefer my cell phone to be off."

"If that's the case," said Neeka, driving her theory in harder, "you could have stayed in the parking lot and slept until I was finished shopping. It's not like I've been gone for half a day. Would it have killed you to do that? Would it?"

"Miss Neeka, for your information," Braxton replied in a controlled tone, "mall security showed up and informed me that I had to move the vehicle from the lot. It was taking up too much space. And that's what I did: I moved it. I mean, you might try being a little understanding of the fact that I've been driving for over twelve hours, and I just might be, I don't know, a tad tired perhaps."

"Obviously you've had no training on how to treat a lady, because that's still no excuse for you to leave me stranded in a strange city, Mr. Dupree." She noticed the bulging veins at his neck. He was getting upset. *Good*.

"Well, Miss LeBeau, El Paso is not a strange city, and you're not stranded now. So let's get over it." He paused, knowing that more would be coming. "Now, would you like me to help you with those packages?"

"Don't you dare tell me when to get over it! You're not the one who has been waiting out here in the cold and the dark for almost an hour. And no, I don't need your help with my bags." Neeka adjusted the strap on her new Prada purse and struggled with bags as sheer stubbornness motivated her steps up into the vehicle. "Why act so concerned now? I've been waiting forever for you to show up. You weren't concerned then."

Clutching as many bags as she could, she stomped up the steps into the RV and flung packages onto the leather sofa. A few bags tumbled to the floor. Stomping back down the steps for a second haul, she could feel Braxton's eyes on her. Foolish man. He obviously didn't have the common sense of a turnip to know that it's rude to make a woman wait for so long. Neeka continued her rant: "No sweater, no jacket. I'm cold and I'm hungry, while you're all warm and cozy."

"Warm? Yes. Cozy? No," Braxton retaliated through clenched teeth.

"That's not the point, Braxton!" Her eyes were daggers aimed at him.

"Look, I said I'm sorry. I'm here now. What more can I say about it? I'm sorry. It won't happen again."

Silence hung heavy between them. "I know it won't because the next time we stop, I will take charge of the keys."

Braxton looked skeptical, then allowed his face to grin. "I don't know about that part. Driving your cute little Lexus SUV is one thing, but driving this RV is another. Without training and experience, you're an accident waiting to happen."

"Don't make me laugh. You obviously underestimate the power of a woman. If you can drive this thing, I certainly can, and I can probably drive it better than you."

"Maybe in your dreams," he chuckled. "But for now I'm in charge of this vehicle. And if you're not sure, I suggest you take out your cell phone and call and ask somebody."

"Well, let's look at it like this." Neeka frowned, aggravated by his words. She couldn't believe how confrontational she was being. Never in her life had her feathers been so ruffled. "If you work for my mother, you are also working for me. And oops, she's not here right now, so that makes me the boss. In fact, that makes me your boss." She pointed a thin finger at him.

"My boss?" He couldn't help shaking his head. The woman was too much. No sense in starting a war. "Okay, you're the boss lady. I apologize again for being late."

"Hmph. That's better."

Suddenly they went quiet. The feeling, to Neeka, was much like sparring fighters going to their prospective corners. Any second, a bell would sound somewhere in her head, and they would come out from their corners swinging.

"Dang, woman." Braxton flashed a sincere smile. "Looks like you bought up the whole mall. Sure you don't need some help?"

"Do I look helpless?"

Braxton threw his hands up. "I just asked."

"I can handle it." On her last climb into the vehicle she lost her step, tripping on the top step, but her fall was cushioned by large and decorative shopping bags.

"Be careful. Here, let me help you." Braxton was out of his seat in two heartbeats, only to have Neeka shoot down his efforts by trying to slap his hands away. Not one to give up so quickly, he took a firm hold of her arm and pulled her up the steps and into his arms. The smell of her hair in his nostrils. The softness of her skin against his hands. Her face was right at his, their lips lined up. Damn. He wanted so badly to see what those lips felt like against his. So soft-looking. The feeling was so tempting. "Are you okay?" He released her and stepped back.

The woman was like a mind reader. "If you dare put your lips on mine, I will bite them off and spit them out. And I'm not playing."

"Sounds painful."

"It will be." Her eyes dared him.

"I was just trying to help boss lady up, that's all." The spell had been strong, but thank goodness it was broken. For a minute he almost lost control.

"And thank you, but no thanks. Please don't touch me again. I don't need your help. I'm perfectly capable."

"Sorry, Miss Boss Lady. I didn't want you to fall and hurt those cute knees of yours."

"I said I can handle it." She took her bags to the sleeping quarters and returned to buckle up in her seat. Just thinking about how he had kept her waiting in the cold made her temper heat up all over again. Despite Braxton's nonchalance about the matter, Neeka felt that she had been a perfect target for a robbery. True, a purse snatcher wouldn't have gotten much in the way of money. She rarely carried a lot of cash. But thanks to her high-limit credit cards, the bounty would still have been plentiful: new shoes, a chocolate Gucci tote bag, a new black dress, a bad-assed two-piece suit by Anne Klein, blouses, more shoes, not to mention a cache of beautiful unmentionables. Her weakness.

"Hope you left something for the other shoppers."

"My money, my prerogative." Neeka heaved a light sigh. She lived to shop, but that croc Kelly bag on sale for ten thousand had to be put on hold. Such an exuberant amount would have exhausted even her credit limit. All the same she felt pleased with her selections. Something about shopping was such an uplift to her spirit. If it wasn't for the nice things she'd purchased, she could strangle Braxton with her bare hands. "Let's just go. I'm all set."

In an attempt to humor her, Braxton saluted with, "You're the boss."

An hour later they were hooked up at the RV park for the night. From her sleeping quarters, Neeka couldn't see much of the place through the darkness of her window, but from what she could see, it wasn't the best one she'd stayed at. But it would have to do. Besides, how the place looked on the outside had nothing to do with the elegance on the inside of the vehicle. By morning they would be pulling out, and the RV park would be a thing of the past.

With a deep sigh Neeka looked up at the flat-screen television that played some local news. After the turkey burgers, fries, and drinks they had for supper, Braxton was already tucked in for the night on the leather sofa that let out to a sleeper. From the vehicle's rear quarters, she could hear the muffled drone of his television program. A couple of times, she could even have sworn that she heard snoring. The man was probably sleeping like a baby, which was a good thing. For the long trek ahead, he needed all the rest he could get. The first sign of daylight they'd be back on the road to their final destination: Austin.

She was a little tired, but far from sleepy. Sleep would be nice, but for the time being it wasn't an option. Neeka sat up in bed and stretched. Why was it so hard for her to fall asleep in an unfamiliar environment? For as long as she could remember, she was plagued with this same problem. A warm shower hadn't helped.

She felt restless as she aimed the remote and flicked through channel after channel. It was still early, only eight-thirty, and the more Neeka thought about it, the more she realized that staying in for the night wasn't what she wanted. Clicking the television off, she reached for her purse on the small stand next to the bed. Maybe she was crazy or coming down with a bout of adventure fever, but she put her hand into her purse and pulled out two colorful business cards, one for a local cab company. Earlier, when she had gone looking for an ATM at the mall, she had come across a bulletin board with a host of cards for local businesses: places to eat, places to stay, and places to buy all kinds of items, not to mention cards for shuttle buses, limousine services, and cabs. She had pulled off not only the card for a cab, but also a brightly colored one for Jumping Jiggy's, a local bar and grill. The best that she could hope for was that the place wasn't some tiny hole in the wall, and filled with drug-hazed dropouts. Nevertheless, some grilled fish and vegetables and some peppy music sounded pretty good to her. She used her cell phone to call a cab. A quick dressing act and some primping with her hair, and she was ready.

The last thing she expected when she opened the accordion-type door was for Braxton to be awake and watching television. His eyes were bloodshot, with the beginning of dark circles beneath them. Poor thing looked exhausted. Good. He was still fully dressed like he was sitting sentry. *Too bad.*

Smelling heavenly and dressed to kill in her little black dress, which clung to her petite frame like skin, she strolled past him, went to the door, and peered out the window. No cab in sight yet. Neeka removed her compact from the shiny clutch bag that matched her sling-backs, and began examining her reflection. *Perfect.*

"May I ask what you think you are doing?" Braxton inquired with one eye open. His words were followed with a weary yawn.

"I'm restless. I'm going out for a short spell," Neeka said. "You get some sleep. I shouldn't be too long."

"Excuse me, but wasn't it just a few hours ago that you were complaining about being in a strange place all alone?" He sat up, forcing alertness. "That *was* you, right?"

"Yes, but, this is not the same, Braxton. I'm taking a cab straight to a public place where there will be others. I'm not sitting alone on a cold bench waiting for someone to come rob me."

"And may I ask boss lady what kind of place would this be?"

"Are you my daddy now?"

"What kind of place did you say?"

"A bar and grill. A place to eat, dance, and be merry, if you must know. Frankly, it's really not your place to be asking me where I'm going. After all, I am a grown woman." No sense in mentioning that she'd never gone to a bar and grill alone in her entire life. Once with a close friend from high school, and once with Mercy for her birthday. Even that last time they had to sneak off. Her mother didn't approve of such behavior, but now, miles away from home, what Mama didn't know didn't concern her. "Don't worry, it's all under control. Get some sleep."

Braxton was looking at her incredulously. "Are you by any chance taking some kind of medication I don't know about? Because if you are, please let me know now so I'll know how to deal with you."

Neeka put a hand on her hip. "What's that supposed to mean?"

"It means that this is not home, Neeka, and you cannot be out carousing around like you live here."

"Excuse me, but the last time I checked my birth certificate, I was over twenty-one. And if I feel like going to a bar or to a strip club to learn pole-dancing"—she paused to point a finger at her chest—"it's *my* business."

"Well, you might be grown, but you're never too grown to get robbed, kidnapped, raped, or killed."

"You wouldn't hurt me, would you?"

"Woman, I'm not talking about me. I'm talking about some deranged person who could be at the club you're going to."

"And how would that be your problem?" Neeka stood with her arms crossed. If he thought he was going to control what she did, he had another thought coming.

"Look, in case you have forgotten, I was hired to drive and look after your safety on this trip. I know that it's not safe for a young, attractive woman to go barhopping in an unfamiliar city all alone. I'm

sorry, but I can't allow you to go out to some bar. End of discussion."
He snorted and pointed the remote to turn up the volume on the television.

"If you say so," Neeka replied, rather flippantly. "Ooh, looks like my cab has arrived. I'll be back. How do you open the door?" She was at the control panel. "Braxton, let me out."

"Woman, I will not let you leave here alone. You must be crazy." Throwing off covers, Braxton was up and looking for his shoes, while Neeka tried buttons and switches at the cockpit, looking for the one that opened the door.

"My cab is waiting! Show me how to open this door. Braxton, the driver can't wait forever." Outside, a yellow and black cab blew an impatient horn.

"Neeka, I don't think so." Braxton fetched his black leather jacket from a closet before opening and securing the RV's door. "This is ridiculous. What kind of churchwoman goes to a club looking for a good time?" He followed her out to the waiting cab.

"The kind that feels like living life every now and then. Just because a person is a Christian or regularly attends church don't dismiss the fact that they still live in the physical world, Braxton. You can never completely isolate yourself from worldly things until you're dead." Neeka gave him a mock smile. *Good. That should shut you up for a while.*

"Like it or not, I'm going with you."

"Fine. But just because you're coming along doesn't make us a couple." She waited for him to open the cab door for her.

"Heaven forbid." Braxton climbed in next to her, acutely aware of his thigh seeking out the warmth from hers. Churchgirl or not, she crossed her legs, giving an ample view of her honey brown thighs that made his heart speed up a few beats. As hard as it was to keep his eyes straight ahead, he couldn't resist a few sly peeks.

"As far as I'm concerned, I'm riding solo tonight." Neeka rattled off the address to the cabdriver.

Too tired to argue, Braxton shook his head. "Whatever the boss lady says."

CHAPTER THIRTEEN

Looks harmless enough." Braxton eyed the modest-looking establishment with the large red neon sign that read Jumping Jiggy's, but secretly wished for the warmth and comfort of a bed. His eyes were hot and red, and if his energy level could be measured, his was down to a fourth of a cup and dwindling. Keeping up with Neeka was proving to be more than he had bargained for. The fact that the woman didn't understand that he required a certain number of sleeping hours was disturbing. He was beginning to see why Neeka wasn't married or involved; clearly she was too into herself. It had to be about what Neeka wanted or nothing at all. *Wonder who she takes that from?* he mused.

Braxton made an attempt at conversation. "You do realize we have to be on the road early?"

"You could have stayed home," Neeka replied. She felt excited to be doing something so out of character.

Braxton found her lack of concern disconcerting. But even more disturbing was that she had figured he would be too tired to be her escort. Any other sensible fool would have allowed her to go hightailing out there and stayed behind to hope that she returned in one piece. But no, not him. He had to be the big brother, the protector. Maybe because he felt strongly that if anything was to happen to Neeka during the trip, he would never be able to forgive himself.

For several months now his company had been handling odd jobs for her mother, and the two of them had talked about everything under the sun. Adeena had mostly talked about Neeka having a hard time finding a nice man to settle down with. Now he could definitely understand why. Her sweet and precious Neeka was self-centered, spoiled rotten, and used to getting her way. The more he sat with Adeena, the more fond of the older woman he had grown, and he had come to think of her as his own mom. Mom or not, it was obvious that Adeena didn't play when it came to her daughters. If he was expected to drive and protect, then drive and protect is what he damn well better be doing.

A light drizzle had begun to fall as they climbed out of the cab. Braxton paid the cab driver, while Neeka sought shelter under the building's awning. There appeared to be a mixed crowd of people standing out in front, coming and going. Loud music blared from a door that constantly swung open and shut.

"Keep the change," Braxton told the driver as he folded his wallet and placed it back in his rear pocket. Seeing how the bar-and-grill excursion had been Neeka's idea, she could have at least offered half for the cab fare, but maybe that was too much for him to expect. As a gentleman, he didn't mind paying, but it was the principle of the thing that bothered him. Fatigue gripping his body, he hurried over to her side, thankful that Neeka had at least waited for him before entering the place. "I hope you're not planning to stay long," he said plaintively. "I could stand some sleep before we hit the road in the morning."

"Like I said before, you could have stayed behind and slept."

"And have you roaming around El Paso unescorted? I think not."

"Well, then, don't complain." She tossed her shoulder-length hair back and walked ahead of him as if she were a regular at Jumping Jiggy's. Loud reggae played in a rhythmic tempo as he followed her up to a bar where she found an empty stool and sat. "Don't worry, Braxton. I'm a big girl and I can take care of myself."

"I suppose that's your cue for me to leave and find my own spot?" Even in the room's dim light, her skin held a shimmer to it like it had been polished. She was beautiful without having to work hard at it like some women. He wondered if she was a good kisser? What kind of underwear did she prefer, cotton or sexy? Tired eyes or not, he could look at her all night.

"I suppose you're right. The night is young, and I plan to have some fun. So if you don't mind." She twirled away from him and motioned the bartender over with a finger up. "Let me see now . . . I'll have a virgin Shirley Temple. No, wait . . . on second thought, make that a Sex on the Beach."

Braxton studied her with mild curiosity. "Have you ever had Sex on the Beach before?"

Neeka was insulted. "Of course not. I'm not that type of woman."

"I was referring to the drink."

"Oh. I knew that. No, not really, but there's a first time for everything." Neeka toyed nervously with her fingers.

"Thought you didn't drink?" Braxton ordered a gin and tonic for himself. No doubt the drink would last him the entire night, because a mere two sips and he would be asleep on the counter. One of the things he disliked about bars and clubs was that all patrons were expected to buy at least one drink to be allowed to sit at a table. "I'd be careful if I were you. A drink like that is nothing to play with, it's pretty potent."

"Are you my daddy?"

He smiled devilishly. "No, but I could be if you let me."

Another sexual innuendo. She let it slide. "Thanks for the information," Neeka said, removing her credit card from her purse. "But I'm away from home, I'm bored, and I would like to try something different. If that's okay with you." She turned her attention to some dancers keeping the beat with a reggae tune.

"It's like you said: You're the boss," Braxton said. She was obviously trying to be funny, as if what he thought actually made a difference. "But if a classy woman like yourself were my date, I would order you something like a glass of wine or, even better, a wine cooler."

"If I wanted wine, Braxton, I would order wine." She looked away again. "And thank goodness we're not on a date."

"Okay, okay, Jeepers. I'm not trying to tell you what to order, merely suggesting." He could do without that little smirk of a smile she had plastered on her face. "I'm just saying that if you're not accustomed to a strong drink like Sex on the Beach, you probably shouldn't have it tonight."

"Well, I'll be the judge of that. Thank you very much. Now," she paused to give a tiny wave of her hand, "if you don't mind, I'm supposed to be solo."

"Don't say I didn't warn you." He paid the bartender for his drink. "I'll be in the eating area. Let me know when you're ready to leave."

"You can count on it."

He strode away, mumbling under his breath, "Spoiled brat. Cute, but still a brat."

Braxton noticed that the place was much larger than it appeared from the outside. The dining room was adjacent to the bar area. Large and clean, the room had antique paraphernalia suspended from the ceiling and anchored to the wall. One thing for certain, it didn't look like the place was hurting for business.

His drink in hand, Braxton found an empty table and took a seat.

Attractive females were all over the place. He even glanced at a few winking in his direction, but as tired as he was, he wouldn't be good company. In no time, a pink and plump waitress was at his table with a menu. The alcoholic beverage he had ordered he could do without, but maybe some food would help. The turkey burger he'd eaten earlier had been enough, but he couldn't occupy a table and not order food. "Hot chicken wings and a Diet Coke. Thank you."

Two hours later, loud music booming through his head, smoke finding its way to his eyes, Braxton couldn't stop yawning. He'd gone through two orders of chicken wings and two Diet Cokes, and he was ready to leave. Barely able to keep his eyes open, he paid his tab and went looking for Neeka, but to his dismay, she was not where he had left her. *Oh, that's just great,* he thought.

Braxton found one of several dance floors, and weaved his way through scantily clad females and overly cologned men seeking to get lucky for the night, all bumping, swaying, and gyrating to the music. He didn't see Neeka among them. He took the stairway to discover that it led up to another dancing area. More sweaty, hip-swaying, booty-shaking, and gyrating people. *Dang, these folks can really party.* Still, no sight of Neeka.

Back downstairs he headed for the front entrance. What if the woman had left and went back to the RV? *What kind of game was she playing now? Ditch the escort?*

Outside the drizzle was now solid rain. Dark clouds assaulted the sky as the water cleaned the cool night air. Standing under the awning, Braxton removed a single cigarette from his pocket and ran it under his nose. The sweet stench of tobacco helped to relax him, but not as much as firing the thing up and smoking it. He hadn't smoked in over three years, but every now and then the urge was strong, especially when he felt stressed. The way he was feeling now, a good smoke would probably do the trick. With the inclement weather, not as many patrons were standing out front as when they'd first arrived. *Oh, what the hell. One last smoke won't kill me on the spot.* A lighter. He needed a lighter. Braxton looked around for someone who could give him a light, when he spotted Neeka. He had to do a double take to make sure that it was actually her. She was standing a short distance from him where the parking lot began. Shards of rain illuminated through the lot's overhead lamp. Standing next to her were two men—one held an umbrella over her head, while the other appeared to be holding a pencil and writing something down. "What the hell . . . Neeka! It's time to go!" Ready or not, this boat was sailing back to the comfort of the RV. "Neeka. Come on, let's go!"

Braxton threw his unlit cigarette down and started in their direction. It all happened so fast, he couldn't be sure of what he was seeing. The umbrella holder lowered the umbrella to his side and grabbed the expensive watch along Neeka's wrist. The two struggled for a split second, Neeka yelling at the top of her lungs. The second assailant appeared to be dislodging her purse. By the time Braxton made it to her side, the watch snatcher had run one way, and the other guy had dropped the purse and run the opposite way.

Braxton took off after the watch snatcher. Rain stung his face as he shortened the distance. Luck must have been on his side because the perpetrator slipped on a wet oil spot on the asphalt and went down. Braxton was on the young punk like a bad suit, trying to remove the watch from his clutch. The two struggled on the ground for half a minute. From a distance he could hear Neeka's shrill screams of, "Braxton, watch out! Braxton, look behind you!" What he didn't see, he felt. A sharp pain to his left buttocks pulled a loud yelp from him. Hot pain ran through him with the force of a locomotive, making him release the perpetrator, who scrambled up with the help of his accomplice. More fancy footwork in the struggle, but to no avail. The watch in hand, the two assailants ran off into the night, laughing.

Retrieving her purse, Neeka made her way over to Braxton. She could barely stand straight as she helped him up. "Are you okay?"

"I'll live." Braxton couldn't believe that the young punk had gotten the best of him. The guy couldn't have been more than nineteen or twenty, and Braxton outweighed him by at least forty pounds. If it hadn't been for the accomplice sneaking up and jabbing him in the flesh of his buttock, he wouldn't have gotten away.

Braxton looked at Neeka. "What about you? Did either of them hurt you?"

Neeka was shivering wet. "No, I'm okay."

He fumbled for his phone but recalled he'd left it in the RV. "Use your cell and call the police." His hands were shaking and his legs felt wobbly. None of this would have happened if they had stayed in, but what good would it do to tell her that? "Young punks probably scoped you the minute we stepped into the club."

"Braxton, I don't feel so good. I want to go home." Rain slicked Neeka's hair to her head, and the cold highlighted the nipples of her breasts.

"Neeka, you've been robbed. We need to call the police."

"No, I just want to go. I feel weird." Rubbing her stomach, she made a face.

"But your watch."

"Forget it. It's not like I can't get another watch."

Her words sounded slightly slurred, probably from that darn Sex on the Beach drink he told her not to mess with. Obviously the drink had clouded her judgment as well. "What about calling the police? We can't just let them get away with this."

"It's only a watch, Braxton. Let's just go . . . oh, my head." She clutched her stomach with one hand, the side of her head with the other. "I don't feel so good, and I'm cold. Let's get a cab and leave."

A part of him wanted to convince her that staying around for the

El Paso police was the right thing to do, but another part of him knew that it probably wouldn't do any good. Petty crimes happened to out-of-towners twenty-four/seven, and most of them went unsolved. Besides, it was half-dark, and he didn't get to see the assailants' faces well enough to identify them. All he knew was that they were two young hoodlums. One white, one black, both with short dreadlocks.

"Are you sure you don't want to wait for a police report? I mean, an expensive watch like that had to be insured."

"No. It wasn't. But I don't care about that. The only thing I want is a cab so we can get back to a warm, dry place."

"Alright then," Braxton sighed with defeat. "I know that watch had to cost a couple of grand. But if you don't want to call the police, you don't want to. Like you said, you're the boss."

CHAPTER FOURTEEN

Man, *stop thinking about it and do it! Help the poor woman out of those wet clothes!*

Braxton stood over her, stalling, trying to will himself more courage. Neeka lay half-conscious on the leather sofa, where he had to almost carry her. No ordinary drink should have rendered her so inebriated. If she wasn't so out of it, he would be giving her the third degree. Had she accepted a drink from a complete stranger? Or perhaps a more common scenario had occurred: Seeing a woman alone and not paying attention to her drink, someone had slipped something into it. Neeka was barely conscious, but her slurred speech, glassy eyes, and unfocused gaze were suspicious enough.

"You know what? You're not so bad-looking if a woman looks hard enough." She giggled like some silly schoolgirl. "Downright handsome actually."

"Thank you . . . I guess." Braxton helped her out of the leather jacket that he had given her. He doubt if it had helped much. What had started out as a mild drizzle when they first headed out for Jiggy's was now a full-fledged thunderstorm, Texas-style. That weird Texas weather he'd experienced more than once on many of his truck runs. "We both need to get some sleep now. We have a long drive ahead."

"You want to kiss me, don't you? Admit it," she slurred. "You know you do. That's all you men want. Sex, sex, sex. The good stuff."

"The good stuff? Woman, stop talking nonsense." The deep rumble of thunder found their ears. Normally the sound of pelting rain hitting the roof would be a soothing comfort, but Braxton felt reluctant to undress her. Both of them were dripping wet, and there was still the matter of that pain radiating from his left buttock. He needed to get out of his own wet clothes and investigate what was causing the mild pain in his backside, but first he had to get Neeka settled. He couldn't very well walk her to her bedroom and allow her to collapse on the bed soaking wet. That wouldn't be right. *Good grief,* he mused, *how could one little woman be so much trouble?*

"I'm a dancer, you know. And a darn good one too. I haven't told one soul yet, but I'm going to open my own dance studio someday. That's right."

"That's nice, but let's get you out of these wet clothes before you come down with a cold." He tugged at her dress, but she pulled away. One thing he felt certain of, one measly drink couldn't have produced the behavior he was witnessing. He'd never seen what the date rape drug "ruffie" could do up close and personal, but he'd heard enough stories from some of his drivers who had. And from what he'd heard, it wasn't pretty. During the cab ride back to the RV, Neeka kept complaining that her head was woozy and her stomach felt upset, like any second she could throw up. Now she was loud and giddy. It was all his fault. He never should have left her at the bar alone.

"Neeka? Just how many drinks did you have?"

She mumbled something back. "Who blinked? Huh?" She fell back on the bed, grinning, her head rolling from side to side. "And fly, I can fly too."

"Drinks. I said drinks. How many did you have?" *Oh, what the heck*. He sucked his teeth. She was obviously too out of it to comprehend. "Look, you can't stay in those wet clothes."

"Huh, you met some hos? Wanna see me dance? Dance with me."

"I said clothes. Just forget it. You can thank me in the morning." Braxton stooped and pulled her shoes off, stopping momentarily to marvel at her small feet. Her new shoes had to be cheaply made. One of the heels had broken off. Obviously it couldn't stand up to a few puddles of water. He tossed the shoes aside. Then he tried removing her dress, but again Neeka pulled away from him. She was quick to her feet, balancing herself as she stood on the bed.

"Watch me. I'm going to be an exotic dancer one day. Watch."

"Come down before you fall off the bed." She ignored his request. Braxton had no choice but to watch in silent fascination as she peeled the tight dress down exposing small but perky breasts. Beneath she wore no bra, but he could see that the dress was the type that had built-in support. "I think you should settle down before you fall and hit your head." The last thing he needed was having to take a possibly drugged female to the emergency room.

She did a little wiggle to get the dress over her slim hips. "No, you watch me now. That's what I really want to be—a fancy dancer." The dress off, she kicked it from the bed, almost losing her balance. To music heard only in her head she wiggled her hips in slow motion. "Like this."

"Neeka, maybe you should get some sleep. Sleep it off." He licked his lips at the sight of her exposed breasts and slender hips moving around in red satin underwear. Outside, thunder roared. Lightning flashed against the drawn curtains of the RV.

"I need my head to stop spinning . . . Oh, Lord, my head." The powerful hands of thunder clapped. Neeka shivered and moaned about being cold as she hurried and lay back down on the bed. "I'm scared. I hate storms. Sleep with me. C'mon, right here." She patted a spot next to her. "Braxton, you can sleep in here with me. You want to. I want you to."

Braxton thought about it. He swallowed hard thinking about it. He wanted to. He needed to. Good Lord, he needed it. "No," he declined, his better judgment kicking in. "I'd better not."

"What's the matter? Thought you wanted me so bad." She batted her eyes and pouted, her head resting on a pillow. "You want me or not?"

"I want you. Hell, I want you bad. But not like this." Why lie about it? From the time he'd laid eyes on her again, dancing with that towel around her, she had his interest. Once he engaged her eyes, then heard her speak, it all came together to ignite his desire. "You're a dancer alright. But what you need is some sleep. We can talk in the morning."

At first it was hard forcing himself not to stare at her natural beauty, but then it became impossible. Despite his own wet garments a heat began rising in him as he allowed his gaze to linger on her breasts. Small pyramids with perfect nipples a shade darker. His eyes moved down along the taut plain of her stomach to find a faint trail of baby-fine hair leading a path from her navel to her . . . She would have to have on some damn red satin panties. Oh, God, his weakness. Why couldn't she have on some plain white cotton panties like most sensible women? Hell, for a churchgoing woman, she should have on big unattractive bloomers. Why sexy red ones?

"Thunder and lightning makes me a little nervous. Just lay next to me. I won't tell if you won't tell."

He was aroused and tried moving his hand over the area of his erection to hide it. Served him right for allowing too much time to pass since being intimate with a woman. Thanks to that nasty ordeal with Sheila. "I don't think that's a good idea," he said.

Neeka went quiet.

"Neeka?" Braxton moved in closer. For crying out loud, now she was asleep. He pulled her arm up and let it collapse to her side. "Neeka? Hey, you." Out like a light. Knocked out with wet underwear on. *That's just great!*

"Okay," Braxton mumbled, gazing down at the valley of her golden brown thighs. "I'm a gentleman. I can do this. It's just a pair of underwear."

He looked around for a blanket. One lay rumpled on the floor where he'd left it before heading out to Jiggy's. He could cover her up and then slide her wet underwear off beneath the blanket. Good thinking. Give the woman some privacy.

Lifting the velour blanket, he placed it over her and then reached beneath it to grip the rim of her scanty underwear. The wet material rolled easily from smooth skin. There. Wasn't so bad after all. He took the wet garments to the restroom and hung them on anything that would hold them. Back at her side it came to him that she should have a sheet over her first, then the blanket. The velour blanket itself might be too warm against her skin. Braxton lifted the sheet from beneath a sleeping Neeka and pulled it gently to dislodge it. *Damn. What a lovely sight! Good baby-making bone structure. Strong-looking hips. Nice derriere too.* Neeka shifted and groaned softly as he placed the thin sheet then the blanket on top of her.

As much as he wanted to climb in next to her, allow her warmth to meld against his, Braxton fought the urge. She was beautiful, like a sleeping child the way her silky straight hair spread out along the pillow. *Such beautiful lips.* Now would be a good time to see what those soft-looking lips would feel like against his. What could one little kiss hurt? But, nah. If it were him under the influence of some substance, he wouldn't want someone to take advantage of him. *One more little peek can't hurt,* he mused, lifting the covers. "No. That's not right either." He put the covers down. "But one little peek . . . what could it hurt?" The covers went up. "Man, shame on you. It's wrong." The covers went down. *Man, get a grip on yourself. It's not like you haven't been around a naked female before.*

It was an odd thought to be having, but he could see her as his wife. Mrs. Braxton Dupree. He really could. "Girl, you something else." He felt a warmness as he stared down at the sleeping form beneath the blanket. He could watch her sleep all night if it wasn't for his own body pleading for a cold shower, some kind of relief.

"Sleep tight, my boss lady, my princess."

CHAPTER FIFTEEN

R ise and shine, sleepyhead." The sound of light rain drifted in through open wooden blinds as Braxton set the small tray on the nightstand. After seven hours of sleep, a good breakfast, and a hot shower, he felt great. He shook Neeka softly, then slightly rough, and when she still did not rouse he shook her harder. A toothpick dangled from a corner of his mouth. "Hey, boss lady, wake up!"

Neeka's eyes fluttered before easing open. Her expression was one of being disoriented, with sleep still pulling at her. "What?"

"Made you some breakfast," Braxton said, easing himself down on the side of the bed, careful not to sit on a limb. He had driven for several hours before pulling the RV into a rest stop for a much-needed break and time for the rain to lighten up. From time to time he had checked on her. He gazed at her with mild fondness. Obviously, Neeka had slept harder than usual because her hair was half-matted down and the rest was sticking straight up from her head. A few wild strands dangled in her apple-red eye. The look was in no way offensive, but it did give meaning to the phrase "a bad hair day." This was what Braxton needed to see, the real Neeka before the morning fix-up. She was good-looking with a few grooming efforts, but right now she looked a hot mess. "Look, we need to talk about last night."

Neeka bulked her eyes, still trying to focus. "What?"

"Last night . . . what happened last night? It's been bugging me like crazy, and I have to ask. Did those guys pull you from the club? Or did you know them from somewhere?" He knew enough about her to realize that she didn't appreciate him trying to butt into her business, but curiosity about what had happened was getting the best of him. A smart, sophisticated woman like Neeka—not to mention a little snobby at times—hardly seemed the type to talk to any Joe who popped up in her face. The two assailants last night hardly seemed like the type of men she would accept a drink from, let alone step outside the club with. Braxton figured that it had to be more than a drink that was in her glass.

Braxton picked up the glass of orange juice and handed it to her. "We could have been killed. You could have been kidnapped. Anything could have happened." The mild pain in his left buttock was a constant reminder. The area was slightly swollen. During his cold shower he had tried his best to examine the spot that was causing him discomfort, but the location of the small injury made it impossible for him to see. He'd tried using a mirror, but even with that he could only see a small puncture wound about the size of a BB. The flesh around the puncture was stiff to his touch, and there had been a round puncture hole in his slacks.

"What guys? Last night?" Reluctant at first, Neeka eased up, took the glass, and turned it up, gulping down the whole eight ounces of juice. She was mad thirsty. *Goodness. Breakfast?* How could he possibly think about eating when her head felt like someone had filled it with cold soapy water and forgotten to drain it off? "What . . . what time is it?" Out of habit she raised her wrist to check her watch and then gasped. Gone. "My watch . . . where's my watch?"

"One inquiry at a time, please. It's about two in the afternoon. Your watch was snatched."

She looked at him curiously. It was a look that made Braxton feel like a suspect.

"Why you looking at me?"

"Snatched? Snatched by who?" She sat up straighter, pulling covers to her bare chest. Braxton was dressed in black, in a turtleneck and slacks that fit his muscular physique to a tee. Not only did he look good, but a fresh soapy scent and cologne wafted from him.

"Two thugs you were socializing with." The look in Neeka's glazed eyes conveyed that she wasn't fully recovered. Braxton continued, "Dang, woman. You must be plenty dehydrated. Would you care for some more juice?" He took the empty glass from her hand.

"Where's my . . ." Neeka peeked beneath the covers again to confirm. "Okay . . . and someone took my watch, and then they took off my clothes?" The juice seemed to revive her, bring her senses back to order. Neeka took inventory of the room to confirm where she was. The bedroom, the RV, in bed, Braxton in the room with her and acting cocky again by sitting on the bed like it was his duty. It finally sunk in that she had no gown on. Hell, she had no bra on. No slip. No nothing. And that man was in the room with her. *Oh, hell no. What did he think this was, the all-you-can-eat buffet?* "Oh, no. Where the heck are my clothes?"

"Oh, so now you have questions." Braxton stood up holding the empty glass. "If you want to talk about something, let's talk about what happened at the club."

"As soon as you tell me where my clothes are."

"Look, Neeka, that stunt you pulled last night was dangerous. I'm not trying to control what you do, but as adults, we have to make wise decisions to keep ourselves as safe as possible. I mean, if you knew those two guys and went outside the club with them for some fresh air, that's one thing, but if they were complete strangers and you went outside, that's . . . that's pretty serious. Dumb and serious."

"Someone took my clothes off." The look on her face was that of a kid pouting because his favorite candy was taken away.

Didn't look like she was listening to a word Braxton was saying. "You do remember last night, right?" He could see panic mounting in her face with each word that came from his mouth.

"Ohmygawd. What have you done? You didn't! Did you? Why am I totally naked?"

He expected her to be concerned, but he didn't expect her to freak out about it. Braxton stood his ground. "I think that's what happens when you take your clothes off." He placed the glass back along the tray where scrambled eggs, coffee, bacon, and toast grew cold.

Neeka gasped. "Ohmygawd. You had your way with me!"

"You wish," Braxton snorted. Squaring his jaw, he moved around the bed to open a window to allow in more fresh air. The rain had slackened, but dark and threatening clouds still patrolled the Texas sky. "How soon we forget. Perhaps you don't recall what happened last night, but I do. It was raining pretty hard when we left the club, you were robbed, I tried to help, and we both got soaked."

"And that was your cue to take my clothes off?" She struggled up from the bed, clutching the blanket to her body. "How dare you! What kind of deprived pervert would take advantage of a woman when she's—"

"When she's what?" He smirked. "Dazed and confused? Or perhaps intoxicated out of her cute little head?"

"When she's . . . I was . . ." Words caught in her throat. What exactly had she been? Drunk, delirious, unconscious? Her thoughts were still a bit fuzzy. "Okay, okay. Let me think here for a minute." She remembered getting dressed to go out. Right. A cab came to the RV park. Right. Braxton insisted on going. Okay. That part was clear. And then at the club . . . and then. The rest was a blank. *Unbelievable. He probably slipped me something in my drink when I wasn't looking.* "I don't believe this!"

"Well, believe it. You were robbed. And stop trying to make it sound like it was my fault. I didn't want to go out to begin with." Braxton shook his head for emphasis. He didn't want to be the one to say I told you so, but it was coming. "Thank God they didn't get your purse too."

"You took my clothes off!"

"No, I'm afraid I didn't. Undergarments, yes. But your clothes, no." He smoothed back the waves of his hair. "I removed your panties because they needed to come off." *Dang. That didn't come out right.* "Uh . . . the rain . . . you were soaked."

"Oh, I'm sure. And you probably couldn't wait to take them off!" She blew out air almost as thick as smoke. "And my mother said you had matured into such a nice guy. Obviously she doesn't know you as well as she thought, or she would know that you're now a pervert who strips a woman butt naked and takes advantage of her!" Climbing out of bed, she wrapped the top blanket around her tighter.

"Hey, you are talking too crazy, and I'm trying to explain."

"Explain what? You being a horny pervert? I think not. You should be ashamed of yourself." She all but stumbled from around the bed. "I knew this trip was a bad idea. I knew it. I should have stayed my behind in California where I belong."

"I agree." Braxton sniffed. He couldn't believe what she was accusing him of. Him! No wonder the woman didn't have a husband or even a steady boyfriend. She was crazy! "No one put a finger on you, and I'm sure that if you think hard enough you can will those damaged brain cells back. Then you'll remember what happened."

"You better hope I don't file charges against you!"

"Woman, you are too much, you know that? There's nothing to file charges for. I did not take advantage of you."

Braxton was standing in Neeka's way, blocking the narrow entrance to the bathroom. Neeka hip-bumped him out of the way, then marched toward the restroom and stopped. "I hope you got a good look with my clothes off. Did you fondle my parts too? You can tell me, Braxton! Did you like what you saw?"

"Heck, yeah, I liked what I saw! . . . I mean, no, I didn't see . . . I mean, I did see but didn't like. Oh, hell, woman. Now you have me all mixed up! Think what you want; I have driving to get back to!" He turned to walk away, then turned back. "And if you really want to know who took your clothes off, you took them off your damn self!"

Neeka headed for the restroom, took a large bath towel, and secured it around her. She located her shampoo among the clutter. Apparently Braxton hadn't taken too long to have a shave and a shower. Typical bachelor, he had left a mess, with his personal toiletries strewn about the compact vanity. *I know he don't think I'm his maid too.* Peeved, she wet her hair and began shampooing, rubbing her scalp hard enough to tear out a few roots. The nerve of him! She couldn't think of the last time she was so upset with a man. At this point she didn't know what to believe.

"This whole thing is your fault," Braxton called back to her. "If you hadn't been so persistent about going somewhere last night, this whole incident wouldn't have happened and we'd be at our destination by now. So if you need to blame someone, blame yourself." He appeared at the door.

"Go away, Braxton!" Neeka knew he was right about staying in opposed to going out to the club. But that wasn't what she needed to hear. And true, she never should have had that drink, that Sex on the Beach concoction. Drinking alcohol was never one of her strong points. But despite all that, he didn't have a right to strip her and do heaven-knows-what to her. What kind of sicko would do that to a woman?

Braxton stood at the door watching her, blowing air that could have been steam for the way he felt. What she was accusing him of was appalling. What kind of person did she think he'd turned into? He didn't want to stoop to her level by giving it a title, but one thing he knew for sure, he wouldn't be able to rest until he convinced her that he wasn't the kind of man who would force himself on a woman or take advantage of a situation like the one she was in last night. "I guess it's all my fault then. You drinking at the bar. You out in the rain with those, those hoodlums, and one snatching your watch. All my fault."

"That gives you no right to take advantage of me."

"Woman, please. If you really think that you've been tampered with, maybe you should lock yourself up in the restroom and examine the goods. I mean, can't you women tell if your goodies have been tampered with?"

"Maybe I'll do just that! I just want this stupid nightmare to be over with so I can get away from you. So, do what you say you do best, Braxton. Drive as fast as you can." Neeka turned on the water in the tiny shower stall.

"Fine with me," he said, walking away.

"And fine with me!" At the sink Neeka rinsed shampoo from her hair. It was her habit to do one washing and then add protein conditioner and don a plastic cap before stepping into the shower. *Silly man could have cleaned up after himself. And there'd better be enough hot water left, or there'll be hell to pay.* She fished a plastic shower cap out from the drawer and found another large towel to turban-wrap her head.

"And furthermore," said Braxton, reappearing at the restroom door, "I think I have a splinter or piece of lead embedded where I was jabbed on the butt with something sharp, a pencil or something. I can't reach it. I need you to remove it. It hurts when I sit."

"Are you for real?" Neeka snorted. "Negro man, please. I suggest you stand and drive this vehicle the rest of the way. I am not removing anything from anyone's butt today, especially yours. I shouldn't even be speaking to you." She snatched the towel from her head.

"You're a very difficult woman, you know that?"

"Ooh, I wonder why?" she spat back, picking up a tube. She uncapped it, squirted a glob of cream into her hands, and used both hands to apply it to her hair. "And speaking of difficult, we'll see how difficult it will be for you to keep grace with my mother once we get back to California! Now leave me alone!"

"Hey, wait a minute!" Braxton made a move in her direction. "That cream's not what you think it is—"

"I said, leave me alone!" Neeka slammed the door in his face, but that didn't stop him from banging on it. "Braxton, stop being a pest. Go away means go away!"

"Neeka, please open the door. It's important. I'm not playing around here!"

Agitated, Neeka wrestled the plastic cap onto her head. *What a jerk. Obviously, the man thinks that just because he has those sexy eyes and that deep sexy voice and that rock-hard body that he can always have his way. He'd better think again!*

"Woman, open this door! You need to hear what I have to say! C'mon now, stop being childish and open the door."

What a persistent fool! "I'm not listening to you." Singing as loud as her voice would carry, she removed her towel and stepped into the warm stream of water. With the shower going full blast, her voice rising and falling with "La, la, la," Braxton's shouts were muffled mumblings.

From the opposite side of the door, he called, "Okay then. Have it your way. I just wanted to tell you that it's not a good idea to use depilatory cream on your hair."

CHAPTER SIXTEEN

See? It's not so bad." Hair clippers in hand, Braxton stepped back and admired his work. Maybe he was in the wrong line of business. Instead of being in trucking, maybe he should consider opening up a chain of barbershops. "Not bad at all." Not all women had a perfectly shaped head like Neeka. Hair or no hair, she was still gorgeous. "I think the short look on you is more becoming than long hair."

Neeka sniffed. "Braxton, stop lying. You're just saying that." Red-eyed, she stood at the restroom mirror agonizing over her short-short coiffure. The close-cropped look had worked well on Anita Baker and Halle Berry, but never in her wildest imagination had she thought about cutting all her beautiful hair off. Not when she enjoyed the idea of having longer hair. "I look like a thirteen-year-old boy."

"No, you don't. You look gorgeous, and I wouldn't tell you something if I didn't mean it. You're lucky you have a good grade of hair that lies flat. I mean, look at you—you're stunning, and you'll be fine for the presentation tomorrow morning."

"Ohmygawd, no! The presentation! I can't do it. I have to call it off. I am not going to stand up in front of a bunch of women and talk about how to make yourself more beautiful when I have no hair. I'm not doing it!"

"Neeka," Braxton sighed as he placed his clippers down. He could understand a little concern over her new look, but that pouty-kid act he could do without. If he could just find the words to make her see that she was still attractive, even with her hair cut short. In fact, the look enhanced her doe eyes, adding to a more innocent look. "You know that wouldn't make sense. We've come all this way to take care of business. You can't let your mother down, and I know enough about you to know that you're not a quitter." He chose not to verbalize his next thought: *Besides, it's only hair.*

"Easy for you to say because it's my hair that's missing and not yours. This is all your fault, Braxton. I look like Peter Pan having a bad hair day."

"It's all in your mind. You still look good to me."

"Maybe with some makeup on. Some face cover, and some eye-liner. I need my lipstick . . . where's my lipstick?"

"Neeka, you're overreacting. It's really not a bad look on you. You're working yourself into a frenzy over nothing."

"It might be nothing to you, but being half-bald is something to me."

"You're not bald. It looks like a short haircut you had done at a beauty salon."

Paying Braxton no attention, Neeka opened her makeup bag and started applying foundation. After a light application of sheer-matte formula to smooth out her complexion, she darkened the rims of her eyes with eyeliner, then picked up her Roses Are Red lipstick. "I can't go tomorrow. I have to call and cancel. I mean, look at me. I'm a mess. I'll call Mama later and tell her. She'll just have to understand."

"You'll do no such thing."

Neeka ignored Braxton. He was standing to her side, looking on with that silly look on his face like he didn't understand what she was going through. Feeling confident with hair one day, and feeling naked without it the next, was serious to her. Well, if he couldn't be more understanding, the least he could be was more sympathetic. It was all his fault for leaving his depilatory shaving cream on the counter near her hair conditioner. By the time she'd realized her hapless mistake, clumps of her hair were rinsing away from her head. Her only solace was that the hair loss wasn't completely down to the scalp.

"Look," said Braxton, his tone as weary as his expression, "I really feel bad about this."

"You feel bad? What about me, Braxton?" she yelled, jabbing a pointed finger to her chest, fighting back tears.

"Maybe this is not the right thing to say, but it's only hair and it'll grow back."

He was right—it wasn't the right thing. She had been holding back a dam, but the floodgates opened. Her shoulders slumped as the tears flowed. She didn't care if she did look like a big baby crying. What was wrong with him? Every woman has something about herself that she takes pride in. Some women have pride in their shapely legs, while others take pride in their pretty eyes or their large breasts. Her glory had been her shoulder-length hair. But now, thanks to Braxton, that too was gone.

"This is all wrong." Neeka sobbed uncontrollably. She sniffed. "All of this. This silly trip I let Mama talk me into. You driving me. And the way I've been acting so hateful, and then saying you molested me when I know you didn't." She paused to accept his offer of a tissue.

"I do remember what happened last night. I said those awful things about you molesting me so you'd get mad enough to hate me. It feels so wrong now." Sniff, sniff. "I never should have come. It's been nothing but stress, and I can't . . . can't take any more."

"Hate you? Oh, woman, please. Don't cry. I could never hate you."

He fought a natural impulse to comfort her with a hug. "I think we just got off to a bad start, but everything will work out. You'll see. Stop crying." It tore at him seeing her this way. Heck, where was all that hotheaded sassiness she'd been displaying? *Maybe losing hair brings out the softer side in females*, he mused. *I might be onto something.* "Stop worrying about your hair. You'll be fine." He took a chance by stepping closer, pulling her into his arms. For some reason he had a strong inclination that there was more to her emotional breakdown than she was telling, but he wouldn't press her for it.

"I never wanted to do this," Neeka was saying, crying softly against his chest. "I tried to get out of it, but no. Mama insisted that I was the only one who could represent the company in a professional way. I'm not such a terrible person. I'm really not. Now look at me. I'm being punished. I lost my favorite watch, made a complete fool of myself by taking my clothes off, and now I'm almost bald." She paused before sobbing harder. "I deserve it."

Deserve it? "No. Look, you listen to me," Braxton said. He pulled her away from his chest so he could look into her red eyes. Face-to-face and so close that he could smell the aftermath of the drink she'd had the night before. Funny, it wasn't a good smell, and it wasn't entirely bad. "You have to believe me when I tell you this. It wasn't all your fault. I should have stayed by your side last night. You're just not a drinker."

"But I've been so mean to you. I wouldn't blame you if you had taken a cab and left me at that place. I was behaving so badly. I feel so ashamed."

He stopped her short. "No. You shouldn't be."

She tried turning her head like it hurt to hear what he was saying.

"Listen to me," Braxton said, pleading. "Look at me. I want you to look into my eyes when I say this. You have nothing to be ashamed of.

I know that wasn't the real you last night." He eased her chin to alignment with his. He could see the depth of her pupils, dark and knowing. "Last night got crazy. I mean, I may not know the whole story of why you were outside at that club, but I believe that someone might have slipped something into your drink. I spotted you standing in the rain with two men. One tried to snatch your purse; the other grabbed your watch and ran. I ran after him."

"I remember. You chased him."

"Of course I chased him. He had your property and I wanted to get it back."

Neeka studied his face. It was filled with sincerity. "You did that for me?"

"Well, yeah. But he still got away with your watch. And it was raining pretty hard. That's why you took your clothes off. But nothing happened."

She lowered her eyes. "Now you probably think I'm some common slut for taking my clothes off." How could she have made such a fool of herself? Realizing that she had done so made her feel even worse.

Braxton grinned. "I assure you, there was nothing sluttish about the way you did it. And 'common' is not a word that fits you. I didn't refuse your offer to join you in bed because I didn't find you desirable, because I do. You're very desirable. I turned it down because I respect you."

"Unbelievable," she mumbled.

Braxton lifted her downcast chin again. He wanted her full, eye-locked attention. "I have to admit that you looked pretty tempting lying there. Shoots! Like an angel sleeping. Every inch of you. Any normal man would have been tempted."

Neeka felt speechless. Foolish and speechless. His words were so tender, and so soothing as his eyes searched hers.

When she said nothing, Braxton said, "And you're still beautiful."

"Don't look at me. I must look terrible." Her hand went up, feeling for the hair that was low and fine and close to her head, a wisp of curl at her neck. "How can you stand to look at me this way?"

"Because you are who you are." Braxton took up the face towel she had used during her shower. He ran warm tap water over it before ringing it out and applying it softly to her tear-streaked face. The gentleness of his touch was like that of a doting mother soothing an upset child. "You know," he said, as softly as a manly voice could, "it's not always about the fancy clothes we wear. It's not always the long, beautiful hair hanging from our heads that makes us who we are. Nor the fancy makeup we use to hide what we think are imperfections." He wiped her face clean. "It's about being comfortable with the beauty that lies within."

That was all fine and dandy coming from him, but still Neeka shuddered to think of what she must look like without makeup and with her hair so short. The total look had to be unpleasant, but there was no indication of such in Braxton's smiling eyes. "But my hair—"

"Natural beauty shouldn't be covered up. It's a flower that's meant to be enjoyed. Try being yourself."

She needed to try turning her face away from his. That's what she needed to do. The heat from his body felt soothing next to hers. His eyes pulling her in. *Goodness, I must be losing my mind*. She stared at his lips. It felt like his lips were magnetized, pulling hers to his. Closer. Then closer until they met. And then he was kissing her back.

Tension rolled from her as she relaxed into the flow of it. Thoughts of her hair were gone. Thoughts of the presentation pending the next day, gone.

"Brax, maybe we shouldn't," she whispered, coming up for air.

"If I'm going too fast for you, stop me." His lips brushed lightly against her collarbone, before nibbling at her ear.

He kissed her again, and it seemed to her right then that the longer they kissed, the more she wanted to know the feeling of him inside her. A small tremble rumbled through her body. And then his lips were on her neck and against her ear, his breath bringing more heat to her body. She hadn't even felt herself walking, but when she realized it, they were alongside, the bed, the towel she had wrapped around her being undone. Their lips never unlocked as Braxton slowly laid her down.

Rain pounded the roof of the RV, its rhythm almost in sync with her racing heart. Neeka had the sensation of floating as her head sunk into the soft pillow and Braxton kissed her exposed breasts, one and then the other. His mouth made juicy sounds as his tongue painted warm wetness around her erect nipples.

"Stop me if this isn't what you want," Braxton whispered as his warm tongue painted a wet trail down to her stomach. "Just say stop." He kissed her stomach gently.

Neeka felt a storm raging inside her. The word 'fornication' screamed in her head, but not loud enough for her to want him to stop. Her mind was telling her what they were about to do was wrong. But if it was so wrong, dang, why did it have to feel so good? Twice, her lips tried to utter one of two words—"stop" and "no"—but they didn't. Couldn't. Instead, she closed her eyes as her back took on a slow and sensual arch. A long moan floated from her lips. Her lips melted into bliss as Braxton moved down to her silken brown thighs, causing a mild shiver from her core as her valley opened.

"Tell me if you want me to stop." He paused for a moment as if it were the last chance for her to stop him. When no protest came his way, his tongue explored her most tender part.

CHAPTER SEVENTEEN

The wig itched. Her palms were sweaty. "I can get through this," Neeka mumbled under her breath as she stood in front of a group of women in a conference room at the Hilton Hotel. She couldn't have been happier for Friday to come. Friday meant that after the presentation, she could shed her two-piece navy blue pantsuit for something more comfortable. It also meant that they could turn the RV around and head home.

The thought of home was warm and fuzzy. "And with Diva Four Cosmetics," she explained, fighting an urge to yank the cap of hair from her head and stomp on it, "you can rest assured that all our products use only premium ingredients that have been tested over and over to ensure that they are hypoallergenic."

Neeka glanced around the plush and spacious room that had been meticulously set up with tables, chairs, and makeup stations complete with lit mirrors. Lavender and pink balloons hugged the ceiling. The coordinator, Mrs. Perry, a thin and overly made-up woman in her late fifties, had certainly gone out of her way to make her comfortable. Despite it all, Neeka didn't feel right. Her new pumps felt too tight, the pantsuit felt a little too warm, and the wig—well, Lord have mercy. Braxton had tried talking her out of wearing a wig, but the idea of standing in front of a crowd with her hair so short ignited a feeling of standing naked before strangers. She just couldn't do it. She tried scratching in between the cap's mesh. *How on earth do some women wear these darn things daily?* The dang thing felt like a nest on her head, with baby spiders dangling on tiny webs.

"If there's anything you need, Miss Lebeau, please don't hesitate to ask."

"Thank you, Mrs. Perry. I'm fine." Neeka composed herself and smiled graciously. She wished the woman would stop saying that. Miss Lebeau. Made her name sound old. She was already two hours into the event, and almost at the end of demo status. Two new accounts and one pending. Her verbal presentation had been flawless, and now as she moved between the various stations, monitoring makeup techniques, Neeka couldn't wait for it all to be over. Another hour and she could wrap it up and get to the signing of the contract with Hope in Healing. She'd be home free. Hopefully there wouldn't be a problem with the signing part. After all, wasn't that what the whole trip was about? The way she was feeling, Braxton could start the RV engine now.

Braxton. Neeka bit down lightly on her bottom lip wondering where he had disappeared to. Even though her mother had paid him to drive her, he had been a real sport in making sure that every box of product was unloaded and brought to the conference. He'd even helped with setting up the demo stations. The room had been all hustle bustle for a spell, and when Neeka had looked up to thank him, he was gone. Nowhere to be found.

Braxton. *What a nice guy,* she mused as she played with the thin gold chain around her neck. *A little cocky, but nice.* Heat radiated from her feet up to the top of her head thinking about him and last night. Last night had been . . . unbelievable. Rain tapping on the roof, the two of them making their own heat beneath the covers, Braxton's gentleness. Last night had been wonderful. Not only was the man a skilled lover, but he also knew how to take his time, seeing that her own experience was no match for his.

What they had done had been good; at the same time it shouldn't have happened. Last thing she needed was for him to get the wrong idea and think that one night of pleasure meant that they were a couple, or even worse, that her mother would be getting her way with plans of courtship and marriage. *Boy, would Mama flip her lid if she knew about the hot stuff.*

"Oh, no, sweetie. Not too much eye shadow." Neeka took a tissue and gently wiped the face of a middle-aged woman who obviously knew nothing about applying makeup. "You want to enhance the eyes with a slight bit of color." The silly woman applying the makeup had enough oil on her subject's face to fry a small chicken. It took five minutes for Neeka to take the woman's skin back to bare and start all over again. "Now try this shade of lipstick."

Back to Braxton. *So what if it's a bunch of woman painting their faces? He could have at least hung around for moral support.* "Here, try this color on her complexion," she said, handing another demo artist a small tube of foundation. "See how it blends so nicely? That's much better." After their lovemaking last night, she had agreed to remove the small piece of pencil lead that had been embedded in his left buttock by one of the hoodlums who stole her watch. *Nice backside.* Taking a closer look had only sparked more lovemaking. Later, he'd made hot cocoa so they could sit in front of the television and listen to the weepy sky. She couldn't recall ever experiencing such moments of total peace and relaxation, like it was them against the world.

Her scalp itched again, and Neeka tried to slip her nail in between the mesh. "Ooh, this darn thing!" she hissed lowly. A few eyes were probably staring at her, but so what? She could care less.

Behind her, a sexy male voice whispered, "If it bothers you, take it off."

Braxton. "Well, it's about time—" The second she turned around, her breath caught. Her eyes widened as they locked on Braxton's clean-shaven head. "Oh, my God! What have you done? You shaved your head!" Without hair he could almost pass for Montel Williams.

Braxton looked pleased with the results. "You like it?" With buttons undone on his black knit shirt, curly black hair peeked out. He held a covered plastic plate out to her. "Here. Thought you might want some lunch. Some of my barbecue ribs and slices of sausage I had marinating. That's where I've been, to the market for chicken, then back at camp cooking and making a few phone calls to check on business."

Neeka couldn't stop looking at his perfectly shaped head. "I can't believe you shaved your head." Apparently she wasn't the only one looking. Almost every female in the room was gaping. She could hear little catty comments of approval being made from somewhere in the room. Someone even did a low cat whistle. *Dang, what's wrong with these hoochie mamas? They act like they've never seen a handsome man with a shaved head before!* "Why would you do such a thing?"

"Because," said Braxton, giving her a quick kiss on the forehead, "I didn't want you to feel so alone with your sexy new look. And it's like I said before, it's not the clothes or the hair that makes us who we are. It's what's inside."

"Amen!" someone shouted from the side of the room.

Her eyes felt like tearing. She took the plate of warm food from him. "Thanks." So that's where he went. To go cook in the RV and get bald for her. The look was more than good; it was sensuously pleasing. She scratched at her head again. "No has ever shaved their head for me. You're so full of surprises."

"Neeka," said Braxton soothingly, "obviously that wig is making you uncomfortable. Why don't you take it off? No thinking about it. Just do it."

A voice from the back of the room said, "Yeah, girl, just take it off!"

"Be proud of your short hair or your baldness!" Braxton rallied.

"Preach, brother," came another feminine voice.

"You know," Neeka said with final resolve, "you're right. Why should I be embarrassed about my hair? I am who I am with or without it!" She could feel a charge in the room as the women began to chant, "Take it off! Take it off!"

It was her move. "You think I won't?" Two pins removed, Neeka snatched the thing from her head. Finally her scalp could breath. There. She had exposed herself down to the raw, something she never would have done on her own. What they saw was what they got. She stood there holding the wig up like a prize. To her amazement, another woman took her hair off, then another, then two more. The ripple effect spread through the room. Soon, a whole room of females stood with fake hair in their hands. Some heads were completely bald, while a few others had patches of hair clinging for dear life after chemo or radiation treatments.

"Unbelievable," Neeka mumbled as she scanned the room. Cancer survivors. She had known that Hope in Healing had something to do with women who had experienced some kind of illness, but Adeena hadn't divulged that it was a nonprofit organization that catered to women who had survived a deadly disease. And here Neeka was worried about hair, agonizing over how she looked, when she was standing in front of a group of women seeking to prolong their lives. She fought back tears thinking of how shallow and self-centered she'd been. She felt even worse for not doing her research first.

"Life sure has a way of making you stop and take a serious look, doesn't it?" Braxton asked, glancing around the room. "Look at all these beautiful faces."

Choked up, Neeka couldn't answer, but her silent nod told him she agreed.

Braxton turned his attention to her. "I hope you like barbecue."

"I do. I don't eat it often." Her mother had never encouraged the eating of much meat. As a result, Neeka ate meat about twice a week. It was well after noon, and she hadn't eaten since early morning. She was hungry enough to eat a whole pig with a side order of cow. Meat, baked beans, garden salad, and a slice of white bread. It all made her mouth water. Removing the plastic from the plate of food Braxton had brought her released the tantalizing aroma of barbecued ribs, and links in the room. She found a vacant table and sat.

"Smells good," Mrs. Perry commented, eyeing Neeka's plate. Before Neeka could dig in herself, she shared some of her food, passing out meat chunks pierced with toothpicks. Braxton came to the rescue by offering to go back to the RV and get more food. He returned with a whole platter of succulent barbecue, and soon a whole roomful of women were smacking their lips and licking sauce from their fingers.

"The meat is heavenly. So tender, and the sauce is to die for. Did you make the sauce yourself?" Mrs. Perry asked, dabbing a spot of sauce from her beige pantsuit. Without her heavy-looking wig, the woman's cinnamon face took on a more youthful appearance.

"Yes, ma'am." Braxton beamed, cutting up more pieces of meat. Initially he'd cooked enough to last a couple of days, but now he could see that wouldn't be happening. "My own special mix."

The event turned into more than a party, with Mrs. Perry offering Braxton a business card. "My husband is an investor who's always looking for a new business venture. This is the best barbecue I have ever tasted. And being here in Texas, the barbecue mecca, that's saying a lot. You call my husband, William, when you get a chance. Your sauce should be in the stores."

"Thank you," said Braxton, accepting her card. "I'll keep that in mind."

Later that evening, after she'd cleaned up the kitchen area of the RV, changed into an oversized black sweatshirt and some black spandex pants, Neeka climbed the metal ladder at the rear of the RV to where Braxton was set up with a small radio, two blankets, and a telescope. The Texas air smelled clean after the rain, and even the slight chill in the air was tolerable. Firebugs flitted about with the natural sounds of the night. Neeka couldn't recall feeling so at peace with the world. She tapped his shoulder. "Here, this is for you." She held out a small gift-wrapped box.

The mellow jazz playing on the radio made it seem romantic with the moon being so full, the sky so clear. Stars appeared small and so close that you could reach up and pull one from its tether. Braxton feigned surprise. "For me?"

"No, for your sister," she teased. "Of course it's for you, silly. Open it."

He wasted no time in removing the blue ribbon and bow. Inside he found a digital camera, one that was nothing like the one that had been destroyed. This one was far fancier. "Wow. You shouldn't have." Braxton removed it from the box to study it. "Now this is what I call a digital camera." He knew enough about cameras to know that she had paid more than twice the price of what his previous one had cost. "Does this mean that I can take your picture now?"

"Only if you want to get tossed off the top of this vehicle." Neeka gave a quick grin to assure him she was only kidding. "Maybe later."

"You sure you're not hiding out from the law? Like I said before, criminals hate getting their pictures taken."

"Look," she said, pausing to heave a sigh. Moonlight glistened from Braxton's smooth head. "I want to apologize for how awful I acted when we started this trip. I also want to apologize for destroying your camera. I wasn't myself, but I had no right to do that."

Braxton placed the camera back in its box. "No big deal. I'm sure you had your reasons. I had no right assuming it was okay to click you up." Patting a spot next to him, he scooted over to make room for her to join him on the blanket. "You look cold. Here," he said, "let's get some blanket over your shoulders."

"Thanks." Being fussed over was something Neeka hadn't experienced for a while. It felt good. She could get used to it. "Can't say if it's a blessing or a curse, but my mother is a photo freak. She loves to snap pictures of some of the most bizarre and inappropriate things." She went quiet, reflecting. "I think it has something to do with the fact that her own mother never kept pictures. Her mother was very superstitious. Suffice it to say, my mother chose to make up for not having photographs of herself. But she sure overdid it. I grew up with that."

"I think I understand now." Braxton looked away and said nothing. He took up the powerful telescope and gazed through it.

"Imagine being sixteen and trying to be intimate with a boy for the first time and your mother barging into your bedroom and snapping a picture of the scene. I needed therapy after that, and so did that young man. Then imagine your mother taking a picture of you crying over some silly boy who broke your heart when you were seventeen, or you getting caught in the act of stealing ten dollars from your mama's purse."

"Sounds like a set-up to me."

"No doubt. Still, one picture after another." She went quiet, staring up at the sky.

"Here. Take a look through this." He helped with holding the telescope to her eye. "Can you see the Big Dipper?"

"Oh, yeah," Neeka agreed. "The little one too."

"If you think it's been so bad for you, imagine being four years old and your mother taking you to a large department store. Your favorite place in the whole world, the toy department, where she knew that toys would take your attention away from her walking out of your life. Then try to imagine crying so hard as you searched for her until you could barely see a foot in front of you."

"Oh, no, Braxton. Your mother did that?" Constellations forgotten, Neeka lowered the telescope to look over at him, realizing that even though they'd known one another for years, she really didn't know much about him. She thought of a couple of things she could say, but neither seemed right. "That's awful. I'm sorry to hear that. I mean, I had no idea." That explained why she had never seen his mother at school.

"It's life." Braxton brushed at imaginary lint along the velvet blanket. "Happens more than you know."

Her heart was melting in her chest. "That's awful. How could a mother leave her young child in a store?"

"Anyway," he sighed, "she never came back for me, but the store security did." He looked down at his hands. "Then a nice pink lady came and took me to a place where they take little boys whose mothers don't want them anymore. Then came a few foster homes before I landed in my last home. They became the closest thing I had to a family. That's where I met my foster brother, Quamee."

"I never knew that." Neeka lowered her head.

"Lot of things you don't know about me. Like I was the first man to send you flowers."

Neeka shot him a look like he had changed colors. "No way."

"It was two days after your thirteenth birthday. Two roses tied together were left on your doorstep with a note saying, 'To Neeka with love.' Remember that? Your mother didn't play even back then, and you could say that I was too chicken to knock on your front door and hand them to you. But I watched from the bushes. I saw you."

"You're kidding. That was from you?" Of course she remembered. She'd kept the roses until they literally crumbled. "I kept wondering who my secret admirer was. Why didn't you say something back then?"

"I don't know. Fear of rejection maybe." The two went quiet.

"But back to you." Braxton perked up, attempting to lighten the mood. "You speak a lot about your mother being too involved in your life and too controlling. In a way you're lucky. You have a mother who really cares about you. But in another way, I can see why you have a problem with it. But when you think about it, Neeka, it's really your own fault."

Excuse me? "What? How's that?" He was judging, and she didn't like it.

"Because the best way to take control of your own life is to grab the reins. Face it, you're not that sixteen-year-old girl anymore, Neeka. If your mother has been pulling the strings all your life, she's pretty darn good at it by now. Why would she just step aside?"

Her silence proved she had no answer.

"All I'm saying is that if you wait for control to be handed over to you, you'll never have it. You have to reach out and snatch it for yourself."

"You don't understand. My mother is different. She's not like most mothers."

"Neeka, she might seem like she's the rock, but I assure you, she has a weak spot like everyone else. And once you get control of your own life, you keep it."

Above, a thin light streaked across the night sky. She went quiet thinking about what he'd said. She had known it all along, but hearing a neutral party voice it gave it strength.

Cut the apron strings, snatch the reins. It didn't matter how; that's what she had to do.

CHAPTER EIGHTEEN

They had just started on their return trip when Braxton pulled off the interstate to shop at Ralph's Market for needed food and supplies. He stood up from the table where he had been making a list. "We have eggs, but no coffee or bread. You sure you don't want to go inside with me?"

Neeka declined his offer by shaking her head. Attired in her yellow sundress and yellow footsies, she was relaxing on the sofa with a bag of potato chips. She was watching the *Ricki Lake Show.* The show was addictive. Normally Neeka preferred a more intelligent platform like *Oprah*, but she was fascinated with how people could appear on national television and reveal the intimate details of their private lives. The show's topic was "Who's the Baby's Daddy?" "You go ahead." Neeka waved Braxton on dismissively. She wanted to stay to find out who the baby's daddy was. "I'm sure you know what to buy, but don't forget my bottled water and some almonds."

"Sure thing," Braxton replied happily as he went out the door.

"With your good-looking self." Neeka watched him from a window a few seconds before her attention was pulled back to the television program. "Unbelievable," she mumbled to herself. *What would make a woman sleep with two, three, or four different men in the same month without using protection?* she wondered. Her phone chirped. She tossed the bag of chips aside and answered.

"Nee? Nee, how's it going so far?" Mercy's voice was loud and clear over the fancy walkie-talkie device.

"Everything is fine. We got the account, and a few others are interested." She should have known that the first caller from home would be Mercy. The two were not just sisters; they were hangout buddies. That girl had to be missing not having Neeka around to harass and barge in on. "What took you so long to call?" Neeka took up the remote and lowered the television volume.

"Girl, you won't believe this, but somebody is getting married in December for real. I saw the bill for the wedding planner, the caterer, and something about some stupid birds flying over. Heck, I don't know. All I know is that your mama crazy!"

"Mercy, calm down, and it's *our* mama, not *my* mama. Besides, she's been talking about planning a wedding for months now, and it still hasn't happened. Don't fall for the game. She's all talk, and those bills are probably phony documents to fool you."

"Nee, I don't think so this time. This is for real. I checked the bills out and called the caterer, and they wanted to know if I needed any changes in the menu."

"Well, it must be her own wedding because she can't force any of us to do something we don't want. And when I get back, we'll have to sit our dear mother down and talk about it until she understands just that."

"Nee, when will you be back? . . . Heck, I could be married and on my honeymoon by then. You know how she is. She's insisting that I go to some stupid dinner party at her house . . . and she—"

Another phone rang somewhere in the vehicle. "Mercy, hold on a minute." She could still hear Mercy's muffled voice prattling on about nothing when she located Braxton's phone and answered it. She probably shouldn't have, but what if his secretary was calling about something important? "Hello."

A very sexy female voice asked to speak to Braxton, not to Mr. Dupree.

"May I ask who's calling?" Neeka bit down lightly on her bottom lip. She was so wrong and had no business trying to find out who the woman was, but too bad.

"Yes. This is Layla Marshall, his girlfriend. I would like him to return my call to confirm our date on Saturday night."

"Oh, I see. Well, he's not available at the moment, Miss Marshall. But I'll make sure that he gets the message."

And then the voice asked, "Is this his mother?"

"No, I'm afraid not," Neeka replied stiffly. She could feel her blood begin to heat up.

"His sister?"

"No. Not quite."

"A cousin perhaps?"

"That's a negative." *Just like a man*, she thought. Braxton had specifically told her that he was not involved. Obviously he didn't know what being involved was or it had been a bald-faced lie. "I'll let Mr. Dupree know that you called."

"Well, whoever you are, it's not important. Just remind him that I'll see him on Saturday."

"I certainly will."

Neeka punched off, feeling like a fool. Stupid woman didn't know not to be so free with information. The nerve of her. When the phone rang again she drew a deep breath, preparing to play the same catty game. She could think of a few things she could tell Miss Layla, but the voice on the line was that of another woman asking to speak to Braxton. Before Neeka could take control of her emotions, she half yelled, "He's not here right now," then clicked off.

I'm not involved right now. Yeah, right. Arms folded, she stood wondering, just how many women did he need? She should have known. Once a player, always a player.

Braxton was back in half an hour with three bags of groceries. "I found two kinds of almonds," he announced cheerfully as he stepped up from the stairwell. "I wasn't sure which one you wanted, so I bought both." The change in the atmosphere was evident the moment he spotted Neeka sitting in the captain's chair looking tight-lipped. "Neeka? What's wrong?"

"Give me the keys," Neeka demanded. She kept her gaze straight out the window.

"The keys to what?" She couldn't possibly be referring to the RV.

"Braxton, don't play dumb. Give me the keys so I can get myself back home where I belong!"

"I don't know what's gotten into you, but it's obvious that you're upset about something. Neeka, you know I can't allow you to drive this vehicle." He walked to the kitchen area and set his purchases down on the table. "You've had no training, nor do you have the proper license to drive it."

"Fine!" Neeka got up to go to the rear sleeping quarters, anyplace to keep from having to look at him, but Braxton blocked her path. "I'm not in the mood for your silly antics right now, so move."

"Not until you tell me what's wrong. You were okay when I left."

"And maybe you should take your phone when you leave, or better yet, tell your girlfriend, Layla, to wait until you get home to call."

Braxton snorted. "Layla? My girlfriend?"

"Oh, yeah, she wants me to remind you of your date on Saturday." She couldn't look him in the eyes because she was so upset.

Braxton was grinning, but the look on Neeka's face conveyed that she was serious. "Oh, so I'm away, and you answer my phone and now you're mad at me?"

"Move out my way, Braxton." She tried moving around him.

"Oh, no, you don't. You're not getting away that easily." She struggled against him, but his strong arms were tight around her in a playful squeeze. "First of all, you wrong for answering my phone. That's privacy invasion, but I'm not mad atcha." A quick kiss to the side of her cheek was confirmation. "Secondly, when I said I wasn't involved with anyone, I was being honest. That Layla woman is someone I met and dated three times, and she's a little confused, thinks we had some kind of strong relationship going. I haven't called her in months, but she hasn't stopped calling me."

Neeka lowered her eyes. Darn him for making her feel so childish and silly. "And there was another woman who called. What about her?"

He angled his head with a quizzical look. "What other woman? Did she leave a name?"

"No, she did not." She folded her arms stubbornly at her chest.

"Probably my new temp secretary. She's young and not exactly what you could call professional. I bet she called me by my first name." He reared back to look at her. "You are one complicated woman, you know that? First, you can't stand me; then you let me make love to you; then you say we can only be friends; and now you're acting jealous."

"I am not jealous!" Neeka snapped. Her words came out strong but didn't sound truthful.

"Okay. You're not jealous."

She didn't know what she was feeling. It was more like confused. "I'm sorry," Neeka sighed, as if the weight of the world were on her shoulder. "I don't know. I just don't like to be lied to. Had enough of relationships filled with lies." *What the heck am I saying?* "I mean, of course you have women calling you. You're young, handsome, a man of means. Some woman would be lucky to have a man like you. I mean, it's not like we're in some kind of relationship."

"Of course not," he said. Words she needed to hear. Words that said he understood when he really didn't. "But I wouldn't have a problem if we *were* in a relationship."

"I'm just homesick," Neeka sighed. "I need to get back to my own space." And what was she making a big fuss about anyway? It's not like they were a couple. Getting too involved with Braxton would only confirm that her mother had won again. Something she wasn't about to let happen. She was facing him. "Sometimes people just get weak and caught up in the moment. This thing with us. That's all it is."

Braxton's throat felt tight. His eyes had a glazed-over look. "If that's how you really feel, I can accept that," he said, kissing the side of her neck. "You can't deny that you're looking for someone special, just like I am. It's normal to want that one special person, Neeka. We need it."

"And what are you saying?" Her eyes locked onto his.

"I'm saying that I feel like I don't have to search any longer."

"Braxton, we cannot keep—" A kiss, long and probing, cut her off. The words, "Don't let yourself slip," scrolled in the back of her mind. But it was too late; she was already falling from the feel of his hot tongue up against hers. She felt helpless to stop his hand from cupping her breast, more helpless to stop his other hand from sliding up her dress and touching places that sent a quiver through her body.

CHAPTER NINETEEN

How about this one?" Princess held the third dress up for Mercy's inspection, a red chiffon sheath. "You can be the lady in red," she said. "Wear this one."

Mercy shook her head. "I hate it." The red dress, a designer original, was undisputedly beautiful, but the red she was seeing wasn't on a dress.

"The right shoes, the right purse. You'll be gorgeous."

"Purse? Prin, what would I need with a purse at Mother's? In fact, if you like it so much, you wear it. I like to choose my own dresses, thank you very much." Mercy sat back against the padded headboard of the queen-size guest bed at Adeena's house. The shot of Chivas Regal she'd had earlier was mixing with her sour mood, leaving a bad taste in her mouth. The nerve of her mother demanding her presence on a weekday night. She could think of better things to be doing on a Wednesday.

"C'mon, Mercy, try being grateful. I mean, look at these beautiful clothes." Princess gestured toward the portable cart where four more designer dresses hung in wait of inspection. "I mean, honestly, how many mothers do you know who can have her personal designer drop off five beautiful dresses for you to pick from?" The happier she looked, the worse Mercy felt. "Tell me how many."

Mercy shot daggers with her eyes. "Who cares. It's just a dress." Princess was a slave to designer clothes, as if wearing someone's name sewn to a label made you better. "Probably the same number that would summon you to her house to meet some snob-acting jerk she thinks you need to hook up with and marry and spit out a bunch of snot-nosed babies for. This is so unnecessary."

"Maybe it's not so bad. It's kind of cute when you think about it. Arranged dating is quite popular." Princess paused and looked reflective. "If Mommie finds a suitable husband for me, I plan to go with it. Being madly in love with a man isn't the strongest ingredient of a happy marriage."

"And you know what is?"

"Trust. Honesty. Communication. Respect. Love is like the icing."

Mercy stared over at her like she had announced that the pope had asked for her hand in marriage. "So what are you saying, Prin? That a woman shouldn't marry for love?"

Shrugging her shoulders, Princess kept her attention on the red dress. "I don't know." She sniffed while fingering the delicate material. "Some folks should marry for love and only love. But then there are others, you know, others who should marry because it's the right thing to do at the right time. Love can always come later."

"Prin, I swear, you sound just like Mother. That's something that she would say. But you know what? Mother can plot and plan all she wants. I swear, one of these days that old woman is going to yank the wrong cord at the wrong time." *Marry first and love will come later.* This was a side of her baby sister she had rarely seen. A side that showed the woman was capable of thoughts deeper than what color pumps to wear with her new suit, or which Fashion Barbie to add to her growing collection.

Princess nodded. "She's a good mother."

"Who said she isn't? But it's not like I don't have a life or can't find a decent man of my own. Heck. I just want to go back home." The more Mercy thought about being at her own condo, the more agitated she became. Of course, if Adeena called and said to come, you didn't hang up and continue your one-woman party. You put your drink away, clean yourself up, and you go.

Mercy's defense had been lame and futile. "But Mother, it's Wednesday, not the weekend. And what about Neeka?" Like that would make a difference. "I thought we didn't have family meetings unless all members of the family could be present."

Neeka had been gone for days, but it felt like months. Mercy felt that she could spend only so much time with Princess before craving more substance. Neeka was being missed something fierce. Occasionally her mind ran wild with the possibility of what sort of things were going on with her sister and that fine-looking Braxton during their excursion to Texas. Once Neeka was back, the two could sit down and have a good "share day."

"Your sister should be back late tonight or early tomorrow, Mercy. In the meantime life still goes on. I need you to come now. It's an emergency. Will you be driving, or should I send a driver?"

"Sure. A driver would be nice." Before she could ask what was so important that her presence was required on a Wednesday night, Adeena had hung up. "Dammit! That woman is driving me crazy!"

Mercy had hung up the phone with clenched teeth. "Silly ole woman. Of course I want to come to your silly party. Wouldn't miss it for nothing in the world." Unlike Neeka, who always sought a way around a challenge, Mercy usually welcomed it. Especially one from their mother.

It was no family secret that she was a control freak just like her mother, and if twenty-three years of practice had taught her one thing, it had taught her that one of the best ways to deal with a control freak like Adeena was to go along with the program and give her exactly what she wants. Then give a little more until she's had enough. It was the perfect plan to show Adeena that she could play her game.

"Ooh, this one, this one!" Princess squealed, doing a little foot dance. Her eyes were like saucers as she held up the lavender silk. The sequined bodice of the dress slipped easily to thin spaghetti straps. "The right shoes. Your hair pinned up. You'll be ready for a presidential ball."

Mercy looked unimpressed. "Or the nuthouse," she said. For days now her mother had been hinting around about some friend of hers having two sons who were eligible bachelors. Like she needed help in finding her own man. It was bad enough that Adeena had the three of them tripping over this December wedding madness, but it wasn't enough. Unlike Neeka though, Mercy had a good mind to accept the first man Adeena chose. Just like that. No questions asked. *Give me the ring. Get the minister. Let's get it over with now.* Handsome or not, short, bald, toothless, old, small penis, no penis. Whatever. She refused to be intimidated. All to show Adeena that she too could play hardball. "Oh, God, I need a drink."

"Mercy, you need to pick out a dress for dinner. Everyone is dressed already except you."

Mercy didn't hear a word she said. "My bag. You seen my bag?"

Princess stopped ogling over what dress Mercy should wear. "Behind that pillow next to you," she responded, then closed her eyes for a few seconds and clutched her stomach.

"Girl, why your face twisted up like that?" Mercy questioned, removing her silver flask from her Gucci bag and uncapping it. Her sister didn't look too good about the eyes, but her skin was positively glowing.

"A little indigestion. That's all." Princess took a seat at the edge of the bed. "Shouldn't have had tomatoes at lunch. The acid reeks havoc."

"What's wrong? You feel sick to your stomach?" Mercy eyed her with casual interest.

"Just a tad. Don't worry, it'll pass." She sucked in a breath and held it, then released it slowly.

"Prin, you need to start eating better. Toast and cherry tomatoes is not a balanced meal." She waited for Princess's excuse. The girl always had one. And if she didn't know any better, she could almost swear that her little sister was picking up a little weight, especially in the chest area. Must be some new push-up bra, she reasoned. Actually, a few pounds looked good on her, seeing that Princess was such a picky eater.

Even though no one else believed her, it was Mercy's strong belief that Princess had a clandestine eating disorder. But every time she tried to broach the subject, her younger sister became an expert at switch-up chatter and turned the conversation to another topic.

"Citrus bothers my stomach at times." Princess smiled weakly.

Yep, Mercy thought, *sounds like an eating disorder*. The thought tried to nag at her, but she wasn't having it. Two swigs would take the edge off, but four short swigs were better. The half a fifth she'd consumed before leaving her house was trying to wear off. "You need me to go find you some Pepto? I know Mother has some in this house. She swears by that stuff."

"No. Please. I'm okay." Princess held the lavender dress up again. "Don't let Mommie see you drinking that stuff. She'll be in a mood the rest of the evening."

"So darn what? I'm a big girl, and so are you. Too big to still be calling your mother Mommie. I mean, get real." Mercy took a few gulps and waited for the liquid to do its trick. "And I'm sure our dear mother will be serving some kind of cocktail or wine for this grand dinner party of hers. Everyone can't be the devout and perfect Christian woman that she is." Bold words, but she had sense enough to put away her flask of Chivas Regal at the precise moment that Adeena strolled into the pastel pink room.

Adeena loved pink, and the flowing, pink silk pantsuit she wore was evident of such. Her hair was French rolled, with hanging side tendrils.

"Mercy, sweetie, you're not dressed. Our dinner guest will be here in fifteen minutes."

Mercy snorted, then turned her face away to roll her eyes. "A dinner party on a workday?"

Warmness radiated from Adeena's eyes. "To eat daily is a blessing. The weekend has nothing to do with it."

"Mother, you could have said what this was about and I still would have come over. You don't have to try being sly and secretive all the time." Her bag still in hand, she stood up and pulled a tin of Altoids from it, popped the lid, and removed one. "You know how I am about surprises."

"I know, sweetie. But now you're here, so hurry and get dressed. Aren't the dresses lovely?" Adeena moved close enough to smooth back a few strands of Mercy's hair. "Chazz has really outdone himself this time. Gave me a delightful price on the lot. All for you being such a wonderful daughter. We don't want to keep our guests waiting."

"And who might these people be that we will be dining with?" Mercy bit down gently on her lower lip. It was all she could do to keep from pulling her trusty flask out and taking a much-needed drink in front of Adeena. "Nice-looking with his own money, I hope."

"You are such a picky person," Adeena said. "It's no surprise though, but I assure you, you won't be disappointed." Adeena strode confidently to the mirror of the soft-pink dresser and admired her reflection. "You have to hurry, dear." She turned to Princess. "Looks like those multivitamins are finally beginning to work. You look radiant in that outfit, sweetheart. Peach really brings out your complexion."

"Thank you, Mommie."

An hour later, Mercy was a vision of loveliness dressed in lavender. Even with Princess still fussing over her hair, she managed a smile as she stepped into the dining room to greet their dinner guests. Sarah, the housekeeper, had prepared a feast of lemon duck with wild rice, honey-blanched vegetables, and stuffed mushrooms. Soup and salad preceded the main course.

Adeena's friend Rosalind Anderson sat between her twin sons, who to Mercy were large and beefy, but not too bad on the eyes.

Mercy tried to recall their names: Mingus and Marvon. The Andersons. A few side glances to the one called Mingus. A little on the plump side, but not too bad. She looked to his brother. Not much difference. "So," she said, oblivious to the alcohol-induced drag in her voice, "which one of you big handsome men is my knight in shining armor that's come to sweep me off my feet and rescue me? Huh? Which one?"

All eyes turned to Mercy. "Mercy," Adeena chided gently. Fire hid behind her eyes. "Mercy, sweetie, please try to behave yourself."

"Of course I will, Mother." Mercy raised her glass of chardonnay. "Here's to a long and happy marriage," she toasted before gulping her drink down. She reached for another wine-filled glass, but before she could lift it, her head slumped forward and landed in her bowl of soup.

CHAPTER TWENTY

Neeka was in her office the earliest she'd ever been on a Thursday morning, beating even her secretary to her desk. She had thought about waiting until Monday to return, but somehow the Texas trip had rejuvenated her. She felt like she could conquer the world. Good thing too, because there was a pile of paperwork waiting for her.

Around nine, her office door blew open like a strong wind was behind it. In walked Mercy, who took one look at her and yammered, "Oh my God! What did you do to your hair?"

"Thought I'd try something different," Neeka announced proudly, smoothing a hand back along her short curls. "You like it?"

"Hell, no. Did you suffer a mental breakdown while you were gone?" Mercy held a tall thermos in one hand, two Styrofoam cups in the other. Closing the door with her foot, she stood staring across at her sister. "What would make you do something like that?"

Pen in hand, Neeka went back to signing off on accounts to be paid. "I was thinking that I'm a grown woman and I wanted a change."

"What? You changed your mind about looking like a female?" Mercy was frowning.

Bad enough that Mercy had barged into her office again without knocking. But now she was tossing insults. "My head, my hair," Neeka said. "Get over it."

"You have been obsessed with your hair since you were old enough for your first Barbie. Don't think I don't remember how you used to cut the hair off those black Barbie dolls and glue it to the back of your head. For you to cut off your own hair must have been some trip."

"Look, if you've come here to be insulting, I have work to do. It's my hair. I cut it off. Change the subject, or bye-bye now." She waved with her hand. *There. Maybe you'll hush up now so I can work.*

"Okay, okay. Don't bite me over it. Anyway," Mercy said as she set down the cups, then straightened the jacket of her burgundy pantsuit before fluffing her pink blouse away from her skin, "Mother will freak over you looking like Peter Pan's brother." Opening the thermos, she took a seat.

Neeka pointed her pen at her. "I'm warning you. Don't make me call security and have you removed from my office."

Mercy grinned at her. "Security? Who? Big Al? Girl, please. Big Al has a bunion on his left toe big enough to squash a raccoon with. The man can barely hobble out to the lunch truck, let alone come see what you want."

"Girl, stop!" Laughing, Neeka balled up a piece of paper and threw it at her. "You need to stop. You're going to hell for making fun of folks."

"It's not making fun when it's the truth. It's gotten worse since you've been gone, but the man is too afraid to go to the foot doctor and have it removed."

"Can you blame him?" Neeka challenged. "That would mean time away from this wonderful job." It was nice to be back, but she could do without the piled-up work. What happened to the promise that Princess would monitor her workload while she was away? "I know you guys missed me." Neeka watched as Mercy pulled out packets of artificial sweetener from the pocket of her jacket. "It took me a few days to get homesick, but shopping helped me through it."

"I can't speak for anyone but myself," replied Mercy, exaggerating her comment by batting her eyes. "I missed the hell out of you. Mother has been driving me crazy. She's found me the perfect man to start up a courtship with. Like I can't find my own damn man."

Neeka rolled her eyes. "Oh, Lord, here we go again. Anybody I know?"

"No. And this is nothing to kid about. We all sat down to dinner last Wednesday. His name is Mingus, and I have to admit now, Mingus would have it going on if I liked greasy-looking chunky men." She slid a cup of tea in Neeka's direction. "And he must be real smart because his head is huge. I might have to marry the man just to show Mother that I can play her game. I'm not afraid of her."

"Yeah, right. And what about the business trip you were going on?" Neeka inquired. "How did it go?"

Mercy scrunched up her nose. "Cancelled. See Mother for details on that one."

Neeka sipped her tea. "That figures. There was no Vegas business trip to begin with." Even as Adeena mentioned that Mercy would be going out of town for business, Neeka had suspected it was a fabrication meant to pacify her. "Moving along, what else is new?" she asked.

"Let's see now." Mercy looked contemplative as she stirred the sweetener into her cup. "Deacon Horteese took me out to dinner and a movie. Strange-acting man outside the church. He seemed nervous the whole time. Felt like I was on a date with somebody's husband. We haven't got busy yet, but I can feel all that fornication juice building up inside me. Heck, I might have to marry him too. He is so sexy."

Mercy paused for a reaction, then continued. "Mother wants me to pick out invitations to her mystery wedding in December. That should be interesting seeing as how we don't know who the bride is yet. Who knows? Maybe she's the bride. And my third secretary quit on Friday. Prin is pregnant, and I'm thinking about trading my Infinity in for a BMW. I have a hard time choosing between the two."

"What?" Neeka put her cup down and stared at Mercy.

"Yeah. A new car. I can see myself in one of those little two-seater models with my hair blowing in the wind. I'm leaning toward baby blue, but silver is nice too."

For as long as she could recall, Mercy was good at playing practical jokes. Not one member of the family managed to escape her unexpected escapades. But frankly, Neeka didn't think that a joke about Princess and pregnancy was very funny. "Mercy, stop lying," she said.

Mercy brushed specks of lint from her pants. "What? Mother promised to buy me any car I want for my next birthday. A little perk to help me over that salary issue."

"The heck about a car! I'm referring to Princess. What's this about being pregnant?"

"Oh, that. Yeah. But you didn't hear it from me." She finished her tea.

"That's not funny, Mercy."

"Do you see me laughing?"

"Does Mama know?"

Mercy helped herself to more tea. "No. I don't think Princess knows it yet herself."

"Excuse me?" Neeka shook her head as she sipped, studying Mercy's expression. She half expected that jokester to break out laughing any second. "Unbelievable. You had me going for a second or two. I go away on business for a week and a half. I come back, and you're a psychic. Will wonders ever cease?"

"Look. Just don't say anything about it yet. Wait until you see Prin for yourself. She's picking up weight. We talking fuller breasts here. She's getting a little tummy, and her face is glowing like Rudolph's nose. Just in time for Christmas, I might add."

Oh, God, please don't let it be so. "No, Mercy. You probably looked at her the wrong way." The news gave Neeka a sinking feeling. Her baby sister was a good person and all, but still she was like a child trapped in a woman's body. She couldn't see Princess raising a child because that girl still needed some raising herself. *Poor Prin.* Neeka wanted to elaborate on the subject, but there was a hard knock at her office door and in walked Adeena in a tailored, double-breasted pink suit, looking every bit the diva boss she was.

"Good morning to my two lovely daughters." Her tone and expression spoke volumes of her good mood.

"Mama." Neeka stood up and walked around her desk for a hug.

"So happy my baby is home. We missed you—" Taken aback, Adeena put a hug on hold and stared at Neeka's head. "Child, who did this awful thing to you?"

Oh, Lord. Here we go again. Once again Neeka was a ten-year-old girl standing in the line of her mother's disapproval. Her knees felt wobbly, and her voice cracked under the nervous tension she felt. Remembering what Braxton had said about snatching the reins back, she forced herself to stand straight and be strong. "I cut my hair."

"You poor dear." Adeena patted her back as she hugged her. "Were you ill at the time?"

"No, Mama, I wasn't. It's just hair; it'll grow back. I really don't want to talk about it anymore." Neeka waited for the next insult.

"I'm sure you don't, dear. This is a good example of the devil being busy in this family. Idle minds. We need to go back to having prayer at the beginning of our day." She gestured for them to move in closer. "Come. We need a prayer moment."

Neeka heaved a weary sigh.

"Mother, please," Mercy drawled. "What about Prin? I believe she needs some praying for."

"Princess is not your business," Adeena snapped, "but since you inquire, your sister called in sick this morning."

"Umph. Wonder what's gotten into her," Mercy mumbled, turning her head to snicker.

Neeka jabbed a quick elbow at her. "Hush up."

"Now, let us pray. Take your sister's hand and bow your heads."

"Yes, ma'am," Mercy snickered.

"Gracious Father, we come to you asking forgiveness for all our sins and bad decisions. Keep us focused and on track with your divine will. Let all impure thoughts be cast away as Satan seeks to make his claim. We ask for strength against the powers of sin, lust, and worldliness, as we stay afloat in your grace. In Jesus's name. Amen."

"Amen," Neeka and Mercy chimed simultaneously.

"That's what wrong with the world. People think they're too good to start their day with a prayer. But now back to you, my dear. I'm very proud of you. You handled business well. Mrs. Perry called and raved about what a wonderful job you did. You really made a big impression at the presentation. The signed contract is in the mail. And she was highly impressed with Braxton. Something about his meat being the best she'd ever had."

The last statement made Neeka's eyes go dreamy. "Amen for that." His meat had been the best *she'd* experienced too.

"What's that dear?"

"Barbecue meat, Mama. Braxton makes the best."

"Oh, of course. But anyway, how did the trip part go? Did you enjoy the RV? It was top of the line, you know."

"Great," replied Neeka as she moved back to her desk and stood. "Can't recall the last time I spent so much time with a man I can't stand." She didn't see the sense in bringing up everything that had happened. Braxton. Funny how she couldn't wait to be rid of him, but her mind kept slipping back to how he had kissed her, where he had kissed her. She felt a warmness between her thighs wondering what he was up to.

"Nonsense. You should give the poor man a chance. He seems to be very fond of you. I trust that Braxton was the perfect gentleman."

"You trust right, Mama. He was. And very boring." A few small lies couldn't hurt. She didn't see the point in spilling details about the trip, the good or the bad. "Drive, cook, and watch television. That's all he wanted to do."

"Wonderful." Adeena beamed. "I felt confident that you'd be in perfect hands with Mr. Dupree."

There was a thick silence in the room.

"Neeka, once again, welcome back. We can talk about your bonus later. And Mercy, I'm sure you have work to do."

"Of course, Mother. No such thing as a free ride in life."

"Absolutely." Adeena made a turn to leave. "One more thing, Neeka. The planner will meet with you and your sisters tomorrow afternoon to pick out your dresses for the wedding. Around three. We don't want to wait until the last minute."

Good Lord. This woman will not stop with this madness. Neeka twisted her mouth. "The planner?"

"Yes, dear. The wedding planner. I only wish I had time to do all the planning myself, but I'm quite busy these days with meetings and seminars. Friday after next, I'll be leaving for my Christian Leadership seminar in Palm Springs. Instead of two, it will run for three days this year. Honestly, it's getting longer and longer."

"You're going away during inventory?" Mercy exchanged a knowing look with Neeka. "For three whole days?"

"You ladies have been well trained. We have inventory every year, and by now I'm sure you know exactly what to do, or we can postpone it until after the wedding."

Neeka plopped down in her executive chair. When the morning started, she had been feeling so good. Now there was a gnawing feeling in the pit of her stomach. "Mama, stop it. There is no December wedding." No doubt Mercy was thinking along the same route. And Adeena's going away for a few days would provide the perfect opportunity to get into her house and look for the photo album. Of the dreaded photos they had grown to hate.

"Mother," said Mercy, feeling the awkwardness in the room, "maybe December is too soon for a wedding. Not only that, but don't we need a willing bride first? I mean, maybe you should plan it for later next year."

"Don't be silly, dear." Adeena waved her words on as frivolous chatter. "I know very well what I'm doing. Dreams are like tiny windows into the future."

Neeka said nothing. *Let Mercy talk her talk.*

"Mother, all I'm saying is that December might not be the best time for any woman to get married. With the holidays and all. There's so much shopping to do. Maybe a wedding in May or June would be better, that's all I'm saying."

"Or maybe no wedding at all." Neeka quickly sifted through some invoices on her desk. She sought to keep her gaze down but couldn't help looking back up at her mother. The look on Adeena's face, the glow in her eyes. They made a shiver run up her back.

Mercy examined her nails and shook her head. "Because you don't have a bride, Mother. No bride, no wedding."

Adeena strode to the open door, then stood and smiled. She glanced from one face to the other. "It's all about faith. You see, I dreamed of a December wedding, and that's exactly what I'm paying for."

Neeka rolled her eyes. "Mother, you can't be serious. No one that we know of is getting married in December."

"And Neeka, I beg to differ. I don't have vivid dreams all the time, but when I do, they have a powerful meaning. Oh yes, there will be a wedding in December. I really don't care who the bride is at this point, but there will be a wedding. You two can count on it."

CHAPTER TWENTY-ONE

Neeka, I don't know about this."

"We're here now, Mercy. We might as well see it through." Neeka powered up the windows in her Lexus. She set her emergency brake and cut the engine.

"We can always change our minds," said Mercy, delicately biting her bottom lip as she sat across from her sister. The two simultaneously opened their door and climbed out. "Seemed like a good idea when we were at your place sipping on those wine coolers, but now—"

"Maybe I should have asked Princess to come with me instead." Neeka clutched the ring of her keys tighter as they exited the SUV.

They looked at each other and chuckled before starting the trek up to the house. "Princess. That's a good one," said Mercy, tucking in her skimpy T-shirt and pulling the drawstring to her black sweatpants tighter. "You know the saying, 'If you believe it, you can achieve it.' I can always go back home and tell Princess to come meet you here."

Neeka stopped short and pointed a finger at her. "Don't you dare chicken out on me now, Mercy. If you do, I will never speak to you again."

Mercy stopped and rolled her eyes at her. "Promises, promises.

Like I said, sneaking into Mother's house seemed like a good idea at first, but now I'm not feeling it. You know how she is about her personal effects. Once she finds out we've been rummaging, she could be on the warpath for weeks. Maybe even months."

"And you know how I feel about those darn pictures Mama has been collecting forever! You want this as much as I do, so stop your panty-whining! Besides, it shouldn't take us long. We get in, we seek, we find, we get out. No big deal."

"Okay, okay. Stop fussing at me."

"I will if you stop trying to chicken out, Mercy. Just take a deep breath and relax."

It was well after nine P.M. on Saturday, nine days after her return from Texas. She shouldn't have waited this long, but Neeka knew the timing couldn't be better, with Adeena out of town and the housekeeper on vacation.

"It just seems odd that you never wanted to do this before. I don't know what's happened, but you've been a little different since you returned. Maybe I need to take a trip with Braxton," said Mercy.

"And maybe you need to hush up. It has nothing to do with Braxton." Another tiny lie. That week and a half away from home had been the longest ten days, painful in the beginning but, oh, so pleasurable in the end. After Braxton had made it clear that there was nothing going on between Layla Marshall and him, there was no rush to get back to California. Friends again, they had stopped off in San Antonio for a few days so he could show Neeka around. Together they had walked down Riverwalk and dined at a couple of quaint cafés. Neeka hadn't realized how much she had needed both some TLC and some time away.

"I can't speak for you, but I'm doing this because it's time," Neeka insisted. The evening air felt crisp along her face. Christmas was near, her favorite time of year, when her mother went overboard with decorations of red, yellow, blue, and green. Not to mention her mother's exuberance for shopping. No one picked a gift like Adeena. No matter how old she got, thoughts of Christmas always filled her with deep warmth. The decorations, the shopping, the gifts, the food, the shopping. She loved it.

"As long as we make it clear that this was your idea. Not mine, but yours. I'm only here for support."

"Mercy, give me a break. Do you want to find the pictures or not?"

"Hell, yes, I want to find those stupid photos," Mercy answered as they made their way up the driveway that led to Adeena's exquisite front door. It made sense not to park close to the house in case one of her mother's nosy neighbors was peeking from a window. Back along the tall hedges, Neeka felt certain that her vehicle was out of sight from snooping eyes. Driveway pebbles crunched beneath their sneakers. "I don't know why I'm tripping," Mercy said. "She'll blame me anyway."

"You're being ridiculous."

"If you let Mother tell it, I'm to blame for everything wrong in the world."

"You get blamed because you're usually the one doing something wrong. Like that time you took Mama's car for a spin when you didn't have your driver's license because you were only fourteen." Neeka shook her head at the memory. "When you finally came home with her dented car, I thought she would never stop fussing."

"You would have to go there." Mercy grinned and shook her head. "And who would think that as I lay crying on my bed, our sweet and loving mother would snap up a picture? The woman is crazy, I tell you! She needs to be stopped."

"You still feel like turning back?" Neeka asked, knowing her sister's answer.

"Hell, no! Let's find those damn pictures and burn every single one of them! Burn 'em! Hell, burn the whole damn house, and let Mother try taking a picture of that!"

"All right now, Mercy. Let's not get carried away here," Neeka said. Maybe it was a bad decision to choose Mercy as a copartner in crime, but it was one she had to live with.

"If Mother blames me, she blames me."

"Stop saying that. She won't blame you." Neeka zipped up the matching jacket of her brown velvet warm-up suit. The fragrant air was chillier than she had expected. "Mama has three daughters, Mercy. Why would she automatically assume you're the culprit?"

"Because that's how it is. That's how it's always been, and you know I'm not lying."

"Okay, okay. Stop obsessing about it."

"Hell, I think we'd do better to find the pictures and burn 'em in the closet. That way it could look like a fire broke out from faulty wires and burned down the house."

Neeka stopped in her tracks and focused on her sister. She didn't say one word for a few seconds, but her incredulous expression said, *Are you crazy?* "I don't know about you, Mercy, but I came to find pictures, not to burn my own mother's house down!"

Mercy raked a nervous hand through her loose, silky straight hair. "I don't know. I shouldn't have let you talk me into coming at all. You mark my words, Neeka, that old woman has a thing about me."

"Mercy, your problem is, you have a thing about yourself."

Looking hurt, Mercy asked, "What's that supposed to mean?"

"You'll figure it out." They made it to the stone porch. "We're here now, so stop worrying about it. We'll remove the photo album and a few small items. It'll look like someone broke into the house and took a few things."

"You mean a few things like some snapshots of young snaggletoothed girls with nappy hair standing straight up? Or that one of me and cousin Keith playing doctor in that closet?"

"This is la-la land, Mercy. Anything is possible in California."

"Yeah, you right. I can see why a burglar would want those pictures. And I suppose the burglar knew the alarm code as well. What if Mother comes home early, Neeka? Did you think about that? What then?"

"Then we scream and run like hell."

"Oh, I see. This is all fun and games to you."

"Mercy, stop whining! Mama won't be back until tomorrow. Sarah is gone. Now is perfect. We're in charge here. It's just like Braxton said. You can't wait for someone to hand the reins of your life over to you. You have to snatch the reins yourself!"

"Braxton?" Mercy whipped her head to the side at that one. "Braxton said that? Lord, girl, don't tell me that a week and a half of being on the road with that man put this idea into your head."

"No, it didn't."

"You never thought much about Mother's picture collection until Braxton came along. What's up with that?"

"Let's just say that after listening to him—I mean really opening up my mind and listening to him—he makes plenty of sense. Good thinking going on in that head of his. He helped to open up my mind."

"Uh-huh." Mercy raised a perfectly shaped brow. "He opened your mind? I see. And what else did he help you open up?"

"Forget you, Mercy." Neeka grinned. "I'm just saying that the man has his head on tight. He's full of solid hard wisdom. That's all I'm saying." She wasn't about to give details of what really happened.

"Tight and hard. My two favorite words. So you two are feeling one another now?"

"That's none of your business. And for the record: No, we are not." Neeka replied with a half-grin, half-smirk. She hated lying, but she wasn't about to tell. Sometimes telling Mercy was the equivalent of taking out an ad in the *National Enquirer*.

"Mother's dream might be on the money. Wedding bells are getting louder and louder if you ask me."

"You should have your ears examined. Just because I said that the man has his head on tight don't mean I want to marry him. And don't bring up that stupid dream Mama had."

"You're keeping something from me. You know I can tell."

"I'm just saying that Braxton has a tight outlook on life. That's all."

"Uh-huh. You like a man with his head on tight. We'll see how much you'll be liking Mother's tight hands squeezing around your neck when she finds out you been snooping in her house behind her back."

"Ooh. Now you have me shaking in my boots." She located Adeena's door key. "This won't take long at all."

"You sure Sarah's gone? You know how she is. If she witness a mouse taking a poop in the corner, she'd tell Mother about it."

"I'm not listening." Neeka jiggled the key in the lock and waited for the tumbler to click. The key to Adeena's house had been hanging on her key ring for years, but she'd never used it. Normally she held the utmost respect for her mother's privacy. But tonight she was beyond normal. She was determined.

"I know it's cold out here and I could be home somewhere in my warm bed and waiting for my friend to come over," Mercy said.

"Anybody I know?" Even though her sisters lived in the condo next to hers, she made it a point to stay out of their private business as much as possible. Young and attractive, she saw no reason why Mercy wouldn't have a boyfriend or two, but one or two never seemed to be enough. On the other hand, if a butterfly fluttered at her own front door, Neeka was sure that both her sisters knew about it.

"Tell the truth, Nee. Did you and Braxton do the wild thing while you were away?"

"Mercy, stop it."

"There you go. You don't tell, I don't tell." Mercy rubbed her bare arms. "Hurry up. I'm cold."

"Good. Nobody told you to be walking around like it's summer. Hold up a minute; this lock is stuck or something. I have the key in right. Oh, wait a minute, here it goes." Neeka got one of two deadbolts unlocked.

"Hurry up before I change my mind." Mercy tapped her foot impatiently.

"Okay, okay. One more lock to go. Stop rushing me. I hate when you do that."

Mercy tried to rub the chill from her arms. "Yeah, right. Like we're in the habit of breaking and entering Mother's house."

"Mercy, be quiet. You are giving me a headache. I can't think straight. Something is wrong with this stupid lock. I think the key might be bent."

"What? Looks like a bad omen to me. We tried. We failed. That's it. Let's go."

"What about your key. Where's yours?"

"Are you sure Sarah's not here? If she is, we can just ring the doorbell and wait for her to let us in."

"Oh, that's real funny, Mercy. Forgive me if I forget to laugh."

Adeena herself had given all three of her daughters a key to her house to have in case of an emergency, or in the event that they needed something from the house in her absence.

Neeka heaved a weary sigh as she thought of all the years she had been tortured with Adeena's photos. Finally, it was going to end. Snatching the reins to her life had to start one day. That day had come. "Wait a minute. I think I heard the tumbler click. I got it."

"Let the burning begin."

"Once again, Mercy, we are not here to burn or cut up stuff. We want to find Mama's stash of pictures and get out." Finally she was able to swing the massive wood and glass door open.

The house was silent. Neeka couldn't recall too many times that she had been in her mother's home when there wasn't a bevy of people present: the housekeeper, guests, mooching relatives, the gardener, or some new caterer preparing weekly meals to keep her mother's low-carb diet on track. "Now try to think," she said, "if you were Mama, where would you hide some pictures?"

"Depends on the kind of pictures. Everyday family photos I would do what most normal people do, put them in a family album to be kept on a shelf in a den. But when it comes to our mother, obviously, we aren't dealing with a normal person. I would have to say they're probably in a box under her bed."

Smiling, Neeka nodded. "Sounds like a place to start looking."

CHAPTER TWENTY-TWO

T his don't make no sense." Neeka plopped down along the rumpled bed and wiped sweat from her forehead. Who knew that violating someone's privacy could be such hard work? Her back was beginning to hurt from bending down to look in every possible nook and cranny for the family album she knew would contain the dreaded prize. The whole process was akin to two hours at the gym. "I have to give it to Mama. She's good. Dang, she's good."

Mercy wiped her forehead with the back of her hand. "Remind me again why we're doing this."

Neeka glared at her and said, "Because we're taking over our lives, and destroying those pictures is the first step." After two hours, Adeena's bedroom looked like a tornado passed through it. "Where the heck could it be?"

"Beats me." Mercy raised her wineglass and slumped into a nearby chair. "Maybe Mother got rid of the pictures herself. It's been over a month since she's pulled that damn album out." She took a swallow of the pink blush wine. "I know one thing for sure, this is more work than I signed up for. I'm too tired to clean this mess up before we leave. We might have to stay all night." She mopped her forehead with the back of her hand. "Better yet, let's change into some swimsuits and go cool off in the pool."

"Swimming is the last thing on my mind. I can't believe we've been through this whole room and can't find what we're looking for. This is the room Mama comes to when she breaks out her collection. It has to be somewhere in this room."

Mercy fanned herself. "Ooh-wee. Either I'm starting early meno-pause, or it's really hot in here. Are you hot?"

Neeka's chest heaved with exhaustion, but if she allowed herself to be stationary for too long they'd have to call it a night. "Maybe it's the alcohol. Maybe you're drinking too much." She hadn't wanted to say anything at first. But there, she had thrown it out there.

"And you have some nerve. Didn't we both have wine coolers at your place before we got the bright idea for this witch hunt? Don't be the pot calling the kettle black."

"True, I had a wine cooler, but only because you brought them over and I wanted to be sociable. I don't keep alcohol in my house." Not that she was pointing a finger, but Neeka had noticed that before Mercy could even begin helping her with the search, she had had to have a couple of glasses of wine.

Back at Neeka's place, before the excursion, Mercy had shown up, uninvited at that, with a four-pack of chilled wine coolers. By the time Neeka had finished one bottle, Mercy had polished off the remaining three. It wasn't Neeka's intention to come off sounding like she was some Goody Two-shoes, but it nagged at her that Mercy might be overindulging. "I could see if we were at a club, a house party, or some other social gathering, but we're not. We're supposed to be on a mis-sion here."

"Well, consider this," Mercy said. "My part of the mission is com-plete. We searched; we couldn't find. And don't be worrying about what I drink. I like a little wine from time to time. It helps to relax me. With a mother like mine, it could be worse. No big deal."

Neeka was too tired to debate. "Whatever," she said, refusing to start a tiff over it. The tone of Mercy's voice confirmed that it was a touchy subject. Neeka got up and went back to the massive walk-in closet. Every stacked hatbox had been pulled out and searched, and all the built-in drawers had been assaulted. It would take hours to pull the room together again. Hands on her hips and staring at the floor, Neeka thought about pulling up the carpet.

"And for your information, Neeka," Mercy called out, "Jesus drank wine. Did that make him a boozer?"

Paying little attention to Mercy's ranting from the adjacent room, Neeka looked around the well-lit closet. The space was big enough to put her small bedroom in. It just didn't make any sense that her mother needed so much space. Elegant evening gowns lined one side; the opposite held more casual attire. A wall of shoes loomed directly in front of her.

"I guess it's no secret that Mama's a shoe freak." She had to have a hundred pairs, some still new in their boxes and stacked neatly. Neeka reached up and pulled down two boxes from the top and flipped each lid off. Not only did she find a pair of four-hundred-dollar sling-backs in the second box, but nestled beneath them was a golden key.

Mercy appeared at the closet entrance. "You think you're better than me because I care for a glass of wine every now and then? Is that it?"

Ignoring her, Neeka held up the key. "Look what I found."

"Where did you find it?"

Neeka held up the shoe box.

"Ooh, let me see. Let me see." Mercy hurried over and lifted up a shoe. "Damn, these are some kick-ass shoes!" The black pumps had a diamond shape and double ankle straps all of sparkling zirconium. "Mother may be a pain in the butt from time to time, but dang that woman can pick out some shoes. A damn shoeologist. That's what she is."

"Stay focused, Mercy. We're here to look for pictures."

"The hell with pictures. Girl, look at these badass shoes! Now tell me, what does Mother need with shoes like these?" Keeping her balance against a wall, Mercy struggled out of her sneakers and socks and slid her feet into a pair of Adeena's shoes. "These are the bomb! And a perfect fit too. I'm keeping these."

Exasperated, Neeka covered up the first box and slid it back along the shelf. "You can't keep the shoes." She moved over to the rack of fancy gowns and began pushing the top garments back to peek behind them. Maybe there was a wall safe to be found.

"And why not?" Mercy challenged. "Shoes like these are meant for young sexy legs like mine. Not the tired aching legs of a fifty-eight-year-old woman. These are my shoes now."

"Enjoy them while you can. Those shoes are not leaving this house," Neeka said sternly. She proceeded to the lower rack of fancy skirts and tops, pushing items aside until she spotted something. A golden half-sized trunk. The way the trunk was wedged far back into the corner behind a curtain of garments, no wonder she hadn't spotted it before.

"Nee, you obviously need some kids to boss around. With all the shoes in this closet," Mercy gestured with a wave of her hand, "I hardly think Mother will miss one stupid pair of them!"

"Coming from the same box that contained this key, I'm sure she would. The shoes stay." Neeka pulled the trunk out and tried the key. A perfect fit.

Mumbling under her breath, Mercy wrestled off the shoes and tossed them back in the box. "Get on my damn nerves. Act like you somebody's mama or something. Honestly, Nee, I don't know who you think you are . . ." She moved in closer to watch Neeka open the trunk lid.

"Looks like we found the mother lode. No pun intended." She felt like spinning around with joy.

"Look at you, little Miss Detective," Mercy replied, shoes forgotten. She pursed her lips before stooping down and reaching inside the trunk to pull out the large family album. "Let's burn this baby now, clean up, and get the heck out of here."

"No. No burning it here. It's too risky. I'll take it with me. Besides, I want to go through these pictures with a fine-tooth comb."

"Girl, please. You have seen every snaggletoothed, sin-doing, butt-naked picture in this album a hundred times. Let's start a fire in the fireplace and burn it like we came to do."

"Do me a favor and go fetch a trash bag. We'll take the album home and go through it at our leisure. One last look before the flames."

Mercy shot a look of protest, then turned to go get a trash bag. "Heck. First you want to burn it; now you want a hellish trip down memory lane. I wish you would make up your mind. You are one weird sistah. I know that."

Neeka reached down into the trunk and pulled up a manila envelope that had been beneath the picture album. The label was addressed to Adeena, but the return address was from San Jose, California. Curious, she angled her head to examine it. To her knowledge, they had family in Louisiana, South Carolina, and plenty of cousins in San Diego. Who could her mother possibly know in San Jose? The envelope had already been sliced at the top, so it wasn't like she was opening her mother's mail. Wasting no time, Neeka slid the contents out. A few letters. A few pictures. The State of California. Adoption papers? *What the heck?*

From a distance, Mercy was hollering something about having to use the restroom. "No hurry, sis! Take your sweet time," Neeka called back to her.

There wasn't time to read the entire document, but from the little Neeka could grasp, one of Adeena's children had been adopted. It was right before her in plain writing. Her mother's name in black, her mother's signature. Adoption. A male child, which meant that . . . *We have a brother? Ohmygawd.* A quick panic filled her at the thought of Mercy knowing what she'd found. She couldn't trust Mercy with the information until she was certain of the truth herself.

Neeka folded the letter-sized envelope in half and tucked it in her pants at her backside. Her velvet jacket did the trick and concealed her find. She thought about the look on her mother's face when she confronted her with the truth.

For years—all of Neeka's life, it seemed—Adeena had preached about the virtue of living a sin-free life, especially the importance of marriage before sex. Fornication this, fornication that. Now it looked to Neeka that her mother wasn't the pure and perfect example of Christian sainthood that she wanted all to believe. Not when she was concealing that she had another child somewhere. With her claim to perfection, Adeena probably had plans to control Neeka's life forever, but now it didn't look that way. *Looks like the tables might be turning in my favor. No more perfect mother. No more interfering with my life. Time for the truth.*

"I don't know about you, but I'm getting sleepy." Mercy entered the walk-in closet with a large black trash bag. "Let's bag the loot and put everything back in its place so we can haul our pretty tails out of here." She stopped short and studied the sly look on Neeka's face. "What's with you?"

"Nothing. I'm just happy to be taking charge for a change, that's all."

Mercy gave a short snort. "You look more like the cat who swallowed the canary. Stop wasting time, and bag it so we can leave. I got things to do."

"Now you talking." Neeka nodded in agreement. Once she was in a private place, she could examine the contents of the envelope more closely. "The truth will set you free," she said quietly.

Mercy looked at her quizzically. "What? What truth?"

"Never mind, my dear sister. Never mind."

CHAPTER TWENTY-THREE

Braxton was a jumble of nerves as he stood at the door of Neeka's condo and rang the doorbell once. The Thursday evening air was cool as the sun slipped behind a reddish horizon. He had been in the middle of a game of chess with Quamee when Neeka had called with an urgency to her voice. She gave no explanation, but wanted him to come to her house right away. Quamee and chess forgotten, he was out the door in five minutes. Had she missed him that much? Roses in his hands, he tapped an impatient foot, wondering what was taking her so long to answer. But before his finger could push the lit bell again, the door swung open. Neeka grabbed his hand and pulled him inside so fast that he almost lost his balance. He heard the snapping of the long stems he carried.

"Hurry up. Get in here."

"Hey," Braxton protested, "not so fast." There was nothing too serious about his tone. In fact, her finally returning his phone call and inviting him over was a good thing. Obviously the woman had some feelings for him. He had some strong feelings in return. He wondered about the pensiveness in her face. The half dozen red roses in his hand were smashed. Two of the buds hung by broken stems from bumping against her. "What's going on?"

"Nothing is going on," Neeka lied. His fresh-showered smell mixed with a woodsy cologne was intoxicating. She needed to talk to someone about her find, and that someone couldn't be a family member. "Please have a seat . . . I mean, make yourself at home."

Braxton did as he was told, even though inwardly he had a problem with being bossed around. He removed his black leather bomber jacket before sitting. Since their return from Texas he'd been missing Neeka enough to brave calling her up to ask her out for dinner, but on each occasion all he had gotten was her answering machine. The least she could have done was phoned him back to say, "Drop dead." But he'd known that it was all a matter of time. She wanted him. That playing hard-to-get was part of her way.

"Give me a minute," Neeka said over her shoulder, closing and locking not one, but two locks on her front door, and two dead bolts. "One can never be too safe."

"So how have you been?" Amused, Braxton set the flowers on the table and watched as she walked to her kitchen and brought out two wooden chairs, leaning one up against the doorknob and fashioning the other precariously over the top of the first chair. A barricade? *What in the world is going on?* She was drawing all the blinds, peeking out from one side of the large window and then the other. "Neeka? Is everything okay?"

"Of course. Nosy neighbors. Did you park your car around the corner like I asked?" She turned to face him, rubbing her hands along the dark silk caftan she wore.

"Yes, I did," he replied, watching her with a quizzical look.

"Did you make sure no one seen you walking up to my condo?"

"Check."

"Did you tiptoe up to the door?"

He had to laugh at that one. She was so mysterious. "Sorry, but I'm a grown man. I don't tiptoe. But I did walk as softly as I could. Neeka, why did you want me to tiptoe? What's up?"

Neeka turned and peeked out the window again. "You know how it is. When you have sisters who live next door, your personal business is hard to maintain."

"Need me to help move the couch in front of the door?"

"Maybe next time," Neeka replied. "They obviously didn't see you come in, or Mercy would have been over here by now."

"Neeka, enough games. What's the deal? I've been ringing you for over a week now. Then out of the blue you call and tell me to get over here right away." He flashed his sexy grin. "Could this possibly be an emergency booty call?"

"More like a looty call because I found the loot." Light on her feet, she headed for the kitchen area.

"The what?" Braxton got up, went to the counter that sliced through the kitchen area, and took a seat on one of the stools.

"Remember what I told you about my mother being a picture freak and keeping a collection of photos?"

"Yeah." He furrowed a brow, waiting.

"I found them—all those pictures from so many years back. Burned every last one of 'em in my fireplace a few days ago. I did like you said and took charge of my own life by burning the loot!"

"Okay. And you're telling this to me because . . ."

Neeka didn't see the harm in telling Braxton about the adoption papers, the letters, the pictures of her older sibling. The information was burning a hole inside her. She wanted to tell Mercy, but she knew that girl would only break her trust by telling Princess. And Princess was weak as wet spaghetti. All it took was Adeena looking at her baby sister a certain way, and she'd snap and tell everything.

"How about some coffee?" Neeka asked.

"Nah. Too late in the evening for coffee. Keeps me up at night. You have some wine?"

"Of course not. I don't buy alcohol for my home. Tea or cocoa?" Neeka grabbed her hot pot and filled it with water.

"Thought you said you can't drink tea or cocoa," Braxton teased.

"Braxton, don't start with me."

"Cocoa is fine." The room was dimly lit, almost romantic. He looked around, noticing her neat and clean quarters. A large envelope rested on the countertop. The mailing address was to Adeena Lebeau. He wondered briefly what it was about, but didn't pry. "So, what's going on with you?"

"I found something else. Important papers." She stopped talking, leaving him hanging as she plugged in the hot pot, then fetched two mugs from her cabinet. "It's bothering me so much that I needed to talk to someone."

"What? No best girlfriend?" Braxton looked dubious.

"Suffice it to say my sisters are my best friends. At least when they're not getting on my last nerves they are. But this is something I can't talk to them about. Not yet." Neeka moved across the kitchen and found her box of gourmet cocoa.

"I'm listening." He admired her backside turned to him, her high and firm derriere. *Damn, she's built solid. Just the way I like it.* He felt tingly in his center thinking about their last get-together in the RV. She hadn't been the most experienced lover, but he had plans to change all of that. Like a junkie, he needed more.

"My mother has a son. And from my calculations, she had him out of wedlock when she was very young."

Braxton regarded her with a shrug. "So? Your mother's not perfect. It happens—no big deal. The question is, what do you plan to do with the information?"

"I plan to reveal the truth. Stop my mother from interfering with my life once and for all. I plan to do a lot."

"I don't get it," Braxton said. He watched as she first poured hot water into a mug, then opened and stirred in cocoa mix. "Young girls have been having babies without husbands since Adam and Eve. It's not the social taboo it once was."

"It is for a woman who wants people to think she's a saint. Mama has preached about fornication, sin, and sex before marriage for so long that I thought I would need a therapist before I could be intimate with a man."

Braxton gave a devilish grin. "I give great therapy, don't you think?"

Neeka blushed. "Quit it. I'm serious."

"Okay, I'm listening."

"She teaches Sunday school to young girls, and she's considered a role model by many." She slid a mug over to Braxton.

"Now I see where you're going with this. So now she's not so pure as she's led you and others to believe, and you smell a daughter's revenge. Is that it?"

"Got that right. My own mama had sex before marriage, and she can't tell me a thing now about having to get married first. Don't you see, this changes things. Even that silly dream she keeps talking about."

"Dream?" Braxton blew into his steaming brew. "What dream?"

It was too outrageous to share, but how else would he understand? "Okay, but don't laugh when I tell you this." She took a deep breath. "About four or five months ago Mama had this vivid dream of a big wedding for one of her daughters. She claimed it was so real that she woke up with the taste of wedding cake in her mouth. A month later she started planning a December wedding. Invitations are being printed as we speak."

"And who's the bride?"

"Who knows! For all I know the wedding could be for us."

"Woman, you are too much. You know that? I like you. I like you a lot. But I don't recall a proposal of marriage."

"Oops. Thought Mama took care of it for you." She blew on her mug and watched his face for a reaction. "But time for a wake-up call. This bit of information about my mother might be what I need to finally put her in her place—and out of my business."

Braxton removed a cigarette from his shirt pocket and ran it under his nostril. "Neeka, no one can make you get married. And even if she was planning a big wedding for you and me, I wouldn't twist your arm about it. I was hoping that you would like me for who I am. An average guy. Adeena might talk a good game, but she can't make you say, 'I do.' "

"No cancer sticks." She reached and pulled it away and tossed it into the nearby trash. "You don't know my mother like I know her. That woman can make you say, 'I do, I don't, I will, and I won't do it again.' And make you mean every bit of it."

"Well, I don't know what you think you can accomplish by spreading the news you found, but if I were you I'd be careful. Things have a way of backfiring. It might be a good idea to put her personal documents back and wait for your mother to bring up the subject, if that's what she wants to do. Just leave it alone."

Leave it alone? No way. Obviously he didn't understand. "Yeah, maybe you're right. I'll put the papers back," Neeka said, but she knew her words were fake. She had plans that didn't include putting the documents back. Plans like calling the number she found in the letter addressed to Adeena. Plans like inviting her secret brother to Adeena's dedication, now three weeks away. It was all part of her plan to take full control of her own life, no matter what the cost. "I'm sure that Mama is planning to tell us about our brother soon enough."

"Your mother is good to you. I wouldn't take a chance messing that up," Braxton said, getting up and coming around to where she stood. He put his arms around her, pulled her closer. "Now that we have it straight about this marriage thing, maybe we can see one another with no strings attached."

"No strings. No pressure. And you can't tell anyone. It stays between you and me."

"I like secrets. Especially a juicy one like you."

"Braxton, you make it sound so naughty. Good friends with benefits. Nothing more."

"Goodness, woman. You make it sound like ending up with me would be the worst thing that could happen to you. Why does it have to be a secret? What's wrong with me?"

Not one solid answer came to mind. "Nothing's wrong with you. It's just that—"

"Just that what? Talk to me now." His arms rested around her tiny waist, and his eyes were small spotlights of interrogation aimed at her.

"If I had met you any other way—if my mother wasn't putting so much pressure on me—this marriage thing . . . don't you see? She's gotten her way for twenty-four years of my life. I refuse to allow her to win this time. If she knew we were dating, it would be like she won. I'm sorry." She lowered her chin before heaving a weary breath. "I just can't let that happen."

"In a way I understand where you coming from," Braxton said. He kissed her forehead. "If that's how you really feel, I can respect that. If I have to settle for being your friend, then that's how it is. Friends with benefits. No strings attached."

"Exactly. No strings." Neeka ran her hand over his newly shaven head. So round, so perfect. It was something she had been wanting to do ever since he shaved off his hair. "How long you planning to keep this bald look?" His smooth and shiny dome, for some reason, was so irresistible, so sexy to her. It reminded her of something nice and naughty, but she couldn't quite put her finger on it. She pulled his head into her chest, so she could kiss the top of it. That made him laugh.

"As long as you like it. You do like it, right?" He raised his head so that his lips could brush lightly across hers, sending a mild current of electricity between them.

"Like it? I'm loving it." She kissed the top of his dome.

"Okay, so tell me the truth. Did you miss me?" He lifted her chin to see her eyes. "I'll go first. I missed the hell out of your cute, little spoiled behind."

"I am not spoiled," she mock-rolled her eyes. "Well, maybe a little."

"Try 'a lot'." He rubbed his nose gently against hers. "But that's okay too. I can handle it."

"How much did you miss me?" Neeka asked, anticipating his probing tongue next to hers. Her hand reached and found his manhood. The powerful throb of it conveyed that he wanted her bad. She licked her lips with anticipation. She wanted him too.

"I can show you better than I can tell you." He drew his mouth to hers to taste the lingering sweetness of cocoa.

Coming up for air, Neeka said, "As long as you understand that this is not a booty call." But there was no way she could deny wanting more of what she had experienced during their road trip.

"Of course not. I'm a leg man myself." Braxton groaned, his hands full of her taut rear end. "Booty is the last thing on my mind." He kissed her harder, their tongues doing a duel.

"Ooh, goodness. We can't keep doing this." Her body felt helpless in his arms.

"We'll make this the last time." Braxton kept his lips locked with hers as he lifted her up and walked the short distance to the sofa. Gently he disrobed her before removing his own clothing. Kissing the soft swell of her nipples, he trailed down to other sensitive spots. "Tell me you want it to," he whispered as he planted soft hot kisses along her belly, then down to her thighs. "Tell me or I'll stop."

"No, don't stop. I want it. I want all of it."

CHAPTER TWENTY-FOUR

O h, my goodness," Princess squealed as she entered the massive room filled with ivory ribbons and pink flowers. "Look at all this food!" She strolled over to where Neeka was helping one of the caterers place dark pink rose petals along the bottom of a huge cake iced in pink. Not only did Angelic Grace Baptist boast a state-of-the-art child-care center, but it also housed a modern banquet room large enough to accommodate three hundred people for the dedication party for Adeena Lebeau. "Everything is so nice. I can't believe the mayor's wife actually came. I'm so excited."

"Believe it," Neeka said, stopping what she was doing to pan her view around the room and see faces she hadn't seen in years. "Our mama is pretty well known."

"This is something Mommie will remember for the rest of her life."

Funny. I was thinking the same thing. Neeka kept quiet.

The room was peppered with important community leaders. Not in the least surprised, Neeka spotted a couple of city councilmen and their wives, not to mention a few members of her mother's Goddess Club. She didn't know a whole lot about the club, but she believed it to be a bunch of snobby middle-aged women with no husbands who had way too much money and way too much time on their hands. She figured that they probably sat around discussing whose life they could mess up—or control. "Mama hasn't come out of her dressing room yet. Maybe you should go check on her."

"I just did." Princess smiled. "She's a little nervous, but she's radiant in pink. Mama's been looking forward to this event for months. She deserves so much more."

"And Mercy?" Neeka already knew that wherever she was, she was drinking. She didn't dwell on Mercy's shortcomings for long. She'd been meaning to have a talk with her sister about her growing alcohol consumption, but with so much going on, she simply hadn't found the time. "Have you see her?"

"Earlier. In Mommie's room. She's around here somewhere. Hey, you think Channel Seven news will actually come?"

"I think that was a rumor," Neeka said. Standing next to Princess, she took a quick peek at her sister's abdomen to see if there was any credence to the pregnancy theory, but the A-shaped yellow chiffon dress made it hard to tell. Neeka glanced slyly at her face. Mercy was right. The girl's face was radiant, her cheeks fatter. "Prin, can I ask you a personal question?"

"Sure, sis. What is it?"

"I was wondering . . . I mean . . ." Neeka thought about coming right out and asking Prin if she was with child, but the timing was all wrong. This was her mother's day. If she upset Princess, there would be tears and more drama to deal with. "Never mind. We'll talk later."

Obviously, the church members had spared no expense: the food, the flowers, the exotic palm, the caterers. Instead of rolling out the red carpet, it was pink. Several large ice sculptures graced the large buffet tables.

"You have your speech ready?" Neeka asked.

"My poem," Princess corrected. "I wrote Mommie a lovely poem. Mercy has a piece she'll be reading. She says it's not a speech, but what else can it be? What about you? Did you have time to prepare something?"

A small wicked smile found Neeka's lips. "No, I have something even better. A big surprise."

"Ooh, I love surprises. What is it?" Princess asked as her face lit up.

"Prin, if I told you, it wouldn't be a surprise."

"Oh, please. You can tell me. I won't tell a soul."

"Don't worry. You'll see soon enough." Neeka glanced up at the wall clock. Twenty after three. The program was scheduled to commence at three. So typical of black folks not to start on time. She wished they would hurry up and start before she lost her nerve about having her long-lost brother show up. Long-lost. That was a laugh. Newly found was more like it. *It's not a bad thing I'm doing. It's a good thing. He's our brother, and he has a right to be here too.* She kept telling herself that. A good thing. To some it might seem a bit extreme, but to Neeka it was the light at the end of the tunnel. The way to freedom. Whatever it took.

"Did you buy it or have it custom-made? Your surprise, that is."

"Prin, I told you I'm not telling, so don't even try it." With each passing minute she was more and more a ball of raw nerves. What if her brother, Mark Wilkinson, didn't show at the airport? What if Braxton couldn't find the man by holding up a sign with his name on it? The fountain of fruit punch was for after the ceremony, but she needed something now to help the lump in her throat. Careful not to get any on her ivory dress, she ladled a cup of it and was drinking slowly when Mercy breezed into the room.

"C'mon, you two. The program is about to start. Prin, if you pre-pared something, get it ready. The family is up at the mike." Mercy turned to head to the back of the small stage. "There are more people out there than I thought. I'm nervous. I just want to get this over with."

Neeka waved them on. "You two go on ahead. I need a minute. I'll be right there."

"Okay," Mercy replied, "but don't take long if you need time on the mike. Let's get this show on the road."

Princess left with Mercy. Neeka stood by herself, except for a few hired help bustling about, adding a few more touches to the buffet area. She pulled out her cell phone and dialed Braxton. "Hi. Were you able to pick up Uncle Mark?" She chose to lie and say Mark was her uncle knowing that Braxton wouldn't have approved of what she was doing. While he always seemed eager to please, doing anything to get on Adeena's bad side wasn't in his repertoire. She hated involving him in her scheme, but Braxton was the only person available for the job who wouldn't be missed right away or draw suspicion.

"Piece of cake," replied Braxton. "In fact, we're outside the church now. We'll see you in ten minutes."

"Great. Thanks, Braxton. I owe you one for this. Mama will be so happy to see Uncle Mark. She hasn't seen her baby brother in years." She clicked her phone off with a devilish smile. The stage was set. Neeka closed her eyes and counted to ten. Would Adeena be upset? Probably. Would she be upset enough to call off the December wedding? Most definitely. Deep down Neeka wanted to believe that what she was about to do would finally get her mother off her back about marriage, but at the same time she couldn't help thinking about her sisters and how knowledge of having a brother would affect them.

Ten minutes later, Neeka had taken her designated seat between Princess and Mercy on the small stage of guest speakers. The event opened with Rev. Clayton leading a prayer and giving his personal rendition of what a saintly and strong Christian woman Adeena Lebeau was. A selected group of choir members paid tribute by singing a song written for Adeena's big day. Princess followed up with a poem that Mercy had dismissed as simple and childish, but to Neeka's surprise it was very good. Even Mercy had prepared a small speech in Adeena's behalf, mostly about silly childhood memories that had the audience laughing. So far, so good.

Neeka's turn finally rolled around. A fluttery feeling seized her stomach as she rose and made her way to the podium. A sea of smiling faces gazed back. Nervously she cleared her throat. "My wonderful mother. What can I say? Only that for a woman who has done so much, there can never be enough words of praise and gratitude. So, instead of preparing an essay or speech, I seized the liberty to do something different. Something special. I would like to take this time to introduce my brother, Mr. Mark Wilkinson."

A few loud gasps came from the audience as a tall and lithe man in his forties walked from the rear of the stage to the podium with a sheet of paper in his hand. Even as Neeka took her seat, she could hear whispered comments from the congregation: Adeena's son? What son? Thought she only had three daughters?

Neeka took a deep breath trying to relax. Mercy, unable to contain herself, leaned over and tapped her shoulder. "Nee? Who the heck is that man?"

"Shhhh. Not so loud. That man is Mama's oldest son. His name is Mark."

Princess trilled in a whisper. "But we don't have a brother!"

"We do now," Neeka replied, wanting them to save all inquiries for later. She was doing her best to listen to Mark's words of acknowledgment and praise before beginning his speech. The man had gone to the limit to speak words of nothing but admiration.

Mercy tapped her again. "He's not named after an expensive car. He can't be our brother."

Neeka wasn't listening to a word they were saying as she sat craning her neck to catch a glimpse of Adeena's face as she sat at the VIP table. Adeena wore a look of silent shock.

Mercy tapped her again. "Nee, what the heck is going on?"

"Oh, no. Mommie don't look too good." Princess went quiet.

"Will you two please hush up and listen to the man's speech!" Neeka whispered harshly. She spotted Braxton at one of the guest tables. He wasn't the happy camper either. The look on his face confirmed that he was aware that he'd been lied too. "Good," she mumbled, "that's what he gets for being in the family mix."

Once the dedication was over, Neeka grabbed her purse and light jacket and hurried out of the building to her car. She didn't bother to inform her sisters, who had chosen to ride with her once again. They were right behind her as she walked fast and hard through the parking lot. Mercy was half running to catch up.

"Neeka! Girl, wait up. What's going on?" Mercy yelled at her back.

"I can't wait. I have to leave now. I have things to do." Neeka waved her keys in the air. "I'll talk to you later. Back at the house."

"Hold up!" Mercy caught up with her as she climbed into her SUV. "In case you have forgotten, we rode here with you, and we're riding back the same way."

"Mercy, I don't have time to argue. You and Prin get in or get left. I have to go."

Princess climbed in the backseat. "Nee, what's going on? What about the dinner? Mother looked like she was ready to kill somebody. Who was that man?"

Too many questions, too little time. "Prin . . ." Neeka sighed. "Can you hush up? I can't play twenty questions right now."

"No, I will not hush! I want someone to tell me what's going on?" Princess yelled, half-crying as she powered down the window. "What's wrong? Why are we running away like this?"

"Prin," Neeka yelled, starting up her engine, "I can't talk about it right now. Just buckle up!"

CHAPTER TWENTY-FIVE

You guys want ham or bacon with those eggs?" Back at her place Neeka couldn't find enough to keep her busy. Ever since she was a young girl, cooking had always been a way to calm her nerves. "What about some pancakes or waffles?"

"Hell, no," said Mercy with an attitude. Her hands were crossed at her chest. "Neeka, if you feel like cooking, cook up some explaining."

Skillet in one hand, wooden spoon in the other, Neeka paced from one end of her kitchen to the other. Nervous energy wouldn't allow her to sit. *Everything will be fine,* she kept telling herself over and over. But each time her mind replayed the scene at Adeena's dedication—the hushed whispers and sly glances from the congregation, the shocked look on her mother's face when her son, Mark, stood and walked from the rear of the banquet room to read his speech—she experienced a shiver so deep it produced goose bumps. "If you guys are hungry, I can have some homemade biscuits ready in half an hour. Prin, you know how much you love my biscuits with some boysenberry syrup."

Princess sniffed and shook her head. "No, thank you. I'm not hungry." She used her crumbled-up napkin to dab at red eyes. She'd been teary-eyed since they arrived at the condo. "I'm worried about Mommie. I've never seen her so upset. I called her cell, but she hung up on me." She rose from the sofa, went to the window, and stood looking out.

Neeka sat the skillet down on the stove. "You two are the best sisters a girl could have. Thanks for riding home with me. I mean, as long as we stick together, we're a unit. Right, Prin? Mercy? Right?"

"Yeah, right," Mercy agreed. "We're one united front until Mother gets here; then you're on your own. I knew about the missing pictures, Neeka, but I had absolutely nothing to do with that man claiming to be our brother. Probably another gold digger looking for a payday."

Neeka was quick to the defense. "Mark isn't like that. It's not like he didn't know how to contact Mama or where she lived, Mercy."

"If that's so, why hasn't he popped up before?"

"That's not important now. As long as we remain a unit, everything will be fine. We need to start standing up to Mama. Enough is enough!" Looking from one sister to another, Neeka smiled weakly.

"Unit my behind," scoffed Mercy. "Neeka, you may as well face it, you have messed up big time. Brother or no brother, what were you thinking calling him up and inviting him to Mother's dedication? I would think that if Mother wanted him to come, she would have sent a car for him. If I were you, Nee, I'd be looking for a good hiding place."

"You think she's that upset about it? I mean, we could stand a brother or two in this family, don't you think so?" Neeka fiddled with the hem of her black organza apron over her sheath dress. And poor Mark. She'd left the man in the hands of Braxton to be taken back to the airport for his flight home. She couldn't imagine how he must have felt not being able to spend some quality time with his own mother and sisters. "I just thought it would be a nice surprise for him to be part of the event."

"Well, looks like you thought wrong. But you keep telling yourself that, Nee. Maybe someone will believe it." Mercy got up and went to the refrigerator to look in.

"I think his speech was nice." Princess dabbed at her eyes again.

"I know one thing: All this drama is making me thirsty. I could stand a drink. All I know is," added Mercy, a tall glass of orange juice in her hand, "usually I'm the one who push Mother's buttons, but the look in her eyes at that dedication was harsh enough to raise the dead." She sat back down and pushed away a plate piled high with cooked food. "How many times do I have to say this? That man is our brother and his name is Mark. Mark Wilkinson." Driving back to her place, the more Neeka explained about finding the adoption papers and contacting Mark, the more her sisters chose not to believe the obvious.

"That man is our brother, and his name is Mark. Mark Wilkinson."

"So you say," Mercy said, rolling her eyes. "Nee, he could be a fake. You would think that if he's really Mother's son, he would be named something practical like Bentley or Rolls-Royce, or Hummer. You know how Mother adores expensive cars."

"I don't think the Hummer has been out as long as Mark has," Princess added quietly. "Could be fake papers you found."

"That makes no sense at all, Prin. Who would go through the trouble of hiding fake adoption papers?" Neeka looked reflective. She should have listened to Braxton. But no. "The adoption papers were authentic and legal."

Mercy stood up for a second trip to the refrigerator. "You could have told me and Prin about those papers. If you had, we wouldn't be here waiting out the storm. And that Mark guy is no spring chicken himself. Mother would have had to be a baby herself when she had him."

"She was fifteen."

Mercy stopped pouring juice. "What? Fifteen?"

"That would make Mark forty-three," Neeka said, rubbing her hands along her apron. So far her cooking wasn't helping her to relax. "I know. I'll bake Mama a chocolate cake. She loves my chocolate cakes." She got busy pulling out the necessary paraphernalia.

Princess sniffed. "When Mommie looked straight at me, she gave me an evil look, and I haven't even done anything. I would never do a thing like that."

"Prin, put a mop in it," Mercy snapped.

"Leave her alone, Mercy!" Neeka felt awful. Not only had she involved Braxton by asking him to drive Mark to and from the airport, but she had also aimed suspicion at her sisters who feared Adeena the way some people fear the law. "I know it seems bad right now, but once this blows over, everything will be fine. We have a brother and that's that." Maybe after she baked a cake, a batch of her oatmeal raisin cookies for Princess would be nice. "Mama always said that I could solve peace treaties with my chocolate cake. And she should know."

"That was before she went on low carb," said Princess.

"Neeka," Mercy droned, admiring her long manicured nails, "instead of going into your Betty Crocker mode, you should be trying to find a way out of town for a while. Mother will be looking for you for sure. But once time has passed, maybe she'll calm down. And then again, maybe she won't."

"You're right." Neeka stopped stirring the cake batter. "I should go away for a while."

"Girl, yeah. Save yourself." Enjoying every moment of it, Mercy lifted a piece of toast and bit off the edge. Then she removed her flask from her purse and poured some into her juice. "Too cold for the Bahamas. But I hear Florida is nice this time of year."

"I better go pack now." Nervous energy propelled Neeka out of the room and up the stairs. Ten minutes later she was back with a small suitcase so crammed that a few items hung out haphazardly. "Can you drive me to the airport? I can't leave my car in storage."

Mercy took another sip. "Sure. I can drive you."

The sound of screeching tires halted outside her condo. "Oh, God," Neeka trilled. "Sounds like her now. Oh, Lord, help us." Eyes wide, Neeka stood clutching her suitcase.

"It is her," Princess announced. She closed the blinds and moved away from the window as if a bomb might come flying through any second. "I'll be going home now."

Neeka was too beside herself to peek out, but Mercy was out of her chair and at the window in a flash. "Ooh, girl. It's her alright. Damn. She looks madder than a pit bull after being neutered. I love you, sister, but I am not taking the blame for this one. I have my own issues with Mother." Mercy moved away from the blinds. "Where's my purse?"

"Don't open the door!" Neeka yelled. What was she saying? Like her mother didn't have a dozen keys to her place. She felt the air change the moment Adeena turned her key in the lock and charged into the room. Her face was as hard as stone; her eyes, embedded red rubies.

"I have to go pee," Princess announced, sprinting for the restroom.

"I think I left my iron on." Mercy stepped toward the front door, but Adeena was blocking it.

"Princess, get back here! No one is going anywhere for now." The tone of her voice was as grating as a fingernail being raked across a chalkboard.

"Mama. The ceremony went well." For what she had done, Neeka was expecting some kind of reaction. Adeena mad, yes. Adeena furious, no. The most she had hoped for was her mother being upset enough to cancel those crazy December wedding plans and stop talking about weddings and babies. "Everything turned out okay. Don't you think so, Mama?"

"I'm only going to ask once." Adeena narrowed her eyes as she paced back and forth before her three daughters, now lined up like soldiers. She pulled off the fancy new hat that matched her champagne-pink dress and shoes. Tossed it to the sofa. "Who is responsible for Mark showing up at church today?"

Neeka could have heard a pin drop if it wasn't for her heart pounding in her ear. *I'm a grown woman for heaven's sake! Why does this woman still have such an effect on me?*

"I asked a question. I demand an answer!" Adeena stopped at Princess. Stared into her eyes. Unblinking. The girl looked like she would collapse. "Was it you?"

Princess answered with teary eyes and a fervent shake of her head.

"I didn't think so." Adeena moved to Mercy. "I know we've had our ups and downs, but I didn't think you despised me so. How could you do something like this?"

"Mother, I don't despise you. It was Neeka. She did it!"

"How dare you lie about your own sister!" Adeena's eyes never blinked. "Of all my children you were always the one who was hardest to deal with. Always challenging me! Always disobeying me! Always!"

"Mama, she's not lying," Neeka said. "Prin and Mercy didn't know. I found the papers and letters at your house. I called Mark up and invited him. I did it." There. She confessed it. It was time to be a woman and step up to the plate. Neeka held her head up. She clutched her suitcase to her tight chest, her heartbeat knocking against it.

Adeena moved around to face her. "You went through my personal belongings?" The most incredulous look played along her face. Tears pooled in her eyes as she felt a spot over her heart. "You?"

"I thought it would be a nice surprise to have Mark there. I realize now that I shouldn't have. I . . . I made a bad choice. Mama, I'm so sorry."

"Sorry? You're sorry? Maybe I should show you what it feels like to have one's personal effects violated. Let's just see how you like it!" Pivoting, Adeena trudged up the stairs.

"Hope you're satisfied," Mercy muttered. "You have finally made her lose her mind."

"Mercy, shut up and go home!" Neeka dropped her suitcase and followed Adeena, hoping to deter a snooping. "Mama, I said I'm sorry. Can't we talk about it?"

"Go home? Are you kidding, and miss the festivities? I don't think so. This should be interesting." She followed Neeka and her mother for the thrill of it.

"Can we all stop fighting so much? I can't stand all this fighting." Reluctant, Princess rushed up behind them, hoping for peace. "Maybe we should all pray."

"Snooping through my things . . . I'll show you snooping." Adeena headed straight to Neeka's bedroom and begun pulling out drawers, tossing clothes out. Garments flew high and low. Old bills hit the floor. Receipts. A new box of condoms. Her mother stopped and held it up. "Fancy that. Large and ultrasensitive." She tossed the box to Neeka. "Is this what good Christian girls keep next to their beds?"

"You go, girl," Mercy cheered. "If they don't want to get pregnant, it is."

Neeka felt she would pass out. "I have had those for months now. I forgot all about them."

Adeena turned to Mercy and narrowed her eyes at her. "Mercy, I'm warning you." She went to the closet and slid the mirrored door open. The force of the door made a harsh scraping sound against its track. She pulled out hatboxes and shoe boxes, along with anything capable of hiding something.

"Okay. Okay, Mama, you've made your point. I was wrong!" Words to deaf ears. Who would have thought that her mother could move so fast and have so much energy? Neeka ignored Princess standing in the doorway looking sick to her stomach, while Mercy was right next to Adeena gawking and obviously enjoying every minute of it. Mercy's eyes reminded her of children at a Ninja Turtle movie, bright with excitement. The only thing missing was a bag of popcorn in her hand. *Ooh, that girl makes me sick. Nothing but a traitor!*

"Why should I stop now?" Adeena asked. "One violation of privacy deserves another." Going straight to the nightstand Adeena pulled out drawers, picked up documents and read them, and tossed them aside. Beneath some papers she found a pair of edible panties still encased in their clear wrapping. She held them up. "Oh, my. Looks like someone fancies a raspberry-flavored crotch. Could these possibly belong to you?"

"Mama, those have been there forever." If Neeka had a big rock in front of her, she'd crawl under it. She could feel her face blush red. Humiliation in front of her family was something she hadn't expected to feel. Her mother was being plain cruel. "Those panties were given to me as a joke by someone at work!" Neeka explained. "I meant to toss them out. I guess I forgot."

"Yeah, right," Mercy mumbled, stepping in closer. She looked away to snicker.

Adeena wasn't listening. With her rear end in the air, she was on her knees pulling a large hatbox from under Neeka's bed.

"Mama, stop! You've made your point already!"

"I will stop when I am ready to stop!" Adeena stood. She flipped the hatbox lid and found more papers. Beneath the papers she reached in and withdrew the biggest, the blackest, the thickest dildo she'd ever seen. All eyes focused on it. All eyes focused on Neeka, then back to the monstrosity.

"Please don't fight," Princess pleaded. "Oh, my goodness, sweet Jesus, have mercy." She held her stomach and hurried to the adjacent restroom and slammed the door.

Adeena sniffed. "I suppose that this thing is a Christmas token from someone at work as well?" She waved the dildo in Neeka's face.

Dang. She shouldn't have kept that thing. "Well, actually . . . it was a gag birthday gift for Mercy. A joke. But I didn't give it to her because the more I thought about it, it seemed too tacky. I gave her a new Gucci bag instead."

Mercy snorted. "Who wouldn't need a new coochie after using something like that!"

Adeena shot her a look. "Mercy, you hush your potty mouth now!"

"That was almost two years ago. That"—she could barely point to it—"that thing has been in storage since." The darn thing had dust on it by now. Funny, she didn't recall it being so . . . so darn huge.

"It doesn't feel good, Neeka, does it?" Adeena stared into her eyes.

"Mama, I wouldn't know. I didn't use that thing!"

"I'm talking about having your privacy invaded!" She thrust the monstrosity at her. "Here! Take it!"

Neeka lowered her eyes. "Oh." Folded hands pressed the monstrosity to her chest. She had it coming. "No, Mama, it don't."

"Dang," Mercy said, feeling her cue. "With that thing, it's more like having your privacy inflated." She grinned wide. "Girl, you are a true freak!"

Adeena raised her free hand and slapped the girl so hard Mercy heard her teeth clink. "Mercy! I thought I told you to shut your filthy mouth!" The hit left a red blotch on her skin.

"You didn't have to hit me!" Mercy yelled, clutching the side of her face. Looking hurt, she moved to the bed to sit at the edge.

"Enough of this nonsense." Adeena shoved the shoe box at Neeka. "I can see Mercy doing something like this. Lord only knows, that child has been like a thorn in my side for all her life. But you, Neeka? How dare you bite the hand that has fed you for years!" She looked over at a silent Mercy. Her eyes dared her to make a comment.

"Mama," Neeka pleaded, "all I wanted was for you to stop pressuring me about finding a man, finding a husband. That's all I wanted."

"And it took embarrassing me?" Adeena sniffled, then threw her head back like a diva, with pride. "True. Mark is my son, and I should have told you girls about him sooner. But telling your daughters about Mark is one thing, and telling the whole congregation is another." Her eyes filled with tears. "Still, you had no right to exploit my personal life, Neeka. No right! And I doubt if I'll ever forgive you."

"Mama, please . . . I wasn't trying to hurt you—" It was hard to explain what she had been feeling. If only Braxton were there. He always knew what to say or how to handle the situation.

"But you have hurt me, Neeka." Adeena headed out of the room full of heartache and disappointment, then paused at the door. "You really have."

Neeka looked on in disbelief. This was no joke. Adeena looked as serious as cancer. In all her twenty-four years of life, Neeka had never seen such a look in her mother's eyes. "Mama, do we have to be so dramatic about this? So what if the church knows you have a son? It's not like it's the end of the world."

"It is for you and me."

"Mama, please," Neeka said. "All this drama over having a son?" But the look in Adeena's eyes told her it was useless.

"I suggest you start looking for a new job and a place to live. Diva Four is owned and operated by my daughters and me. I don't take much to outsiders mingling with family business. As far as I'm concerned, I have no daughter named Donneeka."

CHAPTER TWENTY-SIX

The weekend went too soon. Neeka didn't see the point of going to church on Sunday if her mother wasn't speaking to her, which probably meant that her sisters wouldn't be speaking to her either. She figured that all Adeena needed was some time to cool off. So Neeka spent part of the day pampering herself with deep conditioning of her hair, a manicure and pedicure, and the deep-pore facial that always left her skin glowing. Her hair was growing back fast. In another two or three months, it would be back to its normal length.

By noon, she was at the Fox Hills Mall, shopping. Not many things had the power to make her feel better like a few new pairs of shoes, a few new power suits, some new designer fragrance, and a new purse did. She should have a degree in shopping, seeing as how she loved it so much. Later that evening she called Braxton to get his home address because she wanted to apologize in person for getting him involved in the Mark scandal. He hadn't been thrilled about it, but was still happy to see her. Needing to be alone, she made excuses for why she couldn't linger.

When Monday morning rolled around, Neeka stepped into the office of Diva Four Cosmetics early with her head held high. The disaster of Saturday was not forgotten, but pushed aside. *Mama's always mad at one of us for something. She should be over it by now,* she mused as she made a slight adjustment to the pink silk scarf around her neck. Her dark purple suit was the perfect blend of style and comfort. Her confident stroll in her new, black leather boots made the statement, "I'm the boss's daughter. Let's keep busy."

"How's it going, Al? A beautiful day it is." Smiling, she did a little wave over at Big Al, who guarded the building's entrance. Over the monitor on his desk he stared at her like he was seeing her for the first time. Even though the slightly plump man had on his customary blue and gray uniform, when he stood up, she could see that his left foot was wrapped in a white bandage. The moment he spotted her he was on his phone.

Her day was all planned out. After she finished going over a few accounts, she'd have her secretary type up a few letters to shake up a few clients who were slow in paying. She'd check on the contract for the new account, and for lunch she'd slip away for a clandestine luncheon with Braxton out at the marina. The thought of Braxton was comforting. What they had was the budding of a good friendship, spiced with a pinch of sensual secrecy. With no strings attached, they couldn't be considered a couple. She preferred it that way.

"Good morning," she called over to a few clerks gathered at the watering hole. *Gossiping about their weekend, no doubt.* The four of them, huddled tight, looked at Neeka suspiciously but quickly went back to talking in low voices. Neeka paused outside her closed office door waiting for her secretary to hand her any messages. The cinnamon-hued girl was younger and had worked for her for about nine months. It was her very first job, but surprisingly she was good at what she did.

"Good morning, Silvie."

Silvie kept her head down, typing.

"How was your weekend? Any messages?" Still no answer. *Okay, I guess not. Perhaps she had a bad weekend too.* Neeka was shocked to find her office door locked. "What in the world . . ." She kept trying the door, but yep, it was locked up all right. Neeka never locked her office door. The employees of Diva Four were like one big family, and there was no need to. "Uh, Silvie, can you call over to maintenance? Something appears to be wrong with my door."

The girl never looked up as she typed feverishly. "That's because you don't work here anymore."

"Excuse me?" She couldn't have heard the girl correctly.

"Sorry, Miss Lebeau. I can't talk to you. Miss Adeena had someone change the locks, but I can't talk about it. Please, I need this job. I have a car note to pay." Silvie was close to tears.

"Girl, what in the world are you talking about? . . . Who told you I don't work here anymore? Who locked this door?" She tapped her boots impatiently.

"I'm sorry, Miss Lebeau. She told me not to discuss it."

"What? Who? Never mind. I'll just see about that!" Neeka turned and headed straight for Adeena's office, only to learn from the secretary that her mother wasn't in yet. If she didn't know any better Neeka would have thought the braided-hair secretary was being downright snooty. "When will she be in?"

"I suppose when she gets here, and not a minute sooner."

She walked down the hallway to Princess's office to discover that she had called in sick for the day. "This is ridiculous," she mumbled under her breath. "Where the heck are they?" She marched down to Mercy's office to find that she'd been given a few days off. "Unbelievable," she muttered. "A family conspiracy."

Neeka turned and scanned the spacious office for malicious faces. Not one face was smiling in her direction. Heads were down, like they too knew of her shame. Her fall from Adeena's grace. "Oh, so it's like that now? No one wants to talk to me? Fine! You're all a bunch of puppets waiting for my mother to pull your tired strings!" She stood there feeling too embarrassed to storm out. Finally, Big Al came over, half hobbling in her direction. He told her she had to leave. Tried to usher her away.

"Al, so help me, don't put your hands on me!"

"No need to be getting all uppity with me, Miss Neeka. Doing what I'm told, that's all. Just going through the motions."

"And you'll be going to the emergency room when I stomp my size-seven boots down on your sore foot! I'm not playing—don't touch me!" Al's dark face looked serious.

"Look." Big Al tried to reason. "The boss lady says you no longer work here. She didn't say what it was all about, and I didn't ask. All I know is you have to leave."

"No problem." Neeka held her head up high and allowed herself to be ushered to the door like some stray puppy that no one wanted anymore. She couldn't believe how childish and petty her mother was being. The minute she stopped outside, Big Al called her name. The second she turned around, frowning, he snapped a digital picture of her. Didn't even give her a chance to close her mouth. "Darn you!"

"Sorry, Miss Lebeau, I'm only doing as I'm told." Half smirking, he used a large key to lock the huge glass door and stood watching her through it.

"Who needs this stupid job anyway?" She pivoted around in time to see her SUV being pulled away by a tow truck. "Hey, wait a minute! That's my car!"

CHAPTER TWENTY-SEVEN

It's all there, little brother," Quamee said, looking very proud. "Every cent I've borrowed over the years. Didn't believe me, did you?"

"I have to admit, you amaze me. I never imagined you winning this kind of money playing some darn horses." Braxton raked his eyes over the stack of crisp one-hundred-dollar bills pyramided along his dining room table. God, he'd never seen Quamee with so much cash. Over a hundred and sixty thousand dollars in bundled bills, all brand-new. "Looks like I was wrong about you and those horses. Maybe I should take up gambling."

"Go on now," Quamee prompted with a gesture of his hand. "Count it. Don't be afraid of it. It's good money. Your money. Even threw in a little extra because you've been a real sport about the money you loaned me. Didn't hound me about it one bit."

"And it's all legit?" Braxton wanted to make sure that he wasn't being involved in something illegal. It was no secret that in the past his brother had been involved in a slick scheme or two. "No drug money, and you swear that none of it is stolen from the Mafia? They don't play. They'll break your legs clean off."

"Mafia, my foot!" Quamee pinched up his face. "Man, please. I won that money fair and square at Hollywood Park on an awesome tip. Hell, you can call up there and ask if you like. The cashier ladies know me by name right now." Seated at the table, he went back to cutting up the filet mignon Braxton had prepared. "I keep telling you that there's money to be made at the track, but you never listen."

Braxton poured hot sauce on his scrambled eggs. He looked up with a raised brow. "The racetrack?"

"No. The train track. Man you know me. I love the horses, and the horses love me. Be happy that I know what I'm doing and can pay you back. Not that you need the money."

"I am happy. I think I'm still in shock. But now that you have the means, you might want to think about investing that money." Braxton went for more orange juice. His plate in hand, he moved back toward the table, but his doorbell sounded before he could sit down.

"Something like what?"

"We can start a business together. You know, I've been telling you this for years now."

"And I've been listening. Let me kick the idea around some more."

"Man, hold up." Braxton grinned, unlocking his front door. That Quamee was something else. The man had an excuse or flip remark for everything. The thick door squeaked open to reveal a teary-eyed Neeka dressed all in purple except for a pink scarf.

"Nice boots," Braxton said. A cab pulled out from the driveway.

"I hope I didn't come at a bad time." Neeka used a tissue to dab at her red eyes.

"No, of course not. Come in. I wasn't expecting to see you until noon. What a pleasant surprise." He could see from her distraught expression that something was wrong. "I was just having some breakfast and kicking it with my brother. You remember Quamee, right?"

Neeka nodded.

Quamee stood up. "How you doing?"

"Okay, I guess." Embarrassed, Neeka turned her face away to keep him from looking at her slightly swollen eyes. "Nice seeing you again." She noticed the pile of money on the table. "You sure I haven't come at a bad time?"

"Miss Neeka, it's never a bad time for you. Have you eaten? How about some steak and eggs?" Braxton proceeded to remove the cash from the table, hand-sweeping it into a large bag. "Let me clear this table off. Here, have a seat. Relax."

Eyeing the money, she asked, "What's going on? Somebody rob a bank or something?"

"Oh, that's funny," Quamee snapped, with egg hanging from his mouth. "That's real funny."

"No. Quamee here won big at the track. Finally." Braxton pulled a chair out for her. "Have a seat. Can I get you some tea?"

"Thank you. I'm really sorry about coming by without calling first. I should know better, seeing how I hate when people do it to me." She went quiet.

"No problem," Braxton said, going for an extra plate of scrambled eggs and biscuits. He set the plate down in front of her. "I was thinking about calling you to see if you could extend your lunch break today. I have a special place in mind I wanted to show you. I can have you back at work by two." The next thing he knew, she was crying. Not soft quiet tears, but chest-heaving sobs. "Neeka? What is it? Is your mother okay?"

Quamee was looking uncomfortable. "Hey, man, check this out; I'ma split. Got my grub on. Got some business to take care of. Got some spending to do. I'll catch up with you later." He stood and headed for the door. "Nice seeing you again, Miss Neeka."

Maybe she said good-bye, maybe she didn't. Neeka couldn't think straight.

Braxton stood over her, gave a head tilt. "Thanks, Quamee. I'll talk to you later." Once the door closed behind Quamee, he turned his attention back to a distressed Neeka. "Now, tell me what's wrong."

"My lunch breaks are extended forever now that Mama hates me. She fired me!"

"She what? Fired you for what reason?"

"Because she can be petty. She even had my SUV repossessed, and when I took a cab back to my condo, the locks were changed and the windows were boarded up. She hates my guts."

"Don't be silly. Your mother loves you too much to switch just like that. Is this about that Mark guy you said was your uncle? Because if it is, Adeena's pretty upset with me too for driving the man to the church. She thinks I put you up to it."

Neeka nodded. "I didn't think she would hate me over it."

Braxton pulled up a chair and sat facing her. "I know. I tried to explain that I was doing a favor for you, but she wasn't hearing it. Said that you've been different ever since you returned from Texas, and it's my fault. It appears that I'm a bad influence on you."

"What?" She shot her attention to him. "Different how?"

"I don't know. Something about you've been acting cocky, and it's all my fault." He squared his jaw. That was only half of the story. He didn't see the sense in telling her that before Adeena had hung up the phone, she had given him strict orders: "Stay away from my family!" No problem though. He needed to concentrate more on starting his new business. "She'll probably forgive you, but thanks to you, I don't see it happening for me."

"I'm sorry I got you involved, Braxton. I don't know what to do from here. I was riding around in the cab for an hour. I didn't know where else to go."

"Don't worry about it." He got up to get a clean tissue and passed it to her. "Adeena might be pretty incensed right now, but she'll be okay. Time heals all wounds." Braxton didn't voice what he was actually thinking, that they could now be open about seeing one another.

He was crazy about Neeka but wasn't sure if the feeling was mutual. "Years from now, this whole thing will be something for your family to sit down and laugh about."

"Mama's not just mad; she's insane. I have no place to stay, and I can't get money out of my own checking account because her name is on it and the account is frozen."

"But why is that, Neeka? I mean, you're a grown woman. Why would your mother's name be on your bank account?" He waited for an answer that made sense.

Neeka's lips twitched. "The account was opened when I was thirteen. There's never been a problem with her name being on the account. For Christmas she likes to deposit money as a surprise. There was no reason not to trust my own mother—that's why. But now I can't get to my own money."

He looked incredulous. "She can do that?"

"She did, didn't she? I can't get cash out for a hotel room or a burger with fries. Can't call on my sisters because they're afraid of her. I guess I'm homeless." Neeka stopped to reflect on that word. Homeless.

"Don't be silly." Braxton took up her hand and kissed it. "I have plenty of room here until I find a buyer for this house. It's just me. I'm sure everything with your mother will be okay. In the meantime, you're more than welcome to stay here with me. But you have to promise me one thing."

"What's that?" She sniffed.

"No more lies. I don't appreciate being used like that."

"It won't happen again. I promise." She dabbed at her eyes. "I can't impose on you. I don't want to be a bother." She removed the scarf from around her neck.

"And I wouldn't have a good friend of mine staying at some sleazy motel when I have a five-bedroom house. I'll prepare the guest bedroom. You can sleep in there." Just because they'd been intimate, he didn't want her thinking that he considered her an all-you-can-eat buffet.

"You sure it's no trouble?"

"I'm positive. Now go and freshen that pretty face. No sense in sitting around here being gloomy about things we can't change for the moment. We're going out."

Neeka seemed to be having second thoughts. "I don't know."

"Don't worry," Braxton said soothingly, kissing her fingers. "I haven't forgotten our agreement. No strings attached."

CHAPTER TWENTY-EIGHT

Three hours later, after their brunch of baked fish, fresh salad, and baked potatoes, Braxton headed his panel van south on the Long Beach Freeway, got off at Ocean Boulevard, and headed for the romantic attraction known as Gondola Getaway.

"This is really nice." Neeka smiled from ear to ear as she sat back in the majestic gondola and sipped Dom Perignon. A basket of fresh French bread, cheese, and salami sat in wait.

"I made reservations a couple of days ago, but I wasn't sure if you'd be able to get away from work long enough to enjoy it."

"This is something new for me. I've been on large boats, but never a gondola. How did you find this place?" A light sea mist tingled at her face. Located on Naples Island, Gondola Getaway owned a dozen or more genuine gondolas that bobbed and floated along a half-mile stretch, each with a basket of snacks, Italian music, and a singing gondolier.

"A friend told me about it. I came out one evening and took a ride by myself. Weird, but still romantic. You're the first woman I've brought here."

"Ooh, I feel so special." She sipped.

"And you are," Braxton complimented. "Here's a toast to endless possibilities."

Neeka raised her fluted glass.

"You know, Neeka, this thing that's happened with you and your mother might not be as bad as you think. I mean, think about it. You wanted to be able to run your own life and take complete charge. Maybe this is where it starts."

Neeka said nothing, only sipped and listened.

"All things happen for a reason, that's all I'm saying. Take, for example, me driving you to Texas on business. If I hadn't done that, I never would have decided to purchase my own RV, sell my trucking business, and move to Texas. But Mrs. Perry got me to thinking about putting my sauce on the market and opening up my own restaurant."

She looked puzzled. "Mrs. who?"

"Mrs. Perry, at the presentation. Remember she gave me a card and told me to call her husband about the possibility of going into business?"

"Oh, yes. I recall that. Your barbecue sauce."

"Well, I've been talking to Mr. Perry, and let's just say that he's sounding pretty good about striking up a joint venture to get my sauce on the market. I have it all worked out in my head. I even have flight reservations for next week to scout out a place in Austin. Looks like I'll be leaving old crowded California after all."

"That's wonderful." Her head felt light. For some odd reason his good news didn't feel so good to her.

"No time soon though. A month or two from now. I don't know. I'm just saying that sometimes things happen for a reason. I may not know everything when it comes to the ways of life, but when opportunity knocks, you have to open the door."

"Here's to success." Neeka held her glass up, but her heart wasn't in it. It was hard to feel excited about Braxton's news when her own life was so down. The gondolier steering the graceful vessel behind them started a new song. His melodious voice floated above them.

"One thing I do know, I feel good when I'm around you." He turned to kiss her, a peck to her cheek before his mouth sought hers. "And I've been doing a lot of thinking about you . . . about us, actually. I was thinking that if I did relocate to Texas, how nice it would be to have an assistant. Someone by my side."

Neeka gazed into his eyes. "What exactly are you trying to say?"

"I'm saying that you could come with me. We could be a team. You could work for me. I probably can't pay you the kind of money your mother was paying, at least not starting off. But perhaps later I could, when the business starts turning a profit."

"Sounds like we'd be a couple." Neeka turned her eyes away to look at some seagulls overhead. She was amazed at how such large birds could glide in the sky.

"Would that be the worst thing that could happen to you?"

"Braxton, we've talked about this before. You know I can't."

"Neeka, yes, you can. We can do this. It feels so right to me. I think it feels right to you too. I think you know that I'm crazy about you. Tell me one good reason why we can't be a couple. Once we're settled in Texas, who would know?"

Neeka drew a weary breath and exhaled it slowly. She closed her eyes for a few seconds. There was no doubt that when she was with him she felt safe. She felt respected and cared about. But at the same time, the thought of her mother meeting him first, picking him out to be her husband . . . She couldn't seem to get beyond it. "I can't be with you like that."

"Not if you keep fighting it. Neeka, I know you feel something for me. You can't admit it, but I can feel it when I'm around you." He sat his empty glass down and faced her. "I was afraid to tell you this at first, but I'm in love with you. I knew you were special when I sent those roses to you on your thirteenth birthday. I couldn't tell you then because I didn't know how."

"Braxton, please . . . don't."

"And then when I laid eyes on you again, that day at your condo, seeing those big brown legs of yours dancing with that towel around you. I swear before God, you were so beautiful to me." He paused and shook his head. "I can't help how I feel. The more I'm around you, the more—"

"I can't marry you, Braxton."

"I didn't ask you to. But if I did, what would be so bad about marrying me? What's so terribly wrong with me?"

"Nothing. I mean, everything. No. I mean it's not really you; it's Mama. Don't you see? If we married, she wins. Mama wins, Braxton! I do care about you, but you just don't understand what I've been dealing with for so long. I can't let her win. I won't let her!"

"Neeka, you're not making sense. You keep saying how you want to make your own decisions for your life, so what's stopping you?"

"It makes sense to me, so please don't push me on it. I have enough stress right now." Stubbornly, she looked away.

"Alright. If you say so." He took up the bottle of champagne and poured himself another glass. The gondolier was singing his head off in an exquisite operatic voice.

Braxton felt like a fool for opening up to her and telling her how he felt. *Another stupid and foolish move.* He took two large gulps, and his drink was gone. "You say you want to be in control of your own life, Neeka. Your mother isn't speaking to you, and thanks to you, she's not speaking to me either. Yet you still worry about what she might think or how she feels. So tell me, Neeka, who's winning now?"

CHAPTER TWENTY-NINE

That woman is the most stubborn person I have met in my entire life!" Neeka slammed the phone down in its cradle. She had been calling Adeena for three weeks now. Either Sarah, the housekeeper, answered and informed her that her mother wasn't accepting phone calls, or the answering service picked up and recorded her message. So far she'd left two dozen messages, and still Adeena hadn't returned a call.

"You'd think my sisters would be more concerned." She had tried calling Princess, but there was no answer there either. She left Braxton's phone number and address on Mercy's answering machine, hoping she'd at least bring her mail over since she lived right next door. "I could be dying for all they know. What kind of mother just stops caring about her own child like this?" She tightened the sash on her black silk robe.

"I wouldn't know," Quamee said. "I never knew my real mother."

Neeka looked over to where Quamee and Braxton sat playing chess. Her stay at Braxton's place wouldn't be so bad if it weren't for Quamee coming over every other day. She didn't have anything against the man except for the fact that he smoked like a chimney, told tall tales, cursed like a sailor, and talked entirely too much. They may have been raised as brothers, but thank God, the two were as different as night and day. "The way I feel now, knowing one's real mother isn't all it's cracked up to be," she said.

"Stop being impatient," Braxton told her between mouthfuls of popcorn. "Adeena will come around in due time. She's probably worried about you too."

"If she is, she's certainly not acting like it. I could be living in a cardboard box in an alley for all she knows. I should call a cab and go over there."

"Don't," Braxton advised, keeping his eyes on the board. "She might not let you in her house. What's the point? She's upset right now, and you can't blame her. The trick is to give a person time to miss you. Then she'll be happy to see you."

"It's like they say," Quamee announced, "absence makes the damn heart grow fonder. Had this lady friend one time that I didn't call or visit for a whole month. Hell, when I finally did step to her place, you would have thought I was some kind of celebrity."

"Yeah, you right. And that house of hers is like Fort Knox once the windows and doors are locked." Neeka sauntered over to the table to watch them. "I just think that this has gone on long enough. I need to get back to my job and my own condo." It was Saturday morning, and already she'd been staying in Braxton's spare bedroom for three weeks. While it was a comfortable arrangement, she knew it wasn't permanent. Braxton had proceeded with his business plans by selling both his home and his trucking business. With everything in escrow, Neeka knew it was all a matter of time now and something had to give. "I feel so in limbo," she said.

"You're doing fine," Braxton assured her. "When your mom misses you, she'll come looking."

Neeka blew out an aggravated sigh. "You obviously don't know my mother very well." Still, she felt grateful. Braxton was such a sport about everything, even going out of his way to make her stay as pleasurable as possible. Perhaps a little too out of his way when he slipped into her bed at night to keep her warm. Heck, if it hadn't been for him taking her shopping, she wouldn't have clean underwear or casual clothes to put on. Once she got access to her account, she planned to reimburse him for every dime he'd spent. "I don't know where Mercy could be. I'll try her number again later." She picked up the ashtray where Quamee had a cache of butts. "How about some sandwiches?" Later she would show off her culinary skills with braised leg of lamb and mushroom risotto. Maybe a nice salad. Cooking was her way of relaxing.

"Sounds great." Braxton was concentrating on his chess game. "Some soda would be nice too. If you don't mind."

"Of course I don't mind." She found herself doing a lot of cooking and cleaning lately to earn her keep. She had the notion that if she stayed busy, she wouldn't have so much time to think about the mess she made with her family. "Two turkey sandwiches and two Diet Cokes coming right up."

Mercy showed up at Braxton's place around two dressed in a short wig, dark glasses, and a long black leather coat. "It's so like you not to call first," Neeka said when she opened the door and found her standing there. "Dang, Mercy, where have you been? I've been ringing you like crazy!"

Mercy did a quick look behind her before stepping inside. "I've been to the Bahamas, thanks to Mother. She's been awfully generous lately. I just got back yesterday. Then I had to wait until the coast was clear." She looked around like she was casing the place. "Here's all your mail. I had to take the long way to get here. I thought I was being followed." She removed her coat. "Mother has spies all over the place.

And right now, fraternizing with you would be like George Bush sitting down and breaking bread with Saddam Hussein."

"Hey, Mercy," Braxton said, walking back into the den with a bowl of popcorn. "Care for some lunch? We have sandwiches."

Neeka closed the door and waved Mercy to a seat.

"No, thank you," Mercy replied, eyeing Braxton's attire of brown silk lounging pants, his matching shirt open. A chest full of dark curly hair. "I'm not horny . . . I mean hungry. I'm not hungry." She pulled a chair to the table, then snatched off her short wig. Bouncy curls tumbled to her shoulders. "Mother hired a temp to do your job, but it's not working out. She's been on the warpath, and she needs you at work. You know how stubborn she can be."

Neeka huffed. "If she needs me, you would think she'd call my cell. For all she knows, I could be sleeping in a trash bin every night. Honestly, I can understand being fired and her taking the car back, but locking me out of my own condo is going a bit too far."

"Nee, you know how Mother is. She's the queen of control. Why do you think she continues to pay the note on our condos when she could have paid all three off and bought three more for the fun of it? It's all about control. And having too much pride don't help. You two need to sit down and talk. This whole thing is ridiculous."

"She's not the one being punished." Neeka folded her arms and pouted.

"But I see you not doing too bad. Look at you, all glowing and all. Living in sin becomes you." She nodded over to Quamee staring at her. "Hello."

"I have to live someplace. Oh, I'm sorry . . . Quamee, you remember Mercedes? Mercy, I'm sure that you remember Braxton's brother, Quamee." The man could at least close his mouth while staring. Act like he's never seen a pretty woman in tight jeans before.

"Don't pay Quamee no mind," Braxton said, studying his next move. "I think he's too pleased to get to see you again."

"I think Mother is ready to come around now that there's a more pressing matter on the table."

Neeka was all ears. "What kind of matter would be more pressing than my being shut out of the family?"

"Prin's pregnancy."

"Oh, no." Neeka made a face. "You mean she really is?"

"Didn't I tell you? I knew it. Anyway, Princess broke down and told Mother. Mother screamed and fussed. She hooped and hollered, and then she got over it. I mean, what else can she do? She wanted a grandchild, and she'll be getting her wish. Who cares how the child came to be?"

"That's . . . wow." Neeka couldn't decide whether she felt glad or sad.

"Neeka, get dressed," Mercy ordered, putting her dark glasses back on. "I'll drive you to Mother's house. Enough is enough."

"What for? So she can slam the door on my foot?" Neeka stood looking stubborn, but she knew it wouldn't work with Mercy. That girl could be as persistent as Adeena.

"If the mountain won't come to you, Nee, you have to go to the mountain. Get dressed."

"Mercy, Mama don't want to see me."

"But do you want to see her?"

Neeka hung her head. "You know I do. This whole thing has been a nightmare. I feel awful."

"Get dressed then. I have to go there anyway to pick up something. Once I'm in the house, I'll let you in. No worry. Sarah can't stop me, and if she tries, I will slap the black off her!"

Two hours later, Mercy opened the rear door of Adeena's house and let Neeka in through the servants' entrance. "Now, girl, Mother is in her bedroom. You go on up there and get this mess resolved. Cry, plead, beg, pray. Whatever it takes. Tell her you're not leaving this house until the two of you make up. Go on now."

"Thanks, sis." Neeka took the stairs two at a time and headed for Adeena's master suite. Sarah was on the first floor doing laundry. Even with two other bodies in the house, the place felt empty, like a place she didn't belong in. She found the door to Adeena's suite slightly ajar. She stood for a few seconds gathering her composure. Like most Saturdays, her mother loved to lounge in bed, with Sarah waiting on her head to foot. She found Adeena propped up in the massive bed, sharp scissors in hand, cutting out pictures for a collage.

"Mama."

Adeena looked up. A pinched look came to her face, but after a second or two dissipated. "Neeka. Why are you here?"

So far so good. Nothing thrown in her direction. Neeka eased into the room, came closer, then took it upon herself to roll the wingback chair next to Adeena's bed. Neither spoke for a few seconds.

"I had to see you, Mama." She touched her mother's hand gently. "I can't stand for things to be like this between us. I can't. I don't know how many times I can say I'm sorry and that I was wrong."

"How did you get in this house?" Adeena placed the scissors down. Her eyes narrowed. "Did Sarah let you in?"

"No, Mercy did. But don't be mad at her."

"You shouldn't be here. There's nothing for us to talk about."

"Why, because you hate me now?" Neeka took up the scissors. She aimed the sharp end to her chest on target with her heart. "Here, Mama. If you hate me so much, you might as well take my life. Go ahead, take it!"

"Neeka, stop this foolishness."

"If you can't forgive me, do it! Go ahead, Mama, just do it!" She lifted Adeena's hand. Placed them on the scissors. Warm tears streamed down her face. "The Bible says that God forgives us for all our sins. But if you can't forgive me for this one thing, Mama, I'd rather go be with the Lord." She allowed the tears to flow.

"I will do no such thing! You stop this nonsense now!" Snatching the scissors, Adeena tossed them to the plush carpet. Neeka lay her head in Adeena's lap. "You crazy child of mine. I don't hate you. You're my flesh and blood. I could never do that. The things I said to you, I said because I was upset. Upset at you and . . . upset at myself. . . ."

"Mama, I swear, I never meant to hurt you. I wanted you to stop trying to live my life. That's all I wanted. I have always done what you have wanted. Always. But now I'm tired. I want to do it my way now. Is that so wrong? I shouldn't have brought Mark into this."

"I know," Adeena said, "and I should have told you girls about Mark years ago, but I thought I was doing the right thing by keeping my past in the dark."

"No one has a right to judge you. No one."

"That's how it should be, but unfortunately, Neeka, life isn't like that. My own mother never forgave me for having a child out of wedlock." Adeena looked off, tears in her eyes, reflecting. "I was fifteen. Young and stupid. Didn't know a thing about sex until . . . Anyway, when Mother Deedee found out I was pregnant, it seemed to take all the life out of her. She took to her bed and stayed there. She was a preacher's wife you know. Well-known and respected."

"I know," Neeka said quietly, but truly she didn't know enough about her grandmother. Many times when she had tried to ask about her, it seemed to be subject that her mother didn't care to elaborate on.

"She said that if I didn't agree to a termination, she didn't want to live." Adeena paused, staring into space before looking down at her hands. "I couldn't kill my baby. I just couldn't."

"Mama, you don't have to talk about this if you don't want to."

"I was so afraid. My own father stopped speaking to me. I found out later that Mother Deedee had been right. Sin could change your life. Two weeks after Mark was born, my mother passed away peacefully in her sleep. The doctors couldn't find a reason for her passing. I gave Mark up for adoption. Daddy never told a soul and neither did I. I didn't start looking for Mark until I was married to your father. Mark and I always kept in touch."

"You were young, Mama. Even devout Christian girls sometimes have relations with men. Granny should have been more understanding." Neeka had a vague recollection of her grandmother. What little she knew came from photos, as well as bits and pieces of stories her mother had tried sharing when it wasn't so painful. "No one is perfect in life."

"I know," Adeena said sadly. Her lips trembled. "But my mother never forgave me. And then there's Princess. I thought we could talk about anything, but my own daughter was afraid to tell me she was with child. Afraid to tell me! I don't know. Maybe I haven't been a good mother after all."

"Mama, please," Neeka said quietly, "you've been the best. We just grew up, that's all."

"I see."

The room was quiet for a spell before Adeena said. "Looks like my job is finally done. My baby birds are ready to soar."

The two talked long into the night. Around midnight, Neeka took a cab back to Braxton's place. She was emotionally tired and a little hungry, but at least her mother was speaking to her again. It was a pleasant surprise to see Braxton waiting up for her on the sofa.

"How'd it go?" he asked, stretching his lithe body. The television played on mute.

"We're not ready to sit down and break bread yet, but she's talking to me. She's planning a big family dinner next week. Brother Mark will be back down, so we all can sit down and talk. You know, get to know one another."

"Sounds great," Braxton said, fighting off a yawn. "It's a start."

"It really is. I'm glad I let Mercy talk me into going to Mama's place. I got to see a side of my mother I never knew existed. She's just like everyone else, vulnerable. And then we prayed. Well, she prayed for me."

"Didn't I tell you it would all work out?"

Neeka took a deep breath. "I should be able to get back in my place in a few days. Have my job back too. Might even get a new car."

"If that's what you really want." He aimed the remote and clicked the television off.

Neeka caught the change in his mood right away. The room was suddenly cold. "Don't be silly, Braxton. Of course it's what I want. You've been more than generous, but I can't live off you forever."

"And why not? I'm not the one trying to control your life, Neeka. And personally, I don't have a problem with you living here. In fact, I'm liking it. But the ball's in your court now. Whatever you decide."

"Sounds like somebody might get to missing my good cooking." Neeka put her purse down and moved over to the sofa, sat along the edge. "You know the answer. The longer I stay here, it goes against our rule of no strings attached. That's why." She kissed his forehead. "We can still see one another. I mean, if you still want to."

"And what would be the point if it can never go any further?" He looked away like he couldn't bear looking into her eyes.

Neeka made a face. *What in the world has gotten into this man?* "Why all this attitude, Braxton? Isn't this how 'no strings attached' goes?"

"Oh, yeah," Braxton said, keeping a straight face. "No strings attached. You're right. We wouldn't want to break that rule."

CHAPTER THIRTY

Mercy held her flute of sparkling apple juice up to her lips. "You think Braxton will come?"

"Not if he wasn't invited." The mere mention of his name made Neeka's heart pound. She took a sip of her Cristal to steady herself. She hadn't seen or talked to Braxton in the three weeks since she moved back into her own place. They'd both agreed that it was better to stop torturing one another with a relationship that couldn't go any further. Unfortunately, Neeka couldn't get him out of her mind. His adventurous eyes, the safe feel of being in his arms. The way he had kissed her, like his kiss alone could make the whole world a better place. "Plus, Mama says I should stay away from him. Says he's a bad influence."

"Nee, please. We are grown-assed women. That old woman need a man in her life so she can stop trying to run ours. It's not fair for her to blame Braxton for Mark being at that darn dedication. He only drove him there because you asked him to."

"Mercy, don't you think I know that?" Neeka pretended to pick pieces of lint from her off-white pantsuit. Thank God she had had the presence of mind to bring a change of clothes for the wedding reception. "Apparently it's not just that. She insist that I haven't been myself since the Texas trip, and that Braxton is putting too many wrong ideas in my head."

"I know one thing," Mercy lamented, dabbing at her ringlets. "The next time that old woman hits me, it's on. I don't care whose mama she is. When I get through dusting the floor with her behind, she'll need plastic surgery to reshape it."

That was something to laugh at. "Okay. And I'll make sure the ambulance has your correct address." From the window of the Lake Perris house Neeka could see the mingling wedding guests. Most were gathered along the huge floating platform, surrounded by floating lights that bobbed and swayed. Dance music floated up to the master bedroom window where they gazed out. Despite Princess's swollen-with-child physique, she looked radiant in her off-white wedding dress of satin and pearls. Mercy wasn't doing so bad in her vanilla crème gown. However, her pushed-up cleavage was a bit risqué. "I'm surprised Mama didn't ask you to wear a sweater to cover up those puppies."

"What? My weapons of mass attention?" Mercy used one hand to push at her heaven-bound bosom. "Forget it. She can go lay an egg because if I'm to quit drinking, I have to take up something else in its place. Like more sex. I need these babies to help me find a new man to cherish them."

"You are so crazy."

"But seriously, about Braxton being a bad influence. That's Mother's opinion. How do you feel, Nee?"

"God, I don't believe I'm saying this, but I really miss him. Braxton is like no one I've met before." She heaved a sigh. "I don't know. He has this cocky way about him. Like he just don't give a darn what other people think. He does what he wants when he wants. Careful, unpretentious. I like that about him."

"You like—or you love?" Mercy sipped and studied her sister's face. Neeka lowered her gaze, shook her head. "Makes no difference now. I'm just trying to keep the peace with Mama. That's what's important right now. Making amends for what I did in digging up Mark."

"It wasn't so bad. You know your mama is a drama queen. I mean, look how it all turned out. Mama's dream of a December wedding came true. Prin married her baby daddy. We now know about Mark, and he's getting to know us too. Look at him out there cutting a few steps." They both went silent, gazing out from the second floor. "Hell, for an old dude, he can dance."

"He is nice, isn't he?" Watching from the window, Neeka could see that the wedding reception was in full bloom. A December night was closing in. Christmas decorations were methodically mixed with wedding decor, flowers, lights, balloons, red-berried holly. Mostly white and red. Small boats sailed guests back and forth across the lake to the floating platform, the center of the reception. A few guests chose to float along in private conversations, a single, lit boat dotting the darkness.

Mercy heaved a sigh. "Such imagination Mother has. I never would have thought of renting private boats for a wedding reception two weeks before Christmas. You have to give it to her. That ole gal has vision and taste."

"And I'm surprised she didn't order a Christmas tree for the wedding."

"What makes you think she didn't?" Mercy asked with a sly grin. "It's downstairs in the living room."

"Whatever it takes. I'm just glad Mama's back to her old self again. I have my job back, my condo back, my SUV. I opened a bank account in my own name and moved my money, just in case. One big happy family again. That's all I need."

"Neeka," Mercy said, turning serious again. "We all love Mother. But we have our own lives to live too. I've seen you and Braxton together. You two have chemistry. Chemistry is something that some of us never find with a mate. So what if your mother picked him out. Don't go by that. Go by what you feel here." She patted a spot over her heart.

"I know," Neeka said quietly. It was a time when she should feel happy. Her baby sister was now married to Deacon Horteese, the baby's father. And her mother would finally be getting what she had been wanting all alone, a grandbaby to spoil. Not the pick of a son-in-law, but her first grandchild. Goodness, she was going to be an aunt herself. It was a warm thought. But at the same time, melancholy kept running its hands over her heart. "What about you? How you holding up, with the man you had your eye on marrying your baby sister? How you feeling about that?" A weak smile tugged at Neeka's lips. *Looks like everyone is getting what they need or want except me.* Trouble was, she wasn't sure what she wanted.

Mercy's expression went from mild to intense. "Girl, when I first learned that man, the Deacon, had slept with my own sister, I wanted to choke all the whore juice out of him. We actually dated a couple of times. Thank God he didn't get to the booty, but it was coming." She stopped to make a face. "Eeeww. Every time I think of it, I want to puke. That dog! And with my own sister knowing I had my eyes on Deacon Horteese, it was a stab in the back."

"Mercy, please. You have your eyes on every man you see."

"I'm telling you, when I realized who the baby daddy was, I wanted to put her anorexic behind over my knees and pound on her bottom until that baby popped out! That's how I felt! Damn her!"

"Dang. I'm glad you're happy for her." Neeka stared at her like she was crazy. "That *is* happiness you're experiencing, right?"

"Oh, yeah," Mercy piped up, "in my own jealous-as-hell kind of way. I love my baby sister." She gulped her juice. "And if that Deacon whore ends up dogging her out and hurting her, I will hunt him down and kill him. Well, maybe not kill him, but hire somebody to tie him up and beat the bottom of his feet with bamboo sticks."

"Good thing it's apple juice in that glass."

"I know. I'm through with drinking. I thought about joining a support group to help me along, but I have all the support I need right here with my family, the church, and prayer. First we crawl; then we walk. I tell you, sis, I feel so much better already."

Neeka fought back a tear. "Good for you, Mercy. I'm so proud of you. I know you can do it."

Mercy heaved. "I'm proud of me too. But enough of talking dreary. Let's get down to the party and show those folks that good Christian girls can shake a tail feather too."

"Shake what?"

"Dance, Neeka. It means to dance."

"Oh, okay. I'm right behind you."

From the lake-house dock they took one of many small boats over to the main festivities. Couples danced to slow music as wine stewards weaved perilously between them, with trays laden with the finest champagne and wine. Watching guests in small private boats out on the water made Neeka think of Braxton and their gondola ride. What was he doing? How was he feeling? Was he missing her?

"This is all so nice." Mercy beamed, standing beside her, taking it all in. "You have to give it to Mother; she knows how to handle a wedding."

Neeka nodded in agreement. "Just think, instead of Prin, this could have been my wedding. Braxton's and mine."

"It's not too late." Mercy watched for a reaction.

The statement made Neeka spill some champagne on her blouse. "He's a good guy to have for a friend. But—"

"But what, Nee?"

"He needs a wife. Someone to be his life partner. I guess I'm not ready to be somebody's wife. Plus, he's selling his house and trucking company and heading out of state. I doubt if I'll ever see him again." For some odd reason she couldn't explain, the thought of him being so far away from her was painful. The day she'd packed up her few items and went back to her condo, he'd made his good-bye kiss seem like it was absolutely the last. They both had agreed that a relationship against a brick wall was futile. That was twenty-one days ago, and every time she thought about him, which was three times a day—morning, noon, and night—she couldn't deny that she missed him. "I should at least call to say good-bye, huh?" *What harm would it do to call him?* No. Why torture herself more?

"Of course." Mercy finished her juice. "That's what a good friend would do." She looked around for a steward so she could request another glass of apple juice but reminded herself that she was overloading on carbs and her hips would pay for it later.

"I left my phone at the house. You have your cell?"

Mercy opened her silver-sequined clutch. "Here, Nee-nee. Knock yourself out. I don't know about you, but I hear my song playing. Excuse me while I go get my grove on."

Neeka dialed Braxton's cell-phone number and stood at the platform railing. Lake water glistened under a full moon. The more the phone rang, the more she lost her nerve. What was she doing? Why call the man if they couldn't be together? If she could just talk to him one last time. Even if it *was* to say good-bye. Maybe she was too late. Her nerve lost, she hung up.

Just call the man! Neeka pressed redial. The phone rang three times. "Good grief. Where could he be?" A finger tapped her shoulder lightly. "Not now, please. I'm busy." Two more rings before she could hear his sexy voice on the answering service saying, "Please leave a message."

Leave a message? She squeezed her eyes shut, keeping back a flood of emotions. "Uh . . . Braxton, uh . . . This is me. Neeka. If you're there, please pick up. I'm at the wedding. About us. I just wanted to say that it's not you. It's me. You're a good man, and some woman is going to be so lucky to have . . . Uh . . . What I'm trying to say here is that despite all that's happened with us, I think you're special."

A deep voice behind her asked, "How special?"

She pulled the phone away from her ear and looked at it. "Wow, such clarity." Back to her ear. "The kind of special I'll never forget."

"I hope not, because I think you're special too."

Neeka swerved around. He had been standing right behind her, looking handsome as ever in all black, except for his caramel leather jacket, standing there all the time listening to her leave a message. And here she was blushing like a fool who should know better. "Braxton. When did you . . . I mean how long have you . . . How did you know where the wedding would be?"

"A little bird told me." His eyes engaged hers with an intensity that forced her to look away. When she looked into his face again, his look was softer. "Besides, I couldn't leave without saying good-bye."

"A little bird, you say?" Neeka gave a quick look over at a guilty-faced Mercy, who turned her head away while doing some dance like the funky chicken. "Like mother, like daughter."

Looking around, Braxton said, "This would have been a magnificent wedding for us. I'm impressed." He took her hand up. Kissed the back of it. "Now, what were you saying on the phone?"

Suddenly tongue-tied, Neeka said, "I . . . uh . . . I just wanted you to know that I think you're a special guy."

"But not special enough for you to come with me?"

She chose not to answer his inquiry. "You won't be that far away. I don't see why two good friends can't stay in touch. When will you be leaving?"

"My things are packed in my van as we speak. The rest will be shipped by Quamee once I'm settled in. Can't wait any longer. Found a nice house already. I can move in in about three weeks. In the meantime I'll be staying at a nice hotel. I meet with Mr. Perry on Monday about our business venture. They'll be calling me the barbecue sauce king before it's all over."

Neeka felt her heart slump. "I see."

"Neeka, I really wish you would reconsider my offer and come with me. We'd make a great team. I'll provide the financial backing for the restaurant. You have the business savvy. It can work."

Something inside her wanted to say yes. But she couldn't. "Braxton, you make it sound so easy, but you know I can't."

Somewhere on the opposite side of the platform small cages of white butterflies were being released into the night sky. They both looked up at the same time to watch a white cloud of fluttery wings rise in flight. The music played louder. Glasses were clinking, laughter rode the air.

"Look," he said, "I know I can't provide for you like your mother can, but I'll do my best to make sure you never want for anything." He pulled out a small golden box and held it out. "I won't lie about it. I do want more."

Neeka stood looking at the box in his hand. Fanning her face, Mercy left her dancing partner and hightailed it over. "He bought you a ring? Oh, my God. He's proposing!" It looked like Mercy wanted to take the box from Braxton's hand the way she was squirming and making faces. "It's the ring. He bought the ring. Neeka; this is serious here. I knew it. Girl, you better take that box. Take the box!"

When Neeka didn't go for it, Mercy said, "Girl, your mama didn't raise no fool. Here!" She took it upon herself to take the box and open it. But she looked crestfallen as she reached in and pulled out one piece of golden string. A loop was tied at each end. Mercy held it up. "What the heck . . . Is this some kind of freaky thing between you two?"

Braxton chuckled, but Neeka didn't think it was so funny. "Mercy, will you please leave us alone?"

"Sorry about that. Continue on." Passing the box and string to Braxton, Mercy hurried back to her dance partner just as a slow song started.

"Braxton, I am so sorry; that girl—"

"Don't worry about it," Braxton said. He placed one end of the string on one of his right fingers, the other end on Neeka's left finger. "This is to symbolize what I need. I think you need it too."

"Braxton, how many times can I say it? I—"

"Dance with me."

Neeka let her defenses down as soft music swayed them. His cologne was a clean and woodsy mixture to her senses. The sound of his heartbeat was in her ear, steady and soothing. She closed her eyes with a feeling that she could stay in his arms all night. So warm, so inviting.

"Excuse me, Neeka. I want you to meet Mr. Wallace King."

Her mother would have to show up at this moment to break the spell. *Goodness. If it's not Mercy, it's Mama. What is it with these women?* Braxton was trying to be courteous by speaking to her mother, but Adeena wasn't speaking back. "Mama, please. Can't you see I'm busy with Braxton right now?"

Adeena cleared her throat. "You mean the same Braxton who cut your hair off and tried to fill your half-bald head with nonsense about going against your own mother? Or would it be the Braxton who conspired to shame me at my own dedication service?"

Braxton flashed his sexy smile in spite of Adeena's words. "It's always nice to see you too, Mother Lebeau. You're looking beautiful in pink, as always."

"Neeka, please advise Mr. Dupree to save his flattery for someone it might work on. And do inform him that he was not invited to this function. If he refuses to leave on his own, security can be here in one minute."

"Mama, he's not a French poodle I can tell what to do. Stop behaving like this." Neeka gave Wallace King a good looking-over. In his black business suit and with his salt-and-pepper hair, he was definitely distinguished-looking. Aged handsome, the man looked old enough to be her father. "Nice to meet you, Mr. King."

"Neeka, don't worry about it," Braxton said, removing the string from his finger. He straightened his soft leather jacket before giving a quick kiss to her forehead. "I guess this is where I get off. Neeka, I wish you and your family the best."

"Good-bye, Braxton. And good luck with your new business." Neeka swallowed hard as she stood watching him walk down to the docking platform. Watched as he climbed in one of two boats heading back to shore. She could feel the burn of missing him heating her chest. Something was tugging at her heart. She refused to cry. She had played hard-to-get, and now the game was over. Just like that. She looked at Adeena standing next to her, another man for her to meet at her side. The thought was depressing.

"Neeka, sweetie, Mr. King here is single, has his own successful plumbing business."

"That's nice, Mama."

"He's had one bad experience with marriage, but he's still looking."

"That's wonderful, Mama."

"There just aren't enough good girls in the world today. Isn't that right, Mr. King?"

She wasn't listening to a word her mother was saying. Only the echo in her head. *Staying will bring the same. Same job. Same mother. Same drama.*

"Are you listening, dear?" Adeena turned to Mr. King. "My Neeka here can cook up a storm. Never been married and has no children. Not to say that she don't like children. Quite the contrary."

"Mama, please shut up!" This woman was impossible. Just when Neeka had settled into thinking that things would be different between them. Obviously her mother was back to her old tricks. One insane moment Neeka was feeling okay. Now her head felt cloudy, and her breath felt like it didn't want to come. "I am sick and I am tired of you and what you think I should be doing with my life! This is my damn life, Mother! Mine!"

"Neeka, how dare you speak to me like that! What's gotten into you?"

Mr. King was looking at her like she was a filet mignon on a plate. "Let's all calm down. Miss Neeka, perhaps we can share lively conversation over dinner."

"I'm sure she'd love that," Adeena said. "Wouldn't you, Neeka? She's probably tired with all that's been going on. It's not that she's dating anyone of significance right now. So many men prefer the wild and worldly women and overlook the ones with a good Christian upbringing."

Neeka silenced her with a finger to her lips. "Speaking of good girls, Mama. I think this is about as good as it gets. I'd love to stay and chat, but if you'll excuse me, I believe I have a man to catch. And yes, Mama, his name is Braxton!"

Insulted, Adeena scoffed, "I beg your pardon, young lady. You will do no such thing."

"Oh no? Watch me, Mama!" She searched anxiously for an available boat. There was none. Neeka tried calling out Braxton's name from the busy platform. Above the volume of the music, it was impossible to be heard. She headed toward the launching dock where a narrow bridge connected the platform to land. Not an empty boat in sight. If she didn't get away from her mother as soon as possible, she didn't know what she'd do. Her breathing felt so weird, like her heart would stop at any second. *Breathe! I will not let her keep doing this to me!*

Adeena was coming after her, yelling, "You come back here right this minute, young lady!" A few wedding guests stopped partying to gawk. Mercy left her new friend's side to see what was going on. By the time Princess caught on to the commotion, Neeka was removing her shoes, unbuttoning her short jacket, and climbing the railing of the platform to execute a perfect dive. "Neeka, you stop this nonsense right this minute!"

Panic-faced at her mother's side, Princess asked, "Mommie, what's going on?"

"Where's my camera? Your sister has lost her mind!"

Mercy smirked. "Or found her heart." Then seeing that some of the guests were doing it, she joined in to cheer her sister on. "You go, girl! You love that man, you go get him!"

Adeena shot her a stern look.

"That's right, Mother. I said it!"

The three stood along the platform watching Neeka swim like her life depended on it until she reached the boat Braxton was in. Braxton wasted no time pulling her from the water into the boat.

"Goodness gracious, woman! Why would you jump into the water? I could have turned this boat around to get you. Why would you do that?" He could hear her teeth chattering, prompting him to take off his coat. He draped it around her shoulders. "Say something. Neeka?"

"Take too long." Her teeth chattered more. Cold ran up and down her spine. But she didn't care.

He had to shake his head and grin. Living with a woman like her certainly wouldn't be dull. "Does this mean you'll be going with me to help start the new business?"

Neeka nodded her head in response. "I . . . I just have two things to say."

"What, baby? Talk to me."

"Yes, I'll go. And damn that water is cold."

He pulled her in for a hug. "You are one crazy woman, but I love your crazy behind."

Neeka snuggled to his warm chest. It was the best feeling she'd ever felt.

"I love you too."

EPILOGUE

Neeka!" Mercy screamed at the top of her voice. "Over here. Toss it to me!"

The reception was in full bloom in the commodious backyard of Mr. and Mrs. Braxton Dupree's new home. A set-up fit for a queen. After weeks of agonizing over a big wedding or a small wedding, Neeka and Braxton opted for a small gathering of immediate family, some friends, and a few distant relatives. Less stress was the main objective.

"Will you please stop screaming at me!" Nudging and pushing women were at her back, awaiting the age-old tradition of the toss. With pure sunlight streaming down on her head, the bridal bouquet clutched tight in her hands, Neeka closed her eyes and counted to five. Then she heaved her cache of flowers high into the Texas air. "Catch it, Mercy! Girl, catch it!" She turned around just in time to be disappointed by the sight of Adeena hip-bumping Mercy out of the way and claiming the prize. *Almost bumped that girl to the grass. Unbelievable.*

"That's not fair," moaned one of Neeka's young female cousins who had flown in for the wedding. The young woman stood looking hurt. She knew better than to make an issue with Adeena.

"Baby, all is fair in love and war," Adeena admonished, smoothing down her off-white dress. "Maybe next time for you." Dabbing at her upswept hair, she winked.

Looking scorned, Mercy was rubbing the side of her hip where Adeena had bumped it. "Goodness, Mother. You almost fractured my hip."

"Oh, stop your panty-whining. Mother will buy you a new hip when we get back to Los Angeles." Adeena took the liberty of chuckling at her own silliness, a rare moment. She held the flowers up for inspection. "Looks like your ole mother might have to find herself a new husband." Then on second thought she jabbed the bouquet at Mercy. "Here, child. Been there, done that. You need this more than I do."

"If you say so, Mother." Accepting, Mercy made a face the second Adeena's back was turned. They had one more day to get through while staying at Neeka and Braxton's new place, and the last thing she needed was to get on Adeena's bad side. So she put some space between them by walking over to where Quamee was sitting at one of many elegantly dressed tables. The two had become an item after meeting at Braxton's place six months back. The man had a few problems, gambling being one of them. But Mercy felt confident that if she could nip her own personal issues in the bud, she could handle Quamee's gambling. One thing she knew for certain, the man sure loved to eat.

Careful not to get food on his rented tux, Quamee held up a cocktail shrimp. "This is one beautiful wedding. Nice house too. I have to give it to my man, Braxton; they doing real good."

Before Mercy could say, "I know," Quamee guided the morsel to her mouth. "Ooh. Will you please stop feeding me? I'm stuffed." She held up the bouquet. "Look what I got."

"You know, I was thinking." Quamee regarded her with serious eyes. "Now that your sister is married to my brother, does that mean that we have to stop seeing one another? I mean, after all, we're like family now."

Mercy looked amused by his inquiry. "Fat chance," she countered, picking up a shrimp and aiming for his mouth. She followed up with a soft kiss. "Even if you were my father's mother's brother's cousin on his stepdaddy's side, we'd still be together."

"Word?" Quamee liked what he was hearing. In fact, he had been digging everything about Mercy since their reacquaintance. "That's what I'm talking about." He wanted to lay some serious lip-lock on her, but Princess came over with a fussy baby. He could tell that fatness was on its way. The woman was five weeks postpartum, and already he could see from the tight fit of her fancy white dress that her hips were taking on a healthy looking spread. "Hey. What's up?"

Princess kept rocking her precious bundle back and forth. "Trying to get this boy to sleep. I think he wants his daddy."

Mercy's eyes lit up. "Prin, let me hold him. Ahh. He's such a cutie, my little nephew. Hey, Tiker. It's auntie." Spotting her grandson, Adeena hurried over, as usual, to take charge. Mark was right behind her.

"Mercy, it's Tyler," Princess corrected. "Tyler Rashad Horteese. He's a bit cranky right now because his daddy couldn't make the trip. He miss his daddy."

"He'd better get used to it." Mercy rolled her eyes.

"Mercy, you be nice. Today is Nee-nee's day. We don't need you spoiling it," Adeena said.

"Mother, you know I'm just teasing,"

"Better be." Adeena's halfhearted frown turned to a smile as she held her arms out for her grandson. "Here, give him to me. Isn't he precious? The first grandchild gets to be spoiled the most. Yes, he does. And look at you. Such a good boy. Yes, you are."

Princess watched on with adoration, while Mercy looked on like she felt sick to her stomach. It wasn't everyday she witnessed this side of her mother, ogling and cooing over a baby. She leaned in to whisper in Quamee's ear. "This is too much. What a change from being the beast master."

"Mommie, don't rock 'im too fast."

"Prin, hush. You act like I don't know about babies." Adeena followed her chide-up with a mock frown. "After birthing four, I should know a thing or two."

"We need to give thanks for all the good things that have happened to us."

"Like what, Prin?" Mercy asked as Braxton and Neeka strolled over to join them.

"Everything. With all we've gone through. How it brought us closer. I'll go first," said Princess, sounding every bit a grown-up woman. "I'm thankful for having a family that loves and understands me now. Each one of you. You give me strength when I feel weakness trying to claim me. A loving husband. A healthy baby. I'm thankful for that." She paused to look at Mercy. "And you, sis?"

Mercy cleared her throat. "Knowing when it's time to make changes that enhance your life instead of tearing it down. I'm thankful for that. And even though we fuss and fight sometimes, I know that deep down we all love one another with a passion. That's what I'm truly thankful for." She looked over to Mark, who seemed a bit shy about speaking.

"I'm just thankful to be here among you good people. The chance to know my real family. I feel blessed."

All eyes went to Adeena.

"This is what I'm thankful for." Adeena held the baby up. "And to be blessed with four beautiful children who have shown me that it's okay to cut the strings now." She dabbed at her eye. "That's enough to be thankful for."

The photographer waved them over.

"Come on, everybody," Braxton announced. "We'll all be crying in a minute. I think the photographer needs the immediate family members for pictures." Neeka was right behind him, admiring how debonair and handsome he looked in his off-white tux. The hem of her matching sequin-and-satin gown had to be lifted for her to walk properly. Braxton turned to wrap his arm around Neeka's slender waist. He couldn't resist a kiss from his beautiful bride. One quick one, then another one lingering at her lips.

Adeena handed Tyler back to his mother. "Alright you two. You'll have plenty of time for all that later. You know how I feel about taking pictures. Photography is time and money, so let's get to posing."

"Oh, wait. Let me run and freshen my face." Neeka made a beeline for the sliding French door of the four-bedroom brick house. It warmed her that Braxton had found the perfect house. It was nothing close to, nor as big and fancy as, Adeena's house, but it was all theirs—and paid for in full. "Be right back. Don't you guys dare start without me."

"I'll be right back," Princess said. "Tyler needs to be freshened up."

"Don't forget to tell Quamee," Mercy called behind her. "He's family too."

Adeena turned to Braxton. She looped her arm through his and guided him away from the prying ears. "Thank the Lord you two did the right thing. Took long enough, but being married is always better than living in sin."

"I know. I feel like one lucky man." Braxton held nothing back with his smile. "I couldn't have found a better mate. Guess I owe it all to you for reintroducing us."

Adeena smiled demurely, looking back to case the direction Neeka had gone in. "I know things looked a bit shaky there for a while. But nevertheless we're all family now. I would like to apologize for my behavior, but I'm glad everything worked itself out. If you two need anything, anything at all, I'm only a phone call away."

"Thanks, but that won't be necessary. Money is not an issue right now, and once the barbecue restaurant's in full swing, we'll be even better."

Three small kids dressed in their Sunday best scampered by them, their playful squeals lingering in the June midafternoon air. Adeena again looked around to make sure no one was paying them much attention. "I know, I know. I just want to make sure that . . . Oh hell, I'll just cut to the chase." From her clutch purse she pulled out a folded check and handed it to him. "Here. Don't be a fool, Braxton. Take the money."

Grabbing a flute of Cristal from a passing steward, Braxton sipped. He bit down gently on his tongue to keep from saying something he might regret later. "If I'm to be the provider for your daughter, my wife, I plan to be the only provider. Thank you, Mother Lebeau, but I can't take your money."

"Nonsense. It's my wedding gift to the both of you. Take it," Adeena insisted.

Looking refreshed and happy as a lark, Neeka was back at Braxton's side. "What's that?" Her eyes zeroed in on the check Adeena held out.

"My dear," droned Adeena proudly, "it's your wedding present from your mother. It's the least I can do considering I had to give your job to Mercy and rent out your condo."

"I'll take that." Neeka didn't have a problem accepting the check. To her it served as compensation for everything her mother had ever done—or not done. "This will pay for all the family drama I've gone through and then some." Her eyes bulged at the amount: three hundred thousand dollars. "Goodness, Mama. Thanks. Thanks a lot. We can definitely put this money to good use. I'll start a college fund for our first child."

Braxton saw Adeena's offering as well-intentioned. "Thanks," he said.

Neeka stepped closer to kiss Adeena's cheek. "I'm sure you know how expensive it is for a college education nowadays."

"I sure do, sweetie. And that money could also help with your new business. What's the name of the place again?"

"Neeton's Place. It's a combination of our first names. Our motto is Good Eating at Neeton's."

"Yes. Of course. I like the sound of it, and I'm so happy for the two of you. Starting a new business isn't the easiest thing, but I feel confident that you will be a success. Of course, I'll be even happier when I know I have another grandchild on the way."

Neeka blushed. "In due time, Mama. In due time."

The photographer made another attempt to assemble the whole family. Braxton waved back. "Okay, okay. Let's get this party on the road." The three made their way over to where several family members had gathered for photographs.

Snuggled close to Braxton, Neeka could hear his heartbeat almost as if it were in perfect sync with hers. She couldn't recall the last time she had felt so at peace with herself, so happy and content. Too blessed to be stressed. That's what she was. Her own husband. Her own home. A new business starting up. Freedom to live her own life on her own terms. "This is how it's supposed to be," she mumbled to herself, looking around.

"Did you say something?" Braxton leaned in.

"I didn't get to hear what you're thankful for." She kissed his cheek while the photographer busied himself for the right shot.

Braxton kissed her forehead. "I'm thankful for finding a family like yours to call my own. To wake up to your loving smile each morning. I'm thankful for us."

"And I'm thankful you didn't give up on me. Welcome to the family."

The photographer was telling them to say cheese. Before Braxton repeated the word, he turned to his new bride. "Thank you. I'm glad I could make it."